C000212682

ANY
DAY
YOU
CAN
DIE

The Medellín Story

Thommy
Waite

Any Day You Can Die
Copyright © 2020 by Thommy Waite
All rights reserved.

No part of this book may be reproduced in any
form or by any electronic or mechanical means,
including information storage and retrieval systems,
without written permission from the author, except
for the use of brief quotations in a book review.

This novel is a work of fiction. Names, characters,
businesses, places, events, locales, and
incidents are either the products of the author's
imagination or used in a fictitious manner.
Any resemblance to actual persons, living or
dead, or actual events is purely coincidental.

Edited by Dominic Wakeford
Cover designed by Jamie Keenan

ISBN (print): 978-0-6489899-0-5
ISBN (ebook): 978-0-6489899-1-2

thommywaite.com

For K & B

In order to write about life first you must live it.
ERNEST HEMINGWAY

When I'm fucked up, that's the real me.
THE WEEKND

ONE

"Papi! Papi! Papi!"

The prepago screamed as I plunged myself deep inside her gorgeous tight cunt. I was ploughing her from behind like a man who hadn't been laid for three months. She was a proper little fuck-house. Long mane of black hair, arched back, caramel skin, and a perfect Latina *culo*. Pussy juice ran down my shaft coating my ball sack – the best candy apple of my life. I stuck a thumb inside her arsehole and started belting her round cheeks with my spare hand. The room reeked of cheap perfume and bacon fat. More blood rushed to my cock. I felt her clam tighten. We pulsed together and collapsed into a puddle of filth.

/

My story starts here because it has to. There was a short window when Tony, the little over-achieving boy, imagined his life as a successful, engaged member of society. My mother insisted that I would become a lawyer and I believed her. But the fantasy got corrupted at around age fourteen. I'm not too sure why my priorities got rearranged. During my teenage years I decided that regular life wasn't going to work out for me. I wanted something better. I wanted to be original and free, a libertine living honestly outside the law.

So that's the life I chased. Kind of. I've always been held back by fear. Whether it be comedy, music, acting, writing, podcasting… I never had the guts to go balls-deep. Yet breakthroughs happen at the strangest times. The moment I started fucking that whore, I knew in my bones that I'd found my path. It wasn't the sex. It was the *possibility* of my new life in Medellín. I didn't know what I was stepping into, but it felt dangerous and weird and big. Really fucking big.

I dove in, headfirst. No brakes. No Plan B. The last roll of the dice. Everything started to click. The universe bent to my will. I got what I wanted, with change.

And then came the wonkiness. The fantasy began to sputter. I noticed the warning signs, I saw the whole thing spinning out of control, and instead of bailing, I put myself right in the middle of everything. The opportunity to become windswept and interesting, to stand out from the pack, to escape normie status forever… it was way too much to resist for a clown like myself.

Even now, the desire to become infamous burns within me. I should pack up all of my shit, move to the suburbs, eat some egg noodles and ketchup with Henry Hill. Instead I'm here, ignoring very clear instructions, writing all of this shit down.

1

It was never meant to be Medellín. Like a basic bitch, I wanted to reinvent myself in New York. The Big *fawkin'* Apple. Medellín was just meant to be a stepping stone. A thrifty little oasis. The plan was to chill out for six months, sort my head out, get some shit done. Then I'd be ready to take on the world.

The flight was brutal. Including stopovers, it took me thirty-five hours to get from Melbourne to Medellín. I wanted to be excited when I saw the gorgeous rolling green hills of Antioquia, but I was too bloated and exhausted to feel much of anything.

For the first few days I stayed at a hostel in the center of Poblado, aka 'La Zona Rosa', a high-end and muy turistic section of Medellín. The hostel was run by a perpetually tired Canadian dude. I forked out extra coin for a private room and spent a long time in my bed recovering from the trip, aimlessly trawling social media and YouTube. I watched The Brian Jonestown Massacre perform a live set on a French TV show and the first hour of Owen Benjamin and Kurt Metzger on Rogan. I noticed a doco about the tribes of Papua New Guinea in my suggested vids, so I gave it a spin. It was a low budget affair starring a morose anthropologist wandering around desolate islands with a camcorder from the 90s, sponging off poor fuckers who couldn't afford a loincloth, never mind a pot to piss in. Anthropologists have got a lot to answer for. I guess you could say they're the OG couchsurfers.

On my second or third night I got chatting with some Germans at the hostel bar. There were three of them; a lad and two chicks. We got hungry and they suggested a joint called Chef Burger which was walking distance from the hostel. Over dinner they told me about their travels. They'd come down from Mexico and were planning to explore most of Latin America. Legit backpackers on a budget. My plan – chilling in Medellín for a few months to work on creative bullshit – seemed hilarious to them.

As we ate, I marvelled at all the Colombian women walking down the street. Seeing a bunch of Medellín girls in the wild is a sight to behold. There's a standard Paisa look – long, straight black hair that falls all the way down to the beltline, eye shadow, lipstick, caramel-brown skin, ample cleavage, form-hugging pants, high heels, and of course, a big juicy rump. The arse was the ingredient that tied the whole meal together. I caught myself hungrily scanning chica after chica. *Fuck-houses*, I said to myself in my inner Patrick Bateman voice. *Fuck-houses everywhere.*

After dinner we went to a hipster bar called MAD Records and enjoyed a few more bevvies in the beer garden. One of the German birds seemed to be giving me the eye. But I was six beers deep and couldn't accurately read her vibe. That's the problem with Germans – they're efficient in all the wrong ways. My jet lag slapped me in the face. I excused myself and walked back to the hostel.

/

The next day I asked the tired Canadian about finding a room to rent. According to him, all the Airbnb listings were 'gringo-priced'. He told me to check out the expat Facebook group. There were quite a few rooms available online, but nothing tickled my pickle. I wanted the perfect spot. Good location, killer set-up and the right price. I needed my fifteen grand in the bank to stretch for a while.

A couple of days later I saw the ad:

Hola chicos! A room has opened up in our amazing apartment. Brand new building in Poblado, extremely high-end – you won't find many other places like this in Medellín. The room has a double-bed and walk-in-closet, extremely spacious. Shared bathroom. I've posted pics of the bedroom and the rest of the apartment below. You'd be living with three male expats who are all working in Medellín. No couples, unfortunately. $1.2M pesos or $400 USD per month, includes bills, internet and the maid who comes once a week. Minimum three-month stay. One month security deposit. This room will go quickly so if you're interested or have any questions, please send me a direct message ASAP. Thanks, Allie.

I scanned through the photos. The placed looked fucking epic. A proper party pad! And the rent was within my budget too. A bloke by the name of Allie Phillips was the one who posted the ad. I hit him up via DM. Allie responded immediately.

Hi Tony, thanks for your message. I'll be home at 5 today. That work? Let me know and I'll send you the address.

I clicked on Allie's Facebook profile. *Lives in Medellín, Antioquia. From London, United Kingdom. Works at Virtuagym.* A bald bloke in great shape. Looked to be in his mid-thirties. Most of Allie's photos were of him playing five-a-side or posing next to his motorbike out in the Colombian countryside.

I arrived a tad early that arvo. It was only a fifteen-minute walk up a big hill from the hostel. The name of the building was Edificio Forever. As instructed, I waited out the front of the portero's office.

"Tony?"

I turned around. "That's me."

Allie jumped off his bike, took off his helmet and extended a hand. He was a touch shorter than I was expecting. Padded Fox jacket, aviators, pale blue skinny jeans. Clean-shaven and boyish. His mouth and cheekbones made him look a little like Freddo the Frog. "Nice to meet you, mate. Follow me."

Allie greeted the portero in rapid-fire Spanish. We walked through the gate to an underground car park.

"You come straight from work?"

"Yep. Can't believe it's only Wednes-dee," Allie said, with a shake of his head.

The elevator took us up to level 10.

"Four apartments per floor," Allie said. "It's this one 'ere."

The first thing that struck me was the vast amount of natural light. High ceilings, tastefully furnished. There was a killer balcony complete with a BBQ and hammock. Some dude was sitting at the dining table working on a lappie. He jumped up and made his way towards me.

"Hey man!" the dude said in a ridiculously exaggerated Californian accent. "Brian Hartman."

"Tony. How's it goin'?"

"Life's rad, amigo."

Brian was tall, lean and smiley. Man-bun, intense how-now-brown-cow eyes and a well-maintained artisanal beard. The archetypal digital yoga bro.

Allie walked past me. "Let me show ya the room."

It looked exactly like the pics on Facebook. Bathroom was immaculate too.

"So, what's the deal Tony?" Brian said as we walked back into the living room. "You gonna be the new roomie?"

I laughed half-heartedly. "Pretty sweet spot. This your place?" I asked Allie.

"Nah mate. I wish," Allie said. His accent was still proper Cockney, but a Spanish inflection crept in when he said certain phrases. "Belongs to an American fella called Joe. Retiree. Met him years ago at an expat meetup. Asked me if I wanted to rent out the master bedroom when he bought the place. That was in 2016. Been 'ere ever since."

"Nice. Who moved out?" I said.

"Kiwi bloke," Allie said as he cracked his neck. "He does sail tours from Panama to Colombia. Been spending more and more time in Panama City wiv his missus. Last night he let me know that he ain't coming back for a while."

I nodded. "There's one other housemate?"

"Steve." Allie pointed down the hall. "Canadian. Programmer. Spends a lot of time in his room. Don't hardly ever see him."

I couldn't think of anything else. "You got questions for me?" I said.

Allie shook his head. "Not really. You covered everything in your message. I'll get an agreement from Joe for you to sign. When do you want to move in?"

I thought for a moment. "Tomorrow?"

"Deal," Allie said.

1

I rocked up the next day in the late arvo.

Brian let me in. "Buenas tardes, roomie! Let me help you with those," he said, gesturing at my bags.

"I come bearing gifts," I said. "Cerveza?"

"Nice! What are we imbibing?"

"Aguila. I got twelve, so don't hold back."

"Local brew, woot woot!" Brian said, raising the roof with both hands. "Gimme one of those bad boys."

I threw all my shit in the bedroom and then stepped out onto the balcony with Brian. He was twenty-seven, originally from San Diego, and he worked online for a network marketing company. The dude certainly liked to run his trap. I settled into the hammock and let him hammer me with his life story. Brian was into supplements, juicing and holistic exercise. He was also the founder of an AI face recognition app. Brian declined a second Aguila and fixed himself a soda water with ice, lime and salt, known to some as a 'margarita for faggots'.

Allie came home just after five. I signed the agreement and gave him cash for my first month and security deposit.

"What are you boys getting your beaks into tonight?" I said. "Was thinking about grabbing dinner somewhere."

Brian shrugged. "Hell yeah brother. Always down to visit Grub Town."

Allie opened an Aguila. "Sounds good. What do ya fancy?"

"I'm easy," I said. "Any ideas?"

Allie took a sip and nodded. "Plenty of options just down the hill."

Half an hour later Steve wandered into the living room. Based on Allie's description, I was expecting Steve to look like the 'not your minge' fat bloke from the UK version of *The Office*, a techie tub of lard. But I was way off.

Steve was tiny, only 5'3 or 5'4 – a couple inches away from being a legit little person. Perfect posture. Jacked pecs and biceps. Black chest hair poked out the top of his singlet. A flat, simian face with some hardcore *Planet of the Apes* vibes. Hip, Colombian-style fade – I could tell instantly that his haircut was cooler than he was.

"Hey dude. Tony."

Steve offered me a hairy fist. "You're the new roomie?"

We bumped knuckles.

"Yes sir."

Steve went to the fridge and pulled out a pre-made smoothie.

"We're all heading out for dinner in a bit. You're welcome to come if you're free," Allie said to Steve.

Steve drank his milky shake in two big gulps. "OK."

Allie suggested a Peruvian spot on Calle 10. We wandered down the hill a couple hours later.

/

I learned more about the crew. Steve had been in Medellín for just over a year, and Brian had been in town for around six months. Like me, they'd found the apartment through the expat Facebook group. Allie was the grizzled vet – he'd been in Colombia five years.

Over the course of the meal we discussed learning Spanish, the pros and cons of being a digital nomad, things to do as a tourist in Colombia, Paisa girls, Joe Rogan, the cost of living in Medellín, bitcoin, Donald Trump and the best diet for optimal physical performance. Things I would discuss again and again and again for the next eighteen months of my life. Like a hamster on a wheel. There was no getting away from these compulsory parts of the gringo-in-Medellín syllabus.

Brian dominated the conversation, humble-bragging, story-topping and name-dropping at every opportunity. Allie scoffed his grub like Oliver Twist and bristled with manic energy – there was clearly a lot happening inside that shiny head. Steve only spoke when spoken to. It became clear that the three of them weren't that close. It felt like the first meal they had all eaten together. They weren't legit mates – they were just a few gringos who happened to live with one another.

I ate my ceviche and scoped out the girls in the restaurant. It was a pretty boujee spot and they were all gussied up something proper. *Fuck-houses at every turn*, Bateman hissed. I was double-parking myself with cervezas and mojitos. Steve didn't drink and was on the waters. Allie was sipping light beers. Brian tried to cut himself off, but I twisted his arm and he ended up going drink-for-drink with me.

"You know, I find myself listening to nearly every episode of Rogan," I said. "There's obviously some I can't get through. Like the MMA episodes, I don't even bother. But with a lot of them I get to the end and I feel kind of disgusted with myself. Like, I don't know why I wasted three hours of my life to hear Joe talk about coyotes for the five hundredth time."

"That's so funny man," Brian said with a big smile. He was three cocktails in and looking a little flushed. "It's definitely not the most efficient content in the world. But Joe's all about doing deep-dives on some pretty epic topics. Did you catch the one with Ben Greenfield?"

"I don't remember," I said.

"Oh dude!" Brian said. "Greenfield busts *so many* biohacking myths. Same with Dr. Rhonda Patrick."

"I remember her," I said as I swallowed a fishy mouthful. "She's the one who looks like a cute little field mouse."

"And my man Aubrey Marcus from Onnit, the goddamn warrior poet, always brings the heat! I met him at South By a few years back," Brian said as he stroked his beard. "Such a chill dude."

"The only one I listened to was Guy Ritchie," Allie said as he gnawed on a rib. "*Lock Stock* will always be me favourite film. Brilliant director."

We talked shit for a while longer. It took the waiter a hot

minute to bring us the check – something I would grow accustomed to in Colombia. Steve fucked off home. Me, Brian and Allie decided to hit another bar.

/

Brian and Allie led me to Parque Lleras, the epicentre of all nightlife in Poblado. It was a Thursday night, and the streets were poppin'. Reggaeton blasted out from all the different clubs. Street performers juggled next to traffic lights ("Fuckin' Argies," Allie remarked). The smell of fried food and aguardiente hung in the warm air. Hookers loitered about the park. A tasty little number in a black miniskirt smiled in my direction. I gave her a polite nod and kept walking.

We chose an incredibly loud sports bar that overlooked the park. The widescreen TV was replaying some European soccer game. I could barely hear the others. I ordered an icy bucket of six Heinekens which I started pounding. At some point Allie called it quits and caught a cab home. Brian was chewing my ear off about his AI start-up thing. He was well and truly hammered. I started to feel nauseous. We got the check and decided to hit another bar.

Shortly after leaving, Brian was walking backwards across a side street, gesticulating aggressively about the Wim Hof breathing method, when I saw a flash of yellow out the corner of my eye. I pulled him towards me with my left arm. The cab swerved violently, just missing Brian. The driver pounded on his horn and screamed something out the window as he careened down the carrera.

"Holy shit man!" Brian said. "You just saved my life!"

The adrenaline sobered me up. I shook my head. "He wasn't going that fast. You would've just broken a leg or two."

Brian sloppily shook his head. "Damn dude. Y'all Australians know how to drink! The universe just called time on my night, homie. Wanna split a cab?"

I considered the offer. "I think I'm gonna have one more."

Brian bounced. I did a quick lap around the park to check out the different options. I was about to slip into a low-key bar filled with a few middle-aged locals for a nightcap when I ran into the same tasty little hooker from before.

"Hey baby," she said.

There was a look of confidence painted on her face. Desire oozed out of my pores. *A dirty little fuck-house, all yours for just a few Colombian pesos*, Bateman said gleefully.

She looked like a wild animal who had managed to corner her prey. I had never paid for sex before. At least not directly. The age-old question popped into my shitfaced brain; was engaging in prostitution morally reprehensible, or nothing more than an essential service for our most pressing need?

It really didn't matter. Resistance was futile. Whether I liked it or not, she was gonna fuck my brains out.

TWO

I've reached customs. It's time to declare all my baggage. Strengths. Weaknesses. Blind spots. My rampant mediocrity. Being honest is underrated. I wasted so much time in my twenties being a sneaky little bitch. Fooling others with dumb schemes. No more of that. I want all my cards on the table from the beginning. You should know what you're getting into.

This is *not* a novel. This is a stony-faced retelling of my eighteen months in Medellín, spanning July 2018 to December 2019. I've tried to write a novel many times before. Every single time I quickly became disgusted with myself. There is something pathetic and infantile about fiction. Who in their right mind wants to be told a fucking made-up story by some sicko with too much time on his hands? I outgrew novels a long time ago. But I still thought I had one in me. What a tard!

So, with this bad boy, I'm not fucking around. I'm going full Pink Floyd. Comfortably numb. Just the basic facts. Pretend I'm a bailiff, reading a transcript in court. It's important you get all the details. But trust me, you don't need any extra fluff from a bullshit artist like myself. All killer, no filler.

There are, of course, some exceptions.

First of all, at certain moments during my Colombian walkabout I didn't know what the fuck was going on, mainly because of my piss-poor Spanish. It's impossible to show you the full jigsaw when there's pieces missing. The younger, more pretentious Tony would just use artistic license to fill in the gaps. But that was the old me. If we reach a point in the tale where I'm confused about what went down, I promise to let you know.

Next up, and perhaps I'm getting a little carried away here, but if some young impressionable chaps knew exactly what we were getting up to in Medellín, I've got a feeling that some of them might try and do the same thing, which wouldn't be a good idea. This story could end up hurting me, which I'm okay with, but I don't want copycats. There will be some vague language when it comes to describing certain misadventures.

Also, if you're interested in truly learning about Medellín or Colombia, don't read this story. There have to be better options out there for you to sink your teeth into – my ignorance is truly embarrassing. I stopped eating local food two weeks after arriving and shifted primarily to ordering Western grub on Rappi. There were tons of poor Venezuelan refugees wandering the streets of Poblado – I never bothered to learn a thing about that specific political situation. You'll no doubt pick up a few things here and there, a couple facts, the odd phrase. But on the whole, this little ditty is gonzo as fuck, as in everything has been aggressively filtered through my warped point of view.

When you become an expat, you have this glorified vision of your psyche merging seamlessly with a new culture. Hemingway and Fitzgerald and Stein – the *Midnight in Paris* experience. I've come to realize that I was too wrapped up in my own bullshit to be truly curious about Colombia. By default, I've thrown Colombians under the bus too, which I feel kind of guilty about. This again comes back to my own bullshit. If I was in a better headspace when I was in Medellín, maybe I would've met a different type of local. Feel free to cast your judgement on individuals who appear in this story. But save your wrath for Colombia and Colombians in general. Remember who's telling you the tale. Garbage in, garbage out.

Finally, this isn't just my story. There were a bunch of us getting weird in The City of Eternal Spring. I've changed a few names. Which is annoying, because in the era of evangelical personal branding, names are muy importante.

Apart from the pseudonyms, everything else is the real fucking deal.

I

The morning after the night with the hooker I slept in late. It was eleven-ish by the time I stumbled into the living room of Forever. Brian looked hungover – pale in the face and puffy eyes. Wet hair hung down to his shoulders. He was standing near the breakfast bar with a middle-aged man. There was a large cardboard box on the floor.

"The Aussie has risen!" Brian said. "Joe, meet Tony, the new roomie."

I shook Joe's hand. He wore a wifebeater and khaki shorts. A pair of Oakleys rested on Joe's sun-kissed head. "Hey Tony. Joe D'Angelo. Pleasure to meet you."

"Glad you're alive, homie. How was the rest of your noche?" Brian said.

"Chill, man. Just had a few more beers then caught a cab home," I lied. "What's in the box?"

Brian smiled. "You're gonna love this." He opened a drawer and pulled out a knife. "Joe just got back from Florida." Brian sliced open the box. It was a Onewheel electric skateboard. "My last board got wet in the rain, died just before I came over to Medellín." He pulled the scooter out of its packaging. "My precious baby!" Brian plugged the thing into the wall to charge.

"When did you arrive, Tony?" Joe asked me.

"Ah, about a week ago."

"Enjoying it?"

"Yeah for sure," I said as I put the kettle on. "This is a beautiful apartment Joe."

"Thanks," Joe said. He sounded a bit like Vito from *The Sopranos*. "Watch out for the girls, brother. Scopolamina attacks on the rise. The 'Devil's Breath', they call it. Belgian guy was found dead in Envigado just last week."

My heart skipped a beat. "Like a date-rape thing?"

Joe laughed. "Kind of. But in reverse."

It took me a second to figure out what he meant. "Oh okay. Thanks for the tip."

It seemed like Joe wanted to stay and rap a while, but Brian ushered him out of the apartment.

"Joe's a great dude," Brian said after he was gone. "Was cool enough to pick up the package in Florida and bring it back with him. Not sure if you know, but shipping costs from the States to Colombia can get a little cray cray."

"Does he always pop in unannounced?"

Brian shook his head like a dog at the beach. "Not at all. First time I've seen him here. Joe's a super respectful dude."

Brian convinced me to go to a coffee shop called Cafe Velvet for breakfast. He flew down the hill on his Onewheel before expertly circling back around. The guy had perfect balance. Brian asked me if I wanted a go and I politely declined. I felt seedy and was not in a state of mind to learn a new skill. As a kid, the few times I tried standing on a skateboard ended with me slamming the back of my head on the pavement.

At Velvet I ate a very underwhelming panini. Then we headed to Selina, a coworking space and hostel.

The hotdesk area at Selina was jammed – it was filled to the brim with gringos and gringas hunched over lappies. A chubby black American dude with AirPods was talking obnoxiously slap bang in the middle of the room. The dude was pitching some new crypto thing and kept repeating the acronym 'ICO' which made no sense to me. Selina is pretty much ground zero for digital nomads in Medellín. A place to be seen and heard, evidently. Brian zigzagged up and down the aisles on his Onewheel, stopping to chat whenever he recognized a familiar face. I was expecting it to be a total sausage-fest, but one in five were gringas. Compared to the native Paisas, these sheilas looked like absolute bushpigs.

Brian finally sat down next me. He ranted about how his work was blowing up. His boss was about to close a massive partnership, and when that came off Brian was going to be leading the project.

Selina was way too loud for me to concentrate. I packed my lappie back into my bag. Before I left, Brian suggested that I come along with him to Parque Arví the following day. His idea was to use the metrocable to get to the park. I'd seen a bunch of YouTube videos about it – looked dope. We hatched a plan and I split.

That arvo I tried to do some writing back at Forever. But my mind was too scattered. I went to the Carulla and bought some groceries. It was eerie how similar the layout of the supermarket was to Woolies or Coles back in Melbs. Globalization, baby. When I got back from the shops I opened my lappie to do some work but felt overcome by fatigue. I fixed myself a quick bowl of veggie pasta then crashed hard.

/

Me and Brian left Forever early the next morning. We walked down Calle 10 towards the Poblado metro station. The pavement smelt like bleach. 'Diez' is a party strip in Poblado. It's a chameleon of a street, with a bunch of meat market clubs and fondas (small traditional Colombian drinking holes). At night, it looks like it could belong in any modern city's entertainment district. During the day, the 10 looks pathetically quaint and provincial – a roided-up weakling competing in the Mr Universe comp.

Brian was buzzing. He pirouetted around me, doing figure-eights on his Onewheel, monologuing incessantly. It took us twenty-five minutes to reach the metro station. The place was half-empty. I heard a few other voices speaking English, but none were as loud as Brian's.

I was expecting the metro to be a bit sketch. I put my hand in my front pocket, protecting my wallet. But the quiet train was devoid of any unsavoury characters. There were just a bunch of young families minding their own business.

We went north for a handful of stations and then transferred onto the metrocable, a small ski-lift thing that held me, Brian and four locals. As we started to ascend Brian pulled out his phone.

"Wasssssssssup family, it's your boy Bri Bri the Hart Man, and I'm coming at ya from beautiful Med-e-llín! I'm here with my new Aussie roommate, say wassup to the fam Tony…"

"Hey."

"It's a glorious Saturday morning here in The City of Eternal Spring and right now we're riding on the subway system's metrocable. Check out that dope-ass view!" Brian pushed his phone right up against the window. "We'll be cruising up the mountain in this bad boy for thirty minutes, then we're gonna check out Parque Arví. I'll see y'all then, PEACE!" Brian hi-fived the screen with his palm. He turned to me. "How was that bro? Feel authentic? Authenticity is *everything*. It's a huge part of my personal brand."

"Yeah man. Felt authentic."

Brian winked at me. "Appreciate it, bro."

The metrocable hung just above all the shanty towns that were littered all over the mountain. It's a real *City of God*-type of trip. Kids kicking soccer balls, abuelas sitting out the front of their houses on plastic chairs, washing lines filled to the brim, motos zipping about all the winding lanes. Our ride ended. We got on another metrocable that took us all the way to the park.

Brian told me about his YouTube channel, *Bri Bri the Hart Man*.

"Most of my videos are podcast interviews," he said. "I do them over Skype. But since moving to Medellín, I've been doing more travel vlogger stuff. Restaurant reviews, nightlife, walking tours of different neighbourhoods. I've been super stoked with the uptick in engagement!"

At the entrance Brian asked me to record him flying around on his Onewheel. A bunch of snack vendors crowded around him like he was Marty Mc-Fuckin' Fly. He took toothy selfies with a bunch of them. Finally, we made our way inside the park.

I was Brian's gofer for the next few hours as we traipsed around Arví, a huge fucker of a national park with a bunch of hiking trails and lakes. Brian asked me to position myself awkwardly at various places along the trail so I could get cool shots of him riding about. We smashed a huge bandeja paisa for lunch, which is a fuck-off plate filled with beans, white rice, ground beef, chicharrón, plantain, chorizo, arepa, black pudding, avocado and a fried egg. I was ecstatic when the One-wheel's battery finally died and Brian agreed to call it quits.

Once we were in the metrocable going back down the mountain Brian began to film himself again.

"This place is popping off right now, fam," Brian said to his phone. "Do whatever it takes, and get your butts to Medellín ASAP!"

Brian was grinning like a Hillsong preacher on molly. The view coming back down was even better than going up.

"Bro! I'm so pumped right now. I'm in LOVE," Brian said to me. "Can you even believe it? This beautiful city belongs to us!"

THREE

I was set up for success. No job. No girlfriend. No obligations. Dope apartment. Bit of coin in the bank. A fuckton of free time. There was absolutely nothing holding me back.

I wasted a whole week listening to pods, watching YouTube, and lurking on the socials. I got a couple emails, one from Mum and one from Dunc, my best mate since the first day of high school, both checking in, seeing how I was getting on. I read both emails multiple times but couldn't bring myself to respond. My past life in Melbourne seemed surreal. I scrolled incessantly through Insta stories like a curious alien. It seemed wild that there were people in the world with consistent schedules, ongoing relationships. Droids on the grid, gravity and inertia holding them to predetermined rhythms.

I was spending a lot of time at Forever. I began to understand the dynamic of the house.

Steve was studying Spanish at a local uni, so he'd leave for a few hours each day in the mornings, hitting the gym on the way home. Every second or third night he'd nip out by himself for a late dinner, but apart from that, he was a virtual stowaway.

Brian filled the entire pad with his exhausting lifehacker energy. He was constantly pitching ideas at me as if I was some type of bigwig venture capitalist. His main gig was doing cold calls for a mob called The Lifestyle Corporation. Brian also loved to meditate, which looked strangely similar to doing nothing on the couch.

Allie was always on the go. He left the house early each morning and hit the gym before work. In the evenings he'd play fútbol or ride up the surrounding hills on his bike.

It wasn't like the three of them disliked one another – there was just a complete lack of chemistry. This suited me down to the ground. At thirty-one, I was too old to be a frat boy. The vibe in the house was neutral. I didn't want to get sucked into a social circle that would eat up all my time. I wanted freedom and space. I needed to untangle all the complicated ideas inside my head.

That being said, after my week of isolation, by the time Friday rolled around I was ready for some action. Luck wasn't on my side. Steve, as per usual, was in his room, glued to his lappie. Brian was doing a three-day water fast so his plan for the weekend was to mooch about the house and film the 'experience' for his YouTube channel. Allie was out in Guatape for a couple of nights. So, I was on my lonesome.

Every time I left the house that weekend I subjected myself to a major guilt-trip.

What the fuck are you doing, cunt? Walking around by yourself like a fucking loner. You're not getting any younger you fucking waste of space. Think of yourself as some type of artist, do you mate? Well last time I checked it's been a fucking long time since you did anything creative, you sack of shit. You've got all your ideas ready to go, now all you've got to do is sit down and put the fucking hard work in. Imagine shutting down your whole life just to go and wander around a foreign country like a fucking spanner. Get back to the apartment, open your fucking lappie, and get to fucking work!

When I returned to my room a friendlier voice would chime in.

Listen buddy, I know there's a lot you want to prove to every-one, but you have to remember Rome wasn't built in a day. You can stare at this screen all day long and work until you're blue in the face but that won't do the trick. There's a little thing called harmony. If you want to create something incredible, you need a schedule that's going to bring that to fruition. Work smarter, not harder. Finding the time to sleep, exercise, eat right, socialize – you need all that if you want your dreams to come true. You're in a foreign country and there's so much for you to see and do. Why not get out there and enjoy it? You've been cooped up for too long. Go get some fresh air champ – it'll clear your head.

/

At about eleven on Sunday morning I went down to Avenida El Poblado for ciclovia.

In Medellín there aren't too many open public spaces that are good for exercise. So, on Sunday mornings they shut down major roads all over the city so people can have a run about. I fired up '45:33' by LCD Soundsystem and started jogging. After a few slightly overcast days the air was clear and the sun was hot. Ciclovia feels like one big ad for the Medellín tourism board. Every cross-section of society is represented. Yuppies with their puppies, kids learning to ride bikes, clusters of middle-aged women doing Zumba, shredded Jocko Will-ink-looking motherfuckers pounding the pavement. And my oh my oh my, a delectable assortment of muy rica chicas in form-hugging leggings. *Fuck-houses*, Bateman said matter-of-factly as I jogged long. *Fitness enthusiast fuck-houses. Eye candy for days. You lucky son-of-a-bitch!*

I'd fallen out of rhythm with exercise so I couldn't run for more than ten minutes at a time, but I nearly made it all the way down to Envigado. I bought myself an ice-cold coconut water from a street vendor then turned around. It was just after one when I made it back to Forever. I was buzzing. *I just conquered my inner bitch*, I said as I danced around in the shower. I made myself a ham salad sandwich for lunch and grabbed my lappie. I was just about to launch into some work when Allie walked through the front door.

"Fuck me mate," Allie said as he threw his shit down. "Nearly met me maker fifteen minutes ago."

Allie was riding his moto back from Guatape, coming down a huge hill, when a cyclist veered suddenly into his path. Allie swerved around him and nearly lost control. He jack-knifed, nearly went over the handles, but was able to push his weight down and get the bike back on the road.

"Facking dizzy cunt," Allie said as he threw his duffel bag on the floor. "Had a huge screaming match with the prick n'all. Wanted to run the cunt off the road. Should know better by this point. Sunday pedalers are the worst."

I made Allie a coffee and the caffeine seemed to calm him down. We chatted out on the balcony. He was part of some Medellín motorcycle group – once a month they did a trip out in rural Antioquia. Allie showed me a bunch of pictures on his phone of their ride around Guatape. He seemed to be the youngest in the gang by a country mile – the other cats were all grey-haired boomers, Joe D'Angelo types. Allie told me about a five-a-side fútbol game happening that arvo. I had nothing better to do, so I agreed to join him.

/

Me and Allie left Forever just after five and jumped in an Uber. He was wearing a red and blue Independiente jersey, one of Medellín's local teams. Allie was still seething about his close call on the road. He told me about his sales job at Virtuagym. It was a Dutch company that sold software to gym owners in the States. I was heading south on Avenida El Poblado for the second time that day, but this time it was deathly quiet.

"Me and Karen used to live in that one," Allie said as he pointed at an unremarkable block of apartments.

"Oh yeah?" I said. "Who's Karen?"

"Me ex-missus."

I didn't really know what to do with this piece of information. "She still in Medellín?"

"Nope," Allie said as he laced up his boots. "Designer. Fashion. Lives in Bogotá now."

The sporting complex had three AstroTurf pitches side by side. There was a little tienda in the middle that sold snacks and beer. Allie's mates sat on plastic chairs and got kitted up. They were basically all gringos, only two locals from memory, and the core of the group were lads that Allie worked with at Virtuagym. A tall dopey Brit called Justin leant me a pair of boots that were a couple sizes too big.

As I ran out onto the field, I realized that it had been about fifteen years since I'd played a game of soccer. My old man was a local hero back in his glory days, so he got me started young. Growing up I heard countless stories about how brilliant Bob Fletcher was on the right wing for County Durham in the late 60s. Had a trial for Sunderland when he was fifteen, apparently. Bob's old man, my grandad, was an eccentric WW2 vet who didn't give a shit about sports, and according to Dad this complete lack of support was the thing that stopped him from progressing to the big time. When I was a kid Bob did everything to set me up for success. He coached all my teams, made himself available for kickabouts in the park after school. I was a decent centre mid but unfortunately didn't inherit the old man's lightning speed. When I was fourteen, I started getting fucked up at house parties with Dunc, and all of a sudden soccer stopped being cool real quick.

There were twelve of us, so we played six-on-six. Everyone was pretty good – the standouts were Allie and two Dutch lads. Allie was a fucking maniac with a severe case of white line fever. Despite being the oldest fella on the pitch, he had more tenacity and stamina than everyone else combined. For the entire game he barked orders like a hooligan preparing for battle. I was glad he was on my team – he kept wrecking the opposition with crunching tackles. One time he clipped Justin just beneath his kneecap. "Fook sake All-eh," Justin moaned in a thick Yorkshire accent. "Got work tomorrow ya fookin' dick." After twenty minutes I was breathing out of my arse, so I subbed myself into goal and played as keeper for the rest of the game.

We went for just over an hour. I was ecstatic when someone finally called time. Some lads went straight home but most chilled in the dugout area and had a couple beers. They were all nice enough. I necked a bunch of ice cold Aguilas and listened to their office banter. It was identical to office drinks at Fairfax back in Melbs. "This dude's gonna get fired next week, what's happening with our bonuses from last quarter, do you think so-and-so's tits are fake…" Allie didn't start many conversation threads, but he always managed to finish them with rapid-fire rants and exaggerated act-outs.

Allie took me to a Mexican restaurant in Envigado. Turned out he was a giant Arsenal fan. Allie ordered a huge rack of ribs and talked my ear off about his beloved Gooners. He was stoked that Arsène Wenger was finally gone. After a couple of stiff mojitos over dinner I was feeling pretty loose. "Fuck man, it sucks that we're doing this on a Sunday. I'm in the mood to kick on."

Allie looked at his watch. "Well, it's only eight, now," he said. "'How'd you fancy sharing a little bag? Nuffin' crazy. Just a few lines and some drinks at Forever. Could throw some old footy matches on the box…"

The realization hit me between the eyes. Allie was a coke-head. It made perfect sense. His "coffee's for closers" energy was a deadset giveaway.

"Keen," I said.

Allie waved at the waitress. "La cuenta, por favor." He reached for his phone. "Let me text Ricardo."

We caught a cab back towards Poblado and ended up at this beautiful new edificio in Castropol. The portero let us in the building and we caught the elevator up to the top floor. Allie knocked. A dude with long, curly hair opened the door. This was Jhonatan, Ricardo's permanently stoned PA. I shook his hand then stepped inside.

Ricardo's place was out of control. It was a double story penthouse apartment that made Forever look like a fucking dump. Three drunk tattooed chicas were dancing in the living room while Whitney Houston's 'I Wanna Dance with Somebody' played on YouTube. There was a spiral staircase that went up to the second level. Allie led me outside. The view of the city was insane. A few lads were sitting on deckchairs near the pool, smoking weed.

"Alexander! Qué más?"

One of the lads jumped up and started walking towards us. He was big for a Colombiano, maybe 6'2, at least an inch bigger than me. There were a few distinctive moles all around his face and the middle of his bottom lip was pierced with a silver stud. He was dressed in all black like a goth skater dude.

"Ricardo, this is Tony. He just moved into Forever," Allie said.

Ricardo smiled. "Hey man," he said. His English was perfect. "Nice to meet you."

"Likewise. This place is fucking dope," I said, drunkenly.

Ricardo smiled. He lifted up his baseball hat and scratched the top of his head.

"Thanks man. Welcome." Ricardo called out to Jhonatan. "Dos sillas más por favor."

"No, we don't want to intrude mate," Allie said. "Also we're still a bit sweaty from footy. I'll just grab that bag and we'll be on our way."

Ricardo insisted we stay and chill but Allie was adamant. It seemed like a cool scene – the weed smelled delicious and they were playing Flying Lotus on a Bluetooth speaker. But I did feel rank in my sweaty clobber. I tried to give Allie some money for the bag but he refused.

"Alright, we'll be off then," Allie said. "Noche parceros."

Ricardo slapped Allie on the back. "You gotta come to my party later this month. A cool DJ from Belgium is playing Salón."

"Sounds good. WhatsApp me the info," Allie said.

We were about to split when I piped up. "Hate to ask this, but is there any chance I could buy some weed?"

Ricardo smiled. "Of course." He asked one of his buddies something in Spanish. Then he turned back to me. "You like indica or sativa?"

"Indica would be dope."

A Post Malone-looking motherfucker pulled out a bag from his hoodie and threw it to Ricardo. "Here you go Tony, a little present," Ricardo said as he handed me the bag. "Welcome to Medellín."

The bag was as big as my palm. "No way dude," I said. "I don't need a freebie. How much?"

Ricardo waved his hand at me. "Don't worry. It's nothing."

I insisted on giving him a 20,000-peso note.

Ricardo put one of his big hands on my shoulder. "This guy's alright Allie," he said with a smile. "You got a good one."

"Appreciate it man," I said to Ricardo.

"Come to my party Tony," Ricardo said as he stepped back towards his friends. "We'll have a good time."

/

In the Uber back to Forever Allie told me more about Ricardo. "He's a great geezer, Ricardo. Studied in London for a while. That's why his English is so good. Throws parties all around the city. Always sniffs out the best gear. I don't buy from no one else."

The house was dead quiet when we got back to Forever. Allie put on a YouTube mini-doc about Arsenal's 'Invincibles' and racked up some lines on the coffee table. The coke was tremendous – every toot gave me a powerful rush of euphoria. We talked about old school Premier League shit for hours. "When people go through the all-time greats Pires never gets a look-in, it's fucking criminal," Allie said.

I necked more beers. I was surprised how much random shit from my childhood soccer days that I still had in my brain. Allie rationed out the powder with militant precision.

I wanted to smoke some weed but realized there were no papers in the house. There was an empty can of Aguila on the balcony so I fashioned a ghetto pipe and took a big hit. The weed made me instantly anxious and paranoid. Allie kept ranting and racking up, completely oblivious to my predicament. He cued up the next video – 'Liverpool v Arsenal final game of 88/89'. I stretched out on the couch and before long I was gone.

FOUR

The problem with a good memory is that your nightmares are nothing more than vivid flashbacks to the worst moments of your life.

"Still awake?" Dad asked me.

It was late, just after midnight. Mum was asleep in her room. I was in my boxers, sitting at the breakfast bar.

"Yep. Doin' a bit of chem."

Dad scoffed. It was a hot night – summer came early that year. Dad's white shirt was unbuttoned down to his sternum. He staggered past me towards the fridge.

"On a Friday night?"

I pretended to look back down at my textbook.

"My exams are in a few weeks."

Dad poured himself a full glass of chianti. He reeked of booze, perfume and black licorice.

"Shouldn't you be out with your mates?"

Turns out there was a house party that night I could've gone to. Some chick from school. Her folks were over east, and she lived in a double story that backed onto the Joondalup Golf Course. Quite a few of my pals were there, but Dunc didn't wanna go for some reason, so I bailed too. A while later me and Dunc cottoned on to the fact that we'd gone through the exact same experience during our last couple years of high school. Our respective folks were in the process of splitting, but for some godforsaken reason, still chose to live under the same roof. We were both too embarrassed to tell one another until the first year of uni.

"Have you been eating licorice?" I asked Dad.

He took a big gulp and smiled. "Strips all the booze from your breath. Fools the boys in blue with their fuckin' breathalysers. Ain't getting a cent from me."

Prick was smiling like he was some type of genius. For the first fifteen years of my life the old boy had been a schoolteacher, working with special needs kids. And he was good at it too. But there's only so long you can do that type of work before it breaks your spirit. Around 2002 he jumped ship and started selling Holdens. It was the peak of the mining boom in WA, and so old mate Bob started making fantastic coin. Not that me or Mum saw any of it – cunt always pissed it up the wall at the cas or on the trots at the local TAB.

The moment Bob Fletcher hit the car lot and started flogging Monaros, the patient, rational, considerate school teacher quickly withered and died. Believing in some old wives' tale about licorice was one hundred percent on brand with the new version of my father. The urban legend helped Bob justify his chronic drunk driving, and to North City Holden's 2003 Salesman of the year, that's all that mattered.

Maybe because I had my face in a textbook, and I was trying to get my head around how chemicals *actually* interacted with one another, I took umbrage with Bob's drunken pseudoscience. I began to needle him.

"Where were you tonight?" I said. "Sandy's place?"

Bob shot me a death glare.

"No. Brooksy's."

"But Sandy was there, right?"

Bob finished his chianti and poured himself another.

"What's it to you?"

"I heard you talking to her this morning. On your mobile."

Bob took a gulp. "Sandy calls me every morning. To let me know if any leads came in overnight. That's her job. And if you must know, she *was* there tonight. Everyone from the lot was. We're on track to hit our target. Brooksy had us all over for a barbie."

I felt myself quivering. I put my pen down.

"It's alright Bob," I said. "I know you're fucking Sandy. You don't have to lie."

His forehead creased.

"What did you say?"

"You heard me. Don't worry, Mum's asleep. It's just us. Tell the truth. You're fucking the office secretary, aren't ya mate?"

Bob slammed his glass down and ran around the breakfast bar. He grabbed me by the back of the neck.

"Watch what you're saying, son." Bob's sweet, hot breath percolated all around me. "Be *very* careful."

I couldn't keep my shit together a second longer.

"Relax, Bob! I know you're into Asians. I've seen the type of porn you look at on my computer. I think you and Sandy make a cute couple."

Bob squeezed my neck harder. I could feel his teeth gnashing against my hot ears. "Be *very* careful Anthony…"

Electricity tingled through me. I lifted my left arm up off my textbook and elbowed him square in the face. Bob stumbled back. I jumped up off the stool and faced him. He was holding his Romanesque schnoz which was pissing blood. Bob's eyes went white. He lunged for me.

We tussled on the kitchen tiles. Then he used his taller frame and manoeuvred me into the darkened living room. My head went flying over the couch and smashed into the wall. Bob ragdolled me onto the wooden coffee chest. The blunt edge pushed deep into the middle of my spine. Punches rained down on me. Bob's werewolf face was starting to fade from my vision. A bloody goblet of snot fell from his nose down into my open mouth. Bob pushed himself off me, grabbed his keys, and barged out the front door.

I lay on my back crying and panting. Eventually, a good five minutes after he left, I took a few deep breaths and stood up. I was concussed, my spine was bruised, but apart from that, I was fine.

I wandered through to Mum's room and quietly knocked on her door. There was no answer.

I let myself in. She was in the dead center of the bed. Starkers. Graham Hancock book covering her saggy tits. Empty bottle of wine on her bedside table. Sleep mask on. Snoring like a champ.

/

I woke up to the sound of birds chirping. Brian was on the balcony, meditating. Soothing forest sounds were gently coming out of his phone. My bladder was full as a drum. I went to the loo and released a long, stinky piss. Felt like there were shards of glass inside my head.

I washed my face, changed clothes and came back out to the living area. The coffee table was immaculate – Allie must've cleaned up all our mess. Brian finished meditating. He was in the kitchen eating a banana coated in almond butter.

"Tony! What's poppin' player?"

"I'm alright man. Feelin' a little hung."

Brian smiled. "Big night with Alejandro?"

"Yep. Accidental rager. Were we loud?"

Brian waved his finger. "Not for me. The Hart Man uses industrial strength earbuds. Sick sleep hack I picked up from Tim Ferriss. Didn't hear a thing."

"Sweet." I scratched my head. "Was just meant to be a couple beers over dinner. Things escalated."

"Life is for the living, parcero! You looked pretty at peace sleeping on the couch this morning. Maybe you needed to let off some steam?" Brian ate the last bit of banana and washed it down with his black coffee. "Been wanting to get a little cray cray myself. This Friday me and some bros from the Mastermind are thinking of doing a little crawl around Poblado. Maybe hit a few salsa spots." Brian cha-cha-cha'd on the spot. "You down to join us?"

"Yeah, sure."

"BOOM-CHAKA-LAKA!" Brian picked up his backpack. "Gotta jet bro, heading to Selina. Big meeting in forty-five." He unplugged his Onewheel that was charging near the front door. "Me and the Boss Man are about to close a *massive* deal."

"Good luck."

"We're gonna KILL IT!"

Brian left. I made myself a cuppa. I was staring at the patch of forest just north of our building when Steve the halfling came into the kitchen. The dude was so small – he always managed to sidle up on me.

"Steve-o. What's up man?" I said, still in a bit of shock. I offered him a fist.

Steve bumped it awkwardly. "Not much." As per usual, he was wearing a tank that showed off his shredded arms.

I sipped my tea and watched Steve make his breakfast. He fried up eight eggs and several rashers of bacon in a single frying pan.

"You got school today?" I asked him.

"Yep."

"What's the place called?"

"EAFIT."

"You like it?"

"Guess so." Steve slid his sizzling comida onto a plate. "For Medellín, it's expensive. But the other language schools suck. They're for backpackers who wanna learn a few phrases. EAFIT's an actual university. The Spanish school is just a part of it."

It was the most I'd ever heard Steve say. "I've been thinking about getting proper lessons. How much are the classes?"

Steve sat down at the dining table and salted his food. "It's six hundred Canadian for each two-week intensive." He took a large bite and chewed slowly. "Today everyone starts a new module."

I pulled out my phone and did the currency exchange. The Canadian and Aussie dollars were at parity. Six hundo a fortnight. "Fuck it," I said to Steve. "I'm keen. How do I enrol?"

/

Thirty minutes later an Uber dropped me and Steve off at the EAFIT campus. A security guard checked Steve's Student ID. He explained to the geezer that it was my first day.

"Your Spanish is muy bueno dude," I said to Steve as we walked through the courtyard.

"It's getting there," he said.

I was feeling good about my impulsive decision. Since landing in Medellín I'd been half-heartedly trying to learn some vocabulary with Duolingo on my phone. But I knew I needed a proper course and a good teacher. Hearing Steve speak Spanish fluently was cool as shit. A single month at EAFIT, two full courses, would get me going and it wouldn't break my budget. If I could unlock that part of my brain it would no doubt get my creative mojo flowing too.

Steve ogled every girl as we walked through the campus. Near the cafeteria there was an absolute stunner in sexy librarian glasses – a Latina Mia Khalifa. Steve elbowed me aggressively in the ribs, encouraging me to check her out, but I was one step ahead of him. My sick mind's permanent lodger Patrick Bateman was having a field day, saying the crudest things about Latina Khalifa and her boner-inducing sorority sisters. But unlike Steve the hobbit, I was able to maintain an air of decorum and not exhibit any outward evidence of the crimes of passion that were happening within me. I was relieved when Steve dropped me off at the main lecture hall then marched to class.

The orientation lecture was long and boring. There were maybe sixty of us in the room. The head of the language school was a suave bloke in his early forties. He plodded through a PowerPoint presentation about Colombia. Population, biodiversity, food, dance, culture. Yada yada yada. He played a song on YouTube that featured singers from different parts of the country. My favourite was a bloke called Carlos Vives – the Colombian equivalent of Straya's favourite working class man, Jimmy Barnes.

After the orientation I met the head of the language school in his office. He assigned me into the entry level 'A1' class. I went and found the room. A teacher was writing something on a whiteboard and three students were sitting down, taking notes.

"Hi," I said. "Sorry to interrupt. My name's Anthony Fletcher. I just got assigned into this class."

The teacher, Fernando, told me to take a seat. He was a strange-looking cat. Slender, early fifties, massively receding hairline, sparkly eyes like a precocious child. Weirdly effeminate. The bloke carried himself like a ballet dancer.

Fernando asked the students to introduce ourselves. There was Sean, a scruffy Irish lad in his late thirties. Christine, a young uni grad from NZ. And then there was Nia, a fat black chick with dreadlocks from Texas.

Fernando translated all of our basic info onto the whiteboard. We spent the rest of the lesson re-introducing ourselves in Spanish. I started to fade massively towards the end of class. There was nothing in my stomach apart from a single cup of tea and a hangover began to make its presence felt.

Fernando called time. I rushed out to meet Steve by the campus entrance.

"Hey bro," I said to him. "You ready to split?"

Steve's eyes were darting around at the gaggle of chicas on the sidewalk.

"Yep," he said. "I'm ready."

/

That week Steve and I shared an Uber to uni in the morning and then back to Forever in the arvo every day. I got to know him better. Back in Toronto Steve worked in finance, but got completely burnt out, and taught himself how to code. At that point, he was working freelance for various start-ups in SF, building mobile and web apps.

"Do you know much about crypto?" Steve asked me one morning.

"A little bit. I listened to that Rogan episode with that dude Andreas–"

"–Antonopoulos," Steve interjected.

"Yeah. That's the one. Do you own any?"

"Of course." Steve looked out the window. "You should buy some. It's gonna change the world."

There was a stillness to Steve that was unnerving. The guy was real spectrum-y. But his demeanour offered a welcome respite from Brian and Allie's intense extroversion. He was also really generous at times. One arvo we went to the Oviedo mall together. Steve spoke to the people at Claro on my behalf and helped set me up with a Colombian SIM card.

Forking out a good amount of coin to learn Spanish should've motivated me. And it did, briefly. During the first few classes I opened myself up to everything that Fernando was laying down in class. It was bizarre to be back at uni. I was ten years older than most of the Colombian students on the campus. And like those younger students, my future was undetermined. I had a loose plan about how to better myself, but that was about it.

In my head I was an intelligent person with a knack for language. After hearing Allie and Steve talk fluently, the conceited part of me thought, *if these basic fuckers can pick it up, it's gonna be a breeze for Tony the Pony.* Yet ultimately, learning a new language is about humility. It doesn't matter what you're bringing to the table. The fact that you scored 91% on your English Literature TEE exam in 2004 doesn't count for shit. Your love of subtitled foreign language films doesn't count for shit. Your ability to deliver a confident sales pitch filled to the brim with complex technical jargon doesn't count for shit. All of that goes out the fucking window. When you learn a new language, you become a baby again. You start from zero. To get anywhere, you need to fail again and again and again, whilst simultaneously maintaining your determination not to give up. I don't know why I'm even telling you this, because the truth is, I don't really know what it takes to learn a new language. During my eighteen months in Colombia, my progress was absolutely pathetic. Even now, as I write this tale retrospectively, I'm having to lean on Google Translate pretty heavily when I want to write anything in Spanish! Soy un idiota.

The first couple days were fine. Fernando was attentive and drilled down deeply on every concept. By Wednesday he grew outwardly frustrated by our lack of ability, and started phoning it in. Fernando struck me as the type of guy who entered academia with huge dreams. Fast forward thirty years, and the man was teaching four privileged tourists kindergarten-level sentences. Maybe, at the very least, Fernando had aspirations to be the head of the language school. But perhaps he was too old, and that ship had sailed. So instead, he was forced to submit to the system that had kicked the shit of him during his best years. EAFIT, like most unis and colleges, is a business. Employees like Fernando are not learned scholars – they're organic widgets who shake down dumb cunts like me.

Christine and Nia were way more proficient than me or

Sean. Both attacked the coursework with tenacity – they wanted to learn. On the other hand, Sean and I were just hoping for a miracle, that somehow we'd hear the right information in the right order, and then we'd stand up and say "I know Spanish" like old mate Neo in *The Matrix*. To be fair to Sean, he was a nice fella but a little dense. With his yellow teeth and harsh fringe, the poor lad looked like an Irish serf from the Middle Ages. Fernando kept repeating shit over and over again for Sean's benefit, but nothing seemed to be sinking into the man's brain.

I just remembered a small anecdote about how misguided I was during my short stint at EAFIT. For some reason, the word 'tengo' didn't jive with me. When Fernando explained how 'tengo' was used to denote personal possession – "Yo tengo treinte y uno años... I have thirty-one years" – I actively tuned out his instructions. Instead I thought to myself, *Nah, don't sweat it mate, you'll come across another word that means the same thing which you'll like better*. I can only now truly appreciate how moronic this line of thinking was. We cast judgement upon others and make assumptions about how stupid they are. But in this life, the only stupid person you will truly get to know is yourself. We are the only ones who see *all* of our hidden assumptions that are based on the flimsiest of premises and lead absolutely nowhere. So, as I make fun of Sean's ineptitude, don't mistake that for superiority. My crimes against intelligence are equally as heinous.

Each day class spanned from nine in the morning until one in the arvo. It was a tough slog. By the time Friday rolled around Fernando seemed completely sick of us. Admitting defeat, he assigned some homework and let us leave fifteen minutes early. The four of us decided to grab some lunch to celebrate surviving the first week. We trekked up to Parque Poblado to check out a lunch spot that Nia knew about. The joint had standard Colombian lunch fare – hearty soups, rice, beans, grilled meat, simple salads and sugary juices.

"So, like, how do you guys feel about the structure of the coursework?" Christine asked as she picked some meat off a bone with her plastic-gloved hand.

"It's alright," I said. "I feel like I'm making progress."

"Yeah it's okay," Nia chimed in. "I just wish Fernando would spend more time explaining the grammar side of things."

"Me too!" Christine said.

I had a few beers over lunch and was in the mood to keep things rolling. Christine and Nia went home to study, but Sean agreed to join me for a couple more bevvies. We walked up to Lleras, and hit the sports bar right near the park, the same one I went to during my first night out with the Forever lads. Sean told me more about his life. He came from a small town a couple hours outside of Dublin. Of all his friends, he was the only one who "escaped the village". He went backpacking through Europe in his early twenties, working in hostels and pulling pints to get by. Then a few years after that, he travelled his way around Australia and New Zealand. He worked construction jobs in Wellington and then got into call center work. I bought a packet of Marlboro Golds from a street vendor. We chain-smoked and shot the shit for a couple of hours.

"Fuck man, it's nearly five o'clock," I said as I finished another Heineken.

"I know. I should be getting back to Laureles."

I looked across the park and wondered when I'd bump into my hooker again. "Why don't we just keep going? We could grab a few more beers and drink them back at mine?"

"Oh yeah?"

"Later on my roomie is going out with his mates. We could meet up with them."

Sean agreed to my impromptu plan. According to my English parents, all four of my grandparents have Irish lineage, and so I've always felt a close kinship to my Celtic cousins. As I grow older, I wonder if this says more about my fondness for grog rather than any ancestral connection. After I've necked a certain number of drinks I don't want to stop, but only if I have someone to drink with. For the 'craic'.

When it came to conversation, Sean was hardly Christopher Hitchens. But he was able to make noises with his mouth, and sometimes, that's all that you need.

/

We bought a couple of six packs and wandered up the hill to Forever. When we got back, I fired up YouTube on the big screen and put on the 1995 live MTV version of 'Supersonic'. Brian sauntered shirtless into the living room.

"Sup homies," Brian said. "What are we listening to?"

"Old Oasis," I said.

"Oasis? Sa-weeeet!" Brian said, as he bobbed his head. "Love these bros. 'Wonderwall' is my jam. Maybe throw some Chainsmokers on after this one? Nothing like 'Closer' to get the party started on a Friday noche!"

"Brian, this is Sean, mate from uni."

"Brian Hartman, pleasure to meet you bro!" They shook hands. "You fellas keen to head out tonight?"

"Yeah man," I said. "What's the plan?"

"I'm headed to MAD now. We'll be there for a minute."

Brian left to go meet his mates. Sean rolled a huge joint with my weed. I only had a couple of puffs but the green put me on my fucking arse. I remember stumbling to the bathroom, splashing water on my face, trying to calm the tidal waves of anxiety that were sloshing around inside me. I went back into the living room. Sean had put on the music video for 'Dad's Best Friend' by The Rubberbanditz. My red eyes felt like two chili beans roasting in the sun. I was completely hammered but kept going beer for beer with Seany, the little alcoholic leprechaun. At some point I had conversations with both Allie and Steve in the kitchen, but I can't remember a thing about what was said.

I got changed. We caught an Uber down to MAD. Sean didn't have any cash left so I loaned him 50,000 pesos. Brian was standing in the MAD beer garden with his buddies. I remember getting introduced to a bloke wearing a wide-brimmed hipster hat. Someone bought me a shot of aguardiente and then I went upstairs. Sean was jumping around by himself on the deserted dancefloor like a demonic flea, still wearing his backpack filled with textbooks. I stood still, watched him for a few beats, and then slowly backed away.

FIVE

Another nightmare. As real as it happened the first time around.

I finished my meandering speech. Polite applause. I handed the mic to the MC, bearhugged Dunc and Kel, then jumped off the stage. It was time to get shitfaced.

I dug wearing a kilt. The balmy country Victorian air flowing freely around my nether regions felt wunderbar. As many cunts do, Dunc's mother was getting mad into her heritage as she descended deeper into middle age. Dunc didn't give a shit himself but knew it would make his Ma happy as a clam if he wore the traditional garb on his wedding day. So, Dunc, myself and the other groomsmen donned all the gear and bagpipes bleated at various times during the ceremony. The others were wearing underpants, but I was riding free and easy, the way William Wallace intended.

I double-parked myself with a Coopers pale ale and a scotch on the rocks. It'd been a long few days. Dunc and Kel had rented a five-acre property just outside of Daylesford, which is an hour and a half drive north-west of Melbourne. It was a proper DIY wedding with a 'Wes Anderson holidaying in the Scottish Highlands' aesthetic, so me, Di and a bunch of other family and friends had spent seventy-two hours setting everything up. In the lead up the conditions had been atrocious – cold and drizzly. There was no wet weather contingency plan, and for a minute, the whole thing was looking really dicey. But twenty minutes before the ceremony the sun appeared, and everything came together just as Dunc and Kel intended.

Me and Di were not doing well. She was upset because I'd chosen to drink nonstop since arriving in Daylesford. I didn't understand her problem. If I was going to be toiling all day, unloading tables, setting up tents, draping trees in fairy lights, why not do it with a slight buzz? She said I'd regret not being fully present for every part of my best mate's wedding weekend. After all these years Di still didn't know who I was. When I'm sober, I'm never *really* there. My mind is always occupied, dreaming up various flights of fancy, and with all the social obligation rhubarb, I go on complete autopilot. Conversely, if I'm a little tipsy I'm far more inclined to take a genuine interest in the people and situation around me. Me and Di hadn't spoken a word to one another since the first night we arrived in Daylesford. Now I was done with my speech, it was time to put my toe down.

I started caning the brews. There were quite a few lads from high school over from Perth. I remembered how close our clique was back in the dizzay. They were all quality geezers. When the first year of uni came along, me and Dunc began to detach ourselves. It's hard to recall whether this was a conscious decision. I knew we definitely saw ourselves as the 'arty' types who were destined to move over to Melbourne, whereas the other lads were gonna settle in Perth with good jobs and nice girls. And that's what happened. All the high school boys were engineers, doctors, lawyers, accountants. Me and Dunc moved over to Melbourne, but neither of us could honestly call ourselves legit creatives.

At some point during the night I went into the bushes with one of Dunc's dodgy mates from work to smoke some weed. The pungent grass ripped me right out the frame. I stumbled back towards the music. It was a garish scene. Three generations were vibing to 'I Bet You Look Good on the Dancefloor' by Arctic Monkeys.

Fearing that a whitey was on my immediate horizon, I went back to the two bedroom cabin which we were sharing with the bride and groom. I wanted to lie down, but Di had locked our bedroom door, and I didn't feel like trying to find the stupid bitch. So I turned off all the lights in the living room and sprawled out on the rug in front of the TV.

A while later, I heard voices. Woodsy, one of my pals from high school, was standing over me, laughing hysterically. The overhead lights were on. I lifted myself up. There were about twenty people in the room. Everyone was in hysterics.

I looked down. The kilt was askew. And my junk was on display for the whole world to see.

Woody showed me his phone. "Havin' a good dream, were ya mate?"

I pulled my kilt back down. Then my bloodshot eyes settled on Woody's screen. The cunt had taken a video of me conked out on the living room floor. Oh no! In my sleep I must've reached down, lifted the kilt up, and started playing with my old boy.

The crowd roared when they saw me recoil in embarrassment. My face turned bright red. I stood up.

Woodsy put his arm around me. His breath smelt like curry and hops. "Don't worry mate! We've all done it!"

I was about to grab another beer, laugh it off with the boys, when Di walked into the room. Woodsy made a beeline towards her.

Di's face twitched with fury as Woodsy played her the video. She walked over and grabbed me by the arm.

"What are you *doing*?" she hissed.

Di pulled me towards our bedroom. Woodsy and the boys cheered. I gave them a quick thumbs up and followed Di up the stairs.

She slammed our bedroom door shut. The poor girl looked feral.

"What were you *doing* down there?"

"You locked our door."

"You could've come and found me!"

"I just wanted to lie down–"

"–You were touching yourself! What's *wrong* with you?"

Surprise surprise. Di making a mountain out of a molehill.

"I was asleep. I must've had a dirty dream…"

"There's kids here Tony! What if one of Kel's little cousins walked in when you were doing *that*?"

I shook my head. "Relax. I'll ask Woodsy to delete the video. It's not a big deal."

Di paused for a moment. I could tell she wanted to hit me.

"Why do you always find a way to embarrass me?"

I scoffed. "Embarrass you? You embarrass me."

She crossed her arms like a 'boss bitch' negotiating a deal on *Shark Tank*.

"Oh yeah? How do I embarrass you?"

I loosened my tie.

"I dunno… how about by being the MOST FUCKING BORING PERSON TO EVER SET FOOT ON THE EARTH?" I threw my tie across the room. "'TONY, WHY ARE YOU DRINKING BEFORE LUNCH? TONY, WHEN ARE YOU GOING TO CLEAN THE FRIDGE? TONY, HAVE YOU BOUGHT ME A CHRISTMAS PRESENT YET?'" I stared at my girlfriend of four years. "DO YOU THINK IT'S FUN TO BE WITH SOMEONE LIKE YOU? MAYBE IF YOU FUCKED ME MORE OFTEN I WOULDN'T NEED TO TOUCH MYSELF IN MY SLEEP! YOU ACT LIKE YOU'RE IN YOUR FORTIES ALREADY! WHY ARE YOU SUCH A BORING CUNT?"

Kel barged into the room. She looked stunning in her mud-stained wedding dress. Di glanced at her and burst into tears.

"OH HERE WE GO." I started mock-applauding Di. "AND ONCE AGAIN, THE OSCAR GOES TO… DIANA HACKETT… CONGRATULATIONS BABE!"

Kel ushered Di out of the bedroom.

"I can't do this anymore," Di said to me between sobs. "I'm done. I'm *done*."

/

There's no way I'm going back to that dumb fucking school.

The hangover hadn't even kicked in yet. I stumbled to the bathroom. The anorexic in me likes how I look after a huge night. Gaunt. Cheekbones. Insouciant. Then I start drinking straight from the faucet and my face blows up like a pufferfish. The vanity fades, fast.

It was early, and everyone else was still dead to the world. I made it halfway through a slice of buttered toast and then chucked it up. I was sick as a dog for the rest of the day.

Instead of blaming my hangover on the fact that I had too many beers on an empty stomach, I felt unbridled anger towards EAFIT. Why the fuck was I wasting my meagre savings and valuable time on a dumb fucking Spanish course? I was gonna be spending six months in Colombia, tops, and there were a million other things I could be doing with my time. I cursed myself for getting talked into the idea of going to an overpriced uni with a bunch of squares by that fucking little person Steve.

I jerked off to an Antonella La Bomba FFM scene in the early arvo, which brought temporary relief, but then after five minutes my splitting headache got worse. I thought about the Sean Rouse bit, the one about forcing yourself to drink your own cum to rehydrate yourself after a big night on the turps. I shivered. My whole body got enveloped in a cold sweat and then I ran to the dunny to vomit again.

Thankfully by the late arvo I stopped chucking up and I was able to keep down some tea and a few crackers. This bumpy ride definitely gets a guernsey in my Top Five hangovers of all time. Not fun. Not fun at all.

On Sunday I got my shit together and walked down to ciclovia. As I pounded the pavement I sifted through the mess.

What's the problem here, old boy? Are you blaming the school just because you're struggling to become a student again? Or are you genuinely unhappy with the choice you made? Because there's no harm in quitting if quitting is the right thing to do. You'll be unhappier over the long-term if you stick with something that doesn't jive with you. I shouldn't have to tell you that, Señor Fletcher. You didn't come all the way to Colombia to get financially drained by a draconian institution. It's 2018 mate, and you've got Google Translate on your phone. You can live anywhere overseas and not know a lick of the local tongue! But you've only got a certain amount of money in the bank. And that money is buying you a certain amount of time. When the coin's gone, you're gonna have to change things up anyway. So right now, you've got a little window where you can decide how you wanna spend your days. And here we are again, champ. I've asked you this before. And now I'm gonna ask you again. What exactly do you wanna do with your life?

Although I can get pretty crazy, my rational voice is able to swoop in before things get too out of hand. Sanity is all about self-parenting. Scolding yourself when you do something stupid. Early to bed, early to rise. Eat your veggies. Legit mental cases are psychological orphans. Or even worse, they have parental delusions inside their own head, but instead of love or hate, they only deliver and receive indifference.

When I got back from ciclovia I went to my bedroom and listened to *The War of Art* by Steven Pressfield for the hundredth time on YouTube. In the biopic about my life, I would cast Pressfield to play God. He's the epitome of the wise old village elder, sitting by a campfire, telling all the younglings in the village about what went wrong with his life, how to avoid common pitfalls, how to get into good habits so all of your dreams come true.

I lay on my bed and drank some ice-cold coconut water. Old mate Pressfield started preaching about the evilness of

Resistance, the malevolent life force that gets in the way of everything good and pure. I began to retrace my steps.

When I was in Melbourne, I was fed up with my corporate job because it was sucking up all my time and energy. I didn't come to Colombia because I found it intriguing – I just wanted somewhere cheap where I could afford to be creative all the time. But upon my arrival in Medellín, I lost sight of that. There was a compulsion within me to figure out the people, the geography, the language. It was my own fault. I watched too many stupid vlogs. Cunts like Brian yammering on about the beauty of getting immersed in a completely new culture. Let's face it – that's all bullshit. No matter where you go, people are the same. Different clothes, different religions, different music. But people are people. My choice to study at EAFIT was just Resistance. A huge distraction masquerading as a noble cultural pursuit. Sure, I maybe could've done a better job at applying myself, but that was the fiercely independent artist within me fighting back, desperately trying to sabotage the whole affair.

I started to pace around my bedroom.

OK parcero, if the fluent-in-Spanish-dream is going down the toilet, what are you gonna replace it with? Every action has an equal, yet opposite reaction. For the rest of the year there's nothing stopping you from starting something new or picking up something you've put down in the past. What's it gonna be, Antonio?

I opened up my lappie and started sifting through the desktop folder that glared at me every day: 'Tony Art Stuff'. It was full of stand-up jokes, feature film ideas, unpublished podcast eps, web series outlines, stream-of-consciousness dribble. I clicked around for a bit, grimacing hard at my past attempts at self-expression, when I came across *Song & Dance Man*, one of my unfinished novels.

I opened the doc and read the first few pages of the manuscript. I was expecting the words I'd typed half a decade ago to assault me like the most caustic cringe compilation imaginable, but it actually wasn't too bad. A couple of lines actually made me laugh out loud. The book was a parody of the backstage musical. The thing was set in the mid-60s and Bob Dylan was the protagonist. Old mate Bob is completely bored with the music industry and wants a new challenge. So, he 'disappears' from the public eye, starts wearing a disguise around Manhattan, and secretly begins plotting a Broadway musical, even though he's the worst dancer in the world.

The first draft was 85,000 words long. I remember feeling on top of the world when I finished it. The only person I showed it to was Dunc. He graciously read the thing from beginning to end. I knew it was nowhere near complete, but his lukewarm feedback still cut me to the core. Dunc gave me some solid ideas about how to fix it up, and I had every intention of diving into a second draft, but I never followed through. Something else came up, like it always does.

I started mapping out a plan in my head. By quitting EAFIT, I could spend the rest of the year revising *Song & Dance Man*, and by the beginning of 2019, it would be ready to fly. Then I could go over to New York and pitch the manuscript to a bunch of different publishers. And in terms of work, I could lean on my ad sales background and get a job doing something for *VICE* in Williamsburg, and that would get me one of those E3 visas for Aussies in the States. From there, I could start getting back into stand-up and launch a podcast with another up-and-coming comedian.

It's so easy to find a million holes in this plan now. But at the time, I felt completely reinvigorated. A big part of Pressfield's methodology is to show up every day. Some days you feel like shit, sometimes you're tired, on other days you're incredibly tuned up and everything you touch turns to gold. Despite the circumstances, the important thing is to show up, day in, day out. That's how you 'go pro'. It's not about the quality of the work you're churning out – it's the consistency of your practice.

I created a schedule for myself. I'd wake up in the morning early and hit the gym. If I could smash out some exercise first thing, this would get my endorphins going for the rest of the day. Then I'd come back to Forever and work on *Song & Dance Man* until lunchtime. In the arvo, I'd do another sprint and then call it a day around dinner time. Once a week, I'd allow myself to be a basic bitch tourist. This would force me to socialize with new people and get to know Medellín a little better. At the end of the day, if I was only going to be in Colombia for six months, I needed to know *something* about the place, if only to write about it later.

/

That arvo I bumped into Brian in the kitchen.

"Tony! What's poppin' player?"

"Not a lot dude." It was the first time I'd seen him since Friday. "Hey man, I've got very spotty memories about MAD. Hopefully I wasn't too embarrassing."

Brian waved away my concern.

"Chill, homie. You and your amigo were awesome. Y'all were doing some crazy accents. Me and the bros thought it was hilarious!"

"We were? Fuck. I don't remember shit."

Brian sipped his herbal tea. "You left super early. It's a shame you didn't get to properly hang with any of the Mastermind bros. I'll invite you to the next junto."

"Sounds good."

Brian pointed at his lappie. "Can I show you something real quick? Shot a new vid yesterday, would love to get your feedback."

"Sure. But before that, I'm thinking about joining a gym. According to Google the closest one is Bodytech. Just over the road. Do you know what the deal is with gyms here? Can I just show up?"

Brian chuckled and shook his head. "Wow, the universe has been dropping so many frickin' cool co-inky-dinkies on Bri Bri recently." He put his hand on my shoulder. "I actually had the same thought a couple days ago! Yoga at home is getting a little stale. I asked the squad, and one of the bros recommended Bodytech. I was planning to join tomorrow!"

"Oh. Sweet."

"You wanna be workout bros?"

I nodded. "Let's check it out mañana."

/

We were at the gym bright and early. Brian tried charming the receptionist into giving us a free day pass but didn't have any luck. He had a ton of swagger, but Brian's Spanish was far inferior to Allie and Steve's. There were several times during the exchange that the receptionist had no clue what the fuck Brian was saying.

You lucky son-of-a-bitch, Bateman said as we strolled through the air-conditioned main workout area. It was a thoroughfare of bouncing cleavage and sculpted arse cheeks. There were a bunch of tattooed muscular lads grunting as they threw weights about, but my mind's eye expertly photoshopped the fellas out of the scene.

We found a quiet corner. Brian offered to lead me through a workout.

"Today, I'm thinking we work legs and abs," Brian said as he grabbed some dumbbells off the rack. "I don't know about you, but I feel like there's a huge benefit to moderate exertion over a longer period, rather than simply attacking a single muscle group over a short period... As you know, I'm an Onnit guy, and all of their workouts rely heavily on functional movement, things that you actually do every day... By rocking some squats we can get the blood pumping early in the workout, and from there transition to more core-based movements… If you grab a couple mats, I'll go find some kettlebells."

Brian pulled up an Onnit workout on his phone. He started leading me through it. Instead of just going through each cycle, Brian would stop me mid-exercise to correct my form. It took us three attempts to complete the first round of squats. We moved onto plank push-ups.

"I'm noticing your shoulder blades are bunching up at the top of your spine." Brian paused the video. He crawled next to me and put his hands on the top of my back. "You feel this crowding here? No good, compadre. What you need to do is *lengthen* those arms. That'll keep everything level each time you reset."

I pushed myself off the floor and rested on my knees. "Hey buddy, you know what, I think I'm in the mood for some cardio today. I'm gonna hit the treadmill."

Brian's handsome face creased in disapproval. "You sure man? Trust me dude, this program gets killer results."

"Maybe tomorrow dude. I just really want to get some running in today."

I jumped on the treadmill and threw on some Queens of the Stone Age. Brian sulked for a bit and then slowly went back to his workout. Even without me to fuss over, Brian was barely doing anything. He just kept checking his screen, pretending to agonize over form, the lazy fuck. Josh Homme crooned into my ear and I cranked my machine up a few levels. A talking heads-style fútbol show was playing on the TV in front of me. The hosts were a couple of narcos-looking lads in suits and a stunning blonde chica with a short dress.

After twenty minutes I had a brutal stitch across the left side of my torso. As I cooled down, I looked over to see how Brian was getting on. He'd given up on his workout.

"Wassup fam, it's your boy Bri Bri, and today I'm talking fitness! Now, I know a lot of you gym junkies out there have strict diet and exercise regimes and maybe that's a reason why you don't wanna travel. Maybe you think – damn, what if I go travelling and I can't find any dope spots to work out? Sure, that might be a struggle in some places, but not in Med-e-llín baby! Today the Hart Man's coming at ya live from Bodytech in Poblado, Medellín, and as you can see this place has got it all. We got weight machines. Rowers. Step machines for ya booty. My boy Tony's getting it in over there on the tread-mill. Plenty of free weights, medicine balls, kettlebells, all that good stuff. Upstairs, there's a whole another level where they do aerobics and spin classes. Everything is state of the art and it's only a few pesos a month. So... what are you waiting for? Come say wassup to your boy Bri Bri in Medellín! Alright, that's it fam, time for me to get after it, don't forget to like and subscribe, and be sure to drop a comment if you've got any questions about The City of Eternal Spring. Peace!"

I often wonder, *how did we get here as a culture?* Why did observing 'reality' become so popular? We used to stand in front of funhouse mirrors and watch ourselves become bloated and warped. This led to rollercoasters and horror movies and concept albums. Weird, fantastical, escapist shit. But, over time, the peasants became disillusioned. They craved something more relatable. Real people with real lives talking about real problems. Now cats willingly watch slippery cunts like Brian filming themselves talking about absolutely nothing in a gym.

Even a misanthropic dilettante like myself would have to admit there is something weirdly compelling about these glo-rified home movies. But we are unquestionably wallowing in our own shit. This is something I used to argue with Dunc about regularly. According to him, most people are simply trying to find some gentle, non-confrontational entertain-ment that caters to their loneliness. I don't agree. This type of content isn't entertainment – it's softcore porn for voyeurs, a direct by-product of the social media revolution. And it's a sin, for good reason, to covet thy neighbour's wife. We think we're strong enough not to compare ourselves to strangers on the internet. That doesn't account for human nature. The old shows and movies and records have lost their appeal – shit just doesn't taste as good as it used to.

Instead, we watch mindless videos of preteens walking around malls, incels playing video games, Insta-thots doing unboxing videos. These people aren't you, but they *could* be. The viewer, for better or worse, has become the most fascinating show in the world.

/

One arvo I went on the free Medellín walking tour around 'Centro', a recommendation from Brian. I met the tour guide, a nebbishy fella with a Dali mustache, outside a train station a few stops north of Poblado. There were about twenty of us doing the tour in total (roughly half were Aussies). The guide thanked everyone for coming, remembering everyone's first names without having to consult his clipboard. He led us around the downtown area, El Hueco, for the next four hours. I remember certain titbits from his spiel about Medellín.

Apparently Antioquians are considered the 'Jews of Colombia'. This is because during the early days of colonial migration, when Spaniards were coming over to Colombia to start afresh, it was still a pretty hardcore thing to be a Jew in a Catholic country. A lot of the chosen cunts experiencing persecution in España rebranded themselves with different last names when they made it to South America. Over the centuries, Antioquians became renowned for their entrepreneurial skills and a lot of folks put it down to the Jewish knack for hoarding shekels. Which all sounds like total antisemitic horseshit, but when has the truth ever gotten in the way of a solid tale of casual racism? According to the guide, legit testing indicates that many Paisas do indeed have traces of Jewish DNA compared to other Colombians who have none, but no one verified his sources, so interpret that as you see fit.

Of course, someone on the tour asked him about old mate Pablo. He explained that Escobar symbolizes evil in Colombia. Locals are understandably outraged when they see foreigners glorifying the geezer because of *Narcos*. It would be akin to wearing a 'I Heart Hitler' shirt around the streets of Berlin, simply because you dug the cinematography in *Defiance*. The dude terrorized and killed thousands of people over a decade, and permanently tarnished Colombia's rep on the world stage. But the whole thing is more complicated than you first realize. Pablo did do *some* Robin Hood shit, so there are still hardcore loyalists out there. Also, it wasn't like Pablo was the only dangerous geezer wandering about Medellín during that era. Just like old mate Adolf, the bloke had thousands of henchmen willing to do his dirty work, so when he died it wasn't the end of the story. To this day, Colombia is still the world's number one exporter of Prince Charles. So even though your average man on the street isn't brave enough to come out and say it, there's an unspoken understanding that Escobar was just the tip of the iceberg.

Downtown felt a bit sketched out. Dirty and busy, the air was hot with grease and exhaust fumes. We were instructed to keep our belongings safe in our front pockets. There were a ton of street vendors selling mobile phones and cases. A few dirty vagrants held out their hands as we walked, begging for spare pesos. Each little lane in the downtown area seemed to be unofficially dedicated to a certain type of product, whether it be hammocks, moto helmets, curtains or frying pans. We got a few weird looks from the locals, but on the whole our presence didn't cause too much of a stir. According to the guide, 'the hollow' was safe during the day, but not somewhere you'd want to find yourself after the sun went down.

Halfway through the tour we went to this bakery right in the heart of downtown. We bought some buñuelos – deep fried balls of cheesy dough, a typically stodgy Colombian snack.

"Now, please don't make it too obvious, but if you look over my shoulder, towards the church, you'll see something that sums up this country," the guide said.

Outside the church were a bunch of bored-looking working girls. They looked a lot more haggard and beaten-up compared to the sexy prepagos of Poblado.

"This church is the oldest and most holy in all of Medellín," the guide continued. "But for some reason, this has become a place for prostitutes to wait for customers. It symbolizes the 'yin and yang' of Colombia. God is sacred to Colombians, and we need Him because sin is everywhere, even in the most holy of places."

/

I slowly started going through *Song & Dance Man*. There was a sense of stoned irony weaved throughout the third-person narration. It came across like the beginning of *Pineapple Express*, the black-and-white part in the underground testing facility, when Bill Hader smokes the joint and makes sax noises with his mouth.

Although this goofy filter gave the whole thing a surreal edge, all the jokes were pretty same-y. I realized that if I told the story from Bob Dylan's perspective, it would make it a lot darker. I could zero in on the flawed, insecure Jewish kid from Minnesota who's getting pressured from every angle and doesn't know where to turn. Bob makes the worst decisions imaginable, leading him down a rabbit hole of filth, paranoia and delusion. I nodded my head and made a start on the rewrite.

Each morning I hit the gym with Brian. He desperately wanted a workout partner, but I was loving the treadmill. It made chica-watching muy fácil. At Bodytech there were thirst-traps galore, and it was hilarious watching all of the charged interactions unfold. In Colombia the locals greet with a peck on the cheek, Eurotrash style. All the swoll lads would eagerly plant sweaty kisses on the sexy gals as they sauntered around the room between sets. A never-ending game of cat-and-mouse. Hilariously, there were also a few middle-aged gringo dudes who looked completely out of place, like nerds huddling outside the library.

The rest of the week was uneventful. I kept myself on the straight and narrow – gym first thing with Brian, manuscript editing in the morning and arvo, early to bed. A good little boy chipping away at his dream, doing his very best to make old mate Steven Pressfield happy.

/

Saturday rolled around, the day of Ricardo's party.

After dinner I walked down the hill with Allie and Brian to a barbershop bar just off Diez. Justin, Allie's lanky mate from Virtuagym, met us there. The place was doing two-for-one cock-tails so we ordered a round of mojitos. 'Rockstar' by Post Malone was playing. Allie and Brian started getting into it about Trump.

"Optics count for something my man," Brian said as he stirred his mojito with a straw. "The world looks to America for leadership. And I can't say that Trump has been a very good representation of the American people during his time in office."

Allie wasn't having it. "What about his results? Look at the US economy. Unemployment's down, the stock market's flyin'. Do you think you'd be in the same spot if that bitch Hillary was in charge?"

Brian stroked his beard. "But you're assuming Trump was directly responsible for all that good stuff. Confirmation bias, brother. How do you know those things wouldn't have hap-pened anyway?"

Allie sat on his hands and twitched. "It's just the same as you thinkin' Trump's the cause of all your problems! And I'll tell you something, if you care about what other countries think about you, Trump was the much better choice than Hillary.

That bitch would've been up to her eyeballs in SJW bullshit and nothing would've got done! It's the same with Brexit, mate. The mainstream media tries to tell you that a 'Leave' vote was racist. Facking thing had nothing to do with race! It was about helping out average British people, stopping the pricks in Brussels stealing billions of quid every facking year. When the UK finally pulls out it will be a great day. But you just know they'll twist it to make the average bloke on the street feel like a twat. They've got the whole world brainwashed, facking pricks at the *Guardian*. Anything to keep those ad dollars rolling in."

Brian put up a white flag. "I don't know much about Brexit man, but I'm sure your perspective offers a lot of value." He raised his glass. "Damn fellas, super cool to be chillin' with you bros on this fine Sabado noche, let's do this!"

A DJ jumped on the decks and started spinning A Tribe Called Quest. We all clinked glasses. Allie was still furious. He hopped to the loo for a line. Once you're aware that someone is into nose nonsense, their dirty little habit becomes the most obvious thing in the world.

For some reason I started ranting about the Dalai Lama.

"For the love of God, can someone tell me what the big deal is with that guy? The dude seems like an idiot! He just sits there giggling at everything like a schoolgirl. Bloke's a virgin – he's probably never even had a wank! He must have donkey balls under that robe. Isn't it concerning that *millions* of people genuinely find that dude enlightening? There are turkey sandwiches with more to say."

The others knew I was trying to be funny, so they smiled in my direction, but no one was that enamoured with the riff. I took a sip of my drink. Dunc would get it. Over the years, our sense of humour had become identical.

We drank for a couple of hours then headed over the road to Salón Amador. Just before we left, Allie offered me a bump, but I declined. It was only nine but there was already a small queue outside the club. Allie ran straight up to the bouncer and started chatting to him in Spanish. The bouncer made a quick call on his phone then let us in.

The joint was kitted out like a 70s nightclub. Classy broads everywhere. The music (house sprinkled with a bit of techno) was loud as balls.

We were at the bar buying drinks when Ricardo came over. He was wearing the exact same skater dude get-up, all black from head to toe.

"Parceros!" Ricardo said with a smile. "Come smoke." We grabbed our drinks then Ricardo led us around the dancefloor to the small outdoor section near the loos. Jhonatan and some of Ricardo's other bros were standing in a semicircle. Allie introduced Brian and Justin to everyone. "Qué tal Antonio?" Ricardo asked me as he lit up. "You enjoying Medellín?"

"Yeah dude. Loving it. Thanks again for the invite."

"De nada." Ricardo took a long drag of his smoke. "You're gonna love the headliner. I met him at Tomorrowland a few years ago. "

"This is a really cool spot."

"You like molly?"

"Yeah dude."

"Want some?"

I thought about it. I didn't want to get too fucked up. My plan was to do ciclovia the next morning and then work on my book. But maybe molly was a good idea. It would help me drink less. "Sure," I said to Ricardo. "How much?"

Ricardo called Jhonatan over. He refused my cash. "Salud." I washed down the caps with my Club Colombia Dorada.

Ricardo and his crew split to go meet some other folks out the front. Me, Allie, Brian and Justin hit the floor. It was awkward at first, nervously dancing with three other lads. Brian was throwing huge ungraceful shapes with a cheesy grin painted on his face. He kept yelling shit in my ear, but I couldn't hear a word he was saying. After half an hour I felt butterflies flapping about my lungs. Allie kept nipping to the loos to do rails. Big

Justin, who turned out to be the most boring man in the world, kept moving left to right, right to left, gawking like a hillbilly at a hoedown at all the fuck-houses flooding the dancefloor.

Soon I was walking on air. Every so often I'd glide over to the bar and serenely order another cerveza. Then I'd carry on dancing. I was becoming entwined with the music. Brian excused himself early – he was tired and wanted his bed.

At around midnight Ricardo came and found me on the dancefloor.

"Allie's in trouble. Come."

Me and Justin followed Ricardo out of the club. Allie was on the street arguing with a bouncer.

"Ricardo! Ricardo! Come 'ere!" Allie screamed. "Tell this prick 'oo I am!"

Allie's bald head was bright red. There was a lot of yelling in Spanish, so it was difficult for me to understand exactly what the commotion was all about. As far as I could gather, Allie had done a bump of coke whilst waiting to get served at the bar, one of the bartenders caught him in the act, and security bundled him out. The top dog bouncer didn't want to let Allie back in but eventually Ricardo was able to smooth it over. By that point Allie was so pissed he didn't want to go back in. He told the bouncer to fuck off then jumped in a cab. Justin decided to call it a night too. Ricardo apologized to the bouncer, and that was that.

I spent the next few hours on the dancefloor with Ricardo, Jhonatan and their little crew of pals, dancing to the Belgian DJ. I was peaking something proper and all the bad vibes from Allie's skirmish with the bouncer washed away. A pretty girl glanced in my direction, but I ignored the siren's call and kept doing my thing.

Later, Ricardo introduced me to the Belgian. He was a skinny little fella who looked uncomfortably coked up. We smoked a few cigs then the Belgian caught a cab back to his hotel. Ricardo asked me if I wanted to smoke a spliff with him and Jhonatan to finish off the night. We piled into an Uber just after two.

Shortly after we arrived at Ricardo's building, Jhonatan got a text from some chica he was chasing. Apparently, she was down to fuck, so Jhonatan said ciao and split. Ricardo grabbed his weed and rolling papers. We sat down outside by the pool. He put on 'Muy Tranquilo' by Gramatik.

"What's the deal dude," I said as I passed the joint back to Ricardo. "Do you throw parties at that spot every weekend? All the music was really dope."

"I'm actually a part-owner of Salón."

"Whoa! That's sick."

"Yeah, it's cool," Ricardo said. He took a hit of the jazzie. I looked down at the wild neon bowl that is the Medellín skyline. Reggaeton basslines rumbled up from the few spots that were still open on the 10. "I'm actually part of a conglomerate. We run a few bars and restaurants in Poblado. I'm the kid of the group. I do the promotion. PR, social media, artist bookings, influencers, all that shit."

This explained why Allie wanted Ricardo's help with the bouncer. "Is that your main gig?"

"Gig?"

"Like, your job. How you earn money."

Ricardo handed me back the joint. "Más o menos. My father was a businessman. He got killed by the narcos when I was a kid. The government seized some assets. Corruption, you know? But my family was lucky. We got to keep some things. Other families, they lost everything."

I nodded. "Damn. That's heavy dude."

Ricardo shrugged it off. "It is what it is. Life goes on."

We went inside to grab beers. While Ricardo was pissing, I leant on the kitchen counter. YouTube was silently looping on the big TV. The music video for 'Hero' by Mariah Carey came on. I was unwillingly transported back to the mid-90s.

Ricardo came back from the loo. "You okay man?"

A few hot tears were running down my face. "Yeah," I said with a laugh. I wiped away the tears with the back of my hand. "Just feeling a bit fucked up from those caps."

Ricardo nodded. "You want water?"

"Nah man, I'm good." I put my half-finished beer down on Ricardo's counter. "Think I'm gonna call it a night, bro. I'm knackered." I gave Ricardo a hug and then made my way towards the front door. "Sorry for making it weird. Thanks for a top night."

"No problem man. Get home safe."

SIX

"Joseph! How are you today, sir? Brian Hartman from The Lifestyle Corp. I'm calling for our 10am Eastern."

I was in the kitchen making breakfast. For some reason Brian had let his Selina membership expire so he was doing business calls at home. Instead of using a headset, the dumb cunt did the calls through his lappie, so I was able to hear both sides of the conversation.

"Fantastic! Well it's so great to connect with you, Joseph. Whereabouts in the States are you based?"

"Chicago," Joseph said.

I'd done some digging on The Lifestyle Corp. According to his LinkedIn profile, Brian had been with them since 2013. It was difficult to ascertain exactly what they did. Everything seemed to fall under the general banner of 'network marketing', which if I'm not mistaken, is just a euphemism for pyramid-selling.

"The Windy City! Huge fan of Chicago, love me some deep dish… Well Joseph, I'm calling from my office here in Medellín, Colombia and I'm so happy to be talking with you today! Before we get started, quick question. Did you get an opportunity to review the presentation I sent over last week?"

Let me be clear. There wasn't something so utterly intriguing about Brian that prompted me to do a deep dive. I do deep dives on *everyone*. During my first couple years of uni when Myspace then Facebook took off, I became fascinated with people who shared their lives over the internet. My lurking was driven by hormones – social media allowed me to perve on the girls that I was crushing on at the time. But it quickly grew into something far more comprehensive.

It can take years for a person to truly reveal themselves IRL. Yet the internet, and specifically social media platforms, have become 'safe spaces' where you can divulge a lot of heavy shit to a captive audience. We've become lab rats addicted to little red notifications. The promise of something amazing, the insight that will lead you towards success, fame, acceptance, validation. I remember watching the doco *We Live In Public* a long time ago. That flick spelled out the whole mess very clearly: if something is free, that means you, or rather your data, is the thing that's getting bought and sold.

By spending time lurking on social media every day, I've become clairvoyant. Everything is a clue. When a rabid fame-whore sympathy poster goes AWOL: good chance someone just changed their meds and is suffering through a new bout of depression. When a gal swaps out her couple shot profile pic for a selfie showing off her questionable new haircut: good chance her boyfriend's chronic alcoholism finally came to its logical conclusion and destroyed their relationship from the inside out. When your old buddy from high school starts sharing Alex Jones videos and anti-vaxxer infographics: good chance he's back on the bongs and his short-lived goal to complete two marathons and a biathlon by the end of the year has well and truly taken a backseat.

If you pay attention to someone's output on the internet, it reduces the chances of them surprising you. And as a child of divorce, I fucking hate surprises. Lurking doesn't help you get to the bottom of everything. Some cunts have avoided the siren call of Zuck and Dorsey entirely. But compared to the billions of paranoid androids that dominate the Earth, these analogue Amish fuckers are few and far between.

Although I tried to resist when the whole craze kicked off, I eventually got on Facebook, then Twitter, then Insta. I put my shitty garage band music on YouTube and Soundcloud. Me and Dunc's old podcast was on iTunes. Over time I've taken down a lot of stuff that had my name attached to it. Revisionist personal history. There was always a sense of detachment to everything I put out. If the internet was a bar, I considered myself the 'cool' guy, hanging out in the poets' corner with all the wildest cats and kittens, smoking jazz cigarettes, dressed like a member of Sonic Youth in 1991, throwing out layered jabs and jokes, open to everything, attached to nothing, chasing freedom in the most sardonic way imaginable. I've never shared anything painfully honest about myself online. This is why I've never built an audience and hate everything that I've created. Sometimes I catch a glimpse of someone else in a similar quagmire. They've become nothing more than a pathetic clown. I feel pity for these poor souls. I understand them better than most, but I never try to help them. I have my own clown to kill.

"So Joseph, I'd really like to draw your attention to slide seventeen of the presentation. This is where we break down the real benefits of joining Mark's Mastermind. We like to call them the three P's."

Back to my deep dive on The Lifestyle Corp. Brian met this huckster called Mark Tallone when he was a freshman at the University of Miami. Mark sold insurance and mortgages in the late 90s but then eventually pivoted over to blogging.

"The first 'P' Joseph: People. You're gonna meet the highest performers in your industry, and these *super* tight knit bonds are gonna change your life."

In the early aughts Mark Tallone built traction on his blog by regurgitating standard 'just do it' business advice about entrepreneurship and investing. From there, he began vlogging and then this led to public speaking gigs.

"The second 'P' stands for Persistence. Trust me Joseph, I know that being a business owner in the current economy is very draining. Some days, you flop out of bed and think to yourself 'Can I really be the best version of myself today?' But by joining this Mastermind, you're gonna be able to express all your hidden doubts and concerns with trusted peers, and they'll reciprocate by sharing their coping strategies. This will allow you to keep showing up and delivering the goods, day in, day out. Best practices and accountability from world class performers. Sound good, Joseph?"

Right around the time Mark Tallone met young Brian, The Lifestyle Corp was really taking off. It had become a multi-armed organization that made money through events, blogging, content marketing, personal coaching and corporate training. They also sold Lifestyle Corp-branded vitamins, supplements and fitness merchandise. And it was all essentially one big Ponzi scheme. Old mate Mark was adept at recruiting wide-eyed pups like Brian into the cult. The system was designed so that basically any schmuck who wasn't a complete degenerate could make some coin immediately after joining. But then to continue making dosh, the newbs would have to rope in more members.

"And now Joseph, we get to my favourite 'P': Power. Think about all of your talents, skills and experience that has helped you become the person you are today. Yet, there's still so much to learn, and only so many hours in the day! The proven way to accelerate your growth is to partner up with like-minded individuals who also have a wealth of knowledge and experience. If you need help skill-ing up, it's extremely likely that another Masterminder is gonna have the info you need to grow fast. Together, as a powerful unit under the watchful eye of Mark Tallone, you'll quickly become unstoppable!"

I know all of this shit because I watched a take-down YouTube video from a disgruntled ex-Lifestyle Corp member. The funniest thing about the whole affair is that Mark Tallone so clearly wants to be Tony Robbins. But with his disgraceful goatee, spiky gelled hair and 5'7 stature, he's more sewer rat than Adonis-like demigod.

"So, Joseph, how are you feeling about this opportunity? Can I set up an intro call with yourself and Mr Tallone?"

This was the fourth time I'd heard Brian's Mastermind group pitch. So far, he was o and three.

"Look," Joseph began, "This is all sounds great, but I'm pretty busy right now and…"

Ouch. Poor old Bri Bri. Make that o and four.

/

I was beginning to realize how big an undertaking it was to edit a manuscript.

The first few chapters of *Song & Dance Man* were fluently written with a ton of laughs. But by Chapter Six, my prose started getting real sparse. The novel was meant to be a trippy, psychedelic exploration of disguise and self-deception. I wanted the thing to have energy and thrust, edging the reader towards an orgiastic final showdown. Just like Dunc told me all those years ago, the story had potential, but I needed to spend time beefing it up with more substance.

One arvo I caught the metro and a bus and went up to Comuna 13, a neighbourhood in the north-west of the city. The area's famous because it used to be extremely crime-ridden, but now amazing street art attracts tourists from all over the world. When I was riding up one of Comuna 13's infamous outdoor escalators, I bumped into a large group of middle-aged tourists.

"Now if you look behind me, there's some graffiti in English. 'NO TOURISTS'. Do you see it?" the tour guide said to his group. He looked frighteningly similar to the geezer from the downtown walking tour. I wondered if they were brothers or twins. "Now, let me explain this. As I told you before, the locals are very proud of their neighbourhood and want visitors from all over the world to come here. So, this 'NO TOURISTS' sign is not a warning. In fact, it means the opposite! The people from Comuna 13 are trying to say that any visitors will be considered locals. Please don't worry, there's nothing aggressive about the message. It's just a funny translation!"

I looked at the tour group and felt disgusted. Nothing makes a cultural experience less authentic than bumping into fat Americans with their dumb fanny packs.

I was doing a good job of keeping my nose clean. Gym, tons of water and a super-healthy diet. Something I picked up from Dunc back in the uni days was to keep a huge bottle of water by your side when you're writing. When you're in the thick of it, battling Resistance, your brain is going to compulsively demand a distraction, something, *anything*, to take your mind off the soul-crushing task of putting one word after the other. Taking greedy gulps of water fills the void, and it's a pretty fucking harmless habit. Sure, you end up pissing more. But it also facilitates some type of weird psychosomatic connection, and tricks your mind into releasing trapped sparks of genius onto the blank page.

/

One Sunday arvo I went to a party with Brian and Steve. An Uber picked us from Forever just after three. It took us to this older block of apartments just off Avenida El Poblado, near the Dann Carlton. Brian spoke to the portero and we stepped onto the premises.

"I met Mike a couple weeks back. Expat meetup at Mission20," Brian said. "You been to Mission20 yet Tony?"

"Nope."

"Oh dude, you *have* to check it out." Brian did a shoulder exercise as we walked along. "Tons of brews on tap. I know you're a cerveza guy, so you'll be in heaven. Also, they got some amazing food. Ribs, sausage, tons of other keto-friendly options."

"Cool. I'll have to check it."

"Anyway, Mike just moved to Medellín from Bogotá. He's super chill. You're gonna love him. Mike has a roomie, Norwegian called guy called Ivar. He's a rad dude too."

We walked through the courtyard. There were a few young families playing on the communal playground with their children. Mike and Ivar's apartment was on the ground floor. A gorgeous Colombiana opened the door. She said something to Brian in Spanish.

"Sorry dudes, it's gonna be twenty mil each," Brian said to me and Steve. "Helps cover the ice and paleo snacks. My bad bros. Forgot to mention that."

We paid the chica and entered the apartment. It was a sprawling place with strong 80s vibes. The living room opened up to an enormous outdoor deck that was bordered by a tiny strip of lawn. There were maybe twenty or so people milling about outside. Some generic psytrance was pulsing out from a Bluetooth speaker. I noticed a familiar face in the crowd.

"Hey mates," he said. "Thought I'd run into you lot."

"Chris!" Brian said, warmly. "How's it goin', *mate*?"

I realized it was the Aussie travel geezer from YouTube, *Chris The Wanderer*.

"Hey buddy," I said to him. "Tony. I've seen your videos."

Chris smiled at me. "Yeah, mate. You told me about it the other night."

"Oh shit. I did?"

"Yeah dude," Brian chimed in. "You met Chris that night at MAD. You and your Irish buddy from college were lit!"

It clicked. Chris was the bloke in the hipster hat from my brown-out memories of that evening. "Damn, sorry dude. I was fucking hammered that night. Good to see ya again."

Chris brushed it off. He was a friendly-looking geezer with a Grade 4 haircut. About 5'11 and handsome in the most non-threatening way imaginable. Chris was dressed like an off-duty cop. "All good, mate. You were good value that night. Somehow managed to beat me in Jenga too!"

I smiled. "I probably said this the other night, but you're kinda the reason why I'm here," I said to Chris. "I watched your Medellín videos when I was back in Melbourne."

/

After I broke up with Di, I moved into a share house in St Kilda with two loose tradies from the Cenny Coast. It was a Sunday in December, hot as balls, and I spent all day at home drinking VB, smoking jazzies, watching some Test Match cricket. The Cenny Coast boys went out to have a few at our local, leaving me alone. After the cricket ended some retarded Russell Crowe and Meg Ryan movie called *Proof of Life* came on. Old mate Rusty plays a hostage negotiator in South America who gets contracted to save Meg's husband. Of course, Meg with her 2-Minute Noodle hair can't resist Rusty's blokey machismo, and they end up having a sordid affair. The whole thing is fucking farcical – an unintentional stoner comedy of the highest calibre.

The next morning, I cycled into the office and looked *Proof of Life* up on Wiki. Apparently, the producers wanted to shoot the movie in Colombia, but it was too hot and heavy to do so at the time, so they filmed in Ecuador instead. For whatever reason, I decided to do a deep dive on Colombia, and eventually I stumbled upon Chris' travel content on YouTube.

/

"Yeah, you did mention that the other night," Chris said with a chuckle. "At this point, 'Live and Work in Medellín' is our most popular video. Just ticked over 300,000 views! People get a lot of value outta that one."

Brian introduced Chris to little Steve. The four of us stood in a semi-circle, cracked beers and surveyed the scene. Two tall blonde lads were pouring bags of ice into plastic drums. More people started streaming from the apartment out onto the deck. It was certainly a sausage-fest – eighty percent dudes, maybe even more.

Our chat turned to crypto.

"I completely understand the need for making online transactions more seamless," I started. "Like, here's a good example. Nowadays more and more podcasters are trying to monetize their content by putting certain episodes behind a paywall. They'll release one episode a week for free, and then the other one will be for subscribers only. Most of them use a service like Patreon. If I wanna become a subscriber, I have to go ahead and create a Patreon account, find the show on their directory, select my subscription level, enter my credit card, and then I'll get the paywalled content. That's a *lot* of barriers. So, I completely understand how some new type of digital transaction method could be useful. Like if Sam Harris created a paywalled episode, promoted it on Facebook or Insta, it would be cool if I could just flick him a couple bucks and get the ep immediately. This would simplify the whole process and it would be better for both creators and consumers. So I completely understand the need for finding new delivery systems to transfer funds. But here's what I don't get about crypto. *Why does it need to be a new currency entirely?* Like, why couldn't these new payment methods just be linked to my Aussie bank account?"

Steve jumped right in. "Regulations. Right now, all major currencies are regulated by the government. That makes them easy to manipulate. No one can regulate crypto."

I took a sip of beer. "But people only got excited about crypto when bitcoin became valuable compared to US dollars. Do you think most people bought bitcoin because they saw the inherent value of crypto? Or were they just trying to make a quick buck?"

Steve stared at me with his dead eyes. "It won't happen overnight. There's gonna be a tipping point. And then on the other side we'll see the opposite behaviour. Investors will continue trading traditional currency for a while because it could help them acquire more crypto."

"But hang on," I said as I cracked open another beer, "Do you honestly think governments are just gonna roll over and let that happen? Let's assume crypto is a fundamentally better system and more people decide to start using it. Governments are businesses, and businesses need cash to survive. There's no way in hell crypto will stay unregulated if we get anywhere close to that tipping point! The taxman will start throwing cunts in jail if they don't cough up a piece of the action."

Chris chimed in. "Honestly, that's why I've steered clear of crypto. Me and Kat are Australian, our business is based in California, and we live in Colombia. So already, our tax situation's pretty complicated. I read that in Korea last year the government started making people disclose crypto assets. I guess other governments will start doing that soon."

"You've got a kid, right?" I asked Chris.

"Yeah mate. Little boy, Bobby. Just turned two."

"This is all super-interesting," Brian said. "Like, Tony, I totally see where you're coming from. That more traditional set-up definitely has some perks, and a lot of people don't want to change their ways. But Steve is a real expert in this space. Personally, as a creator, I'd love it if my followers had more ways to show my content love. I'm excited to see how things develop!"

Steve ignored Brian's attempt to wind down the disagreement. "You don't understand all the different applications for this type of technology," Steve said to me. "There's challenges during any period of transition. But over time, they'll become less and less significant."

The deck started to fill up. A large group of young chicas arrived – *grillas* with tramp stamps, faded blue jeans and

Adidas trainers. Someone killed the music. Mike and Ivar stood on some deck chairs. They were both giant, athletic dudes with long limbs. Ivar was by far the prettier one with his Nordic bone structure and Ken doll head of hair – he looked like an Olympic volleyballer. Mike was shredded, but a total prawn. The poor bloke had beady Lord Voldemort eyes, and one of the worst sets of teeth I'd ever seen.

"Parceros!" Mike began. "Welcome to our humble abode. I hope you're excited about this communal experience!"

"Raise your hand if you've heard of the Wim Hof breathing method," Ivar said.

Just over half the crowd put their hands in the air.

"Fantastic," Mike said. "Well, for those who don't know the great man, Wim Hof is a pioneer in human performance. He developed a system which uses breath work and cold to reset all of your internal systems. We'll demonstrate the technique shortly with the ice baths. But before that, Ivar's going to lead the whole group through a guided meditation."

"Everyone set your drinks down," Ivar said. "Now, I want you to close your eyes and take a deep breath… And another… And another… Pay close attention to your breath… The breath is your guide… Your compass… Now in a moment, after a few more deep inhales, I'm going to let out a slow 'om'… I want you to join me… And from there, we're going to build up the energy very slowly and see where it takes us…"

Ivar let out a deep, guttural 'om' and we all followed suit. Slowly, the intensity started to build. After about a minute someone in the crowd started making a hissing sound. A couple chicas began whooping like banshees. Someone near me was growling like a bullfrog playing a didgeridoo. I got bored and took a sip of my beer.

The rhythm of the original chant was lost. It descended into chaotic primal howling which lasted for a few minutes. Somehow, everyone got back in sync with one another. The whole thing ended with a violent crescendo. There was a brief moment of silence which was broken by some nervous gig-gling and a polite smattering of applause.

Mike and Ivar were the first to submerge themselves in the ice water drums. Most of the crowd pushed forward to watch but I hung back and cracked open another brew. Mike and Ivar got out after a few minutes and started doing the Wim Hof breathing bullshit. Then, once that was done, Ivar let out a few more primal screams, just for the hell of it. The man was a gobbledygook evangelist of the highest order.

Brian and a loud Texan were the next ones in the baths. Brian hopped out like a bitch after less than a minute and spent the next hour shivering. Chris introduced me to Ivar – he seemed spaced out, like he was on shrooms. As the arvo wore on, the loosest units started to dance in the middle of the deck to a 'Burning Man' Spotify mix. Steve stood and stared at the twerking grillas in silence. He seemed to be des-perately trying to figure out how to stick his dick in one of them without throwing a single move on the floor.

While I was taking a piss, my phone buzzed. Message from Ricardo.

Antonio. Having a little party at my place now. You free?

I finished pissing and stepped back into the living area. Steve, Brian and Chris were chatting solemnly on the edge of the dancefloor. I pulled out my phone and responded to Ricardo.

Sounds good bro. Be there in 15.

SEVEN

Allie's guy pulled up on a moto and we gave him cash. Then we joined the throng walking towards the stadium.

"Technically this is a local derby," Allie explained. "But no one takes Envigado seriously. The real derby is against Nacional. I can't *wait* until we get to play those green cunts again. Ref facking robbed us last time around."

I felt like I was in a *VICE* expose about hooliganism. We marched through a dank, grey tunnel behind a large mob of Independiente supporters. There were tons of police on horses stationed around the perimeter of the stadium. Allie was in his element.

We handed over our tickets and walked through the turnstile. The stadium holds about twenty-five thousand. Allie led me to the home end, which was jam-packed. The atmosphere was wild. It was ten minutes 'til kick off and the whole end was already singing and dancing. Someone let off a flare just behind us. All of the ultras seemed pretty sketchy – gakked out something chronic, borderline street people. The rest of the stadium seemed far more family friendly. Allie belted out a chant in Spanish. The other fans stared at him for a moment but then eventually joined in.

The match turned out to be a thriller. Independiente went 2-0 down early but managed to get level before half-time and ended up winning 4-3. The players on both teams were skilful as fuck but didn't have anywhere near the same fitness levels as the lads in the Euro leagues. I was convinced that number 27 for Envigado was a gringo. I looked him up on my phone and sure enough I was right. *Billy Hughes, born in London.*

It was fucking intense being amongst all the crazies. They didn't stop dancing and chanting for the entire game, including the halftime break. When the Independiente goals went in, the roar was accentuated by hundreds of air horns. A group of young lads right in front of us were swigging from baby bottles of aguardiente and chain-smoking joints. Allie was doing key bumps. He finished his bag just as the ref blew the final whistle.

"Let's go see Ricardo," Allie yelled in my ear. "He's at one of his clubs on the 10."

/

Half an hour later we entered a bar that looked fit for a Kardashian's sixteenth birthday party. It was upmarket with a few garish touches. Grecian pillars covered in plastic vines connected the ground floor with the upper level. It was well before midnight and the main dancefloor was empty.

"He'll be in that private booth over there," Allie said.

Ricardo and about ten of his crew were sipping vodka and chilling. The room was lit with a blacklight. I noticed Marcela immediately. She was wearing a plain white tank top, sitting on the couch, laughing with one of her girlfriends. I first met Marcela the Sunday before at Ricardo's after I bailed on the primal howling party. She had a cute, squirrel-like face and clear braces. Marcela worked as dental assistant in Laureles and spoke a bit of English.

Allie bought another bag from Ricardo and I hoovered up a line in the loos. I got myself a stiff glass of vodka and orange. After a couple of minutes, I boldly plonked myself down on the couch next to Marcela and started chatting. She seemed happy to see me. Ricardo ordered more bottles and I downed more drinks. Allie offered me more charlie but I refrained. 'The Hills' by The Weeknd came on. Marcela grabbed my hand and pulled me into the middle of the room. She grinded on me for a bit. Then suddenly, she bailed.

"Marcela likes you, man," Ricardo said to me later that night.

"She does?"

Ricardo laughed. "You like her?"

"For sure. She's cute."

"I'll give you her WhatsApp. You should send her a message."

Ricardo always had girls around. But he never seemed that focused on pussy, unlike Jhonatan and his buddies, and the vast majority of Colombian men, who are thirsty as fuck 24/7. That night at the Kardashian club all the local lads were trying to pull girls in the club or texting chicas on WhatsApp. The lot of them hardly spoke a word to one another. Ricardo was different. He just puffed on his vape and worked the room. All business, all the time.

/

The next day I sent Marcela a message and we started chatting. Without old mate Google Translate I would've been fucked. For a solid forty-eight hours we were in constant communication – it was like I was fifteen again. Eventually, I worked up the nuts and asked Marcela if she wanted to grab some dinner. She responded immediately in the affirmative. I punched the air and picked an Italian restaurant in Poblado with solid reviews.

In the lead up to the big date, I stalked my way through Marcela's Insta. The pics seemed carefully curated – about twenty selfies and a couple of group shots with her gal pals. No ex-boyfriends to speak of. I looked Marcela up on Facebook, but she didn't appear to have a profile.

I received another email from Dunc.

Hey mate

This hasn't been easy for me to write, and it probably won't be easy for you to read.

For a while now, it's been pretty difficult to be your friend. During your last few months in Melbs you were detached and aloof. This made sense. With such a huge trip on the horizon, I wasn't expecting you to be super-engaged with anything around here.

But the fact you haven't responded to any of my emails or messages since you made it to Colombia has wrecked me. I understand you're probably doing a bunch of different stuff, and that's fine. I just feel slighted that you haven't made time to reach out.

I know I've been busy with work stuff over the last few years. And the whole six months leading up to the wedding was a blur, so I probably wasn't a good friend during this sprint. As you know, Kel's still tight with Di, as am I, but that doesn't mean we value you any less as a friend.

If there's something I've done to hurt you, let me know. I would like to think we could work through just about anything. But maybe that's wishful thinking on my behalf. I'm in the dark here and would love to hear from you soon.

That's it. Just wanted to clear the air.

Hope you're having fun in the sun.

Dunc

/

Wednesday arvo rolled around. I jumped out of the shower and checked my phone. Message from Marcela.

I'm so sorry Tony. I can't see you tonight. I need to see my family in Laureles. Can we try next week?

Fuck. Allie warned me about Colombian girls. They vibe with you hard on WhatsApp but then always find an excuse to bail just before the first date.

I was about to text Marcela back something snarky. But I talked myself off the ledge.

No worries. Next week sounds good. Hope everything's okay with your family. Have a good night!

I walked into the kitchen. Brian was meal-prepping a huge batch of green curry.

"Damn Tony boy, I'm loving that shirt," he said. "Strong *aloha* vibes. What are you doing tonight, homie?"

"I actually just had a date bail on me. So nothing much."

Brian pirouetted on the spot. "In a couple hours I'm gonna head down and meet my buddy Melissa at Dancefree. Thought it was high time I got my ass to a dance class. You wanna come with?"

I thought for a minute. "I don't wanna intrude on your date, dude."

Brian waved me away with his spatula. "Ain't like that, man. Mel's just a friend. Anyway, it's a group class for beginners. They'll be a big crowd down there tonight."

I was all dressed up with nowhere to go. "OK. Sounds good, man. Appreciate the invite."

We arrived at Dancefree just before 8.30. Brian locked his Onewheel out front. We paid and the lady behind the counter gave us wristbands.

"How do you know Mel?" I asked Brian.

"She works at this local chocolate spot, near Velvet. When I feel my productivity lagging, I ride over to her cafe and get myself some bomb dark chocolate. So good bro! I'll take you there this week." Brian waved to someone over my shoulder. "Here she comes now."

Mel waved at Brian. She had extremely heavy eyeshadow and pink streaks in her hair. Mel was walking alongside a beautiful girl who looked like a runway model.

"Brian!" Mel said with her throaty smoker's voice. She planted a kiss on his check. "Cómo estás?"

"Muy bien. Y tu?" Brian said.

"Bien gracias."

Brian put his hand on my shoulder. "Mel this is my Aussie roomie, Tony."

"Mucho gusto, Tony!" She pecked me on the cheek. "Brian, Tony, this is my friend Dani. We've been dancing together for two years."

I looked at Dani. Tall, tanned, shoulder-length brown hair. Deep, intoxicating coffee-coloured eyes. It's so rare to see perfect tens in the wild. Even in Colombia, where there's an absolute abundance of stunning women. Tens have a grace and tranquillity that's unmistakable.

"Hi! Nice to meet you both," Dani said. As a cherry on top, her English was immaculate.

We wandered into Dancefree. The place was packed. A squat little gringo instructor with a headset mic led the class. He barked out orders in English and Spanish. The dancers seemed split right down the middle between gringos and locals. Legit salsa looks like sex standing up. At the other end of the spectrum, beginners resemble virgin dorks at a church dance.

Towards the end of the class, the instructors got all the dudes to split into two separate circles. The gals danced a few simple steps with one bloke and then moved onto the next guy. Finally, I was gonna get an opportunity to dance with Dani. We locked eyes. Just when I was about to put my hand on her hip, the instructor cut the music and moved us onto the next exercise.

For the final few minutes of the class the instructor blasted the music and let everyone do whatever they pleased. The beginners gravitated towards the back of the room. Me and a fifty-year-old American lady just practiced going left to right, right to left. Dani was getting spun around like a sports car by a beefy local. The instructor called time.

"That was dope!" Brian said as Mel and Dani wandered towards us. "Y'all wanna head somewhere and grab a drink?"

"Si!" Mel said as she beamed at Brian.

"Sure," Dani said.

Brian danced on the spot. "Hakuna Matata! What's good near here?"

"How about we try MAD?" I said. "Play some Jenga?"

/

Fifteen minutes later I was bringing three Pilsens and a soda water out to the MAD beer garden. Some Russian blokes had claimed the Jenga set, so the four of us sat on the quaint tree-stump stools and chatted.

"Tony the Pony was crushing it tonight," Brian said as he sipped his soda. "You got them liquid hips, homie!"

I shook my head. "Dude. I was terrible. Don't lie to me."

The girls giggled.

"Did you two meet in Medellín?" Mel asked us.

"Yep. I met Brian when I moved into Forever."

"And what part of Australia are you from, Tony?" Dani asked.

"I grew up in Perth. But I've spent the last seven years living in Melbourne."

"Oh really!" Dani said, her eyes lighting up. "I *love* Melbourne."

Dani started asking me about my past life – where I lived, favourite restaurants, music venues. She visited Melbourne in 2016 and fell in love with the place. Our conversation was so intense that I forgot Brian and Mel were there. I grabbed myself another beer and Dani a water. She was originally from Cali and had moved to Medellín to study. After graduating she started working as a graphic designer for some ad agency.

"Looks like these homies ain't budging," Brian said as he gestured at the Russians. "There's a pool hall a few blocks away. Anyone down for some 8-ball?"

Mel was all over Brian as we walked towards Lleras. They were dancing in the middle of the street for a minute, and then Mel demanded a go on his Onewheel. She was laughing at full volume at every lame joke Brian dropped on her. Bri Bri, the sly old goober, had snagged himself a gimme. There was no way he could possibly miss this shot.

We claimed the one free table at the pool hall.

"Alright let's do two on two," Brian said as he chalked up a cue. "What're we thinking? Chicos v chicas?"

"Me and Dani could be Team Melbourne?"

"That works!" Brian said.

Brian racked up the balls and broke. The music in the hall was like 96FM – Perth's 'Dad Rock' station. Pearl Jam, Nickelback, Nirvana and a shit ton of Guns N' Roses, who are basically living gods in Colombia. Allie told me that one time he was riding his bike near Parque Poblado when he saw a bunch of musos all jump out of an SUV and walk into a jazz club just opposite the park. They looked like pros, so he parked his bike and went into the club to investigate. Turns out old mates Slash and Duff were in town to play a huge stadium show on the weekend and they fancied a strum! Allie watched them jam with the house band for an hour and managed to get a photo with them afterwards too.

Team Melbourne crushed Mel and Brian at pool. I gave Dani a high-five. "Muy bien. You want another drink?"

"No, I have to go," Dani said. "Work tomorrow."

'Like A Stone' by Audioslave was blaring. Mel and Dani decided to share a cab.

"Hey," I said as I followed them out of the hall. "I forgot to tell you. We're having a party at Forever next Friday night. Both of you should come."

"At your home?" Mel said.

"Yeah. Give me your numbers. I'll WhatsApp you the deets."

The girls put their numbers into my phone. Chris Cornell was wailing in the background. A yellow cab stopped out the front of the hall. Dani waved in my direction and then slammed her door shut.

EIGHT

"Joe! How you doin' amigo?"

I ushered Joe D'Angelo inside. His date was a petite little thing who looked *very* young.

"Hey Tony, good to see ya again bud." Joe was drenched in cologne. He wore a bright purple dress shirt. "This is Valentina, my wife."

The age gap between them must've been close to forty years.

"Mucho gusto!" I said to Valentina. "Come in, make yourselves at home." I laughed at myself. "I'm an idiot. This *is* your home! My bad."

Joe chuckled. "Relax. It's your home too, amigo."

"Snacks on the table there. We've also got some steaks to grill on the barbie later. What can I get you guys to drink?"

I connected my phone to the speaker. That arvo I'd created a Spotify playlist. From my deep dive through Dani's socials, it was clear that she was mad into salsa. But I didn't want to pander too much. I still have the playlist in front of me. 'Shuggie', Foxygen; 'Free Your Mind', Cut Copy; 'Good Advice', The Growlers; 'Sacred Sands', Allah-Las; 'I Can't Feel My Face', The Weeknd; 'Melbourne', DMAs; 'Delorean Dynamite', Todd Terje. Then, after about two hours of my bullshit, I lined up tons of pop bangers, reggaeton and salsa-friendly instrumentals.

The roomies were cool with my snap decision to throw a house party. I told them to invite everyone they knew and I'd take care of everything else. Brian was responsible for the most attendees – Chris Volker aka Chris the Wanderer, Mike the primal screamer, old man Joe D'Angelo, and a whole bunch of random digital nomad types. Some of the Virtuagym crew rocked up. A large group of Israeli fellas came too – they all had tech jobs at Selina.

The only person that Steve invited was Tyler Connors. Tyler was a twenty-three-year-old Canadian kid who looked like an overgrown Hitler Youth member. His nose was flat as a pancake. In his blue jeans and plain white tee, the dude looked like he was about to star in a high school production of *A Streetcar Named Desire*.

"Tony," Steve said solemnly, "This is Tyler."

"Pleased to meet you man. Tony."

Tyler looked at me with his wolf cub eyes. His handshake was weak and clammy. "Hey. Tyler."

"You guys meet at EAFIT?"

Steve shook his head. "Nope."

"I'm a coach," Tyler said. "Doing a bootcamp in Medellín that starts Monday. Steve's one of my rockstar students."

"Oh cool," I said as I pulled out a tray of steaks from the fridge. "Is it like a fitness program?"

Tyler checked out Valentina. "No, it's an intensive dating program. Over the next eight weeks I'm gonna help Steve and guys like him start meeting and dating women from a positive place. We've actually got a couple of spots still available. You interested?"

Wow. Steve was so desperate that he'd called in a pick-up artist! The information settled in my brain. It made sense. The autistic hobbit needed a syllabus that he could learn and apply to the letter.

"Sounds cool man," I said as I salted the steaks. "But I'm in the middle of a big writing project at the moment, so I don't really have the time. But I'm sure you'll do well. Lots of beautiful girls in this town."

Tyler stayed on-brand and didn't let my hard 'no' kill his vibe. "OK. But if you change your mind, let me know asap. Got a few people interested in the final spots. By Monday I'll be fully booked."

I took the tray of meat out to the balcony. The Israelis from Selina were leaning next to the barbie, chilling, smoking a joint.

"Does Evgeniy talk to you about crypto all day long?" a skinny lad with yellow teeth asked me.

"Evgeniy?" I said.

"Ah, sorry," Yellow-Teeth said in his French-sounding accent. "Evgeniy doesn't like his Jew name. I meant to say Steve."

Tyler was sitting next to Valentina on the couch. Steve was opposite them on the recliner. Tyler was trying out some cheesy lines in Spanish, and Valentina was blushing, lapping up every word. Brian was showing Joe some standard yoga stretches off to the side and the poor old geezer had no idea that his wife was getting tuned by another man. Steve the eager pupil stared at Tyler with controlled intensity.

"I didn't know Steve was Jewish," I said.

"Really?" Yellow-Teeth said. "With a face like that? Don't let his Canadian accent fool you, my friend! That's a Jew if I ever saw one."

The Israelis offered to cook the steaks for me – barbecuing reminded them of their army days. In Straya, letting another man cook your meat is a cardinal sin. There I was feeling sorry for Joe, and then I went ahead and let some other blokes bring my sirloins to medium-rare! Many take me for a stereotypical Aussie. Loud shirts, boozing, a fondness for the word 'cunt'. I'm definitely ticking a few boxes, I'll admit that. But when I meet a true blue, dinky-di ocker bloke they suss me out immediately. There are a few telltale signs, and the fact that I'll gladly let another man control my barbie is definitely one of them.

I handed over the tongs to the Israeli bros and went back inside. Allie was acting out one of his moto accidents to some blonde American girl. His bald head was newly shaved and shinier than Joe Rogan's. Allie was clearly five lines deep, and the girl was physically pulling herself away from their conversation – it looked as though she'd been trying to leave for a while. As I was grabbing a beer someone buzzed up.

I opened the front door. Mel and Dani were waiting in the doorway. Mel wore a low-cut top – a black pendant necklace was nestled between her B-cups. Dani looked alive and fresh, like an American Apparel girl.

"Chicas!" I said. "Cómo están?"

I led the girls into the apartment and made them mojitos. Hungry eyes scanned Mel and Dani up and down. Fresh meat. There were a few gringas at the party, but compared to the Colombianas, they looked like dull pieces of furniture. Mel ran straight across to Brian and hugged him. I introduced Joe to Dani and went out to the balcony to check on the food. The Israelis were taking great care of my sirloins. I listened to them chat about Selina, sipped my beer, and watched the scene unfold inside the apartment.

Mel was all over Brian – she had her arm around his waist and her head nestled against one of his well-defined pecs. Tyler made his move. He lifted himself off the couch and made a beeline for Dani. Valentina watched Tyler leave and pouted like a little girl. Tyler shook Dani's hand and started playing with her fingers. She smiled luminously. Rage bubbled within me like a hot stew. I opened up my shoulders and took in a deep breath. Tyler was going to stick to Dani like shit for the rest of the night. I told the Israelis that I was going to grab a serving plate and excused myself.

"Dani. Let me show you around."

Tyler glared at me like a school shooter.

"Sure," Dani said. "Nice to meet you," she said to Tyler as we walked away.

I took my time giving Dani the full tour. I struggled to tell whether she was glad that I'd pulled her away from Tyler's formulaic advances. Our saunter ended in my stark bedroom. Dani read the handwritten quote I had placed on the wall above my desk.

"What matters in life is not what happens to you but what you remember and how you remember it."
— *Gabriel Garcia Marquez*

Dani turned and looked at me with doe eyes.
"You like Gabo?"
This was a gift that Dani's Insta feed had bequeathed me. She was a big fan of Colombia's most famous son. This quote was featured in a post from 2015 where Dani was posing in a bikini on a beach in Argentina. Dumb cunts like Steve will pay slimeball PUAs thousands of bucks to participate in ridiculous 'intensives' that teach you how to impress women. But unless you're autistic, you don't need other dudes to tell you what women want. Just listen to what they say, and then say *the exact same thing back to them.*
"I'm only just getting into Gabo," I said, pointing to the new copy of *Love in the Time of Cholera* on my bedside table. "I'm a writer, so it would be ridiculous not to read Marquez while I'm here. I was looking him up online and this quote jumped out at me."
Dani smiled warmly. "I *love* this quote."
"It's pretty special, right?"
I led Dani back to the living room and dropped her off next to Mel. Then I went out to the balcony and helped the Israelis serve up the meat. In addition to the steaks, sausages and grilled eggplants, I also had two fuck-off salads (apple, chestnut, blue cheese and mandarin, cucumber, purple onion) plus mountains of fresh bread rolls from the Carulla.
I could feel Dani's eyes watching me as I laid everything

out on the dining table. My parents made a lot of mistakes, but one thing they did right was teach me how to host a party. There's two main rules. Number one, there is no such thing as too much food. Number two, there is no such thing as too much booze.

I was the last to fill my plate. I went out to the balcony. Dani followed suit and sat down next to me.

"You're a writer?" she said.

I nodded.

"What do you write?"

I swallowed a mouthful of steak. "I used to work for a media company in Melbs doing ad sales, so I've done technical writing for years. But my passion is creative stuff. Right now, I'm editing the manuscript of a novel that I wrote a few years ago."

Dani was eating all the mandarin chunks from her plate first, which I found adorable. "What's your novel about?"

I spent a few minutes explaining the premise of *Song & Dance Man*.

"The plan is to move to New York in early 2019. I've been researching publishers in Brooklyn and there's a few I think would be a good fit for my book."

"New York is so cool," Dani said. "It's my second-favourite city in the US."

"What's number one?"

"SF."

I laughed. "That's the compulsory answer for graphic designer hipster chicks."

Dani raised her eyebrows. "You think I'm a hipster?"

I put my plate down. "For sure."

"No," she said, smiling. "I'm not cool enough to be a hipster."

I took a swig of my beer. "That right there is the standard hipster response."

We finished eating and came inside to get another drink. 'Sea Lion Goth Blues' by The Growlers started playing. Mel ran towards us. She was flushed across the cheeks, lit already. Mel grabbed Dani's hand and pulled her to the middle of the room. They started dancing. Bateman began whispering in my ear.

You can put yourself at the center of your universe. Healthy diet. High intensity workouts. Creative endeavours for the soul. But then out of nowhere, they appear. The hardbodies that have been put on this earth to drain your balls of cum. And it's nigh-on impossible to resist their song, compadre. So don't even think about that. But it takes a lot to tame one of these sirens. Sure, they seem sweet as pie on the surface, but think about it. This Antioquian land is rugged my friend. It's soaked in blood. And that's who's dancing in front you. The direct descendants of the conquistadors! Don't let this fake, globalist reality fool you. These women want a provider. And in the beginning, they ask just for a little, but with each passing day they want more and more and more...

Everyone started getting loose. I had a shot of sweet aguardiente with old mate Joe. Mel twerked on Brian's cock, desperately trying to get his attention, but Brian was busy discussing quality organic content with Chris Volker. A few more of Allie's Virtuagym pals arrived. I got trapped in a boring twenty-minute, one-way convo with a lad from Atlanta about his sales lead business. Someone turned up the music. Joe and Valentina came over, thanked me, then split. Mel and Dani were dancing salsa with a couple of young Colombian fellas, friends of Brian's from the gym, and Tyler was stalking them like a hunting dog. Allie asked me if I wanted a bump and I gratefully declined. I grabbed another beer and began chatting with Brian and Chris. They'd moved onto the future of dropshipping. Chris was wearing his wide-brimmed hat – it looked a bit like the garment that The Undertaker would wear when he entered the arena. Allie turned off my playlist and put on The Prodigy. He started raving with Mike – the pair of them looked like two geared-up degenerates at Glastonbury.

The Israelis started banging on the window from the balcony. They'd lit up a joint, closed the sliding doors and locked themselves out. As I was opening the sliding door for them, there was a bang at the front door. One of our neighbours, a George Costanza lookalike, told Brian to turn the music down.

"Sorry fam," Brian announced, "We're gonna have to move it along."

"Let's wander down the 10," Allie said.

"Sounds good," I said, as the stoned Israelis filed inside past me. "Let's find a club."

"Si!" Mel screamed. "Let's go dancing!"

/

We didn't bother with any of Ricardo's clubs because he was in Miami visiting his mother. Instead, Mel led us to an uber-Colombian place at the bottom of the 10 near Parque Poblado. She spoke to the bouncer and everyone got in for free. It was busy – there were hundreds of cunts inside, and we seemed to be the only gringos in the place.

Most of the lads went to the bar but I jumped straight up on the dancefloor. The music was so loud it made my head throb. There were three chubby girls dancing by themselves. I grabbed the hand of the most attractive one and started dancing. I swayed left to right, right to left until the song ended.

I kissed my partner on the cheek and wheeled around. Result! Dani was standing there, waiting for me. We locked eyes. Without a word I grabbed her hand, pulled her in close. Dani tried to show me some basic salsa steps. But I kept fucking up. So instead she just turned around and nestled her perfect arse on my crotch. I was rock hard. She offered her soft, sweet neck to me. This time, the crafty vampire refused the innocent virgin.

"I'm gonna grab some water," I yelled in her ear. "Want some?"

She nodded at me with hungry eyes.

I could see Mel grinding on Tyler towards the back of the dancefloor. Brian and Chris were perched on stools at the bar, fully engaged in deep conversation about business mumbo jumbo. I weaselled my way to the front of the queue, but it still took me a good ten minutes to get back to Dani. She was dancing with another partner. I sipped my water and waited for the tune to end. Dani made a beeline towards me.

She set her bottle of water down on a table. The beat dropped. Dani put her hand on the back of my neck. She pulled me in close.

My whole world exploded.

NINE

Dani walked into the restaurant. 'Flowers on the Wall' by Tomorrow's Tulips started playing in my head. She smiled. Her expression was unfussy yet dialled-in. I kissed her on the cheek and she sat down.

Over a couple of soda Bretañas we discussed Friday night's premature ending. Shortly after our first embrace, Dani had abandoned me on the dancefloor.

"When I came out of the bathroom that American girl from the party came up to me," Dani said. "Blonde, curly hair. Do you know who I'm talking about?"

I nodded. "Yep. Don't remember her name though."

"Well anyway, she told me that Mel was really drunk and that she was on the street with some guys from the party. So, I ran outside. Mel was super-wasted, she could barely stand. She was standing there with Tyler and... what's your tiny roommate called?"

"Steve."

Dani took a sip. "They were trying to push her into a taxi. I told them to go inside. And then I took Mel back to my apartment."

I relaxed back in my chair. "Damn. I thought you just ran away from me!"

Dani giggled. "No."

I digested this information. "Do you think they were trying to help her get home? Or were they trying to take advantage?"

Dani scoffed. "They're not nice guys. I was super angry. I yelled at them. Called them pigs."

"How did Mel pull up the next day?"

"Just a headache. Nothing serious."

"Do you think someone spiked her drink?"

"No. She just drank too much. Mel has a massive crush on Brian. But he doesn't seem to be interested. Do you think he likes her?"

An ancient waiter took our orders then stepped away.

"Brian's obsessed with Brian." I chuckled. "He's hellbent on becoming the next big digital nomad lifestyle guru. Do you know who Tim Ferriss is?"

"No."

I leant towards Dani. "Tim Ferriss wrote this book called *The 4-Hour Workweek* like ten years ago. He's the one who popularized the whole 'passive income' thing. And so now every man and his dog wants to be an entrepreneur. And Brian is the walking, talking embodiment of a Tim Ferriss fanboy. Every minute he's got a new idea for a multimillion-dollar business. Plus, he's constantly cranking out shitty content for his podcast, blog, YouTube channel. Someone like Brian has zero time for a girlfriend."

"But Mel's really sweet! They'd make a cute couple."

"That's not the point. Brian didn't come to Medellín to find someone to date." I took another sip. "How do you feel about all these gringos coming to Medellín? Business guys like Brian. PUAs like Tyler. Do you find it annoying?"

Dani shrugged. "Medellín is becoming more touristic in general. It's good for the city. Tourists spend money." She spoke slowly and deliberately. "The sex tourism is disgusting. As a feminist, that really bothers me on a deep level. A lot of girls get hurt, and some of them are way too young. Many are from Venezuela. I hate that side of things. Dirty men abusing poor women. But more or less, tourists are helping Colombia modernize. We want them to keep coming. We just have to deal with a few bad ones."

It was impossible not to gawk at Dani. The way she spoke was unbelievably cute. When I speak Spanish, it sounds like nails on a chalkboard. But Dani's sing-song accent took her English to the next level.

"You seemed to enjoy getting to know Tyler at the party," I said.

"What do you mean?"

"He was playing with your hand. Reading your palm or something?"

Dani shuddered. "No," she said resolutely. "That guy is a *creep*. I was just being polite."

I pulled at my stubble. "Is that what you're doing now? Being polite?"

Her eyes sparkled. "Of course. I'm polite to everyone."

Our food came out. Two chicken caesar salads and a bowl of meatballs to share.

"I've got a confession to make," I said as I dabbed my mouth with a napkin. "I've studied every photo on your Insta feed."

Dani looked up from her salad. "You have?"

"You're twenty-five, right?"

"Si. And you?"

"Thirty-one," I said, taking a sip of red wine. "When I was your age, I'd done one little bus tour of northern Europe. A few days in some of the major cities on the tourist trail. That was it. But according to your Insta, you've been everywhere. How's that possible?"

This manoeuvre probably goes against every principle outlined in *The Game*. Disclosing that you've been lurking doesn't put you in a strong negotiating position. Yet, there's more than one way to skin a pussycat. Women get turned on by power, which is handy. But they *love* vulnerability. If a chick reveals her flaws too early, dudes run for the hills. But when the roles are reversed, sheilas view it as a challenge.

Simply bedding a gal has never been enough for me. I've always felt such vitriol for PUA clowns like Tyler. It's not that hard to convince someone to bump uglies. Sex is *always* better when there's feelings involved. Now, I'm not saying you should make a point of catching feelings yourself. To use a zeitgeist-y term, that's 'problematic'. There is, however, a great utility to activating a woman's emotions. She's guaranteed to fuck you like she means it.

"My father's a businessman," Dani said as she set down her cutlery. "He's in manufacturing. Plastics."

"Oh yeah? What type of stuff?"

"Grocery, storage boxes, industrial. He makes it all."

"Nice."

"Anyway, he grew up dirt poor and now he's a very rich man. So, he spoils his daughters. I'm super-lucky. He's helped me travel to many cool places. Especially when I was studying, before I started working."

I nodded. "He has factories here?"

"No. Just near our home in Cali."

"You know my housemate, Allie? The bald guy? He told me that Colombians never leave their hometown."

Dani smiled. "Más o menos, si. I'm a unicorn."

"Why didn't you move home after you finished studying?"

Dani took a beat. "I love my family. Cali as a city, not so much. My sisters, they're older. They're both married. The oldest one, Lina, she has two kids. And they have very happy lives. But it's predictable. They do the same things every week, with the same people. Same church every Sunday. Me, I *love* to travel. I want to go everywhere. And one day I'll leave Colombia. But until then, Medellín is the perfect place for me. I love the weather. The city is alive. The people are super-friendly. And it's only a short trip to get home."

/

I paid for dinner. We caught a cab to Crepes & Waffles in Ciudad del Rio. Hot air whipped through the car. The crackly radio was blasting retro disco. Dani was laughing at the driver, a big fat bloke in a stained white polo. He was ribbing me about something. I heard 'gringo' a few times, but my ear wasn't good enough to understand what was being said.

At Crepes, Dani ordered a banana split and I went for a strawberry ice cream in a cone. Dani insisted on paying. We ate our desserts on the big concrete steps outside the Modern Art Museum. There were a lot of folks out, taking in the night air. La pura vida.

"Do you wanna see my apartment?" Dani said. "It's a brand-new building. I moved in last month."

Her place was a five-minute walk. Dani said g'day to the portero, an old geezer with wispy white hair. Her spot was on the seventeenth floor.

I closed the door behind me. The joint smelt like a new car. An immaculate two-bedroom bachelorette pad. Paid for with Papi's dinero, no doubt.

Dani was leaning against a wall. She stared at me with doe eyes. I swooped in like a vulture, feeling strong and lean after several weeks of brutal cardio workouts. Her sweet mouth tasted like banana. Dani walked me to her bedroom. I laid her down on the bed, took off her jeans and panties, marvelled at her delectable little snatch. My cock was bulging in my briefs. Dani pulled it out and gave it a few generous licks. I slid myself inside her. We locked eyes.

Dani was not the type of gal who would typically let you fuck her raw on the first date. But when you catch feelings, rules go right out the window.

TEN

For the first few weeks, me and Dani spent every spare moment together.

It blew my mind how many hours a week she worked. Her fancy office was in the WeWork building next to the Santafé mall. She was there each morning by eight and didn't get home 'til seven. Dani was definitely not the trust fund kid I thought her to be. She wanted success on her own terms.

I was at her apartment 24/7. We were like two junkies, desperate for the next fix. I couldn't believe someone like Dani had fallen into my life. To win her ultimate affection, my strategy was to go full hipster. Dani wasn't familiar with Jim Jarmusch, so we started working haphazardly through his filmography. *Only Lovers Left Alive. Permanent Vacation. Down by Law. Stranger Than Paradise.* I played her a ton of this Brazilian samba cat called Jorge Ben who I'd discovered a few years earlier. I made Dani watch 'In Ruins', the stand-up special from my favourite living comedian Eddie Pepitone aka 'The Bitter Buddha'.

There was something so goofy and unaffected about Dani's demeanour that was breathtaking. When she was dancing salsa or walking down the street Dani looked like an Amazonian goddess. Yet her intimidating presence didn't match her personality. She was thoughtful and passionate about details. Of all her adorable quirks, the thing I loved the most was how she spoke to her house plants as if they were real people. "Oh no, a bug ate one of your leaves! Did that hurt? Don't worry, have a drink mi amor, you'll feel better soon." The only real strike against her as a person was that she loved the TV show *Girls*.

Dani would seduce me with surprising ferocity. But when it was time to fuck, she'd morph into a submissive little starfish. Let me share a fond memory from the old wank bank.

I'm chilling on Dani's couch, watching a Jarmusch joint. Out of nowhere, Dani pulls my face towards her perky tits. I suck hard on her nipples. She caresses my cock over my jeans. I hit pause on the movie and carry her to the bedroom. We strip. She's up on the bed, on all fours, arching her back, slobbering all over my old boy. I put her nightstand mirror against the head of the bed and swivel her around. I slap my cock on her juicy rump, tickling her clit with my head. Dani bites her lip, begs me to fuck her properly. I tease her for a while longer. Then I start laying pipe. Her great tits are swinging back and forth. Dani's salsa skills are coming in handy – she's twerking on my cock like a stripper in the champagne room. I tell Dani to touch herself. She reaches back with one hand and pulls herself off. I feel a tickle in my balls. I grab both of her caramel cheeks and sink my nails in like I'm fucking Wolverine. She's quivering. I can't hold on a second longer. I pulse, shooting my milky load deep into her soaked cunt.

/

There was another obsession blooming in my life – lurking in the expat Facebook group.

Every day there was some new juicy bullshit for me to fawn over. I couldn't believe the amount of traction each new post generated. It was if everyone in the group was sitting with Facebook open, ready to pounce. The main culprits were the middle-aged retirees, the Joe D'Angelo types. Grey-haired boomers were bailing on Trumpistan and moving to Medellín in droves. The mods tried to keep things under control, but the group was becoming a shitpost cesspit filled to the brim with competing armies of laptop bullies, scammers, conspiracy theory edge-lords, cynical trolls and hapless techno-luddites. Instead of dedicating myself to finishing *Song & Dance Man*, I procrastinated for hours at a time watching the drama unfold.

One day some boomer posted a meme disparaging Colombian women, essentially claiming that the vast majority were nothing more than gold-digging whores. This kicked off a massive back-and-forth. A young SJW-looking Paisa girl with a rainbow-filtered profile pic was furious. The chica attacked the OP for posting something so false and insensitive, and signed off with a memorable rant: *You stupid motherfuckers! Come to Medellín and think you are rich. We are not stupid! If you are rich you party in Paris or Tokyo. You buy women because you are ugly. Dirty grillas from Bello. I hope you all rot in hell. Colombia does not want your money. We know you are losers back home. Fuck off!*

A bunch of other gringo dudes defended the OP in the thread, claiming that if the meme held no truth, why were the local girls getting so offended? Things got so chummy between the gringos that four of them organized to meet up the following night.

It was time to take my lurking offline.

/

I arrived at 37 Park, a popular spot near Lleras with an outdoor beer garden, at about six-thirty. I sat down on one of the stools in the garden, acquired an overpriced mojito, opened my lappie and waited.

The OP was the first to arrive. He was a pale American dude with alien eyes. Early fifties, decent head of strawberry blonde hair, toned upper body, fond of skipping leg day. Fortunately, he decided to sit at a table nearby.

Only two of his allies from the Facebook spat showed up. One was a chubby fella in his early thirties with a dirty little mustache. The other was a fat-necked Midwesterner in a lime green polo that was a size too small.

The three of them got into it. I transcribed the following nuggets from their convo:

"Did y'all go through that dumb bitch's photos? Oh my god. Why the fuck would you show the world your dirty pits? I could smell her stank through my screen!"

"I'm done paying on the first date. So many of these girls just want free shit. It's a test. Trust me, Colombian dudes are cheapskates. If you don't pay, she's *more* likely to fuck you. That's the type of treatment they're used to."

"We need a men-only Facebook group. A place where we can speak our mind freely. No filters. But not gonna lie, feels good to troll a feminist every so often!"

Of course, these three geniuses were all budding entrepreneurs. After they were done trashing Colombianas, they started hatching a plan for an Amazon dropshipping business. Listening to them vibe with one another made me think of Brian. Medellín was riddled with 'wantrepreneur' fuckers just like him, and yet the stupid cunt still couldn't get his shit together.

I've been hate-following for so long now that I'm unsure about what gives me more delight; stuff I genuinely dig, or things that are so bad that they're actually good. In the beginning, the impulse to seek out stuff that made my skin crawl was driven by boredom and some mild schadenfreude. But it quickly progressed to a fully-fledged hobby.

After a few bevvies, the three new amigos decided to wander up the road and get tacos. I settled my tab and decided to scope out Vintrash, a tourist-friendly meat market, which was just around the corner.

Vintrash was busy for a weeknight. I went to the bar on the ground floor and ordered myself a Pilsen. There was a big group of loose Aussie tourists on the dancefloor bumping and grinding to Daddy Yankee. This was probably their big night out in Medellín. When you're on the road, there's no such thing as a school night.

A couple of the Aussies, two blonde sheilas, came over to the bar. As they waited to be served, I thought about introducing myself, asking where they were from, where they were going, what they thought of Medellín. Leaning on the old antipodean connection. The blondes ordered a jug filled to the brim with orange juice and vodka before rejoining their mates on the floor.

Still very much in lurk mode, I sipped my Pilsen and said nothing.

/

Mark Tallone came to visit out of the blue. Brian begged me to have dinner one Thursday so I could meet the dude.

Mark was staying at The Charlee, a boujee 'lifestyle' hotel in Lleras. We met him at the joint's restaurant at seven.

"Mark Tallone. Pleasure to meet you, Tony."

Mark looked even more rat-like in person. Over dinner, Mark explained why he was in Medellín.

"Not gonna lie, Tony, it's pretty amazing to be here. I was scheduled to meet some Masterminders in North Carolina but the event got postponed. I *never* get openings on my calendar, so I thought what the hell, must be a sign from the big guy telling me to come down and hang with Bri Bri. YOLO, baby!"

I remembered from my digging that Mark's wife was somehow involved in The Lifestyle Corp. I asked him about her role.

"Me and Maria are a pretty special team. She's the brains behind the operation, that's for sure! I guess you could say that I'm the hunter and she's the nurturer. Maria anticipates problems before they arise. She makes all of our members feel really loved. And on top of everything, she's an amazing mom."

"How many kids have you guys got?"

"Three daughters," Mark said proudly. "The loves of my life."

As I worked through my underwhelming grilled chicken and sautéed veggies, Mark trotted out his Mastermind pitch.

"Tony, let me come clean. I really get off on helping people. When people think of Mark Tallone, a few different words come to mind. Investor. Influencer. Speaker. Author. But for me, my most important role is conduit. With my Masterminds, I bring likeminded people together and set the right mood so everyone can have raunchy, anything goes idea-sex. It's a really beautiful thing."

Brian was picking the skin off his overcooked salmon. "Results speak for themselves, bro."

"Brian tells me you're writing a book. I know a *lot* of successful authors. I could find an amazing group for you to join, take your writing to the next level. How does that sound?"

I shook my head. "Appreciate the offer, but I'm good. Prefer to do my own thing."

Mark smiled. "I get it. You're an independent guy Tony. That's cool. Pablo didn't like taking orders either and that hombre built one hell of an empire!"

I lowered my voice. "Don't talk about that type of shit here."

Mark and Brian were affronted by my directness. Mark abandoned his pitch. He stared at the fuck-houses wandering around on the street below.

"Now fellas, I gotta ask," Mark started. "How the bleep are you thinking straight with this amount of ass on display? I knew Colombian women were beautiful, Sofia Vergara and all that, but *holy Jesus mother of balls.* Please tell me you're sewing your wild oats?"

Brian looked me in the eye. He wanted to keep things squeaky clean in front of the boss man.

"I'm dating a girl," I said. "Graphic Designer. She's from Cali originally. Speaks English, which is rare. And lucky for me because my Spanish sucks a bag of dicks."

Mark hi-fived me over the table. "Nice, bro! And how about Lieutenant Hartman? You puttin' up numbers?"

Brian wiggled in his chair. "Look, it's undeniable how gorgeous the chicas are here in Gran Colombia. Physically, of course, but they just have an amazing vibe in general. But since getting to Medellín, I've just been busting my ass trying to get my start-up off the ground." Brian looked at me. "This is breaking news, Tony, but Mark's about to become a partner in my app. So, expect *big* things happening over–"

"–Brian's got a lot of admirers," I interrupted. "My girlfriend's got an amiga, girl she dances with, cute little hippie chick called Mel who has a major crush on Bri Bri."

"For real?" Mark said.

I nodded. "Mel was throwing herself at Brian at this party a few weeks back."

Brian's death stare was only partially obscured by his Californian geniality. "Mel's a super cool gal. I actually got to hang with her for a little while today at her work! But we're definitely just good friends. I really value authenticity above everything. And right now, my focus is all about health, business and just pursuing wisdom in general. So, I'm definitely not ready for an intimate union at this point in time. But in the future, I'd love to find a life partner. Y'all know the Hart Man. I'm all *about* stepping into the unknown!"

Mark slapped Brian on his back. "This guy! Wise beyond his years! If I was down here when I was younger… The trouble I'd be getting myself into. Oooooooh-eeeeeeee!"

/

On the Saturday, Brian managed to corral a bunch of us down to The Charlee's rooftop bar for cocktails with Mark. I arrived just after seven with Allie. That arvo there'd been a ton of rain, but all the clouds were gone and there was a stillness to the air. The bar was quiet. A bunch of stony-faced Colombianos lounged by the pool with their trophy putas. We said g'day to Brian and Mark then ordered a round of cocktails. Mark quickly cottoned onto the fact that Allie had blow – they scurried off to the loos to do rails. Steve and Tyler Connors showed up.

I shook Tyler's hand. "Hey man."

"Hey."

"How's the program going?"

Tyler nodded forcefully. "Awesome. I'm really pleased with the progress. My goal is to effectively red-pill everyone who comes under my mentorship. This time around, I'm happy to report that the mission was successful."

"It's over already?"

Tyler nodded. "We had our final in-field last night. But there's so much demand in Medellín at the moment. I'm gonna stay a while longer and run some more accelerators. Steve here is gonna be my full-time wingman."

Steve wasn't listening. He was staring at all the silicon stunners by the pool.

Allie and Steve came back from the loos like two naughty schoolboys. Someone tapped me on the shoulder. It was Ricardo.

"Ricky lad!"

Ricardo hugged me. "Antonio. Good to see you."

"Igualmente, bro. How's things dude?"

Ricardo lit a fag. "Just got back from Miami."

"Your mum's okay?"

"She's good."

"Nice. What else is new?"

"I'm thinking about investing in a new venue."

"Oh yeah. Another club?"

Ricardo took a drag. "It's a hotel, but with a club on the ground floor. It's called Click Clack, it's still under construction. You've probably seen it. Do you know Justo? The vegan place?"

"No."

"Anyway, it's near there. I'm deciding whether to invest. It's a lot of money. I would need a loan." Ricardo lifted up his baseball cap and scratched his scalp. "Allie told me you met a chica?"

"Yeah dude. Met her at Dancefree." I showed him a photo on my phone. "She's from Cali. But she's been in Medellín for a few years. Her name's Dani. You know her?"

"No. She's cute, dude."

"Thanks man. She's cool. You'd dig her. Text one of your chicas, maybe we could do a double-date?"

Ricardo nodded. "Sure. Be careful though man. Cali girls are no joke. Lots of passion."

I downed a second mojito and bid all the lads hasta luego. Tyler and Steve snarled at me with their Men Go Their Own Way brand of contempt.

An Uber picked me up and took me up to Los Balsos. I got to Casablanca just before 8.30. It was a family-friendly steakhouse with a huge playground for kids and a small petting zoo with donkeys and goats. Dani wanted to go because of the amazing views of the city. She was sitting at a table for two wearing a strappy white dress.

"This is pretty embarrassing to admit, but I think *Jagged Little Pill* by Alanis Morissette was the first bit of music I paid attention to," I said to Dani during dinner. "I was maybe six or seven. My best mate's older bro thought it was cool, loaned me the CD. But then I heard *What's The Story* by Oasis. Changed my whole world. Those huge, booming melodies. It's perfect music for a kid because the lyrics don't mean anything, but Liam's voice sounds cool as shit. I've listened to that record more than anything else."

"I know what you mean about lyrics," Dani said. "When I'm dancing, I feel like I'm in a trance. I don't hear the words. But later, I'll start singing the song to myself in the shower. I only remember a few lines. Or the song will appear in my dreams. It's my medicine. My mind wants me to repeat certain things to myself. Like a mantra."

We finished our meal. A waiter took a picture of us against the Medellín skyline.

"If tonight was a song, what would the lyrics be?" I asked Dani.

She thought for a moment then shrugged. "I don't know." Dani smiled. "Time will tell, I guess."

After dinner, Dani took me to this famous lover's lookout place which is by the side of the road that leads out to the airport. There was quite a crowd milling about. Vendors sold drinks and snacks. Some dude was playing J Gomez out of his souped-up little Honda.

We bought a couple of salpicóns, which are these fruit salad pudding things. The city was lit up like a Nikola Tesla experiment. From this wild vantage point I could see everything, the energy and passion and desire that snaked through every inch of Medellín.

For some reason I started ranting about the Proud Boys.

"It was started by this dude called Gavin McInnes. He's one of the founders of *VICE*."

Dani twirled her plastic spoon through her salpicón. "Really?"

"Yeah. It was him and two other Canadian guys in Montreal. In like the mid-90s. Anyway, this dude, McInnes, he controlled *VICE*'s editorial direction for years. The whole Williamsburg hipster thing spawned out of his writing. They called him 'The Godfather of Hipsterdom'. Your mate, Lena Dunham, wouldn't have created *Girls* if it weren't for McInnes."

Dani recoiled. "No! It was *Sex and the City* that inspired *Girls*."

I swallowed a mouthful of fruit. "Sure. But the reason *Girls* was set in Brooklyn is because the whole hipster thing took off. And that's largely because of McInnes. Anyway, *VICE* started getting more and more popular, and that meant more money, more advertisers, and according to McInnes, he started getting pressured by the ad department. They were trying to control what he wrote. And he couldn't deal with that 'coz he's an old school punk. So, he bailed on *VICE* like ten years ago, and got a big payout."

"This McInnes guy," Dani said, "He's not with *VICE* anymore?"

"Correct. Hasn't been for about a decade or so. He ran his own ad agency for a while. But then he got fired because he said some crazy shit about trans people. After that, he started becoming a kind of internet celebrity. He joined this conservative network and started doing his own chat show thing on YouTube. Originally, it was just goofy comedy, lots of dad jokes. Not really political. But then he started leaning hard to the right all of a sudden."

Dani was listening intently. "Like a Trump supporter?"

"Big time. Even though he's Canadian, he really bought into the whole 'Make America Great Again' bullshit. The dude believes in super-traditional values. Like… most women shouldn't have careers, they should just stay home and have kids."

Dani scrunched up her nose. "What a pig."

"But here's the crazy part…" I scoffed the rest of my dessert. "Even when he started doing his internet show, the political one, the whole time he's kind of joking around. He's been on Joe Rogan a couple of times, and both times Rogan said to him, 'Dude, I can't tell whether you're being serious or not'. Like, he clearly believes in some of the things he's talking about, but a lot of what he does is just for shits and giggles."

"So, what are the Proud Boys then?"

I chuckled. "As a joke, McInnes created a men-only group on his show. Everyone wears black Fred Perry shirts, MAGA hats, and you have to get a tattoo when you join the club. There's a bunch of other initiation rituals, just dumb fratboy shit. Anyway, this club became the Proud Boys. And because McInnes had a huge internet following, they got really popular, really quick. There were chapters all over the world. I used to see Proud Boys in Melbourne all the time."

"What do they do?"

"It's pretty much a drinking club. I honestly think that's all McInnes wanted. To hang out with some bros at dive bars, get away from the wife and kids. But then a bunch of 'alt-right' super-racist dudes joined up. They like to go out and get into street fights with Antifa people. And because most of the Proud Boys are Trump fans, they've got a ton of enemies. I just find it crazy that one dude can have a random idea and then it sparks a whole movement."

Dani let out a deep breath. "I had no idea about any of this."

"It's hard to know what's really happening versus what bullshit the media's spinning. But to be honest, with a lot of these gringos in Medellín, I could totally see them becoming Proud Boys. They're all kinda lost. Looking for some type of direction. Dudes like McInnes blow their dog-whistles and a ton of blokes pick up on the signal. It's scary how easy it is to program people."

"What about you?" Dani said. "Do you feel lost?"

I put both of my paws on Dani's fine culo. "I did. For a little while. When I first got here. But not anymore."

Back at Dani's apartment she straddled me, bouncing up and down on my granite cock. She pulsed twice, bang bang, one after the other. I followed suit with a loud grunt after Dani tickled my ballsack with her fingers. We tried watching some movie on Netflix but gave up after twenty minutes. Soon, we were both out for the count.

/

I woke up at 2am with a gurgling pain in my gut. I raced to the bathroom and put my head in the toilet. I was expecting a chunder but instead I farted out some rancid, hot gas. I lapped up water from the sink and sat down on the toilet. I tried forcing a movement. No bueno. It was probably bad meat from Casablanca. Or maybe the salpicón. I knew at some point, there was gonna be a disastrous exit from either my mouth or my arse or both ends at once. I definitely didn't want that happening in Dani's bathroom.

I got changed and gently woke her up. "Hey babe," I whispered.

Dani stirred. "Si?"

"I don't feel good. I think it's food poisoning. I'm gonna catch an Uber home."

Dani sat up. "Oh no. Why don't you stay?"

"No, it's fine. I don't wanna disturb you. I'll call you tomorrow."

I kissed her on the forehead and caught an Uber back to Forever.

/

The elevator door opened; a few cold chills shot up my spine. Armageddon was close. Swedish House Mafia was playing inside the apartment.

I opened the front door. There was an orgy happening in the living room. Tyler, Mark and Steve were fucking Valentina, Joe D'Angelo's spritely wife, on the leather couch. The overhead lights were on – it was impossible not to see everything.

Tyler was boning Valentina from behind with his huge Canadian thickie while Mark throat-fucked her on the other end of the spit. Steve was standing next to Tyler, staring at Valentina's arsehole, playing with himself, waiting for his turn to tag in. On the coffee table there was a half-empty bottle of Jack, lines of charlie, and a makeshift ashtray filled with butts.

"Tony!" Mark yelled over the music. He looked sweaty and demonic. "Want in? I'm nearly done with this bitch!"

Valentina took Mark's cock out of her mouth and looked my way. The dirty slut smiled, letting me know that I was more than welcome to join the party.

I didn't know what else to do, so I burst out laughing. "I'm good fellas." I gave Mark and the other boys a thumbs up. "Enjoy your night."

The four of them kept on fucking and sucking. I went to the kitchen and got myself a glass of water. *Holy fucking shit. That's the landlord's misso! If Steve tags in that girl's gonna be airtight.* I noticed that Brian was out on the balcony by himself.

I was about to head through to the loo when Allie walked through the front door. His face was pale and pixelated. Allie's eyes went wild when he saw that Valentina was the one getting fucked in the living room. He turned off the music.

"WHAT THE FACK'S THIS THEN?"

"Hey! What the fuck man!" Mark said.

Allie took a few steps forward. "All of you. Out. NOW."

"Come on Allie, chill," Mark pleaded. "I got some blow. Want a line?"

"I SAID GET THE FACK OUT OF MY HOUSE YOU FACKING CUNT!"

Brian rushed inside from the balcony. "Hey Allie, it's all good. Party's winding down anyway."

Mark pushed Valentina's mouth away from his cock. He did a really poor man's version of Conor McGregor's billionaire strut and made his way towards Allie. "You got a problem, bro? Can't you see we're in the middle of something! How about a bit of privacy?"

Tyler didn't miss a beat. He kept pumping Valentina from behind with his weapon of a cock.

"Ah... ah... ah... ah," she moaned.

Allie squared up to Mark. He looked like an extra from *Green Street Hooligans*. "Fackin' me landlord's missus? On me couch?" A demented smile crept across Allie's face. "YOU CUNT."

Valentina was getting closer to the Promised Land. "Ahhhh... ahhhh... ahhhh."

Brian stepped between Allie and Mark. "Allie! Chill!"

Allie kept screaming at Mark. "CUNT! CUNT! CUNT!"

Brian raised his voice. "ALLIE! DUDE! RELAX!"

Valentina started to pulse. "Ah, ah, ah, ah, ah... Aaaaaaaaaaaaahhhhhhhhhhhhhhh!"

Mark's dick had shrunk considerably – it was half the size of his nutsack. Wisely, the rodent realized that a fight with Allie wasn't the best idea. He told Tyler, Steve and Valentina to get dressed. A minute later the three of them filed out the door in silence.

Allie went straight for the lines on the coffee table. He efficiently hoovered them up like a top-of-the-line Dyson.

Brian's eyes were glazed with tears. He pulled at his man bun before retreating back out onto the balcony, utterly defeated.

ELEVEN

The food poisoning wrecked me for twenty-four hours. Dani picked up the same bug. Going back to Forever when I did was a smart move. There's nothing quite like loud, projectile diarrhea to wrench new lovebirds out of the honeymoon phase.

The next time I saw Dani was at her apartment on Monday evening. She cooked me valluna (breaded pork cutlets, fries and salad) for dinner.

As she was preparing the meal, Dani threw on 'Apocalypse Dreams' by Tame Impala.

"Tame Impala are from Perth, right?" she said.

/

I was watching a band called The Dee Dee Dums at the UWA tav. Dunc walked into the pub with some chick. She was a bubbly little brunette with a cute smile and gypsy eyes.

I got a jug of Tooheys and the three of us sat down. The band sounded like a cross between Creem and Blue Cheer. After a few more numbers, their set ended.

I chatted with Kel. Like me and Dunc, she was from the Joondalup area. Kel grew up in Ocean Reef, on the 'right' side of Marmion Ave. She liked to paint portraits. Dunc and Kel had met on the train home after O-Day.

The two of them got super-serious very quickly. Uni was meant to be the time where me and Dunc would forge a formidable creative partnership. A steady girlfriend getting in the way was not part of the plan. But any feelings of resentment on my side of the aisle evaporated instantly. Their spark was undeniable and as a fellow creative, Kel understood where we were coming from. She encouraged and allowed for all of our precocious indulgences.

The three of us developed a strange little clique. Despite their steady relationship, neither Dunc nor Kel wanted to isolate themselves from the chaos of young adulthood. So, they used me as their conduit to fun and debauchery. After a while, we self-identified the bizarre dynamic of our chosen family. Dunc was 'Dad', Kel was 'Mum', and I was their mischievous yet well-intentioned dog. Whenever I drank too much or broke something around our share house, Dunc and Kel would playfully chastise me. We laughed all the time and lived by a simple motto: 'if it's not fun, it's funny'.

I third-wheeled with Dunc and Kel for a long time, basically up until I met Di. Maybe this caused some type of arrested development within me. Maybe it prolonged the process of me grieving my parents' split. Maybe it somehow led me to Medellín.

Who knows? I don't have regrets. Regrets are for pussies.

/

"A few months later the three of us went to see The Dee Dee Dums again," I said to Dani. "They were supporting another local Perth band called The Silents. Since we saw them last, they'd gotten a new drummer and changed their name to Tame Impala. The rest, mi amor, is history."

Dani smiled. "Wow. Super cool! We should FaceTime with Dunc and Kel sometime. I wanna meet them."

"Sure. We can do that."

After dinner, as I was loading the dishwasher, I commenced my investigation.

"I've been thinking about something... You've been in Medellín for years now. One night we're gonna be out at dinner, and we're gonna run into one of your exes, and it's gonna be awkward. So why don't we just skip all that bullshit, and you tell me about your dating history now?"

Dani handed me the frying pan. "This is very organized of you. What's the word in English? Prog... Prag...?"

"Pragmatic."

"Si. Pragmatic." Dani sat on a stool opposite me. "This won't take long. I've only had one real boyfriend. Joaquin. I met him at university. He works for a big law firm in Medellín. He comes from a good family. We were together for five years, más o menos. We broke up at the start of 2017."

I rinsed the chopping board. "Why'd you split?"

She shrugged. "Life. There wasn't a single moment. For the last year we were together something wasn't right. And when we broke up, I was a big mess. But after a few weeks, I knew it was the correct decision."

I nodded. "What about now? Do you talk?"

"No," she said. "He wished me a happy birthday a few months ago. But nothing since."

I pulled at my chin. "It's crazy. We build these deep bonds with people. Then they become total strangers."

"What about you?" Dani said. "What's *your* history?"

"What? Afraid you're gonna see one of my exes in Poblado?"

"Maybe... there's more gringas coming every day."

I told her about Di.

Dani seemed happy that there was only one serious girl in my past. "Do you still talk?"

"No," I said. "More time needs to pass."

After we finished cleaning up, Dani FaceTimed with her Colombiana amiga in Melbourne, a pretty little gym bunny with a brick shithouse of a boyfriend. The first signs of a Strayan twang were starting to creep into her mate's accent.

That night, the moment Dani fell asleep, I reached for my phone and pulled up her Insta profile. I looked through Dani's list of Followers.

Bingo. *Joaquin Cruz. Abogado | Ciclista | Nacional FC*. He was a good-looking lad with dreamy eyes and perfect white teeth. Dude seemed like a catch. His profile was public. I scanned through his feed. Lots of cycling trips with his buds, lawyer headshots, family weddings. I scrolled back a couple years and found what I was looking for – Dani and Joaquin embracing tenderly against the backdrop of a Chilean mountain range. Old mate likely deleted all the other remnants of Dani from his feed, but couldn't bear to remove this memory.

It was probably when they were at their happiest.

/

Later that week I was chilling with Brian on the balcony at Forever. He begrudgingly told me about the lead up to the orgy with Valentina.

"Damn dude… Definitely wasn't the most chill night of my life… Well, after you left to go on your date, we all headed to Salón… I think Mark bought some cocaine from Ricardo, or maybe one his amigos… We hung at Salón for a while, then Mark, Tyler and Steve wanted to go check out another spot… So we went to this bar down near the pool hall… Valentina was waiting, I think Tyler told her to go there… Anyway, we all tried to go have some drinks at Mark's room at The Charlee, but security wouldn't let us go up… So, I suggested we come back here, have a nightcap… But Mark and Tyler wanted to keep raging… And then all of a sudden Valentina started getting all promiscuous… It was a real shock man, like, she's a married woman…"

Poor old Joe D'Angelo. I guess that's what happens when you marry someone forty years your junior.

"You seemed pretty upset dude," I said. "You good now?"

Brian's nostrils flared ever so slightly. "Not gonna lie man. I wasn't doing great that night. Mark broke the news when we got back to Forever. Turns out, he's not gonna be able to come in as a silent partner on my startup. Doesn't have the bandwidth right now."

I ran my tongue over my front teeth. "That's what you were upset about?"

Brian put his hands on his lower back and stretched out his hips. "Yeah homie. As you know, I've got a lot of side hustles. But the AI app is my main priority." Brian finished his stretch and rubbed his hands together. "What can I say man. The universe works in mysterious ways! It just wasn't the right moment for that project. It's the Hart Man's job to stay focused and keep my eyes on the next opportunity."

"You're still working for Mark?"

"For sure," Brian said resolutely. "Mark's helped me grow so much. I'm definitely disappointed, but hopefully he changes his mind at some point in the future."

"But dude," I said, "Mark seems like a fucking scumbag. Presents himself as a family man, but then he comes down here and goes crazy with blow. Fucks a whore with a couple of other dudes. You really want to work for someone like that?"

"Sure, sure, sure. Totally valid point man." The prick's diplomacy was sickening. "Thing is, I'm just not in a position to judge anyone. That's on God. Besides, Mark really *is* a great guy, he's just under a lot of stress right now. I think the cocaine did something to his brain chemistry. All I can do is bust my ass, hustle like crazy, and have faith that good things will come my way. How's your training going by the way? Still crushing mad cardio?"

1

One day, Tyler Connors uploaded an extensive thirty-five-minute highlight video about his Medellín immersion program to YouTube. I made some popcorn and watched the whole thing at Dani's apartment. A large portion of the vid was Tyler condescending to his neckbeard students about game theory, 'infield' footage filmed inside malls, and plenty of drone shots of the sensual Medellín skyline. I didn't catch a single glimpse of Steve – the little fella must've been filming everything. Some of Tyler's direct quotes were out of control:

"When you talk with your diaphragm, there's more 'dick' behind your words, and girls pick up on that energy and confidence subconsciously."

"Take doggy for example. In North America you have to go to the ass; in Colombia the ass comes to you."

"If a bitch wants me to spit in her face, I'll do it. And if she doesn't, who cares! At the end of the day, it's just spit."

Bateman scolded me.

Never mind all your Bob Dylan running around Manhattan in 1966 bullshit. Who's gonna be interested in that? A handful of stoned Coen Brothers fans? Stop fucking around Antonio. Look at all this shit going down right in front of your face! You've got pussy hounds having orgies with shady cheaters in your living room. Autistic incels trying to get their dicks wet. Coke fiends snorting the national product like it's an Olympic sport. And every asshole is trying to get VC-funding for their half-baked app! This is the story you should be writing. With your emotional unavailability, your voyeuristic tendencies, your carefully crafted aloofness… you're the only guy in this town who can get this story down properly. Medellín is the next big thing. Or more specifically, crazy gringos in Medellín. Never mind taking yourself to New York. If you get this story on the page before anyone else, New York will come to you!

Colombian feminist bloggers stumbled upon Tyler's video. They were appalled and started writing hit-pieces. Major news outlets picked up the stories and Tyler got caught in a hailstorm of shit. The headlines were bonkers. "The Dark and Dangerous Side of Medellín Dating"; "Medellín 'Dating Academy' Draws Ire From Feminist Sphere"; "Immersion – Medellín's New Kind of Sex Tourism."

After a few days of nonstop public shaming, Tyler turned all of his social profiles to private. Someone on the forum claimed that Tyler had scurried back to Canada.

I was morbidly curious. Late one night, I knocked on Steve's door.

"It's true," Steve said, his eyes black with rage. "He's gone."

I raised my eyebrows. "Damn. People take this internet shit seriously."

"Fucking SJWs," Steve said. The rotten smell of scrotum drifted out of his room. "Marxist bastards. I thought I was safe down here. But no. It's over. They won."

/

I began reconsidering my trip to New York. It was gonna be the middle of winter in January – hardly an ideal time to move. Instead, I could renew my Colombian tourist visa by making a quick trip over to Panama just after New Year's, then spend a few extra months in Medellín.

One evening I propositioned Dani.

"You can visit the US as a tourist, right? You've got a visa?"

"Si," she said.

"You wanna come with me to New York in like... June next year?"

Dani gasped. "Really?"

I smiled. "What matters in life is not what happens to you but what you remember and how you remember it."

She burst out laughing. "Oh my god." Dani kissed me. "I love you."

I kissed her back. "I love *you*."

Dani unclenched her shoulders and exhaled. "What will we do if we can't get jobs?"

"We'll just come back here. Or maybe we could head up to Canada? Doesn't matter. We'll make it work."

Dani pulled out her lappie and started planning.

I showered and caught an Uber up to Selina for Brian's junto. It was high time I learnt more about the machinations of the Poblado business bros.

/

"Thanks to everyone for coming," Chris Volker said. There were six of us in a booth at Selina's main bar. "And thanks to Tony for joining us tonight as a guest. Let's jump in. This week it's my topic. Tonight, I wanna talk about specialization."

I got drunk and listened to them go at it. After an hour and a half, I'd downed several Pilsens and five shots of aguardiente.

I interrupted Chris mid-sentence. "Can I ask something?" I said. "I'm just wondering why you and Kat are targeting individuals who want to sell on Amazon instead of businesses?"

"Brands typically already have ecomm managers in-house," Chris said. "They don't want to spend extra marketing budget on an agency."

"But I'm assuming that whether you're working with some random dude or a huge brand it doesn't really change what your team is doing day to day, right?"

Chris thought for a moment. "Not too much. High volume items usually need a bit more care on the PPC side. But yep, fundamentals are the same."

"OK," I said as I took a swig from my fresh beer. "So rather than trying to get more clients, why don't you just get *better* clients? You'll get way more commission for the same amount of work."

Chris laughed. "Easier said than done, mate."

I shrugged. "Look I'm not a business guy, but there's only so many hours in the day, right? If you're gonna do something, why not make it blow the fuck up?"

TWELVE

"Let's go around the circle."

Me and the three other Forever roommates were at the pool hall on a weeknight. It was early, and apart from one loved-up pair of locals who were shooting 8-ball, we were the only cunts in the place. The tired, middle-aged Colombiana who ran the joint was eating a greasy burger behind the counter. A young waitress with acne was smoking a fag by the entrance, checking her phone. As was the norm, some 90s classics were blaring out of the pool hall's stereo. Bon Jovi, Hootie & The Blowfish, Natalie Imbruglia, and of course, Guns N' Roses.

Across the road there was a Hooters *and* a Colombian knock-off version of Hooters. The counterfeit version had a small army of fuck-houses all dressed in tight-black t-shirts, tiny shorts and white bobby socks milling about the front bar – an obvious ploy to entice thirsty foot traffic inside. Whereas the real McCoy kept all the tits and arse hidden within the establishment. I couldn't decide what was more appealing. Floss a g-string up the snatch so pussy lips spill out over the fabric? Or hide the honey pot entirely with some Bridget Jones-esque knickers? I'm still on the fence.

"Allie," I said. "Why don't you kick us off?"

The tension at Forever was becoming unbearable. Even though I was spending most of my time at Dani's, I felt uneasy whenever I had to go and pick something up. It reminded me of living with my parents during high school. I knew that Dani would have no problem if I moved in with her, but didn't want the pressure of cohabitation so early into our relationship. I was keeping tabs on new rooms getting listed online, but really couldn't be arsed moving my shit. As a final Hail Mary, I organized the sit down at the pool hall.

"Alright," Allie said. He took a swig of his Club Colombia. "I think I'm a pretty reasonable geezer. Stay outta my way and I'll stay outta yours. But to be honest, I'm still facking furious. These two cunts thought it would be a good idea to fack our landlord's missus in our apartment. You're facking lucky the neighbours didn't make a complaint to the strata! If that happened Joe would've definitely found out."

I tried to cut him off, but Allie kept going.

"Talk about shitting where you eat. Facking ridiculous…"

"OK." I turned my head clockwise. "Steve. Do you wanna respond?"

Steve's eye was twitching. I wasn't sure if this was a new tic or something that he'd been doing for a while. "It wasn't my idea. We told Mark that Tyler's place was free. But he didn't wanna go."

"That's true Allie," Brian added. "Mark really did push for a nightcap at Forever."

Allie furrowed his brow. It was early in the night, so he wasn't too gakked out. "So facking what? If I told you to run into traffic, would you do it?"

"Of course not, bro," Brian said. "Mark just really wanted to see my crib. He's been watching a lot of my content."

Allie shook his head. "You could've stopped him."

Brian tucked some tendrils of hair behind his ears. "Dude, things just got out of hand. Caught me by total surprise. No one intended to disrespect you."

Allie stared at Brian. "You serious, mate? Are you being serious right now? You bring a drunk girl home on a Sat'dee night and you think she wants tea and biscuits? Cut the shit, mate."

Steve jumped in. "How much blow do you have in your room right now?" he said to Allie. "One day that spot is gonna get raided."

Silence. Eventually Allie responded in a steady, even voice. "Don't mention that again. I mean it. Keep your mouth shut, you dizzy cunt."

I kept things moving along. "Brian. Why don't you tell us how you've been feeling?"

Brian rubbed his hands together like a gymnast chalking up before a ride on the pommel horse. "Well first of all, I want to thank everyone for coming together today. When you live with others there's inevitably gonna be a few spot fires here and there. It's really awesome to know that we can come together like this and have some open, honest dialogue about the family dynamic. Look, as you know I'm someone who places a really high priority on mental and physical health. I feel blessed to be able to spend time with y'all in this *super* special place. But, it's really important for everyone to understand that intentions matter. If you're waking up each morning and not directing your full attention towards self-improvement, there's a good chance things are gonna fall through the cracks. This lack of mindfulness allows bad vibes to percolate around a home. So, if I could make one small suggestion, it would be that I really want my roomies to get better at loving themselves. If everyone can make a conscious effort to increase their level of self-love, this will make it so much easier to love each other."

Brian sat there proudly like old mate Osho from *Wild Wild Country*. Nobody had anything to add, so I seized the moment.

"OK, well, I think we–"

"–What about you?" Steve said to me. "What are your problems with us?"

The moment. Like a basic bitch, I always thinking of that quote that gets consistently shared on Insta: "And the day came when the risk to remain tight in a bud was more painful than the risk it took to blossom." Not today motherfuckers. Not today.

"I don't have a problem with anyone," I lied. "I *do* have a problem with the vibe in the house. Steve. Brian. I think we can all agree that it was pretty fucked up to have an orgy like that in the living room. Allie's the one on the hook here if shit goes down. I think he needs a proper apology. Let's have a few beers, shoot some pool. Put this dumb shit to bed."

Brian put one hand on his heart. "I've already apologized to Allie, but I don't mind repeating myself. I'm sorry brother. I understand what we did hurt you."

One down.

Steve was staring at the fuck-houses that were slinking around out the front of the knock-off Hooters. His eye twitched again. Finally, just when I thought he was gonna bail, Steve looked at Allie. "I'm sorry. Won't happen again."

I pumped the air like old mate Lleyton Hewitt. "Come on!" I looked at Allie. He was grinding his jaw, fantasizing about his next white caterpillar. "They did something really stupid Al. Everyone makes mistakes. Luckily nothing too serious happened. Can we put this all behind us?"

Allie scratched the bridge of his nose. "Alright. Let's move on."

We all clinked glasses.

"Salud! To Forever!" I said.

Allie ran off to the loos. I stood up, walked to the nearest table and racked up some balls. When Allie came back from his toot, I pitched an impromptu idea to the squad.

"Why don't we do a lads' trip?"

Brian bit his bottom lip and nodded. "Oh yeah. Dope idea bro!" he said. "Like a finca?"

"Nah," I said. "Multi-city tour. Santa Marta, Cartagena. Maybe check out Tayrona. Early Jan."

Brian gave me a high-five. "Love it dude. Count me in. I'll be able to shoot *so much* content."

I turned to Steve. "You haven't been to the coast yet, right?"

Steve shook his head. "Not yet. How many days?"

I shrugged. "Just a quick trip. Nine days, tops."

Steve broke. Balls scattered across the table. "That could work."

I turned to Allie. "You in?"

Allie swigged his fresh beer. "Jan's good for me. Besides, you stupid facks will need someone there to keep you outta trouble."

THIRTEEN

For Dani's Christmas present I surprised her with an over-night stay at this quaint *Lord of the Rings*-inspired boutique hostel near the hippie town of Santa Elena.

I hired a car and we drove out to the hotel early one Saturday morning. The cabins were carved into the hills like little hobbit homes. We spent the day hiking and ate lunch at a place in the town. That arvo there was a huge downpour, so we had to catch a random local bus back to Hobbiton.

At nightfall it got super chilly. It's amazing how much colder it is up in the mountains compared to being at the bottom of the valley. Medellín's perfect weather was turning me into a temperature pussy. Me and Dani went for a walk around the property and smoked a joint. Our little hobbit hole was all cosy with candles and a roaring fireplace. I put on *Proof of Life* but Dani didn't understand why I found it so hilarious. We tried watching *The Fellowship of the Ring* but got bored and decided to have sex.

I loved making Dani pulse with my tongue while she was on all fours. Her body looked borderline mystical in the fire-light. Afterwards we spooned for a while.

"Do you want to come to Cali with me for Christmas?"

Dani's silty pussy juice was all through my stubble. "It's a family thing, right? I don't wanna intrude."

"It's okay. You should come."

"You might wanna check with your mother first."

Dani rolled over and looked at me. She bit her lip. "I already have."

/

We landed in Cali a few days before Christmas. It was hot as balls. Dani's mother, Julianna, was waiting for us. Julianna was a few shades darker than Dani. Despite her age, she was still a beautiful woman.

"Señora Flores." I offered her my hand. "Mucho gusto."

She looked me up and down, before settling on my eyes. "Tony. Señor Azul."

A brand-new white SUV was waiting. Dani and Julianna nattered nonstop the entire journey. When we got to Hacienda de Flores, I was gobsmacked. The place was an immaculate double-storey mansion made out of white stone and marble. There were multiple uniformed workers throughout the house and garden. An infinity pool overlooked a hypnotically green valley.

Dani introduced me to her sisters: Lina, the oldest, and Naty, the middle child. Lina had two kids, young boys both under the age of five. Naty was merely responsible for a slobbering French Bulldog. All the sisters were pretty, but Dani was by far the pick of the litter. Lina and Naty's square-jawed husbands looked like identical twins.

Dani and Julianna led me into the kitchen.

"Papi!" Dani embraced her father. "Esto es Tony."

Her father, Alvaro, shook my hand. He was a slender geezer with a partially receding hairline, dyed jet-black hair that was cut very short. Alvaro looked to be in his mid-sixties and was in great shape. Compared to the average bloke there was more space between his top lip and nose, prime real estate for a bushy mustache, but alas, he was clean-shaven. Alvaro was dressed head to toe in Reebok exercise clobber.

"Bienvenido, Señor Azul," Alvaro said to me. He chewed thoughtfully on a mandarin.

I turned to Dani. "Mr Blue? Like *Reservoir Dogs*?" I smiled. "That's my name here?"

Dani put an arm around her father. "I guess so."

/

That arvo me and Dani played with the kids and the dog around the pool. The whole thing felt like a *Vanity Fair* photoshoot. We ate a never-ending stream of traditional Colombian Christmas food – tons of sweet pastries and processed meat.

I grabbed my lappie and tried to get some writing done. Instead, I procrastinated for a while on YouTube, and then listened to the latest ep of Kevin Brennan's pod 'Misery Loves Company'. For some reason, I found hearing a bitter middle-aged comedian rant about futile bullshit incredibly cathartic.

After dinner, Julianna and Alvaro retired to bed and everyone jumped back in the pool. We tried to play a board game, but the kids were getting ratty, so everyone decided to call it a night.

Dani led me to her childhood bedroom. Four-poster bed, full length mirror, classic off-white walls, no ornaments or decorations. Naty secretly gifted me and Dani some little chocolate edibles. Qué rico!

"Has Naty always been a stoner?"

Dani was sitting cross-legged on her bed. She took a dainty bite of her chocolate. "Si. Naty was the wild one."

"What about you? Did you rebel?"

Dani set her half-eaten edible on the bedside counter. "No. Not really."

"When did you first get stoned?"

"When I had sixteen or seventeen years. Somewhere around then."

"Did you like it?"

Dani's eyes lit up. "Si! I was at my friend's house. Her parents were away at their finca. We smoked a little in her garden. I remember coughing and laughing a lot. And then her boyfriend came and picked us up, drove us into town. It was a perfect night – the air was warm and still. I remember the moment so clearly. I had my arm out the window and I was just lost in the music. And then I stared at the speed. The numbers. How do you say in English... the speed meter?"

"Speedometer?"

"Si. Speedometer. I just stared at the dial as it changed up and down as we drove along. And I don't know why, but I just started having the craziest thoughts about numbers. Not paranoia, more like a debate in my head. I was trying to decide if numbers are a man-made language, like English or Spanish, or if numbers are like the code that controls *everything* in the universe. After that, I became obsessed with numerology for a while."

"My mum is crazy about numerology. At least she was. Maybe she still is. I'm not sure."

Dani looked off the chain in her silk nightgown. I was perpetually dumbstruck by her looks. Empirically speaking, I'm not an unattractive man, yet because I was dating a ten, I felt like a Division 3 side trying to hold their own against Real Madrid. Men's desire for the female form clouds our judgement about everything, especially our own appeal. I believe it was the late, great Patrice O'Neal who said, "Once I realized that women like men for other reasons compared to what I believed in my own head, my women problems stopped". At some point, I realized that Dani wasn't throwing me a bone. If she wanted to fuck a male ten, she'd be fucking a male ten. But she wasn't – she was fucking me.

"Is your mum religious?" Dani said.

"No. She grew up Catholic. I think that put her off religion."

"She's from England like you're Dad, right?"

I nodded. "Yep. We moved to Perth when I was three." I put my arms behind my head. "My mum's main thing is aliens. She fucking *loves* aliens."

"Really?"

"Oh my god. My whole fucking life. There was this one time, I was maybe fourteen or fifteen, asleep in my bed, it must've been around midnight, and she barges into my room and wakes me up, she's like 'Tony, Tony. Come with me. Quick'. So, I put a shirt on and followed her. We're standing on the driveway, and there were these moving lights in the sky. They would flash for a while then disappear, following the same path over and over. I'm fucking pretty freaked out, and then Mum goes, 'go and wake Pat and Keeley up', these people who live over the road. I knock on Pat and Keeley's door and tell them about the lights. Then Keeley says through the flyscreen, doesn't even bother to come outside, I'll never fucking forget it, she just goes, 'it's the new McDonalds, spotlights for their grand opening, tell your mum to go to bed'. Then Keeley slams her door in my face. I look back over the road at my mum who's drunk and waving both arms at the lights."

Dani laughed so hard she snorted.

"Oh my god! Where was your father?"

"He wasn't there. Probably at Sandy's. I think he started seeing her around then."

Dani stroked my chest. "Did it hurt you? The separation?"

"Nah. Compared to some divorces, it wasn't that messy. There's nothing worse than grown men who hang on to teenage pain like fucking emos. Over here there are so many poor people who have nothing. I don't have anything to be angry about."

Dani was looking at me with mournful, puppy dog eyes. I decided to change the topic. "I'm surprised you didn't become a massive stoner after such a cool first time."

She shrugged. "I would like to do it more. Weed just makes

me so tired. Same as alcohol. If I have too much, I just go to sleep." She gestured to her half-eaten edible. "You want the rest of mine?"

"No. I'm good."

"Anyway, my father would go crazy if I had a drug problem."

"Your parents were strict?"

Dani took off her hooped earrings. "Si. We had to be sneaky."

Dani worked her way down my body, gently pecking my chest and torso. Then she slipped off my boxers and took me inside her mouth. I grabbed her by the hips and hoisted her up on top of me. Her exposed clean-as-a-whistle snatch hovered above my face. She gasped as I tongued her clit. With both arms I kept her locked in this uber compromising position until we pulsed together over her bamboo sheets.

/

The next day was more of the same. Food, pool, games, repeat. Me and Dani didn't end up leaving Hacienda de Flores for the duration of our stay. Dani said that the city of Cali wasn't anything impressive and I took her word for it. I tried to do a bit of work in the arvo but again got distracted. I relaxed on a sun lounger and listened to a few episodes of Mike Recine's podcast 'The Sitdown'.

Lina sauntered over with a glass of white wine. She sat down next to me.

"It makes sense now," Lina said. She was the only one in the house apart from Dani that spoke English.

I pulled my headphones off. "What does?"

"I understand why Daniela likes you."

"Why's that?"

"You're exotic. Dani loves mysteries."

I laughed heartily. "Exotic? I'm from the suburbs of Perth, mi amiga. You lot grew up in *this* house!"

Lina took a sip of Argentinian chardonnay and smiled. "No. Not because you're a gringo. She likes you because of how you see the world. You are always thinking, no?"

I leant back into the lounger and let the sun roast me.

"Come visit Cali again before you leave for New York," Lina said.

"We'll be in Colombia for like six more months. We'll definitely make it back here before then."

"We don't want to lose Dani. If you decide to live in the States you still have to come back and visit, okay?"

"Claro."

"At least once a year?"

I held my hands up. "Whatever you say."

Lina stood up and walked back towards the house. "Gracias, Señor Azul."

FOURTEEN

The squabbling started before we even left the tarmac.

"No dude, you don't get peanuts on a plane anymore," Brian said. "A lot of people are severely allergic."

"But what about before?" Allie said. "When I was growing up you always got nuts. No one was keeling over in the aisles back then."

It was the first week of January. On New Year's Eve I went out to Mondongos, an institution of a restaurant on Calle 10 with Dani and a bunch of her mates. They were all exactly like her – successful, attractive yuppies in steady long-term relationships. I was the only gringo, and I got the impression that one gringo was the right number for a public dinner. No gringos was a little backward and provincial, multiple gringos was embarrassing, but a single gringo who knew his place and didn't rock the boat was just right. Although I got along with everyone fine, a part of me did crave a more raucous jamboree. Ricardo was throwing a massive party at a bar in Provenza, and I considered heading there after we finished dining, but I knew it wasn't going to be Dani's scene, so I didn't end up bothering.

"Maybe you could buy yourself something to eat?" Brian said.

"I shouldn't have to buy anything, mate. I want *nuts*." Allie cracked his neck. "Facking cunts. Taking the piss."

I queued up the newest ep of 'Cum Town' on my phone. Despite the bickering I was happy to be heading to the coast with the boys. I was doubtful that the trip would happen. But everyone chipped in. Steve figured out flights. I found Airbnbs. Brian organized Tayrona. And Allie put together the general itinerary. None of the other lads had too much else going on, and we were all buzzing to be on the road as a squad.

"I've got trail mix," Steve said. He pulled the mix out of his backpack and handed it to Allie.

"Steve! You can't open that packet on the plane, there's nuts in there too…"

"Whoops." Allie tore it open. "Too late."

/

Cartagena was hot as a motherfucker.

"Do you feel okay leaving your girlfriend on her own?" Steve asked me.

I took a swig of margarita and wiped my brow. "Yeah dude."

"What about rules?" Steve said, his guinea pig eyes piercing my soul.

"As in, relationship rules? Exclusivity and all that jazz?"

Steve nodded.

"We haven't spoken about it." I laughed. "To be honest man, it's happened pretty quick. We're still in the puppy love phase. It would be stupid to start talking about rules now. There'll be plenty of time for that. Right now, we're crazy into each other, and I can't see that changing anytime soon."

"Sounds like me and Karen," Allie said. "Within a month we were living with each other. Colombian girls don't fack about. If they like ya, you'll know about it."

"It's gonna be a super-dope experience for you to date a Colombiana, man!" Brian added. "She's a great dancer too, dude. There's no way you're not getting really good at Spanish. And salsa!"

I bought a pack of cigarettes from a street vendor. Allie went to the loos for a toot. We were at some cocktail bar. Most of the patrons were tourists and all the waiters were frail old cunts. There was a salsa club over the road, and the music was wafting through the warm air. It was about six in the evening.

"I wouldn't get into a relationship without rules," Steve said.

"Why not?" I said.

"Too much risk." Steve sipped his bottle of water. "I prefer to be in control."

Watching Steve drink water had a sobering effect. "Fair enough." I downed the rest of my margarita in one go.

Brian was scrolling through videos on his phone. Since landing in Cartagena he'd been on a recording binge. "Sa-weet! All that footage from the seafood place looks rad." Brian clenched his fist victoriously.

Across the road two stunning Colombianas were embracing one another out the front of the salsa club. They were standing opposite one another, holding hands, smiling ear to ear. In downtown Cartagena the locals stand out like sore thumbs, such is the industrial level of tourism. My dick moved in my shorts. The chicas were either lifelong pals or bi-curious new acquaintances.

Allie returned from the loo. "What's next?" he said. "Hit another bar then nosh?"

"I don't know about y'all, but I'm down to *dance*." Brian shuffled about in his chair. "Shall we check out this spot right here?"

My eyes followed the two girls as they walked inside the club. "Let's do it."

/

"Hey babe."

I was walking down the street holding my café con leche, wading through an army of sun-pickled fruit vendors. Barranquilla was noticeably less touristy compared to Cartagena.

"Mi amorcito! How are you?" Dani said down the line.

"I'm good. Tired, but good."

The arvo before, we got off the bus in downtown Barranquilla, walked to the Airbnb, dumped our bags, and then went for a wander around our neighbourhood. There was a ramshackle little pool hall a few blocks away with some crusty old dudes playing carambole. The spot had one regular 8-ball table, so we camped out there for a few hours. I got lit on bulk Pilsens and aguardiente shots. For dinner we found a no-frills place packed with locals. When the sun went down things started to feel a little sketch. Allie bought some coke from a young kid with a neck tatt. We walked down a side street, looking for a bar so me and Allie could do rails. Out of nowhere, the dealer kid came running up behind us with a few of his amigos. One of them grabbed at me but didn't manage to pry anything out of my pockets. Of course, Brian was filming himself at the time, so a kid just plucked his iPhone right out of his hands. Allie gave chase for a bit, but the kids reached the main street and scattered amongst the noisy throng of foot traffic.

I told Dani an edited version of this story over the phone.

"Oh no!" she said. "No dar papaya!"

I scratched at my dry scalp. "What can I say... Brian *loves* to give papaya."

Even though we told him it was futile, Brian wanted to make a police report. So, we dropped him at the nearest cop shop. Then me, Allie and Steve ended up at some random heavy metal bar downtown. I ended up going halves on another bag of blow with Al. Steve kept insisting we go find a bar with girls, but me and Allie were really into the 80s YouTube playlist featuring the likes of Whitesnake, Poison and Warrant. The charlie was legit and it perked me right up. I proceeded to get smashed on whiskey and cokes. I didn't remember the cab ride back to the Airbnb.

"How are you?" I asked Dani. "How's work going?"

"It's fine," Dani said. "Not many projects at the moment. I spend my days planning our New York adventure!"

I took a sip. The coffee was weak as piss – way too milky. "Miss you boo."

"Awww! Miss you too bebé! You boys having fun?"

"We are. It's cool to see different parts of the country."

"You'll love Tayrona!"

I went back to our air-conditioned Airbnb. The other lads were still dead to the world. Lucky cunts. I've always been okay dealing with hangovers – it's the lack of kip that always fucks me over.

I pulled out my phone and trawled Facebook. My old boss Col had posted a picture of his young family at the beach, down the Mornington Peninsula. It was the height of summer back in Straya. Fuck. Old mate Zuck has the algorithms tweaked perfectly. When you're feeling weak and vulnerable, he always catapults you unwillingly down memory lane.

/

It was 2014. Me, Dunc and Kel had been in Melbourne for three years. Dunc had a full-time gig doing video production for a corporate training mob. Kel was studying at Swinburne to be a primary school teacher. I was pulling pints at The Espy in St Kilda, and half-heartedly pursuing stand-up and acting on the side.

After a brutal Friday night shift, I hit the wall. I decided that I needed a nine to five. Hospitality hours were killing my creativity. Working behind a bar was ravaging my liver. I would still have plenty of time for arty nonsense at night and on the weekends. Those were the half-truths I conned myself with. Resistance, man. It's a slippery motherfucker.

It didn't take me long to get sucked into the system – I started the ad sales gig at Fairfax three weeks later. After my first full week in the office, I went for an Italian feed on Lygon with Dunc and Kel. We toasted my new start. I sensed Dunc was angry that I'd followed his lead and given into 'The Man'. But like typical long-time friends, we buried any animosity with fake, drunken affirmations. Kel had scored some MD from uni. We all necked caps and headed to Ding Dong.

That was the night I met Di. She was high too. We locked eyes on the dancefloor – a cheesy Klaxons or Fratellis song was playing, I can't remember which. There was an instant sense of recognition. It was like we knew one another from a past life.

I went back to Di's place in Richmond. She took out her fire twirling sticks and gave me a demonstration. Di was a town planner for the City of Melbourne, a corporate high-flyer. But she grew up in Torquay, so there was still a bit of country hippie flowing through her veins. We had nervous but euphoric sex. I stayed the night.

And that was that. I went from slacker barman, to loved-up yuppie in a matter of weeks. I had a good job and a good girl. Just like Dunc.

Of course, a sense of suffocation crept in quickly. My life looked good on paper, but I was having someone else's dream. For the longest time, I felt powerless to prevent my slide towards beige, suburban mediocrity.

Resistance, man. It's a slippery motherfucker.

/

I was sunburnt, chronically constipated and half-cut. Allie was trying to figure out the bill.

"Did we get three salchipapas?" he said. "I thought we only had two?"

"There is also a prob-lem wiz zee drinks," The Frog said. "Why is ziss thirty thou-sand?"

"Pass me zee menu," The Frogette said. "Zee prices are diff-er-ent to the bill."

We met The Frog and The Frogette, a tall married couple from Paris, in the line to enter Tayrona on Wednesday. The Frogs had left their two-year-old daughter back in France with The Frogette's mother and were doing a whirlwind fourteen-day trip around Colombia. It was obvious to everyone that The Frogette had taken an immediate liking to Brian. She gazed at him like a diabetic eyeing up a cream cake. And it seemed like The Frog wasn't bothered by his wife's crush. Apparently, a lot of Euro cunts have a deal where it's okay if your spouse fucks around when they're on vacation. When you get home, life returns to normal.

"What's the difference? I asked Allie as I lit a fag.

Allie consulted the check. "Twenty thousand."

"Here you go," I said as I threw him a bill.

We all stood up. My legs were sore. Upon entering the park, the four of us and The Frogs had walked for miles through the rainforest. We saw countless families of monkeys jumping about at the top of the canopy. Getting to the first beach was like a dream. We climbed over jagged rock formations and stepped onto the brilliant white sand, marvelling at the shimmering blue-green water. Brian filmed everyone running into the surf on my phone. M83's 'Midnight City' played in my head as I launched into the ocean like a fish.

I went to the loo. My post-feed fag did the trick – I was able to push out three days' worth of compacted turd. The campgrounds were primitive; communal showers and hammocks. When the sun went down the mozzies were out of control. On night one I'd been woken up every twenty minutes by the little menaces buzzing right near my ear. For night two, my plan was to get so drunk that I'd pass out cold.

I wiped my arse then found the others. They were sitting in a semi-circle on the sand. The Frogs were eating strawberry ice creams. It was late arvo and the sun was getting lower in the sky. Unlike the first beach inside the park, the playa near the campgrounds was far from pristine. There were plastic wrappers and empty beer cans all over the sand. The water was gasoline-y from all the speedboats that were constantly ferrying cunts over to Santa Marta.

Brian was borrowing my phone to record his content. "Listen to me fam. You *cannot* afford to miss out on Parque Tayrona!" Brian said. He was prancing around like an Insta thot at Coachella. "Look at this place. Nothing compares! Whether you wanna see some beautiful natural landscapes, get some great hikes in, or just chill on the beach with your amigos, this place has it all! Right, that's it for today fam... I'm gonna get myself a cerveza and get ready for an epic last night in paradise. Don't forget to like and subscribe! Bri Bri out!"

The beach was packed with hundreds of tourists like us. We wanted feeding. We wanted fucking. And some of us, namely Allie, had their hearts set on a fight for good measure. In the cities and towns there's a uniformity to Colombian culture. The most tantalizing fuck-house, to the sweetest abuela, to the grimiest bum, all blend together in a rich, sexy kaleidoscope. Dark Catholic guilt and native voodoo and conquistador bloodshed, all congealed like a heavy tapioca pudding. Yet in places like Tayrona there's vulnerability. Tired indigenous women sherpa snacks for miles on foot so they can sell them to lairy gringos with tribal tattoos.

Ah, fuck it. All this shit is someone else's problem for another day. YOLO, baby.

/

"Cómo?" she screamed over the music.

I was entering the void. It was our last night in Santa Marta, the final night of the trip, the penultimate huzzah. After a week of non-stop partying I'd forgotten exactly what I was chasing with all the boozing and the smoking and the snorting. But I desperately needed the show to go on.

"Tu corres bien," I yelled into my dance partner's ear. She was a pretty young thing with big brown eyes and child-bearing hips. I was trying to tell her that she danced well. But I knew from her reaction that, once again, my disgraceful Spanish had let me down. My partner just nodded and continued moving from side to side. I was doing my best to stay in time but kept stepping on her feet. The tune ended. She pushed me away and went back to her pals.

Me and Steve were the last ones standing. Brian and Allie were back at the Airbnb sleeping.

Our last night in Tayrona was fucking crazy. The Frog recognized a bunch of British lads on the beach. One of them, a skinny little ned from Scotland, had a bunch of MD. We all got on it and had an epic beach party. The Frogs even convinced Brian to drop the whole 'my body is a temple' trip for five minutes and roll with us. The only one who abstained was Steve. Huge speakers blasted twisted electronica and the beach went full psytrance. Over the course of the night, The Frogette lost interest in Brian and began fawning over some mouthy git from Bristol. However, the MD seemed to awaken dormant homoerotic feelings within The Frog, and he began lusting after Brian instead. The bizarre love triangle was dismantled instantaneously when The Frogette began projectile vomiting onto the sand.

Brian didn't deal with the comedown too well. The next day on the hairy speedboat ride over to Santa Marta, he chucked up all over himself. As soon as we made it to the Airbnb in the old town, Brian locked himself in his bedroom where he remained for the rest of the trip.

Our first night in Santa Marta was pretty wild. Me, Steve and Allie went to an American burger place in the main square of the historic district. Allie refused to eat anything – he just kept necking Heinekens and snorting charlie in the loos. After dinner we went to an Irish Pub next door and did some drunk karaoke (I belted out a hoarse version of 'Fortunate Son' by

CCR). Then we went to some other bar and Allie nearly got into fisticuffs with a couple of Chelsea fans. All the bars shut, so we went back to our Airbnb and did more lines.

On Saturday, Allie didn't rise, so me and Steve went down to the family friendly beach for a couple of hours around lunchtime. We had a really average and overpriced lunch on sun loungers, then called it quits. I tried exploring Santa Marta on foot with Steve that arvo, but he was so fucking boring. I kept needing to make pitstops into bars for beers and shots of aguardiente. As I drank, Steve sipped on his water canister and stared like a predator at any girls in his vicinity. By the early evening Allie was still dead to the world, Brian was still hiding in his room, so Steve and I freshened up and headed out for one last roll of the dice.

I was sick of dancing, so we left the club and wandered towards the beach. I bought a baby bottle of aguardiente from a tienda. We sat on the steps by the beach and looked at the black ocean. I was at the stage of the bender where it becomes difficult to feel drunk anymore.

"Are you Israeli?" I took a swig from my bottle. "One of the Selina guys said your real name's Evgeniy."

Steve stared at the ocean.

"My parents left the Ukraine in the 80s. They were in Israel for a few years, and that's where I was born. We emigrated to Canada when I was three."

"Do you consider yourself Jewish?"

"No. I'm not religious."

Our conversation shifted to AI. Steve did not share Elon Musk's concern that some type of AI overlord was destined to rise up and enslave us.

"Human intelligence is only powerful because it develops and functions in its natural environment. Even if you could artificially create a brain with infinite computing power, it wouldn't be able to change the world, because it couldn't interact with the world like organic creatures can. I believe that AI technology will definitely be used to enhance human intelligence. But the concept of attaining some type of transcendence is just sci-fi bullshit."

I was disappointed by Steve's sober, logical argument. Maybe some cold alien intelligence was exactly what this world needed? I changed the topic.

"What do you think about hookers?"

"What about them?" Steve said.

"Do you think it's exploitation? Bad for society? You must've seen all those anti-sex tourist posters around Poblado."

"I don't see anything wrong with it. I fuck hookers all the time."

Steve's late-night trips out from his stuffy lair suddenly made more sense. Midnight snacks.

"I've never been with a hooker before," I lied. I finished the rest of my aguardiente. I felt like a tiny, insignificant nail being pulled towards a huge, invisible magnet. "Fuck it. Wanna find a whorehouse?"

Steve considered the proposal. "You got cash?"

"Nope."

"Neither do I. My card's at the Airbnb."

"I've got my card."

We found an ATM and I withdrew 500,000 pesos. Steve already knew where the nearest brothel was. Creepily, he'd saved it as a favourite place on his Google Maps app.

Two black dudes let us into a scungy little bar. It was late, maybe 2.30, and there were only three girls at the bar. They all stood up from a booth and approached us. Before I could get my bearings, Steve went for the best one, a dirty blonde with bad teeth and decent fake tits. He took her hand and asked me to lend him 150k. I gave Steve the cash, then his girl led him down the hall.

The two girls remaining were probably still in their twenties but looked way older. One was slightly cross-eyed, and the other had huge thighs with a shit-ton of cellulite.

They're disgusting, Bateman told me. *This is perfect. Don't be afraid. You know what to do.*

I took a deep breath.

"Quiero un trio."

The three of us went into a gross little dorm with harsh overhead light. The girls wouldn't start getting undressed until I handed over the money. They tried to pamper me – kissing my neck, sucking on my nipples. But I wasn't there for that. I wanted them to desecrate one another. I watched their white dry tongues lash together. Then I made them get on all fours. I lined them up, Human Centipede-style. I pulled my phone out of my jeans and started recording a video.

"Wassup family! It's your boy Antonio and he's about ready to fuck these two dirty bitches!"

I was enveloped in nothingness. Just like I wanted.

"Comida," I said whilst filming the cross-eyed bitch tongue her colleague's filthy brown arsehole. I grabbed the back of her head and pushed her further forward. "Esta es tu comida."

/

Less than a thousand bucks. I couldn't fucking believe it.

"I can't wait to see you!" Dani said down the line. "What time will you be back?"

I was in a panic. Before Christmas I had four grand in my savings account.

"Umm… my flight from Panama lands in Medellín at eleven. So, I'll probably make it to Poblado at around one in the morning…"

It didn't make sense. How the fuck had I spent so much so quickly?

"OK perfect. You're coming to me, yes?"

"I was planning to go straight to Forever, drop my stuff."

"No! I want to see you!"

I looked around the Santa Marta airport. Everyone seemed to be radiating that warm post-holiday glow. Brian, Steve and Allie had jumped on their flight back to Medellín moments before. I needed to make a quick stop in Panama City. By getting off the plane in Panama, my Colombian visa would automatically renew for another six months.

"Are you sure?" I said. "It'll be late. And you've got work tomorrow."

"No, I want to see you. My *body* has been missing you."

I woke up that morning disgusted with myself. The thrill of unlocking my first threesome had evaporated instantly. It was by far the most post-pulse regret I'd ever experienced in my life. The moment I filled the condom with my evil seed I realized the depravity of the situation. I deleted the video from my phone without bothering to watch it.

"I'm glad to hear that," I said to Dani. "I've been missing you, too."

FIFTEEN

I was scrolling through Facebook.

Brian had just posted a new post-workout photo. Before Christmas he'd shifted gyms and was now frequenting a CrossFit down near Parque Poblado. He was going with Chris Volker and Lamonte, a black Texan stud and new Mastermind member. The three of them stood arm in arm, drenched in sweat.

I scrolled down. Mark Tallone playing in his backyard with his wife and three daughters. Just a regular old dad in middle America, nothing to see here...

I kept scrolling. An Irish lad had posted in the expat forum to let everyone know that his online language school was looking for more teachers – 'Earn up to $28 USD/hour teaching Chinese kids English'. I desperately needed some type of income. Since returning from the coast, the only thing I could think of was to create a freelance writing profile on Upwork. I hadn't even considered online ESL teaching. I sent the Irish fella a DM asking for more deets.

Everyone at Forever was back in their regular groove. Except for Allie. The bloke didn't have an off switch. Every night Allie would get home from work, snort lines, have a shower, rack up more caterpillars, and then go out riding on his bike until two or three in the morning.

On the Friday after we got back from Santa Marta, Allie was doing rails on the coffee table at 9am.

"No work today, Al?"

He rubbed his nostrils and shook his head. "Cunts let me go yesterday."

That stopped me in my tracks. "Whoa. Really?"

Allie inhaled a huge caterpillar. "Facking Dutch pricks! I've been their leading sales guy for the last three years, and then they give us the boot outta nowhere. Some facking shit about moving in a different direction with the goals of the company. Tell you what, now that I'm not there I've got no idea how they're gonna make targets for the rest of the year! They think they're being smart when they hire people in Medellín, pay them mickey mouse wages, fack all bonuses, keep the profit margin as fat as possible. Well that only works if you've got people like me bringing in the bacon! Wouldn't be surprised if they close down the office by the middle of the year. That would be facking brilliant!"

I filled up the kettle with some water. "Fuck dude. What ya gonna do?"

Allie waved away my concern. "I'll be fine. Should've left those twats a long time ago." He hoovered up another line. "Gonna put my feet up, enjoy myself. Life's too short, innit?"

I reached for a teabag. "I've actually got an interview next week. Teaching Chinese kids English online. Irish lad on the expat group gave me his referral link. Dude's a good egg. You want me to make an intro?"

Allie swivelled around. He quickly checked that no ninjas were trying to sneak in through the window.

"Teaching chinks English? Nah mate. Fack that. Would rather sell empanadas on the street."

/

The next day was the big Medellín derby. Independiente vs Nacional. Allie put on his Independiente shirt in the mid-arvo and walked out the door of Forever.

That night I went out with Dani to Mission20, which is between her place in Ciudad Del Rio and Manila. We arrived at the bar just as the fútbol was ending. Independiente were getting stuffed 4-1 by the 'green cunts' Nacional. The stadium was completely full, and all the Nacional fans were going bonkers. I pictured Allie, furiously grinding his teeth, swearing under his breath like Joe Pesci in *Home Alone*.

The Mission20 menu was gringo-priced, so I just went for a humble burger and decided to avoid sampling any of their delicious-sounding craft beers. The place was rammed. It took us an eternity to place our order with the waitress. I went for a piss. When I came back Dani was waving around a menu.

"Did you see they have buffalo chicken wings? And fried pickles. I just added them to our order!"

"What?"

"Look at the portion sizes." Dani gestured at someone else's plate. "I don't think a burger will be enough for you."

"But I don't want wings. Or pickles."

"Are you sure? Because I think–"

I snapped. "HEY! I SAID I DON'T WANT ANY OF THAT SHIT!"

Dani's mouth fell open. "OK. Keep your voice down."

I felt my eyes go wild. "DON'T TELL ME WHAT TO DO! DID I ORDER YOUR FOOD?"

Dani put her hand on my arm. "OK! I'll tell the chica. Stop yelling."

"FUCK OFF!"

I stormed out of the bar. The still night air felt nice on my red-hot ears. I walked along the bike path towards Manila.

My phone vibrated in my pocket. I expected it to be Dani, but it was an unknown number.

"Hello," I spat.

"Hola. Cómo estás? Es este Anthony Fletcher?" a female voice said.

"Si."

The voice started jabbering away in Spanish at a million miles per hour. I wasn't in the mood to fuck around. "No hablo Español," I said.

There was silence for a few seconds. "Un momento, señor."

I wanted to hang up, thinking it was probably just a telemarketer, but remembered they'd asked for me by name, which was weird. About thirty seconds later a different woman started talking in English.

"Hello. Is this Anthony Fletcher?"

"Yes."

"Hello Mr Fletcher. My name is Cynthia, I'm calling from Hospital de Madre Laura. It is about your friend, Alexander Phillips."

I stopped in the middle of the bike path.

"I'm sorry to tell you this, but Señor Phillips is in intensive care. Are you able to come to the hospital?"

My vision blurred.

"I'm on my way."

SIXTEEN

A new WhatsApp voice message from Dani. I hit play.

"What's your problem? Why aren't you responding to me? Did I do something wrong? I thought we were having a good time… then you go crazy. Do you realize how embarrassing that was for me? Everyone was looking at me! I don't know what your fucking problem is. I would never treat you like that. I wouldn't treat anyone like that. I'm so fucking angry. Have a nice day, asshole."

I rubbed the sleep out of my eyes.

Hey, I texted Dani. *Don't panic, I'm not hurt, but I spent all of last night in a hospital. That's why I didn't respond to your messages. Call me when you can.*

Dani called me immediately.

"Oh my god," she said. "What happened?"

I sat up in my bed. "It's Allie. He got stabbed after the fútbol last night."

Dani gasped.

"He lost a ton of blood. But they managed to stabilize him just after midnight. He's gonna be fine."

Dani took a beat. "Why did they call you?"

"Allie must've put me down as his emergency contact with his insurance."

"Have you called his family?"

"No. I didn't want to scare anyone on the other side of the world. According to the docs, he'll be conscious again soon."

Dani exhaled deeply. I pictured her crossing herself. "I'm so glad he's okay."

"Me too." I massaged my temple with my forefinger. "Look, I'm sorry for my behaviour last night. There was no reason for me to storm out like that."

The line went cold.

"If I'm honest, I've hit a real roadblock with *Song & Dance Man*." I cleared my phlegmy throat. "When I was with the boys on the coast, I managed to figure out a lot of the structural stuff. And I was excited to make a start on the next round of edits. But ever since I got back to Medellín, I've just felt really blocked. Last week I spent so many hours staring at a blank page. That's why I was so fucking cranky last night."

Dani mulled over my confession. "Why didn't you tell me that you were struggling?"

"I don't know. Coz I'm a man, woman." I sat up and stretched out my crinkly spine. "How about I come over and apologize in person?"

/

Thirty minutes later I was on Dani's doorstep, handing her a bunch of flowers. Dark bags sat under her eyes. We sat on her couch. I reached out and grabbed Dani's hand.

"I'm not sure if you've noticed, but I'm not normal," I said. "I'm trying to finish this damn book. I'm trying to hook up that online teaching gig. I'm trying to push myself. I wanna do something cool with my life. At the same time, I don't want to burden you with all my bullshit. You're the best part of my day. Last night I just lost my cool because all the stress bubbled up at once. I'm sorry for being a dick."

Dani's bottom lip quivered. She began to cry.

"I don't want you to bottle everything up… It's not fair that you don't tell me everything that's going on with you… How can I help you if you keep everything hidden away?"

I inched closer to her on the couch. "No. It's not like that. I don't hide everything. It's just when I'm stressed out. I don't wanna kill your vibe."

"But I'm your girlfriend, Tony. You're *allowed* to kill my vibe. I want you to tell me when you're upset. Or stressed. Or angry. Whatever it is. I want to know. I need to know."

I nodded.

She wiped tears from her eyes. "And if you're so stressed out, maybe you shouldn't do the online teaching thing? I can help you with money. You can move in here. It's not a problem. You should just focus on your book."

"No," I said gently. "Since I got to Medellín my schedule has been open-ended. I've had too much free time. I need some structure. If I teach a couple of classes first thing in the morning, it's gonna force me to be more productive with the book. And we'll have more money for New York."

Dani looked like some type of deity from a fever dream.

"I was so afraid when you told me that you were in the hospital…"

I kissed her tenderly on the lips. Dani's eyes remained temporarily cold and open. Slowly, she began to thaw. My hands moved to her chest. I carried Dani to the bedroom and undressed her. With her engorged pre-period tits and glistening pussy, she looked pornographically hot. Yet when the director called "Action!", my leading man let me down. I felt pathetic as I tried stuffing my floppy cock inside her.

I gave up, apologized, and asked Dani if she wanted me to go down on her instead.

"No." She smiled. "Just hold me."

Allie was white as a sheet.

"How ya feelin', old boy?"

"Parched. Facking nurse wouldn't give me any water before. Pass me that cup."

I obliged then pointed to the stitches under Allie's left eye. "That one's gonna look cool as fuck when it heals up! Chicks dig scars, bro."

Allie took a sip and gave me a half-smile.

"You sure you don't want me to call anyone back home, Al?"

"No. It'll do more harm than good."

Allie went boozing by himself after the derby and got into a verbal exchange with a Nacional fan who cut the line at some fonda near the stadium. Ten minutes later, Allie left the bar and got jumped by the lad and five of his knife-wielding buddies. Allie did his best to fend them off but got punctured in the guts a few times and collapsed on the pavement. In the ambulance he was hallucinating. Three tiny witches were flying about on broomsticks to the tune of 'Satisfaction' by the Stones.

"Glad you're alright pal," I said to Allie. "Call me if you need anything."

"Fanks. Will do."

/

The following week I had my interviews with the online teaching mob.

The first, a ten-minute Skype call with a young admin chick in Beijing, was nothing more than a formality.

The next one, a trial class with real students, was stressful as fuck. There were four Chinese kids on the call, and they were super-young, probably only four or five years old. Some had parents in the background, watching my every move like

CCP operatives. I managed to muddle through my lesson plan without any major hiccups.

Allie got discharged from hospital. The last thing he wanted was tea and sympathy. Allie holed himself up in his room and became the second hermit at Forever.

I tried to divert all my nervous energy towards *Song & Dance Man*. It was futile. I desperately needed a job. If I didn't get the teaching gig I'd be completely fucked. Maybe Mum or Dunc would loan me some cash? The idea of asking for help filled me with dread. If things didn't turn around, I would have no choice.

I would be forced to go full native.

/

Brian invited me and Dani to a house party at the Volkers' on a Saturday night. I was doing everything to avoid spending extra coin at restaurants, so I gleefully accepted.

We arrived just after seven. The Volkers lived on the second floor of an old red-bricked four storey building in Manila. It was a private residence with no portero, a rarity for gringos living in Medellín. A morbidly obese abuela with hairy face moles sat on a plastic chair out the front of the building. She smiled at us and called Dani 'linda'. We walked up a single flight of stairs that smelt like cat piss and knocked on the door.

"The big boy!" Chris said.

"What's crackin', champ?" I gave Chris a hug. "Chris, Dani. Dani, Chris."

The apartment was small, recently renovated and impeccably furnished. Chris introduced me to Kat, who was far more attractive IRL compared to how she looked on YouTube. Kat was from Brisbane, just like Chris. She had a strong jaw, sparkly green eyes, a five-head that would rival Rihanna's, and a banging post-baby body with curves in all the right places. Their little boy Bobby was a cutie pie – he looked just like a young Macaulay Culkin.

Chris gave us a quick tour of his home.

"It's beautiful, Chris," Dani said.

"Gracias!"

"When did you move in?" Dani asked as she admired the plant wall.

"We bought the place in late 2017. It actually used to be an Airbnb, so it needed some fixing up." Chris showed us photos of the renos on his phone. "One day, the old couple downstairs will wanna sell. Our plan is to buy all four storeys and fix up each apartment. The fact that we don't have a building association is huge. Means we don't waste any coin on strata fees. Not many places like this left in Poblado."

Brian sashayed into the apartment, perspiring slightly after his Onewheel journey down from Forever. There weren't many other people at the bash. It was pretty family-friendly. There was an Ecuadorian couple with a small boy roughly the same age as Bobby. And there was a highly-strung American girl, her stoic Colombiano husband and their newborn baby girl. The baby had a shaved head which looked fucking strange. Dani told me later that it was a Latin American old wives' tale that if you shaved a baby's head, their hair would start coming in thicker and faster. If you ever make it to Colombia, be prepared to see tiny skinheads everywhere.

Bobby said goodnight to everybody, and Kat put him to bed just after 8.30. All the other cunts with kids left shortly after that.

Brian and Chris sat on the couch, gossiping about their Mastermind crew. Kat joined me and Dani in the dining room.

"Tony tells me that you and Chris have your own Amazon marketing agency?" Dani said.

Kat took a sip of her red wine. "That's right."

"And your team is based in the US?"

"Some of them. But most of them are actually in Eastern Europe. We're fully remote, so we've got people all over the world."

"Wow!" Dani said.

"I'm really impressed with your business model," I added. "You don't have to worry about commuting, renting an office, all that jazz."

Kat nodded. "For sure. But the real benefit is being able to hire top talent. Most businesses can only hire in a single city. But we can take applicants from pretty much anywhere."

Dani started peppering Kat with questions about Amazon.

"This is probably a little into the weeds, but we offer four core service areas," Kat said. She quickly downed a celery stick drenched in hummus. "Operations. Brand protection. Organic marketing, which is basically SEO. And paid advertising. Every brand selling on Amazon needs to manage these four things if they want to be successful on the channel."

Dani smiled. "It's amazing that you guys figured this all out and built a business."

Kat beamed. "I love it! It's super-fun for a nerd like me. And what's crazy is that this Amazon marketplace model is starting to take over the world. Uber, Rappi... even dating apps like Tinder run on the same principles. And it's the same four service areas every time. In theory, we could probably expand our management service to a completely different marketplace. One day, we probably will."

SEVENTEEN

"Let me see."

Dani was trying on a pair of boyfriend jeans at Pull & Bear. She came out of the changing room sheepishly.

"Oh nice!" I took a photo of Dani on my phone. "You look like you listen to a *ton* of Mac Demarco."

Dani looked at my screen. "Delete that!" she said, slapping me playfully on the bicep.

"Ouch. Alright. Deleted."

"I told you I look stupid in loose pants."

"Doesn't bother me." I winked at Dani. "I'm more interested in what's underneath."

Dani decided to go with her first choice, a pair of distressed black jeans. When we got to the front of the queue, I threw my credit card on the counter and kissed Dani on the cheek.

I was in a fantastic mood. My first online classes would commence the following week, after Chinese New Year. I was only booked for a few hours during the first month, but was assured my hours and money would increase from there. To celebrate, I'd taken Dani out shopping at the Santafé mall.

We cruised over to another store. Malls in Medellín are bizarre. Hardly anyone buys anything. According to Dani, when regular life was really dangerous in Colombia, malls were one of the few safe public places. Even now, they're nothing more than loitering meccas.

Dani bought a pair of silver earrings then decided that she was done. We considered grabbing lunch at the food court, but I pushed to get a Rappi delivered to her place. I was horny as a motherfucker and eager to get my dick wet. We caught the elevator down to the carpark. I enveloped Dani from behind as we huffed exhaust fumes and waited for a taxi.

On the way to Dani's building I thought about Allie. Although he was still recovering from his injuries, he'd left Medellín a couple days earlier to go and do an ayahuasca ceremony up in the mountains. The poor guy was probably sitting cross-legged, tripping his balls off, chunks of vom splattered all over his chest.

Dani pulled up Rappi on her phone. She ordered a chicken salad from one of her favourite lunch spots. I added a fried chicken sandwich, a side of plantain chips, and a Coke Zero before finalizing the order.

We got back to Dani's apartment. I made my way towards the bathroom.

"Hey, can you pass me your phone?" Dani said. "I wanna see how I look in those jeans again."

I handed Dani my phone. The Rappi driver would be arriving with our lunch in about twenty-five minutes. Just enough time for a quick shag. I took a piss, washed my hands, and then made a beeline towards Dani.

"What the fuck is this?" She was standing up. A video was playing on my phone.

My heart dropped. "Hey, don't play that…"

The video continued to play. Grunt-y sex noises emanated from my device. Dani threw it at me. The phone hit me in the gut and fell down on the tiles.

"GET OUT. GET OUT MY HOUSE!"

"Dani, it's not what you think, let me explain…"

Her face was distorted with pain. "I SAID GET OUT!" She burst into tears.

I ran towards Dani and grabbed her by the shoulders. "Let me explain."

She collected herself. "Get out! Or I'll kill you." Dani wriggled away from me, ran towards her bedroom and locked the door.

I picked up the phone and hit pause on my disgraceful homemade porn. Like a wetbrained prize-fighter, I made my way back to Forever.

EIGHTEEN

Apple automatically stores deleted videos in your 'Recently Deleted' folder for thirty days. Dani had stumbled upon the video twenty-nine days after my debased dalliance with those two bushpigs. Twenty-four hours later and I would've been in the clear. If you've done anything heinous over the last month and recorded it, I'd highly recommend you quickly check your own device right now.

"Why the fuck would you cheat on a perfect ten with two nasty working girls?" I hear you asking.

Let me go full Siggy Freud for a moment. As a teen, my innocent adolescent penis looked nothing like the veiny monsters that appeared in standard boy-girl flicks, and therefore I couldn't properly engage with the fantasy on display. The heavenly vision of two nubile ladies going to town on another was all I needed. At drunken high school house parties, I would gawk at girls making out and groping one another on the dancefloor. Eventually I realized that this was more of a burlesque performance rather than a genuine explosion of sapphic lust. Most gals who publicly fuck around with other gals do it to titillate boys. This slight deception annoyed me. Why would a girl be interested in getting poked by an ugly cock when she could find her way into a pretty little pussy? My manhood grew to be as big and angry and ugly as most of the cocks in porn (alright, amateur porn), and so my preference gradually switched from straight up lesbiana to FFM threesomes. All I needed to do was find a couple of bi-curious gals to execute the fantasy IRL…

Yet, I never found them. Or maybe I did, but lacked the nous to sniff out the opportunity and close the deal. The exception was Di. After a couple of years together, I revealed my long-running fantasy. Di told me that she'd made out with some girls in high school, enjoyed it, and would be down to invite another girl into our bed. For some reason I never took her up on the offer. Two years into the relationship we both subconsciously knew it was doomed to fail. Di wanted it to work more than I did, and would've done anything to try and keep me happy. Deep down I knew that fucking another girl in front of Di would destroy us. I wasn't ready for that bombastic level of emotional carnage. With Di, I wanted a slow descent towards distrust and misery. And that's exactly what I got.

Despite the fact our relationship was only a few months old, I genuinely saw marriage and children on my horizon with Dani. I didn't even consider sharing her with anyone, not even another blissful concoction of Latina perfection. And so, the unfulfilled desire to fuck two girls at the same time continued to burn inside me whilst I barrelled towards a lifetime of commitment. Greedy little Tony, the village idiot, wanted to get his rocks off before he settled down with his beloved. But my dastardly plan was scuppered by the army of nameless, faceless nerds who designed Steve Jobs' godforsaken tracking devices.

I tried my best to weasel my way back into Dani's life. Hundreds of earnest, whimpering apologies were sent her way. I repeatedly visited her edificio and office in the hope that I could finagle a face-to-face. But she cut me off, good and proper, and honestly, who could blame her? My first and only foray into homemade erotica was not for the faint of heart. Arsehole licking, clit-sucking, spit-swapping… Call me a one hit wonder if you must, but at least I've been to the top of the charts.

The rotten artifact meant nothing now that Dani was gone. Even the typically stoic Bateman had no advice for me. I was on my own again.

/

The teaching classes should've been a welcome reprieve, but they weren't.

Each morning I rolled out of bed just before 5am, made myself a quick cup of coffee, and logged into the virtual classroom. As per the strict instructions from management, I would then go full Playschool presenter and deliver the lesson with a 'Tom Cruise Talking About Scientology' level of positivity. Everything was recorded. If I made the tiniest mistake with the curriculum, I would hear about it in my end of week report. Never mind my Santa Marta porno – these recordings are the most shameful files of mine that are floating about somewhere in the cloud. Most of the kids were little shits. The worst was a chubby little fuck who went by the Anglo pseudonym 'Sunny'. Young mate Sunny squawked every answer like a deaf parrot and was clearly playing video games on his second monitor. The other pupils learnt my name but not Sunny – to him I was just 'Teacher'.

My classes would finish around 7am. I'd fix myself a bacon and avo smash for brekkie then wash it down with an extra strong mojito. Then I'd go through to my bedroom and listen 'Green Grass' by Tom Waits, 'Jolene' by Ray LaMontagne, Todd Terje and Bryan Ferry's version of 'Johnny and Mary'.

Tears streamed down my face. Eventually the combination of rum, caffeine, melancholy and bitter rumination would send me back to sleep.

I'd wake around midday and feel momentarily more equipped to do something productive with my day. *Song &*

Dance Man was still nowhere near finished. Even though I was filled with sharp, jangly emotions that I could push straight into Bobby D's Broadway odyssey, the pathetic manuscript just felt like a noose around my neck. So I'd smoke a joint, do my habitual trawl of the expat group, and then enjoy the warm comfort of a YouTube rabbit-hole excursion.

Typically, I'd kick things off with something vaguely educational, such as one of Kat Volker's Amazon videos. Then I'd rewatch twenty minutes of an old favourite, maybe Gavin McInnes' first JRE appearance. From there, I'd try out a YouTube recommendation. I recall discovering Lowres Wunderbread's video essay about the Safdie Brothers' flick *Good Time* during this weird period. Then I'd head over to xvideos for a cheeky bat. One of Antonella La Bomba's classics would usually do the trick. I'd start downing Pilsens and search for a post-pulse pick me up: 'Allah-Las at Best Keep Secret 2013', 'Father John Misty Live On KEXP' or, if I wanted to do a bit of low-rent time travel, perhaps 'Queens of the Stone Age with Dave Grohl Glastonbury Festival 2002'. Then I'd be back on the expat forum, spying on new members, giggling at their pathetic YouTube channels with seven subscribers.

Upon nightfall I'd acquire a Home Burger combo from Rappi, maybe a few extra brews, and then I'd venture down more strange dark alleys. Public masturbation and caught compilations on efukt, restaurant fights, public freakouts. Well aware that I needed to be up early the following morning for my next round of classes, I would throw on a podcast to wind down, maybe some 'Legion of Skanks' or the meandering ramblings of 'Ari Shaffir's Skeptic Tank'.

Instead of going to sleep, without fail I would always sneak in an extra couple hours of screen time. More porn, more YouTube, more manic Wikipedia research about the most random shit imaginable. There was no final destination to my incessant trawling; it was all about the journey.

The heads out there will understand. The internet will never be conquered, but that's no reason not to try.

/

My rock bottom was when I saw the video on Nick Tanner's Insta.

"G'day cunts... Nick Tanner 'ere, coming at ya live from the Big Apple... just sharing some good news... Well, it's actually a double whammy really... As many of you know, I've been over here doing shows in the States for the last few months... And I was getting pretty close to my visa running out... But as it happens, there's a visa just for Aussies... And I'm not sure exactly how... But I've managed to snag myself one, ay... Meaning I'll be able to stay quite a bit longer than I was originally anticipating... So that's a bit spesh... Definitely not a bad start to my week... Ahhhhh... Oh yeah, the other bit of good news... So, since I got to New York, I've been performing all around the joint... But the club that's made me feel real welcome, more than anywhere else, is the Comedy Cellar... Pretty lovely place... You may remember it from the start of *Louie*... Anyway, last night I auditioned to be a regular at the club... And as luck would have it I passed... So I guess now Nicky boy Tanner is officially a New York comedian... And the Comedy Cellar is me home club... So that's pretty alright... If you're ever in town make sure you pop in and say g'day... That's everything from me... Hope ewes are all having a sweet day... Catch yas later..."

That fucking fish-lipped piece of shit. Everything about the cunt – the dinky-di accent, the roo-in-the-headlights innocence, the 'I'm dressed like your dad but I'm only thirty-three' aesthetic – it was all horseshit. Nick Tanner was a ruthless businessman. He was playing the role of the unaffected Aussie bloke who was accidentally stumbling towards fame and fortune. And it appeared to be working.

I know all of this because the first time I ever tried stand-up, Nick Tanner heckled me. It was shortly after I arrived in Melbourne. There were comedy comps at my uni, but I never had the cojones. There was something that petrified me about doing stand-up in Perth. Something to do with not shitting where you eat. But in Melbourne, no one knew me.

I went to an open mic. There were thirty blokes in hoodies waiting. The room reeked of BO, weed, halitosis. We all put our names in a hat. I was one of the last to get called up. I bounded up onto the stage, full of piss and vinegar. The lights blinded me. My confidence evaporated. I awkwardly started to deliver my pre-written jokes. Nothing. Absolutely nothing. A vacuum of nothingness.

At these open mics, there's very few actual audience members. Who in their right mind would purposefully go and watch amateur comics fumble through their flimsy acts? When you're starting out, you perform for other wannabe comedians who are doing nothing more than obsessing over their own set. This is the trial by fire. You refine your joke writing and stage presence to a level where it successfully distracts other comics from their own thoughts. At that point, you win their respect. Once you've done this, you band together with other comedians, and make a plan to get some 'real' stage time in front of actual audiences at shitty pub shows.

So, I'm doing my first open mic set, which was only two minutes in length, but it's feeling like an eternity, and I must've been about halfway through, when I hear someone yelling at the back of the room. I wasn't sure if I was hallucinating, I was kind of having an out-of-body experience, but then I realized some bloke with a fat face and curly hair was yelling at me from the back of the room.

"Slow down, turbo!"

I stopped babbling and faced the heckler. "What was that, mate?"

"I said slow down, turbo," Nick Tanner repeated.

"Slow down?" I scrunched up my face. "You a cop or something?"

You have to remember this was my very first time on stage, everything felt very fucking surreal, so looking back this wasn't the worst comeback in the world. But Tanner crucified me for it.

"Not a cop, mate. I'm a comedian. This is a comedy club. We're all comedians here. You sure you're in the right place?"

A lightning bolt of laughter reverberated around the room. The dude running the mic called time.

I jumped offstage and slunk back into my chair. After the last bloke did his set, Tanner got up and did five minutes. His pedestrian, one-dimensional jokes about tram etiquette, labradoodles and cupcakes were delivered at a snail's pace. All the comics in the crowd roared after each glaringly obvious punchline. I cottoned on to what was happening. Tanner had recently 'levelled up' and was now doing shows around town. All the other comedians were trying to get into his good books.

I went to the same open mic every week for a couple of months. Tanner closed out the show with his same five minutes every time. Tram etiquette. Labradoodles. Cupcakes. This is another dirty secret about stand-up; if you want to get good, be prepared to repeat yourself again and again and again. Tanner heckled someone new every single week, but he never went after me again. It made me feel slightly better that his wrath was indiscriminate, but at the same time, I knew that Tanner was just the tip of the iceberg, and that I'd have to deal with an army of cunts just like him if I wanted to climb the ladder.

So instead, I started a podcast with Dunc. Unlike the rigid limitations of stand-up, you can do anything on a pod. Sketches, philosophical pontificating, shit-talking... nothing's off the table. We had a lot of gusto for our first ten episodes, but quickly ran out of steam. I told myself that I'd get back on the stage soon. But I never did.

All the while, Tanner's star kept rising. He started popping up on Aussie TV shows. Then he got a Netflix special. Now the cunt's a regular at the Comedy Cellar! And I can guarantee you he's still telling the same jokes. Except his trams chunk probably got co-opted into a New York City subway bit.

These days, cunts are always talking about mental health. Here's a rotten truth; if you become successful, a lot of your problems tend to go away. If you don't find success, your plight becomes harder. And despite what self-help gurus tell you, there simply isn't enough success to go around.

Make of that what you will.

/

Things weren't going well for Brian or Steve, either.

A full-blown bromance was blossoming between Chris Volker and Lamonte the CrossFit stud. This made poor old Brian last week's news.

Bitcoin's price continued to drop, and although he didn't divulge a thing, it was clear that Steve's personal finances were taking a battering.

With nowhere to go and nothing to do, the three of us were spending a lot of time at Forever. The place was starting to look and feel a bit crusty from all the wear and tear, a far cry from the sparkling palace it was upon my arrival in Medellín.

Allie came home from his ayahuasca retreat and injected some well-needed positivity into the household. I sat on a stool in the kitchen as he told me about his experience.

"There were two shamans. Husband and wife team," Allie explained. "The guy was Swiss and the bird was Colombian. She's from the Amazon region, in the south. And they have a little girl who's five."

"You stayed at their place?"

"Yep. Bloke from Virtuagym told me about their finca a couple of years back. Found 'em on Google."

"And was it just you?"

Allie nodded.

"Fuck. That must've been weird. Tripping balls in someone else's house?"

Allie raised his eyebrows. "You're not wrong. When I first arrived, I felt like the woman was trying to avoid me. Like she was afraid of me for some reason. Whenever I walked into a room, she would grab her daughter and lead her away. And then on the first night, I got woken up by the wife screaming 'GET OUT! GET OUT!' over and over again."

"She screamed that at you?"

"No, she was in her bedroom. Her yells echoed all through the house."

"Whoa."

"The next morning, I asked the Swiss bloke if maybe I brought some bad energy into their home, and that's why his wife was acting weird. But he said no, it had nothing to do with me, it was just a bad dream. So, over the next week they guide me through all the ceremonies. And then after the last one, I asked the lady shaman if she was afraid of me when I first got there. She's a very shy person, but eventually she admitted that she *was* scared in the beginning. I guess she's kind of like a medium, and she didn't like what I was bringing into her home, but she didn't want to tell me because she knew it would just freak me out."

I processed this information. "How were the ceremonies?"

"The nights were 'orrible, mate," Allie said. "I kept waking up every hour or so drenched in cold sweats. The walls of my room would dissolve and turn into animal faces. I was convinced they were trying to swallow me up while I slept."

"Did you receive any type of message?

Allie put his finger on his chin.

"It's hard to describe…" Allie took a beat. "The first few days I was just chucking my guts up nonstop. You don't have a chance to think. The medicine just attacks all the gunk and negative energy that's built up inside ya. All you're doing is riding the wave of nausea, trying to stay alive. But by day four or five, I got a handle on the physical stuff. Then you start dealing with a different type of pain. The ayahuasca spirit begins telling you a story using symbols and metaphors about your life. You're paralyzed – it holds every part of your attention – and you have to just lie there and accept it. So, to answer your question, it doesn't really give you a message. It just smacks you in the face with a profound experience that changes how you see the world. A new level of awareness."

I wasn't sure if I trusted Zen Allie. "I don't want to dig into anything too personal, but can you give me a specific example? Like, what's one piece of awareness that you got from taking the medicine?"

Allie took a sip of his green smoothie.

"When I was in the hospital, the doctor told me that considering the amount of blood I lost, there's no way I should be alive. The only thing that kept me nervous system going was the amount of charlie in my system. I felt dead ashamed. It made me realize how facking addicted I was. Then I retraced me steps. I moved all the way to Colombia, away from all me family and friends, just so I could do as much charlie as humanly possible. When I started doing the ceremonies, I realized I was carrying a lot of guilt. But the medicine showed me the metaphor in what the doc said. Although I considered it a dirty little habit, the coke was actually the thing that was keeping me alive! It was useful to me. But at some point, the drug turned on me. If I kept going, it was gonna kill me. That's why I got stabbed after the football. It was the universe sending me a sign."

I raised my eyebrows. "Wow dude. Deep shit."

"Feel like a new man, mate! If you racked up a big juicy line right now, I wouldn't be interested. Never gonna touch the stuff again."

/

One night, Ricardo invited me to his penthouse. I was happy to be getting out of Forever for a few hours.

"How's life dude?" I said to Ricardo.

"I'm okay. I can't be a part of Click Clack. I wasn't able to get a loan"

"Damn."

"Allie told me that you broke up with your chica," Ricardo said as he lit up a joint. "What happened?"

"Ah, you know. We wanted different things. Wasn't to be."

Jhonatan was out in some neighbourhood called Buenos Aires. Me and Ricardo called a cab and met up with him. Jhonatan was with a big squad, they were all kind of dodgy-looking. We had drinks at this uber Colombian fonda. Everyone was sipping aguardiente, smoking weed, eating salchipapas. Ricardo handed out some bags of powder to Jhonatan's crew. Buenos Aires is a picturesque neighbourhood. There's this tram line that runs down the main strip, and you can see all the mountains in the background.

Those couple hours at that fonda might have been the time I felt most alone during my entire stint in Colombia. Apart from Ricardo, no one spoke English. I just sat there, necking Pilsens, smoking cigarettes, feeling sorry for myself. The artifice of Poblado has the effect of making you think that you 'belong' in Colombia. Whenever I made it out to a more authentic barrio, I felt wonderfully alienated.

I sensed Ricardo felt the same way. He was, after all, a rich kid from an elite family that had been educated at hoity-toity schools all over the world. As a club promoter, Ricardo needed someone like Jhonatan as his right-hand man – a kid from the other side of the tracks who would gladly wade through tricky situations on his behalf. Initially, I took Ricardo as a chronic co-dependent. He seemed to dig weirdo gringos like myself and Allie because we injected some low-rent glamour into his hometown. And I was under the impression that he was desperate for the approval of homely locals too. Yet, like myself, Ricardo seemed completely disconnected from all of Jhonatan's mates. It was like he wanted to fit in, he knew it was important, but didn't completely understand the point. After a couple of hours everyone decided they were going to hit up some salsa bar a few blocks up the road. Me and Ricardo jumped in a cab and went back to his spot.

Ricardo asked me for a good TV show. He was looking to get into a new series. I recommended *The Sopranos*. We smoked a joint and watched the pilot episode on his big screen.

"What do ya reckon?" I said after it finished.

He shrugged. "Okay. Pretty slow."

"What about *Breaking Bad*? You seen it?"

"No."

"Dude… You'd love it."

"OK. Let's smoke again first."

He rolled up another fattie by the pool. "You don't have to tell me if you don't want to," Ricardo started, "But that night we came here to chill after Salón, why were you crying?"

My first impulse was to plead the fifth. Tony, the master of secrets. *And the day came when the risk to remain tight in a bud was more painful than the risk it took to blossom.* I thought about the memory. Why was I always so protective? This is what happens when you keep a lot of bodies buried in your backyard. You start to lose perspective. Fuck it. I let rip.

"It was the song that was playing on YouTube. 'Hero' by Mariah Carey. It made me think of my old man. He's a macho dude, but for some reason he really digs cheesy female vocalists like Mariah. He liked that song when we were growing up, bought the CD. One day when I was like six years old, he grabbed me and started slow dancing with me in the living room. Looking back, I think he must've been drunk. When the song ended, he told me that I was his hero. Memory fucked me right up. We're not on good terms anymore."

Ricardo licked the joint. "Ah. Sorry man."

"It's fine. I shouldn't be bitching to you of all people about daddy issues."

Ricardo lit up the joint. "You know Burzum?"

I searched through my internal wiki. "Yeah… it's that crazy dude… Varg Vikernes, right? The Nazi guy?"

Ricardo giggled. "Yeah. I think he's pagan now. But he used to be a Nazi when he was in prison."

"I saw that doco about him and all the other Scandinavian black metal dudes."

"Yeah, that's a good movie. His music is crazy. Have you heard it?"

"Maybe in that doco. But I don't remember. Give me a taste."

Ricardo teed up a song and hit play. The tune was an apocalyptic anthem that assaulted the sprawling night sky. I was stoned as a motherfucker.

"Do you feel *the pull*?" Ricardo asked me mischievously, as the song finished up.

I saw a swooping vulture out the corner of my eye.

"Yeah man," I said. "I think I do."

NINETEEN

The little cunt's face started turning red.

"Good job Britney! Now it's your turn Sunny. How many monkeys do you see in the tree?"

Sunny didn't respond. He was looking upward with fierce concentration.

"Sunny? Can you see any monkeys in the tree?"

Plop.

The little bastard was taking a shit.

Plop. Plop. Plop.

"Hey Sunny? Are you okay?"

He finished shitting and looked at his screen. "Two monkey in tree."

"That's right. There's two monkeys in the tree. What about the water? How many sharks are in the water?"

Sunny jumped off the toilet and bullishly set his tablet down on the ground. The screen settled – his little codger and balls were on full display. Sunny reached for some toilet paper and started wiping his arse. Britney covered her mouth and started to giggle. I hit Sunny's 'Hide Screen' button, but the damage was already done.

Fortunately, we were on the last exercise of the lesson. I asked Britney a few final questions, kept Sunny's screen hidden and then bid them both adieu.

"Good-a-bye, Teacher," Sunny said.

/

Let's go back to Melbourne for a moment.

Me and Di lived in Abbotsford, which is a leafy inner-city suburb north east of the CBD with a huge old convent. On this particular Wednesday I rode my bike into the office, which only took twenty minutes. It was footy finals time and my boss Col was a diehard Bombers fan. He always tried to chew my ear off about the West Coast Eagles even though I'd told him repeatedly that I didn't give a shit about the AFL. Dealing with Col's incessant droning about soft tissue injuries, high-pressure acts and forward fifty entries was the most difficult part of my workday.

At 5.30 I jumped back on the bike and pedalled straight to Dunc and Kel's place, a chic double storey apartment that was also in Abbotsford. When I got there, Dunc was in the middle of cleaning up some dog shit off the floor. Fray the Great Dane was only a few weeks old but already bigger than a fully-grown Jack Russell. I cracked a beer and Dunc lit a jazzie. I was showing Dunc the Father John Misty Letterman performance of 'Bored in the USA' when Di walked through the door holding Vietnamese takeaway. She was on the phone with one her dumbcunt pals from uni, some vapid banker whore. Di's one of those people who can be friends with absolutely anybody, which made her particularly popular with socially inept miscreants. It was infuriating. If she sees the good in *everyone*, what makes me special? At the time, this guilt-by-association resentment was beginning to fester inside me.

We ate our pho on the balcony and shared meaningless anecdotes about our week. It was unseasonably warm for September. Like usual, I drank more than everyone else, and decided to serve up a few misanthropic musings for dessert.

"What are we doing with ourselves here?" I said to everyone. "In this town. In these jobs. Is this the best we could be doing?"

"My tummy's full of pho," Di said. "Not gonna lie, I'm pretty content right now."

"Content is the right word." I finished off my last Melbourne Bitter. "Have you noticed how everyone in the world has somehow become a content-creator? Content to make you feel *content*. Not amazing. Not happy. Not wild. Not free. Just… content."

Dunc finished rolling his post-dinner joint.

"What are you upset with? Yourself? Or 'the system'?"

I ran my fingers through my hair. "I'm just thinking out loud. Why are things set up the way they are? Do we want these yuppie lives, or are we getting conned? Is any of this actually making anyone happy? Or are we just chasing comfort?"

"Come on T!" Kel said. "You've just got the hump day blues. This weekend you'll be out in the Grampians, tripping your balls off. That'll make you feel alive!"

I shook my head. "Controlled chaos. I know how that rollercoaster works. It's just a ride, babes. It's just a ride."

Di tapped me on the arm. "Come on. Let's go." The poor girl had heard my version of Bill Hicks' act many times before. "I need to get home before this carb coma takes hold."

I stood up. "The mid-week jamboree draws to a predictable close. Time to ride back to my comfy bed to have comfy dreams about comfy things."

Dunc lit up. We locked eyes properly for the first time in a while. "If you're so unhappy, why don't you change something?"

The pup was sitting on Kel's lap. I leant down and kissed the back of Fray's head which smelt like freshly buttered toast.

"Seeing as this world isn't changing anytime soon," I said to Dunc, "I guess I'll probably have to."

I

I gulped back my morning mojito. I wanted to quit the online teaching gig with every ounce of my being. But I was destitute. Unless I wanted to return home, tail between my legs, I needed to keep slogging away.

It had happened. I'd gone full native.

At this point *Song & Dance Man* was officially a lost cause. So instead, I was channelling all my energy into an anonymous Insta account. I was taking all the holy figures of the digital nomad biohacker douchebag movement – Tim Ferriss, Joe Rogan, David Goggins, Jocko Willink, Aubrey Marcus, Noah Kagan, Tony Robbins, Gary Vee, Wim Hof, Elon Musk, Grant Cardone – and viciously roasting them with original memes. My hope was that the memes would become insanely popular with like-minded misanthropes the world over. And once my handle acquired over 100k followers, I would reveal myself as the Banksy-esque author of the posts.

I threw up a meme about Tim Ferriss getting butt-fucked for four hours and then watched a *VICE* doco about buying drugs on the dark web. Kids have it so fucking easy these days. No more relying on dodgy friends of dodgy friends. Everything conveniently delivered straight to your door.

I was smoking a joint on the balcony when Steve wandered into the kitchen to make his morning smoothie. I finished my number and stepped inside.

"Steve-o."

"Hey."

Cotton mouth. I chugged two huge glasses of water then grabbed a Pilsen out the fridge. I was about to head to my room, but instead wheeled around and faced Steve. The new sativa I picked up from Ricardo always turned me into a Chatty Cathy. "Yo Steve-o, you must know a bit about the dark web?"

"Why do you say that?"

I took a sip of Pilsen. "Just a guess. All the crypto stuff. Seems up your alley."

Steve grunted.

"I just watched a *VICE* doco. It's crazy how simple it is to buy drugs online these days."

Steve poured protein powder and water into the Vitamix. "Why do you need the dark web? You're in Colombia."

"No, not for me. I just see a lot of people in the States are buying drugs online now."

Steve turned the Vitamix on. I took a sip of beer. Something occurred to me. Steve flicked the blender off.

"In the doco they said when The Silk Road got dismantled, fifty copycat sites sprung up immediately. All those dark web marketplaces are just like Amazon, right?"

Steve drank some of his smoothie. "I don't do drugs."

"I know you don't. But surely you must know how it works. Is it basically like Amazon? All the dealers create listings, customers plug keywords into the search tool, and the most relevant results are listed on the page? Is that how it works?"

"I guess so."

"Could we pull Tor up on your computer and take a squiz?"

Steve shot me a dirty look. "Why don't you do it on your laptop?"

"I don't have Tor. Come on. It'll take like five minutes."

Steve's room wasn't funky anymore. It was spotless. There was an automatic air freshener on his desk just to the side of his dual monitor set-up. A Jordan Peterson poster and quote hung over his bed.

Face the demands of life voluntarily. Respond to a challenge, instead of bracing for catastrophe.

Five minutes later, we were scrolling through some dark web search results.

"Dude, these listings are terrible!" I said. "Click on this one." Steve clicked on the listing. "Check it out. One shitty photo in bad light. A single line of copy. No indication of estimated shipping costs. Just the absolute bare bones. And this was the third highest result on the page!"

"What's your point?" Steve said.

"This piece of shit product listing is probably generating hundreds of thousands of dollars every single month. On this marketplace alone! But it was clearly created by some dumb cunt drug dealer. Imagine if it was built by someone who knew what they were doing!"

Steve was looking at me like I was a stray dog that might bite him. "Is this gonna take much longer? I need to get back to work."

My heart was beating out of my chest. Everything was coming together in real time. "Let me show you something."

I grabbed my lappie and showed Steve one of Kat Volker's five-minute YouTube videos about online marketplace fundamentals.

"I'm not interested in selling anything on Amazon," Steve said.

"No. Maybe we could follow those principles but apply them to products being bought and sold on the dark web?"

Steve scoffed. "You're stoned. Colombia produces more coke than any other country in the world. No one's gonna buy your stuff online when they can find a guy on every street corner."

I started laughing. "No! Not here. We could sell it to people in the States. Maybe Canada too."

"How would you ship it?"

I cracked my knuckles. "That's the thing. I wouldn't do *any* shipping. I wouldn't need to. I'd find someone in the States who could store and ship inventory for us. Dropship model. Ricardo has Colombiano friends in Miami. I bet he knows a dude."

Steve swivelled away from me. "That might work." He closed down Tor. "But I'm busy. I can't take on any more projects right now."

I saw red.

"You're a *slave* dude. Work work work. All you do is work! You're just trading precious time for money. If you want to keep doubling down on crypto wouldn't it be nice to have a bit of passive income coming in? How are you gonna find a girl if you can't get your money right?"

Steve twitched.

"Let's not go crazy," I continued. "Why don't we talk to Ricardo, see if he knows someone in the States who could help us out? And if he does, we run a little trial. If you give me a bit of your time and help set up some test listings, I'll invest a few grand into inventory. If nothing happens, we shut everything down straight away."

Steve glanced over my shoulder up at Saint Jordan.

"Come on, dude," I said. "Let's roll the dice."

TWENTY

Ricardo was surprised to see Steve.

"Parceros." He shook my hand. "Steve, you like *Breaking Bad* too?"

Steve shook his head. "No."

"Me and Steve just had a little idea." I gestured at the lappie in my hand. "Can I set this up somewhere? We wanna show you something."

Ricardo flicked an unlit cigarette between his fingers. He appraised the different product listings on my lappie.

"Customers place orders online?" he asked. "Or WhatsApp?"

"Either. Depends how each seller prefers to do business."

Ricardo placed the cigarette in his mouth. "What's your idea?"

I leant forward.

"All these top listings are garbage. The sellers aren't doing a good job describing the product. But because more and more people are buying online, these guys are all probably making a killing. I wanna see if I can do a better job marketing the products. Steve's gonna help me with all the dark web shit. I just need someone who can source me top quality inventory."

Ricardo was about to light the fag but changed his mind. He started rolling it through his fingers again. "Look man. I can get good shit here. But trying to transport stuff into the States... that's a different story."

"I don't wanna smuggle anything. I wanna find a dealer in the States who will sell to me wholesale, and then who can fulfill each order for a fee. Dropship model. You must know people in Miami. Is there anyone who could hook us up?"

Ricardo's eyes darted over to Steve. He leant back into the couch and readjusted his cap.

"Sure. I know people. But why would they help you? If they get busted, the cops go to them."

I shook my head. "To your guys in Miami, I'm just another customer. They sell me a few grand worth of product, with a slight discount because I'm buying in bulk. Then when the orders start coming through, I'll pay them a fixed fee to process and ship each one to the customer. The vast majority of drugs in the States get shipped via the postal service. It's the same model Amazon uses with third-party sellers. And when you think about it, it's actually way better for your guys in Miami. They don't have to pay any street dealers commission for moving the stuff. And they get the vast majority of their money upfront. If I don't move the product, that's on me."

Ricardo considered my plan. "What about profit? If you're paying all these fees, how do you plan to make money?"

I caught a glimpse of myself in a mirror behind Ricardo's head. I looked like a tub of shit – pudgy with the first signs of a disgusting neckbeard.

"People who buy gear online pay more," I said. "Think about it. These aren't junkies on the street trying to scrape together some spare pesos for a bag. These customers are happy to pay a premium for the convenience of getting something delivered to their door. Or maybe they want to compare all the different options available and pick the premium product on offer. Even if your dude in Miami doesn't give me a discount for buying in bulk, I'm confident that I could sell the stuff at a higher price online. It just needs to be really good stuff."

"My friends in Miami are legit," Ricardo said. "They're probably already selling online."

"Doesn't matter." I shifted on the couch – I didn't want to see my dishevelled reflection. "Like I said before, if they're selling online, they're probably not doing a very good job. The economy's flying in Trumpistan. There's plenty of demand to go around."

Ricardo finally lit his cigarette. "Look man. I know we party together, but I'm not too deep in that world. I sell a little, but that's about controlling what happens in my house. I just wanna run my clubs, throw cool parties… I don't think I want to take on a new project right now."

I scratched at my neck. Time to go in for the kill.

"Thirty-three percent, dude. Thirty-three percent. You intro-duce me to your guys in Miami, place a test order, and then that's it. You get one-third of all the profit. No investment. No risk. A completely new revenue stream. American dollars. If it works out, you could get a lot of money for making a few phone calls. And then once you have all that cash, maybe you'll be able invest in Click Clack after all?"

Ricardo mulled it over. He took a monster drag. "One test order?"

"That's it," I said. "If it doesn't work, we shut it down."

Ricardo looked at Steve. "What about risk? No one could trace this back to us?"

Steve looked thoroughly bored. "Everything I do will be encrypted. I'm not incriminating myself in anything."

Ricardo lifted his hat up and ran his fingers through his hair. "Let me call my guy. No promises."

TWENTY-ONE

"Let's drop some acid!"

Life is different when you work for yourself. At no point are you ever really 'off the clock'. But if you've found your true calling, there never seems to be enough hours in the day.

Ricardo looked at me. "Now?"

"Sure," I said. "Why not?"

Ricardo looked out the window. "It's nearly dark."

"So what? Tripping at night is the shit. Scary as fuck."

Ricardo lit a cigarette and laughed. "You love being paranoid. What the fuck is wrong with you?"

"I grew up in the safe suburbs of Perth, dude. Scary fucking place. I'm a victim of my environment."

It'd been a month since I placed the first order with Ricardo's guy in Miami. My brain was fried from weeks of nonstop analysis and tinkering. A Tim Ferriss cock-rider would conclude that I was in need of a 'reset'. Fuck that bullshit. I'm a more primitive communicator. After a month of hard slog, I wanted to get properly fucked up. Ripped right out the goddamn frame. Annihilation was the destination. All aboard the crazy train!

Steve was hunched over his lappie.

"Steve-o, my Commonwealth cousin," I said. "Here it comes. The perfunctory question. Are you interested in imbibing some Class A gear with us this evening?"

"No," Steve said without bothering to look up from his screen.

"Ha ha! Just as I suspected! Well in that case, would you be so kind to handle all the work bullshit so I can trip my balls off?"

Steve grunted an affirmation.

My phone buzzed in my pocket. Email from Mum.

Hello darling

Just listened to a v interesting interview with Graham Hancock on Joe Rogan's podcast. You listen to him, right? A lot of pyramids/Ancient Egypt talk. I will make it over there one day if it kills me!

Life is the same for me. Uni break is coming up so I will get quite a few days off. Coming at a good time – weeds are out of control in the front garden again.

Check out the podcast if you get a chance. Love and miss you darling.

Mum xxx

Fucking hell. Even Mum was on the Rogan bandwagon! Surely that's a 'jump the shark' moment. Bald cunt was taking over the world. I put my phone down and locked it. My sack prickled with anticipation. When was the last time I tripped? Probably 2016-ish, a weekend camping trip with Dunc, Kel and Di.

I wheeled towards Jhonatan. "Mi amigo. Quieres ácido?"

Jhonatan had a joint hanging from his mouth. He smirked. "Si, parcero."

I punched the air. Jhonatan knew we were doing something shady online but didn't appear to give two shits about the details.

"Come on, dude," I said to Ricardo. "Don't leave me and Jhonny Depp hangin'! Let's cook some food then grow our heads!"

Ricardo lit a cigarette. "I like tripping during the day, man. All the visuals. It would be a waste at night, no?"

I pointed towards the garden. "This place is heavenly. The moonlight will look fucking amazing on that lake."

Ricardo looked out the window. "Fuck it," he said. "I'll take half a tab."

The four of us had decided to get out of Medellín for the weekend and come to Ricardo's dope finca, which was about twenty minutes outside of Guatape. Ricardo's old man built the place in the 70s. The house was dated but still completely functional. The property itself was huge. At the back of the house there was an outdoor deck which led down to a completely private patch of lakefront. There were no other properties around for miles. An old caretaker dude from a nearby village maintained the garden. According to Ricardo, no one in his extended family used the finca very often. His mother was in Miami all year round. There were no family photos on the walls, just a few old paintings, but the ghost of Ricardo's old man lingered.

Jhonatan offered to cook dinner. I blasted 'Pop Crimes' by Rowland S. Howard out the Bluetooth speaker. I stood on the deck, sucked on some ice-cold hoppy nectar, stared at the pre-dusk light hitting the lake, and reminisced about my crazy month.

Ricardo's pal in Miami, Diego, said the minimum for a bulk order was five grand, US dollars. In order to come up with the coin, I was forced to draw cash out from a couple of credit cards. Then I worked around the clock to create three SEO-optimized product listings – coke, MDMA caps and some LSD. Steve helped get my content live on a marketplace. The first buyer message came through after just fifteen minutes. There was a bit of customer service malarkey, but on the whole everything went smoothly. Whenever I ran into a new problem, I consulted Kat Volker's Amazon playbook. The moment a customer transferred over funds I would WhatsApp the details to Diego and his team would ship the order. I sold through all my inventory in less than seventy-two hours.

Steve and Ricardo were blown away. For the next batch I convinced them to match my $5k investment, and we bought

$15k worth of stuff. It was even easier the second time around. Some of our first customers came back and made repeat orders. The real game-changer was our first few seller reviews. Initially, I was relying on my copy and images to convince every new customer to take a chance on my products. The reviews, which included glowing feedback about the quality of the gear, the buying experience and short shipping timeline, helped spike our traffic volume and on-page conversion percentage drastically.

We sold through the second batch in a matter of days. We went again. And again. And again. And again. Each time we bumped up our collective investment. After the third batch I paid off my credit cards and quit the online teaching job.

Have you ever uncovered a hidden talent? It's a trip. In hindsight, it's easy to sift through my biography and align all the puzzle pieces. Although my time at Fairfax was lackadaisical, I was in theory working a sales job, and this definitely helped refine my skills of persuasion, which no doubt helped get Steve and Ricardo onboard. And after spending eight months living amongst all the digital douchebags in Medellín, I was no doubt suffering from a mild case of Stockholm Syndrome. This likely influenced my decision to throw a crazy Hail Mary in the form of a crooked dropshipping business. If you can't bear to join them, beat them.

The most illuminating part of my success was the revelation about kneecapping oneself in order to get ahead. I believe I can boil it down to a simple equation; opportunity plus desperation equals success. I always fought to maintain a certain level of comfort throughout my entire adult life. Never truly fulfilled, yet never completely destitute. It was a sad state of affairs. I was afraid of chaos, the most reliable fuel known to man.

We chowed down on Jhonatan's starchy grub. Steve retired to his room. Rather than acid, Ricardo convinced me to neck some molly instead.

We fixed ourselves scotches and sauntered out to the deck. I put on 'No Voodoo' by Allah-Las. Ricardo said it sounded like The Beatles which was completely off the mark but I didn't call him on it. The half-moon made the lake look like a large, tepid bath. There was a throwing knife set-up in the backyard so we did that for a while. Jhonatan sparked up a joint and we started giggling. Soon I was laughing so hard that I thought that I was gonna break a rib. The Allah-Las record finished and 'Loser' by Beck came on. I ventured down to the water to collect myself. I considered going for a paddle in one of the kayaks, but I was feeling pretty loopy, so I decided against it. It was getting a bit cold so we went inside and put on *Breaking Bad*. Ricardo and Jhonatan fell asleep halfway through the episode. I switched off the TV, then went upstairs to my bed.

/

Because of the paper-thin old curtains I woke up early. I dozed for a while but wasn't able to properly go back under. I was scattered but happy as a clam.

Downstairs, Steve was working on his lappie. I made myself a cup of coffee and Steve showed me the plugins that he was attempting to customize. We worked on a few auto-mated sequences together for an hour or so. Ricardo sauntered into the kitchen.

"What should we do today?" Ricardo asked. It was bizarre to see Medellín's prince of darkness so early in the morning.

"It's a gorgeous day out there," I said. "Maybe we could jump in the kayaks, go for a paddle on the lake?"

"Let's order some girls," Steve said.

"*Eso*," Ricardo said as he applauded Steve's suggestion. "I like that idea."

I wasn't so sure. "I'm still feeling a bit rough after last night, lads. Not sure if I'm feeling strong enough to satisfy a chica. Got a bit of pebble dick going on."

"What the fuck is *pebble dick*?" Steve said.

"It's what it sounds like," I said. "Always happens the morning after I take molly. My cock looks like it belongs to a seven-year-old right now."

Ricardo laughed. "It's cool, man. We can get some dick pills. There's a farmacia in the town. It's an older guy. Friend of my family. We can get anything."

"Really?" I said.

"Yeah, man. You want anything else?"

"Maybe some Valium for later?" I said. "To help me sleep."

"Sure." Ricardo pulled out his phone. "What about chicas? How many? My treat."

We decided on five; a girl each and one extra for good luck. Ricardo made a call.

/

Three hours later a tattooed Colombiano pulled up to the front gates in an SUV. Five young grillas from Bello stepped out of the vehicle. Steve and I leered at them on Ricardo's security monitor. They were all wearing tank tops, daisy dukes and Adidas sneakers. Ricardo gave the Colombiano a wad of cash and led the gals onto the property.

That arvo we drank and frolicked on the shore of the lake, blasting Maluma. The girls grinded on our dicks like their lives depended on it. Every second of our idyllic fiesta was uploaded to Snapchat. We started to pair off.

Jhonatan was the first to take his bitch, a twerking little fiend with Pocahontas eyes, up to his bedroom.

Ricardo went for the brooding, emo girl with astrological tatts who looked a bit like a Latina version of Neve Campbell. Many times during our *Breaking Bad* binges I was petrified that Ricardo was going to try it on with me. I felt a great sense of relief when I saw him making out with his chica on a deckchair.

I hit off with the 'negrita' of the group. She had an amazing butt and dick-sucking lips. The first black girl of my life, I ate her purple clit from behind until she pulsed on my face. The Cialis was working miracles – that day I'd gone from a pebble dick to a sixteen-year-old's 'I'm too embarrassed to stand up from my desk in History class' cum gun. I lay down and let her ride my chemically enhanced cock. She pulsed a couple more times. "Mi culo, papi, mi culo," she kept pleading, so I wet my index finger and then jammed it right up her stinker. She began moaning like a born-again fanatic. I clamped down hard on her nipple with my molars. I pictured my finger and fat cock taking turns entering her orifices and this pushed me over the edge. I pulled her off me, held her down by the neck, ripped the condom off and emptied my balls all over her face.

Me and the negrita fell asleep for a while. She was still dead to the world when I woke up a couple of hours later. I went downstairs. Ricardo and Neve Campbell were smoking cigarettes, listening to house music on the deck.

"Tony Soprano," Ricardo said. "You should go check on your boy."

"Where is he?"

"In his room. He's putting on quite a show. The door's wide open."

I grabbed myself a Pilsen and walked towards the very front of the house. I could hear Steve's chicas giggling as I walked down the hall. I peered around the corner and looked into his room.

Steve was standing on his bed completely naked, and the two girls were taking turns sucking his cock. They had their bare arses arched high up in the air facing the lappie that was set up opposite the bed.

Ding. Ding. Ding.

One of the chicas jumped down and made her way towards the lappie.

"Gracias mi amor!" she said before blowing a kiss at the webcam. "Más? No hay problema."

The bitch made her way back onto the bed and started fingering her amiga.

Steve looked like a little Greek statue, caught in the riptide of nirvana. He looked over at me standing in the doorway. I winked at him, raised my Pilsen and mouthed "salud".

/

I was stoked when the girls left early the next day. I could tell Ricardo and Jhonatan were equally relieved. The first fuck with the negrita was great, the second was okay, but my balls were fresh outta juice by the third rodeo. But Steve the halfling was insatiable. He was up all night fucking and sucking. The following morning, his two poor camgirls could barely walk.

The four of us drank coffee and giggled about the prior evening's exploits. Jhonatan went out for a paddleboard on the lake.

"You need to call your guy," Steve said to Ricardo. "I just sold the last of our inventory."

"What the fuck?" I said. "A hundred grand worth of stock. Gone already?"

"Yep," Steve said. "Look."

Steve showed me the spreadsheet. We'd sold the fucking lot in four days!

Ricardo smiled and called Diego to place another order. As he babbled away in Spanish, my balls started to regenerate.

Holy fuck, Bateman said. *A hundred grand in four days! That's twenty-five grand a day. 750k a month. And don't forget Tony the pony, this is just the beginning. You're only on a few marketplaces right now – imagine what you can do when you expand your catalogue, launch everywhere. You think that black fuck-house from last night was something special? You'll be able to have a hundred of those bitches in your bed every fucking night!*

Ricardo got off the phone. "He wants to set up a face-to-face."

My cock hardened. "Diego?"

Ricardo shook his head. "No." He lit a fag. "The boss. El Mono."

TWENTY-TWO

"Must be water damage, mate." Allie was inspecting Brian's Onewheel. He reconnected it to the power socket. "Yep, still nuffing. Some water probably got in and started mucking about wiv the electrics."

Brian was at the end of his tether.

"Goddamnit, man. Y'all know any mechanics?"

Allie grabbed his backpack off the dining room table. "For a Onewheel?" He scrunched up his face. "Nah. Call the number on your warranty. Maybe they'll send you a replacement?"

At this point, Allie was working as a pub crawl guide. The old Forever roommate before me, the Kiwi fella in Panama City, had managed to hook him up. Against all odds, the control-alt-delete impact of the ayahuasca ceremony was still holding firm. Despite leading groups of coke-obsessed degenerates around Poblado six nights a week, Allie was still fanatically sober. He got smashed with a bad hospital bill (insurance didn't cover it because he got fired by Virtuagym), so he sold his moto but was still underwater financially. Working a five-hour Medellín pub crawl shift was likely netting him $40 at the most. Despite everything, Allie was chipper as fuck.

"Sorry I can't help, mate." Allie bounded towards the door like a kid headed to school. "Catch ya later, lads."

I poured a bit of honey in my coffee. I was all bunged up from too much fast food.

Brian finally gave up on resuscitating his beloved chariot.

"What's your gameplan for the noche, Tony Pepperoni?"

"Trading."

"Damn! You fellas are putting in the *work*."

Brian's situation was rapidly deteriorating. He was still working for The Lifestyle Corp. But it seemed like he'd been relieved of any sales responsibilities and was now nothing more than Mark Tallone's full-time bitch. Everything about Brian was faded. Some cats can go full Bukowski and make their destitution look glamorous. But life was beating the shit out of Bri Bri, and there was nothing he could do to hide it.

"I've been doing a lot of research about new currencies myself," Brian continued. Old mate was morbidly curious about what me, Steve and Ricardo were getting our grubby fingers into. "I'd love to buy you and Steve lunch some time. Would be cool to swap notes. Y'all free tomorrow?"

I took a sip of coffee. "Not sure, man. I'd have to check with Steve."

"No sweat, homie. Let a brother know!"

I took my coffee through to the loo. Since getting back from Ricardo's finca, Steve and I hadn't left Forever. It never stopped. Customer messages. Inventory forecasting. Order management. SEO research. Content development. Steve was constantly pulling cash out from PayPal and Venmo and dumping it into 'ForeverCoin', the sham currency we built that allowed us to wash everything we earned from the filthy venture.

It was a deluge. We were working twenty-hour days in our frenzied little boiler room, scrambling to stay afloat.

Notification on my phone. Email from Di.

Hey Stranger

Medellín, hey? I'm surprised, but at the same time, it makes perfect sense. Can't say I know too much about Colombia, but from what I've seen, it looks beautiful.

I'm writing because I have some news and I want you to hear it from me before you hear from someone else. Last weekend Peter asked me to marry him and I said yes. We don't have too many details locked in at the moment, but we're thinking of doing it in 2020 sometime, probably down the peninsula somewhere.

I see that you're not very active on social media anymore but wanted to let you know before the news starts getting shared online.

Apart from that I don't have too much else to report. Work continues to be insanely busy and so I'm not really looking forward to planning a wedding! But I'll find the time I'm sure.

I don't know how long you'll be in Colombia (Kel mentioned something about a New York trip later this year?) but I hope it's everything you want it to be. If you're ever back in Melbourne it would be great to catch up. In my head I like to think that we could be friends one day. But maybe that's wishful thinking. Not sure if it matters to you, but these days I'm very happy.

Take care.

Di xxx

The news took me out of the present for a few moments. I'd done plenty of digging on Peter when they first got together. Seemed like a nice fella. Big, jovial fucker with a dad bod and a mop of curly black hair. A solid guy that a sweet girl like Di deserved. They'd get married, have some sprogs and build a castle in the suburbs. The Strayan Dream, baby.

The coffee did its thing and I was able to push out a long, dense crap. My prostate tingled with relief. I navigated to WhatsApp. It was high time I tried Dani again.

Hey. How are you? I know you probably don't want to hear from me, but I'll die wondering so here goes nada. I'm really busy at the moment. A few weeks ago, I started trading crypto with Steve (yes, I have become one of 'those' guys). Things are going incredibly well. I'm doing a LOT better financially these days. When we were dating, I was feeling very insecure about the amount of money in my bank account. I knew you came from a wealthy family and it fucked with my head. I stupidly withheld my fears from you, and it started to make me very anxious. Of course, this doesn't excuse any of my stupid behaviour. But hopefully it gives you more insight about the things that I was dealing with. Is there any chance you would be open to having dinner with me? No strings attached. I just want to clear the air. Any time. Any place. My treat. Let me know if you would consider this. T xxx

I hit send. Dani read the message straight away but didn't respond.

/

Steve liked to play porn on a constant loop while he worked. In the beginning, this weirded me out. But I quickly realized that Steve wasn't getting off on it – he just enjoyed being surrounded by sex. To Steve, all the grunting and the slapping and the squelching was nothing more than bawdy muzak.

Ricardo dropped by just after half-eight at night.

"Special delivery," Ricardo said as he waltzed into Steve's room. He handed me a big box of Frisby takeout. "OK, I have news. Number one, the Miami trip is locked in. Mono wants to meet with us next Thursday. So, let's fly in Wednesday."

I took a bite of my chicken burger. "Sounds good."

"And Click Clack is launching next month. Big party on the first Friday. Save the date."

I nodded my head. "Nice. Congrats, dude."

"Wait 'til you see the sound system." Ricardo showed me a few pics on his phone. "It's insane. Finally, I have a room that will impress the best DJs in the world."

"What about The Chainsmokers? Maybe you could fly them out?" I joked. "Brian would lose his shit!"

Ricardo let out a raspy chuckle. "Never, my friend." He rubbed Steve's shoulders. "How about you, sito? Everything good with Diego?"

"Ya. I'm getting close to figuring out the new version of the autoresponder. Number system instead of text analysis. More efficient."

"Nice," Ricardo said. He made his way towards the door. "I have to go back down to the hotel. Just wanted to drop off the food, say hi."

"Before you go," I started, "We need to talk about something."

Ricardo sat down on Steve's bed. "What's up?"

I put my half-eaten burger back in the box. "Even if this new sequence saves us time with customer service bullshit, the overall workload isn't going to slow down anytime soon. I don't know about you Steve, but I'm close to burning out."

Steve didn't interject so I kept going.

"We need to keep this show on the road. Most start-ups would hire other people to share the load. It's not like we can put an ad up on the expat group. But there's another option." I stood up from my chair and pointed towards the living room. "Brian and Allie. Two broken toys. Easy to manipulate. Easy to control. They're broke as fuck. Right now, we could give them both a salary of $20k a month. Do you realize how much $20k can get you in Medellín? They'd both fucking *kill* to be dragging that in every month. We'd have their total loyalty. Plus, neither of them have a mind for business. There's a bunch of snakes in Medellín who'd take our idea and start their own thing. Brian and Allie won't do that. They'd be the perfect employees. Allie could be the worker bee. Steve could train him to do all the customer service jazz pretty quick. And Brian could be our office bitch. I wouldn't want him anywhere near a laptop, but he could make our lives a lot easier." I pointed at the Frisby box. "Food. Booze. Flights. Girls. Admin." I looked at Ricardo. "Kind of like what Jhonatan does for you."

Ricardo mulled it over. "We definitely need more people?"

I shrugged. "We don't *need* more people. But if we don't bring in fresh blood, we can't scale."

The two of them grilled me for the next half hour. Emboldened by my impromptu expansion plan, I swatted away all their concerns with ease. With Ricardo and Steve I had business partners. But this frisky little captain was ready to start managing some *human capital*. The two impossibly flawed morons that slept down the hall were the perfect candidates.

"What about security?" Steve said. "How can you guarantee adding Allie and Brian won't cause problems?"

I rubbed my eyes. "I'm exhausted man. You are too. There's no way we can keep doing this by ourselves for much longer. We need to take a chance now, otherwise we're gonna burn out. I'm not stupid. I'm not gonna tell them everything all at once. If they're interested, which they will be, we'll reveal things slowly, piece by piece. I'll make them swear on a copy of *The 4-Hour Workweek* to keep their fucking traps zipped. First rule of ForeverCoin is that there's no such thing as ForeverCoin. Second rule of ForeverCoin is that there's *no such thing as ForeverCoin*. Trust me. I know how to run this. I understand Brian and Allie. We hold all the power."

Ricardo was nearly over the line. "I could see Brian liking the money," he said. "But won't Allie have a problem with what we do? He's sober now."

I guffawed. "Dude. At this very moment, like literally *right* now, Allie's acting as a sherpa for some gakked-out tourists in Poblado. If he can deal with that, he can handle marketing some dodgy listings online! Trust me. And Brian's a pushover. He wants validation more than anything. Anyway, I'll just tell them both that the dark web stuff is temporary. Which it is. One day we'll retire or go legit. It'll be fine."

Ricardo and Steve looked at each other. Done deal, baby.

"You'll talk to them?" Ricardo said.

"Yep," I confirmed. "When Allie gets home from work, I'll wake Brian up, sit them down, feel 'em out."

Ricardo stood up to leave. "That's it, okay? Just Allie and Brian. No más."

"Agreed," I said. "Just Allie and Brian."

TWENTY-THREE

Hola papi, gracias for your message.

I couldn't fucking believe it. Antonella La Bomba, the sexiest pornstar in the world, my dream girl, was actually writing me back!

Usually I don't do privates.

Haha, of course you don't, you sneaky fat-titted slut!

But you seem cute...

It was mid-morning. Our plane to Miami was about to take off. Brian sat next to me, editing one of his narcolepsy-inducing video podcasts. Ricardo was on the other side, sleep mask on, snoring gently.

The price to have me for one night is 10k.

I responded straight away.

$10k is fine. What's your Venmo? I'll send you the cash right now.

La Bomba forwarded her deets immediately.

Gracias Papi! I got your money. Let me know where you want to meet tomorrow. Shau! xxx

Result! The following evening, I'd be dining on my favourite pornstar's arse. I put on the latest episode of Bill Burr's 'Monday Morning' podcast and relaxed. The plane took off.

/

"Me and my boys just arrived at our pimped-out penthouse at The Conrad in beautiful Miami. Let me show you round, *MTV Cribs*-style!"

Brian filmed himself as he sauntered around the place.

"There's one bedroom by the door right there... Here's the bar complete with a sweet-looking mini fridge... Two other rooms right here... Living room, TV, sunken couch, very nice... You know we got the AC blasting to deal with that next level Florida humidity... and here's the real prize... an amazing balcony that looks right out onto the golf course, you know I'm gonna be out there first thing tomorrow morning, getting in that *muy importante* meditation and yoga sesh to really kick-start my day!"

Steve sent me a message on Slack. Everything was under control back in Medellín. Allie was learning the ropes quicker than expected.

"Well, this is a business trip, so I'm gonna get busy with some crypto stuff with my bros, I'll check in with y'all at dinner time. Ciao pescao!" Brian sat down on the couch. "So, what's the verdict bros? You diggin' this suite or what?"

I looked up from my lappie. "It's pretty far from the action, dude. It's gonna take us an hour to get to South Beach."

"An hour? No way dude. Gotta be like twenty-five minutes at the most..."

"Look it up."

Brian pulled out his phone. "Damn. One hour, five minutes. Hopefully the traffic won't be that bad. I'll let Nathan know we'll be a little late."

I closed my lappie and looked over at Ricardo. "You wanna talk through tomorrow's game plan one more time?"

Ricardo put his phone down and sat up. "Let's do it."

"Alright," I started. "We introduce ourselves. I'll explain our system. You talk about security. Just repeat what Steve wrote down. And then I'll close things out with the pitch."

Ricardo nodded. "Intros. System. Security. Pitch." His phone dinged. "Meeting's confirmed. 10am."

"What do you want me to do?" Brian asked.

"You can just chill here tomorrow." I stood up and patted Brian on the shoulder. "We'll get you involved in the next one."

/

Lean and muscular, Nathan Condie looked like a cast member from a CW show.

"The podcast is just a front," he said. "It's an excuse to talk to every private B2B SaaS founder. My pitch is, 'Come on, get exposure'. On the show, I charm them, ask for their core metrics. Then I sell their data."

Nathan was dressed immaculately in loafers, chinos and a crisp white shirt rolled up to his elbows. There was a swarthiness to his facial features – he looked part-Turk or maybe even Persian. Outrageously gay, Nathan spoke like a Valley Girl doing a TED Talk.

"I make each guest sign a disclaimer so legally, they can't touch me." Nathan took a bite of his dressing-less salad. "And before I release the episode, I force them to introduce me to three other founders."

The four of us were eating dinner at an upmarket Mexican joint on the South Beach strip. It was a people-watcher's paradise. Miami has a jarring, sloppy sexuality that socks you right in the face. A procession of chubby, horned-up animals ambled along the footpath next to our table, faded from day-drinking in the Floridian sunshine. There was the occasional beautiful girl sandwiched amongst all the monsters. But in terms of general fuck-housery, Medellín was streets ahead. If I was retarded and thirteen years old, I would perhaps consider Miami a bastion of erotic glamour. Alas, in this particular incarnation, Miami didn't do a thing for me.

"Damn, dude. Really interesting strategic play!" Brian said. "I'm sure your guests must be stoked to be on the show. You got that magic blue checkmark. Those download numbers must look awesome!"

Nathan scoffed. "A few thousand downloads per episode. No bueno. I don't give a shit. You have to be crazy to try and make money off of podcasting. There's gotta be something happening on the back-end. Otherwise it's a *total* waste of time."

Brian let out a half-baked laugh. The impossible was happening – Brian's bottomless reserve of enlightened positivity was running dry! I did him a solid and changed the topic.

"You met Brian at Florida State right?" I asked Nathan.

"Uh huh."

I squeezed some lime on top of my average carnitas burrito. I once heard Ari Shaffir describe Mexican grub as 'dirt food' on a podcast. Shaffir's rationale was that no matter how you dressed it up, a burrito is fundamentally nothing more than a humble working man's lunch. When you go to a fancy Mexican restaurant you pay more for better cutlery, crisper linen on the table, a more considered Spotify playlist. None of the extra money you spend makes it to your plate in any meaningful way.

"Is he still the same dude? Or was Brian different back in college?"

Nathan stopped eating and looked over at Brian. He seemed a little taken aback by my question. "Looks pretty much the same to me. The whole crypto thing is a surprise, though. I just assumed Brian would be with Tallone forever."

Brian's positivity was back. He was smiling like a goober.

"Well I can't disagree with you there my man! It was a tough decision to leave The Lifestyle Corp. Me and Mark have been close for a long time now... But, I've been dabbling in crypto for the last year, and recently I've been getting super-excited about its potential! When Tony and Ricardo asked me to be a partner I couldn't resist."

I was about to correct Brian's revisionist history when Nathan jumped in.

"What are y'all doing exactly?" he asked.

"We're called ForeverCoin," Ricardo started. "It's free to sign up. Every month our members get a thousand coins. Like a Universal Basic Income. Our value-add compared to other currencies is that you don't have to be a crypto expert to start mining. In the future, everyone will be using crypto, so we want to be ahead of the curve."

"How many users do you have right now?"

I gave up on my burrito. "Not a lot. Just a few guys in Medellín. But that's why we're here. Big meeting tomorrow with a potential partner. We're planning our ICO."

Nathan unleashed a catty diatribe. As a hard-nosed capitalist, Nathan couldn't get behind crypto because it didn't provide the world with any real value. He believed in tangible things. Revenue. Employees. Churn. Profit. Data. Shit that could be bought and sold – not some digitized Monopoly money bullshit. Even though no one asked him to open his wallet, Nathan let us know in no uncertain terms that he wouldn't be investing in ForeverCoin. To him, we were just some coconut cowboys slumming it in the third world.

I sipped on my oversalted margarita and relaxed back into my seat. Steve was a fucking genius. Turns out "we run our own cryptocurrency" is a magical incantation. Say it once and your credibility goes right out the window! No one wants to learn a thing more about what you do. Nathan's reaction proved that ForeverCoin was the perfect front. We could safely hide in plain sight.

Nathan began to rant about the stupidity of Andrew Yang and UBI as an economic stimulation tool. I could see Brian squirming in his seat. He was desperate to tell his old chum the truth. Brian wanted Nathan to know that we were crushing the drop-shipping game on an inconceivable level, albeit on the dirty side of the internet. Unlike a lot of douchebags in Medellín, we weren't selling shitty private label products on Amazon. I see your garlic press, and I raise you my ounce of world-class cocaine grown and manufactured in the foothills of rural Colombia, shipped out through the port of Buenaventura, and drop-shipped to happy customers all over the mighty USA!

Brian took the condescending browbeating from Nathan like a champ, and kept his mouth zipped shut.

/

"What do you know about this Mono dude?"

Me and Ricardo were sitting on the balcony, enjoying a nightcap, looking over the darkened golf course below. Brian was zonked out in his room.

"Not much man." Ricardo lit a cig. "Like I told you, he's a gringo. Lived in Colombia for a while. Now he's here. I think he's married to a Paisa. That's all I know."

I sipped my whiskey. Someone laughed loudly down on the ground floor, and the noise echoed off the hotel walls. "Are you sure? Diego didn't tell you anything else?"

Ricardo shook his head. "Diego's a soldier. Poor kid from Envigado. I used to see him at my clubs. We're friendly. But he's loyal to his boss."

Cold feet. Why had I agreed to meet a drug trafficker in person? Maybe the whole thing was a set-up? I downed the rest of my whiskey.

"How do you feel about meeting someone like Mono? Considering what happened to your dad."

Ricardo took off his baseball cap. He took a long drag.

"Did I ever tell you what they did to my father?"

"No."

Ricardo took another impressive drag.

"He was moving from one safe house to another, going through the countryside with his driver. They passed some cops who were waiting on one side of a bridge. The cops let them cross the bridge, into this little town. They were driving through the town when they got ambushed. Guys on motos. The driver got shot. He died in the car. My father got moved to some other building. They wanted a ransom. So, they called my mother, but we were at my grandmother's house in Bogotá, and she didn't pick up. They killed my father in the most brutal way possible, to send a message. To let all the other rich guys in Colombia know that they were in trouble. They hung my father by his arms for a few days. And then they cut off his dick, stabbed him hundreds of times, left him for dead."

Another laugh echoed up from the ground floor. Terrible timing.

"Fuck dude. That's heavy."

Ricardo stubbed out his cig.

"The cops on the bridge told the narcos in the town. Probably got a few pesos for the tip. Literally five, ten dollars. That was normal back then. The cartels controlled everything. No one was safe."

It was a fucking trip. While I was playing soccer in the safe suburbs of Perth, Ricardo and his family were behind enemy lines in a warzone.

Ricardo stood up and made his way inside.

"You ask me if I'm afraid to meet a guy like Mono. A gringo who sells a bit of powder in Florida." Ricardo laughed. "As long as he's not Colombian, I think we'll be fine."

/

We waited for about an hour.

Google Maps had directed me and Ricardo to a warehouse in a depressing commercial district on the outskirts of Miami's city limits, about ninety minutes from The Conrad. Diego, an unassuming geezer in a blue polo, met us out the front. Diego patted us down, opened the gate and led us inside what turned out to be a dusty pet food factory. There were stray packages lying on conveyor belts – it looked like it went out of business not too long ago. The place reeked of sawdust and Styrofoam. We climbed up some steel stairs and sat down in a barebones office that overlooked the factory floor.

Diego was friendly, but not in the mood to chat. He confiscated our phones and stood just outside the office door.

Footsteps. A bunch of people were walking up the stairs. Three young Latino dudes, all clones of Diego, made it to the top of the landing. A moment later El Mono appeared.

The dude looked like he could be Allie's father. They both had the same shiny bald head and were roughly the same height. Mono wore expensive snakeskin boots, dark jeans, a tan belt with a flashy cowboy buckle, and an embroidered Western shirt. Silver aviators hung from his top button. The guy looked to be in his early-to-mid-sixties. Apart from his slight paunch, he was in great shape.

"I'm sorry for keeping you waiting, fellas." Mono entered the office and sat down on the other side of the desk. "I've had a hell of a morning."

Mono spoke with a thick Brummie accent, which was jarring. His outfit suggested that he was some type of Texan oil baron.

"These things are always a bit awkward, aren't they?" Mono said merrily. "You don't know me. I don't know you. I'm sure Diego let you know that I'm known to many as 'Mono'. Have to say, originally, I wasn't that fond of the nickname... It's definitely grown on me."

The cunt was lathered up in aftershave. His powerful scent filled the space.

"How about an icebreaker? Me youngest is just starting to get into riddles, came across a cracker the other day." Mono smiled. "Alright, pretend you're escaping a labyrinth, and there are three doors in front of ya. The door on the left leads to a raging inferno. The door in the center leads to a deadly assassin. The door on the right leads to a lion that hasn't eaten in three months. Which door do you choose?"

My memory kicked in.

"Door on the right."

Mono looked at me. "And why's that?"

"A lion that hadn't eaten in three months would be dead."

Mono was impressed. "Fair play, lad. You figure that out on the spot?"

I shook my head. "I wish. Read it in a book when I was a kid."

Mono chuckled. "At least you're honest, lad. Great memory. Fair play."

Me and Ricardo went through our pitch.

"I like the attitude, lads," Mono said. "Numbers are impressive. If I give you exactly what you want, and you start managing everything I do online, what's the ROI on my investment?"

"We've crunched the numbers," I started, "and based on the results we've already generated with our own listings, we feel 5X across the board is realistic. Obviously certain product categories will be higher than others."

Mono was lost in deep thought. I wasn't sure if my words were sinking in.

"Also, like I mentioned before, if you go with us, we'll give you ownership of our listings too," I continued. "They're already ranking well, bringing in big numbers every month. So that means from the jump, you'll be earning more revenue online. No ramp-up period. In theory, we *could* figure out a way to dropship all of your products. But that doesn't sit right with me. You should own all of your listings. With the fifteen percent commission performance model we're proposing, it keeps things very simple. We're incentivized to grow revenue as much as possible, and you retain complete control of your product line and online distribution."

Mono looked Ricardo's way.

"What about the other players in Colombia?" Mono said to him. "If you start selling my gear, this won't ruffle feathers?"

"No," Ricardo said. "As long as we don't start growing or moving any product out of the country, everything will be fine."

"You'll keep everyone safe in Medellín?"

Ricardo nodded. "Sí."

Mono looked at me with his hazel eyes. We were nearly over the line.

"Why should I do this, Tony? Why can't I just teach my guys to do this themselves?"

I smiled. "Anyone can talk the talk. Pulling the trigger is a different story." I rolled my shoulder blades up for a second, making myself as big as possible, like a grizzly bear. "You've seen our numbers. You know we can do this. And we *are* going to find a way to scale this up. If it's with you, that's great. I've done my research. Fifteen percent is a fair structure for this type of deal. But if you want to walk away, that's cool. We'll find another partner. Your call."

/

I sprayed champagne all over the balcony.

"THIS SHIT'S HAPPENING BABY!"

Ricardo was punching the air. "Puta madre! Puta madre!" He looked my way. "Tony fucking Soprano! You fucking did it, man!"

I pulled the lads in for a group hug.

"Go big or go home, boys. Let's fucking *do* this!"

Brian cracked open another bottle of champers. "You were gone for a long time, bros. I was getting a little freaked out."

I held my empty glass towards Brian. "We were just rappin' with the bloke. Mono's chill, dude. You gotta meet him next time around."

We called up Steve and Allie and told them the good news. I thought it was gonna be a quickie, but Steve had loads of technical questions about how the new setup with Mono's team would work. It was dark by the time we got through everything.

When we were done with the conference call, Ricardo and Brian bolted out the door. Brian was meeting up with Nathan Condie again for a networking event, and Ricardo was going to spend the night at his mother's.

I jumped on my lappie and got some more work done. I had about an hour before I needed to leave. As I whizzed through my spreadsheets, I fantasized about what I was going to do with La Bomba. After a couple of cocktails at The W's bar, I'd take her up to the room that I'd booked. I'd sit in a darkened corner, like Arnie in *True Lies*, and watch the slut play with herself on the bed. Then I'd forcefully ask her to edge herself towards the point of pulsing. After about ten minutes of this malarkey I'd walk towards her, grab her by the hair, and smoosh her face into the puddles of pussy juice that would be scattered all over the sheets. Then I'd rip off her panties and bury my face in that heavenly arse.

I finished my work and knocked back a Cialis with the last bit of champagne. As I ran through to the bathroom, I got an alert on my phone.

Hola Papi! I'm so sorry but I can't see you tonight.

I couldn't believe it.

I got booked for a shoot in LA tomorrow. Have to leave tonight. So sorry :(

I collected myself. She wasn't the only whore in town, after all.

OK. I understand. No problem.

Gracias, Papi. Do you want me to send you back the money? Or we can reschedule... I will be back in Miami soon. I would love to make it up to you... We can meet when I'm back?

Dumb bitch didn't know what she was missing out on.

No problem. Keep the money. I'll see you when you're back. Safe travels.

Poor cunt only had a couple years left in her anyway. Needed every cent she could get.

Gracias Papi! I look forward to meeting you. You seem very sexy… I am excited to play with you. Shau! xxx

I showered and ordered some room service. I still had the room booked at The W. I just needed to get myself a new escort…

Halfway through my cheeseburger and fries the day caught up to me. I was dog-tired. I had a Heineken and watched a bit of ESPN. I stripped and hopped into bed.

/

I woke up in a panic.

There were people in the suite. I sat up, heart pounding, and strained my ears. Yep. There were definitely noises coming from the living space. My head went light.

I edged out of bed. A chemically induced tree trunk hugged against the inside of my boxers. I tiptoed towards my window, cold with worry. Maybe Mono figured out where we were staying? There was nowhere to hide.

Just before I reached the window, I slipped out of my paranoid fugue state, and regained full control of my faculties. My left brain chastised me. *Why would it be Mono's guys breaking in to kill you, and not either Ricardo or Brian returning home, you fucking dolt?* This set me at ease and my heart rate slowed. Still, I wasn't a hundred percent convinced. I opened my curtain the tiniest smidgen and peaked though.

Brian and Nathan Condie were holding one another in the middle of the room. They were rocking back and forth. It looked like they were slow dancing. Brian pulled Nathan closer and put both of his hands on his arse. Then they closed their eyes and started making out.

I turned away. Perhaps I was dreaming. I let a few moments pass and then looked through the crack between the curtains again. They were still going at it like a pair of teenagers. Tongues flying everywhere. Hands through each other's hair. Heavy, heavy petting.

Brian's inability to close the deal with chicas suddenly made perfect sense. He pushed Nathan down onto the couch. Then he got on all fours and put his face on top of Nathan's crotch.

Realizing where things were headed, I turned around and tiptoed back towards my bed. I grabbed my phone off my nightstand and unlocked it.

/

"So bro... You didn't end up heading to The W last night?"

I was waiting for the question all morning. Brian finally worked up the courage just after we got through security at Miami International, as we ambled towards our gate.

"Nah man. My chica bailed. I was wrecked anyway. Such a big day yesterday. Just ordered room service and crashed super early. Slept all the way through like a baby."

Brian was visibly relieved. "Oh. Right on, dude."

"How about you? How was your event thing with Nathan?"

"Great, bro. Nathan knows a lot of folks in Miami, so it was dope to connect with a bunch of rockstars!"

"Did you guys party afterwards?"

Brian scrunched up his well-proportioned face. "We were pretty beat too, homie. We just had a quick nightcap at The Conrad and then Nate caught an Uber home."

At the gate, Ricardo jumped on a call with one of the Click Clack partners. Brian managed to ingratiate himself with some All-American looking family. A call from a private number came through to my phone.

"Hello?"

"Tony. It's Mono."

I stood up and went for a stroll.

"Hey mate. What's up?"

"Not much. How's the riddle-master today?"

I smiled. "I'm good. Just about to board our plane back to Medellín. What can I do for ya?"

Mono cleared his throat. "Just wanted to give a quick call to let you know that moving forward, I'm only going to be talking to you about this project. Alright?"

"No worries," I said.

"Never get into specifics over the phone. But I'll make it out to Medellín in a few months. We can talk more directly then."

"I get it."

"You boys are onto something. I just need you to keep everyone on your side under control."

Ricardo was gesticulating like a telenovela actor as he spoke on the phone. Brian was sitting cross-legged on the floor, playing dollies with a couple of little girls.

"That won't be a problem."

TWENTY-FOUR

If you're looking for a slick tech sequence, a dirty homage to *The Social Network*, you're bang outta luck. I can't do snappy, highly unrealistic, Sorkin-style dialogue either. Instead, you'll get a brief explanation about how me and the boys went big time.

First of all, let the record show, and this cannot be overstated: the four of us at Forever worked our absolute *balls* off.

The moment we got back to Medellín, Mono started bombarding us with requests via Diego. The workload was immense. It took us several days to organize the masses of data into something comprehensible. We prioritized everything and mapped out a bulk content optimization and product launch plan.

Steve prepared the order spreadsheet and sent across our first invoice. We spent a nervous couple of hours wondering if the bald fuck was going to cough up the loot. The money came through. Mono sent me a brief message which I shared with the team: "Good start. Keep going."

There were firm rules about security. Steve got us new phones, email addresses, bank accounts. There were elaborate VPN logins for everything. The laundering involved pushing our dinero through multiple different financial and crypto indexes. I didn't understand nor care too much about the details. I just knew that each provider took a little cut.

But considering the volumes that we were generating, it was a small price to pay. We created a basic company website and social media profiles for ForeverCoin. From the outside looking in we were just another bunch of gringos gambling at the crypto table. Brian and Allie were considered salaried employees on $20k USD a month, and we all agreed that after six months they would receive some type of raise. The three founders took everything else.

In terms of the division of labour, we split into pairs.

Steve and Allie were the tech guys. Steve identified problems with our systems and kept all the cogs turning. It was baffling how quickly Allie learnt new concepts. The geezer was still sober as a judge, and he channelled all of his hooligan intensity into his new vocation. Allie would watch Steve like a hawk, and soon enough he was figuring out shit by himself. All day long the two of them sat side by side, Tweedledum and Tweedledee, slaving over their lappies in silence.

I kept cranking out all the copy. Brian became my full-time bitch. He took care of my diet. We began exercising together. If I felt like a drink, Brian made sure there was plenty of clear liquor, limes and agua con gas on hand. When it was getting late, he sent me to bed. I started to feel fit and strong. My productivity went through the roof.

Ricardo offered to get involved in all the grunt work, but I told him that it wasn't necessary. The dude was already busy as a motherfucker with Click Clack and his other clubs. I sensed he felt a tad guilty about his angel investor status. Ultimately, all he really did was introduce me to Mono through Diego, and this led to a huge windfall. But I wanted him out of the day-to-day. The biggest thing he did was keep things sweet with the local authorities. It didn't seem likely that any of the Medellín piggies were clever enough to sniff out a highly advanced dark web operation from under their noses. Yet it gave us all peace of mind to know that Ricardo had the situation under control.

Long story short: we started making a ton of money selling Mono's drugs on the dark web. You get it. Move on Tony boy. Move on.

/

One day, the four Forever roomies went out for a boozy lunch.

We started with a game of tejo down in Envigado. Tejo involves throwing shit at targets filled with gunpowder. Some call it a sport, but that's a bit of a stretch. It's a novel activity that pairs well with drinking – the spicy, Colombian equivalent of lawn bowls.

After tejo we caught a cab up to this spot in Laureles called Barrio Central Cafe.

"This place was heaving last year during the World Cup," Allie explained. "We all went facking bananas when Pickford made that save."

My memory jogged. That's right. England beat Colombia on pens.

"Who were you cheering for?" I asked Allie.

He looked at me like I was retarded. "England, mate." Allie kept scanning the menu. "They're a funny bunch, Colombians. Back home, if England gets knocked out of a big tournament everyone stays at the pub a while longer, has a few more drinks. Commiserates, y'know? But here, there's none of that. They just shut off the TV straight away and go home in silence. Head in the sand. Furious. They pretend like it never happened."

"In Colombia, we have a lot of passion." Brian took a sip of his strawberry daiquiri and smiled. "Dope line, right? Don't quote me on that bad boy. Belongs to my hombre Maluma. Y'all hear his new song with Madonna?"

We ordered burgers and a ton of drinks. Even Steve had a few scotches which was very rare. It was a beautiful sunny arvo. The atmosphere at the pub was sweet except for the cheesy Colombian music. After lunch, the lads got into it about Spanish.

"I honestly think a lot of locals would consider me fluent, homie," Brian said to Allie.

Allie stood up. "You're drunk Brian." He marched towards the loos. I was amazed how Allie was able to hang with people who were drinking. I half-expected him to come back from the toilet with coke nuggets abseiling from his cavernous nostrils. But the man's resolve was strong as fuck.

I was also drunk and in the mood to push buttons.

"Who do you think is the uncoolest race of people?" I asked the boys.

"What do you mean by 'uncoolest'?" Brian said.

I snorted in my drink. "Brian... top marks for not trying. What do you think I mean? You fucking dolt. Uncool. Not cool. Lacking cool."

Brian held up his hands. He was pissed as a fart. "Sorry homie. Just trying to clarify..."

Steve took a sip of his old fashioned. "You go first," he said to me.

"With pleasure," I started. "Well for me, it's a dead heat. Joint winners in the uncool stakes would be Indians and Jews." I remembered in a flash that Steve was Jewish. "Not you Steve-o. I'm talking about the kosher ones."

Steve didn't bat an eyelid. He was lost in thought. "I know this isn't that original because of Borat," he said. "But I would say Kazakhs. They're definitely not cool."

I punched the air. "Solid fucking choice! I always forget about Eurasian cunts." I turned to Allie, who was checking something on his phone. "Al?"

"What?"

"Who's the uncoolest race of people?"

Allie thought for a moment. "Eskimos," he spat.

I burst out laughing. "Eskimos?"

Allie went back to his phone. "Don't seem to bring much to the table, do they?"

Brian was too much of a woke pussy to answer my absurd hypothetical. I used the question to start a conversation with two Colombian girls who were sitting at a table next to us. The two of them both picked Guatemalans who are apparently a bit rapey. I peppered the gals with questions about Latin American geopolitics and history. They were both wearing office clobber and spoke decent English. We drank with them for several hours. One of the chicas was recently single, and she was eyeing me up as a potential drunken rebound, but her amiga cockblocked me and took her home.

Around nightfall our beer wench went AWOL, so I went up to the bar to buy another round of drinks. The tired Canadian guy, the dude who ran the hostel I stayed at when I first got to Medellín, was unloading a case of BBC beers into a fridge.

"Hey!" I yelled over the music.

"Hey."

"You run that hostel in Poblado, right?"

"That's right."

"I thought it was you! I'm Tony. You helped me out when I got here like a year ago!"

He clearly didn't remember me. The cunt now had dark bags under his dark bags. "Cool, man. Kenny."

I reached over the bar and he shook my hand.

"This your bar too?"

"Yep. Run it with my wife."

"Hey Kenny, any chance I could put some of my music on? This Colombian shit's doing my fucking head in! I could Bluetooth onto your speaker. Or maybe I could jump onto YouTube if you'd prefer?"

Kenny shook his head. "Sorry dude. We play Colombian stuff here. One of the girls will serve you soon." He went back to stocking the fridge.

This wasn't the response I wanted. I ran around the side of the bar. Kenny was shocked when he noticed me by his side.

"Hey Kenny, I'd really like to play some of my music." I pulled cash out my wallet. "We've had a great time here this arvo. Spent a lot of money. Consider this a tip." I handed him 500,000 pesos. "How can I hook my phone up to your speaker?"

Kenny held my gaze. The dude probably wasn't even forty yet. Lines up your schnoz lead to lines on your forehead. Should be a bumper sticker. The man had gone full native. Drunk gringos like us kept his family above water. Like a bitch, he held out his hand.

"Cue up your tunes. I'll play them for you now."

/

It was getting old being at Forever.

Despite what every digital nomad pillock says, working at home isn't all that it's cracked up to be. Maybe if you were on your own it would be alright, but with three other dudes it turns into a grimy frat house real fast. Half-drunk coffee cups, burger wrappers, beer bottles. Here's a fun fact – B.O. still smells like B.O. even if you've got over a million bucks in the bank. Rolling out of bed every morning and getting straight to work is certainly convenient. But 'our little thing' found its way into every crevice of the apartment. It was beginning to suffocate me.

I asked Brian to find me a new place. A party pad. I wanted something bonkers, even better than Ricardo's penthouse. Brian found a dope mansion just to the east of Poblado, slightly up the hill from Santafé.

The Uber dropped me off at two, right on time. It was only a ten-minute ride from Forever – I certainly didn't want to be too far away from the action. In true Paisa fashion, the agent wasn't there when I showed up. I said g'day to the portero,

Humberto, a middle-aged fella with kind eyes and a receding hairline. After five minutes I was about to call Brian and vent about Colombian tardiness when a car pulled up. I was gob-smacked. Marcela stepped out of the vehicle.

It had been close to a year since I'd seen her. A lot had changed. The braces were gone. New tits. Fake arse. Longer hair. Marcela was wearing a dynamite blouse, skirt and high heel combo that accentuated her new figure.

"Tony!" Marcela kissed me on the cheek. "It's great to see you!"

Her English was much better too.

"Hola," I said in shock. "Did Brian know about this?"

She beamed. "Si." Her teeth were immaculate. "I told him not to say anything. I wanted to surprise you!"

Many of us have half-baked notions about the people we could become. These ideas hover above us, like mobiles hang over babies in cots. Visible but totally out of reach. It's easier to stay locked in the pathetic grooves of your own mangled personality. My theory is that it comes down to hatred. It's cool to claim you hate yourself, but I think very few people actually do. When you start becoming aware of your own inadequacies, a knee-jerk repulsion takes place. This tends to happen during adolescence. You realize, *Holy fuck... Maybe I'm not the greatest person the world has ever known.* It's easy to blame your parents for your flaws – the clumsy architects with incompatible wiring. Or your bully. Or your friends. Or your teachers. Or your school. Or Boomers. Or the goddamn patriarchy, maaaaaaaaaan.

Quickly you realize that there's a long road ahead of you, and it would be more convenient to make peace with your own failings. The majority of mouth-breathers experience a form of Stockholm Syndrome. We end up loving our pesky ego. The hate continues to pour out of us in the direction of other people and things. However, there's a lucky few who never succumb. They spend their whole lives getting high on their own supply.

As luck would have it, Marcela is one of those rare individuals. For no good reason, she *hates* herself. She'll spend the rest of her life trying to dampen the pain with new looks, new jobs, new schemes, new people.

"It's good to see you," I said to her. "You look great."

Humberto opened the gate. As we walked through the front door, Marcela told me that she quit the dental practice and started working in real estate at the beginning of the year. The joint lived up to the hype. It was a three-storey, probably built sometime in the 80s. Multiple bedrooms. Gym. Enough space for a pool table. The icing on the cake was the huge indoor swimming pool and sauna at the back of the house.

"And last of all, the kitchen," Marcela said as she wiggled her giant plastic arse in front of my face. "Everything is new. Dishwasher. Perfect if you want to hire a chef."

"Why did the last tenants move out?"

Marcela tilted her head. "They moved back to the States."

"They broke their lease?"

"Si."

I clicked my fingers like Ali G. "Fuckin' gringos. Can't trust 'em!"

Marcela sized me up. Did she get her lips done too? I couldn't remember exactly what she looked like before...

"You like the place?" she said.

I moved towards her. "Yep. I like what I see."

Marcela wet her lips. "That's good."

"What's the rent again?"

"Five thousand US a month."

I held my heart, pretending to be wounded. "Oooooh Marcela. You trying to gringo-price me?"

"No! Five thousand is—"

"—Joking," I said. I took another step towards her. "I'll take it."

She bit her bottom lip. "Perfecto."

"Let me sign now. Then maybe you could show me around the place again?"

Marcela smiled. She pulled out the contract and placed it on the kitchen counter. I sidled up behind her and gently placed my hands on her hips.

This is maybe the fourth or fifth shag scene in this tale. Can you guess what's coming? By this point, do you feel like you know what I'm into, sexually? What tickles my pickle? What type of musical number charms the old trouser snake?

When I was a kid, I had this book by some photojournalist who went on tour with Oasis. Lots of shots of the Gallaghers smoking Bensons, drinking Stella, looking broody on Lambrettas. Fucking loved it, was my pride and joy, used to read it over and over whilst listening to *What's The Story*. Anyway, at the beginning of the book, Liam and Noel got their own page for acknowledgements. Noel penned a brief message thanking the photojournalist, the band, the fans, his Mam. Liam's contribution was more memorable. It was just a single sentence: "A book without pictures is a shit book." And I have to say, I feel the same way about books, except you can substitute pictures with sex. Even though we now live in a world where any schmuck can open up a private browser tab and go to town on xvideos, I'm still rather fond of fornication in the literary format. And I'm guessing there's at least a few dirty bastards reading this right now who feel the same way, so don't worry, here it comes, the highlights reel of my first fuck with Marcela!

I thought about kissing her neck. Instead I just stood there for a few beats, breathing gently into her ear. Then I squatted down on my haunches like a Slavic street urchin and lifted up her skirt. Her big, round culo was staring me in the face. There was just the slightest whiff of a post-lunch dump emanating from her nether regions. A black G-string travelled down her crack towards the promised land. I buried my face between her cheeks and pulled the G-string to the side with my teeth. I tongued her arse and cunt aggressively. There was no shit taste thankfully – the hint of a funky smell is about as far as that kink goes. Then she reached around and pulled my face right into her. I stood up and spun her around and ripped open her blouse, kissed her on the mouth, made her taste her own freshly shucked clam juice. I hoisted Marcela over my shoulder. Instead of walking all the way up the stairs to the bedroom, I took her into the living room and threw her down on the couch. Believe it or not I actually asked if she had a condom in her purse. She said no. Of course, I fucked her anyway. Without the rubber I knew I was going to pulse quick, so I made her touch herself while I gently ploughed her wet hole. I lifted one of her legs up, sucked on a toe, closed my eyes. In my mind's eye, I conjured several geriatrics trudging through the snow, which kept me from blowing my load. After a couple of minutes, Marcela barked like a seal and pulsed. I opened my eyes, fondled her tits and after maybe five or six more strokes, I was done.

Is that the type of action what you were expecting? If not, maybe you should be paying closer attention. I'm cutting myself wide open over here! The least you could do is listen to what I'm saying.

/

Brian lurched in front of the traffic just as the light turned green. I followed suit. We scampered past the furious front row of vehicles and hopped up onto the sidewalk. At the Calle 10A and Chef Burger intersection we took a left, jumped back onto the road, barrelled down the underpass and suddenly we were in Astorga. Brian led me down a little side street and stopped in front of a medium-sized complex.

"Damn, that was dope!" Brian whooped. "The Onewheel will always be my first love. But these bad boys are more powerful than they look!"

We parked our 'Grins', the lime green electric scooters that had started to pop up all over Poblado. Locals seemed to detest them which made riding them that much sweeter. Brian showed me how to end the ride on my phone.

The complex contained a few lowkey bars and bistros. Chris and Lamonte were already waiting at a brand-new Mexican spot in the rear courtyard. It was early on a Saturday night.

"Chrissy boy!" I said.

Chris Volker stood up and embraced me.

"Geez Tony… You look shredded, mate."

I pointed at Brian.

"That's all this guy. Cunt's got me on a new diet and work-out plan." I extended my hand towards Lamonte. "Hey, dude. Tony. Heard a lot about you."

"Pleasure to meet you, bro. Lamonte." There was a little crucifix around Lamonte's neck. Cunt was always praising old mate Dio in his Insta stories. Lamonte spoke with a light Southern accent. "Loving the shirt man. You get that here?"

"Thanks dude." I looked down at my plain white tee with a neon pineapple on the front. "Ordered it online from some skateshop in Bogotá. Surprised that it actually made it to my door!"

We all ordered burrito bowls.

"How's the fam, Chrissy? Amazon keeping you on your toes?"

"Always, mate." Chris loaded his bowl up with hot sauce. Cunt always ate like he hadn't seen food in days. "Things are good. Got a little trip to Florida planned in a couple of months. Gonna drop in and say g'day to a couple of clients. Wanna take the little fella to Disney World too."

"Nice." I took a bite. Decent Tex-Mex. "How'd you hear about this spot, Bri Bri?"

"Medellín Buzz, homie. Those dudes are always dropping truth bombs when it comes to good eats!"

"I know the Medellín Buzz lads," Chris said. Half of his bowl was already gone. "Pretty sure one of those dudes came to one of our first Masterminds."

"What do you do then Lamonte?" I said.

Lamonte dabbed his lips with a napkin. "I'm a personal trainer." His eyes darted towards Chris. "Sorry. Let me take that again. I'm the owner of a fitness lifestyle brand."

"Good boy," Chris said as he ate one of his final mouthfuls.

"I'm trying to get better at that," Lamonte continued. "Like presenting myself in the best manner possible when I meet new people, you feel me? I've been guilty of setting limitations on myself in the past. But Chris and the other Mastermind dudes have added a lot of value across that area. Keeping me focused. Honest. Hungry. I feel grateful and blessed to have such a trusted circle."

Chris and Lamonte looked at one another and shared a tender little moment.

"You been smashing the putas at your CrossFit?" I said, killing the dead air with a blunt hatchet. "I'm sure you must have some fucking thirsty clients?"

Lamonte grinned bashfully. "Aww man. As an entrepreneur, you know how it is. If you really wanna focus on a passion project you can't let nothing distract you. I'm determined to take my brand global in 2020. I'm putting a hundred and ten percent of my energy towards that right now. Not gonna lie, a lot of the chicas at the gym are bad. But I'm just trusting the process, letting things unfold as Jesus intended them to. Feeling blessed to be out here, man."

I pulled my phone out. "Check this shit out." I showed off the nudes Marcela had sent me earlier that day.

Lamonte's eyes went wide. "Damn. She's thick." He slid his bowl over to Chris and let him have a bite.

Chris didn't know where to look. He giggled nervously. "How are things going with your coin, lads?"

"Really great." Brian beamed. "Remember Mark, my old boss?"

Chris sipped his agua sin gas. "Tallone? Of course."

"Well, Mark did me a major solid and introduced me to a few VCs in SF. Fortunately we've been able to raise some capital. It's not a crazy amount, but definitely enough to keep us afloat for a while."

Chris was visibly shocked. "Holy shit. That's incredible, boys." He took off his Undertaker hat and scratched his head. "Congrats. You don't have a background in crypto, do ya Tony?"

"Nah mate." I finished the rest of my Pilsen. "Just picked it up a few months ago. Beginner's luck!"

After dinner Brian led us up to the second level of the complex to a brand-new pool hall. The tables were immaculate – much better than the raggedy old ones at our usual 8-ball haunt in Lleras. I ordered a round of drinks from the pretty barmaid and played a few games of doubles against Chris and Lamonte. We were coming off a huge week of revenue – I convinced Brian to have some cheeky toots in the loos. Usually he couldn't play pool to save his life, but after a bit of charlie he turned into a shark. We decimated the CrossFit lads five games to zip.

"We should bounce pretty soon dude," Brian said to me.

I turned to Chris and Lamonte. "You boys coming?" It was the opening night of Click Clack. "There's gonna be some surprise guest at midnight. Ricardo won't tell us who it's gonna be, so you know it's gotta be good."

Chris and Lamonte looked at one another with doe eyes. In Seth Rogen movies, bromances between men in their thirties are portrayed as cute and admirable. But IRL, they're absolutely pathetic. I was unquestionably one half of a bro-mantic relationship with Dunc during my teenage years and throughout my twenties. At that point in your life you genuinely don't know any better. However, when a man hits thirty he should fill in the emotional hole left by his father with cement. I looked at Chris and Lamonte with utter contempt. These two stupid fuckers genuinely enjoyed spending time in each other's company! It was sad more than anything else. The only thing that would rationalize their longing glances and sweet nothings would be a secret homosexual tryst, but unlike Brian, neither Chris nor Lamonte seemed to be hiding a desire for cock. Their relationship stood above money, pussy, YouTube views, a new personal WOD time at CrossFit. They were mad about each other and didn't care who knew. I love the pursuit of truth, but there's *nothing* worse than modern day 'authenticity'. I could picture Chris and Lamonte holding hands at a Mumford & Sons concert, enjoying warm fuzzies about the prospect of many more years together. Disgusting!

"We're gonna call it a night, mate," Chris said.

We! The dumb fuck actually said 'we'. Chris wanted to go back to his boring family and his poky little apartment. Lamonte wanted to go home and maybe do some push ups to burn a few extra calories, read his Bible. And they would both undoubtedly go to sleep dreaming of one another.

"Suit yourselves."

/

Me and Brian unlocked the same scooters and rode up Calle 10 towards Click Clack.

Just before we hit Avenida El Poblado I noticed a huge graffiti tag on a decrepit dividing wall: *ANY DAY YOU CAN DIE*. In my coked-out state I couldn't recall if I had seen the sign all over the city, or whether that was just something from a dream. Or maybe I saw it up in Comuna 13, when I first got to Medellín? I like to think that I'm an observant person, but certain things definitely fall through the cracks. Logic would strongly suggest that I'm more attentive to certain phenomena. It would be handy if there was a Wiki for the minutiae of your own existence. If there was a God, I wouldn't care if he was good or evil or apathetic; I would really just want him to be a competent, faithful bookkeeper. It would be reassuring if someone was keeping score. There still wouldn't be truth, but at least there'd be answers.

Allie and Steve were waiting at the main bar behind the lobby on the ground floor. Steve had a couple of camgirl floozies on his arm – the same chicas from the weekend at Ricardo's finca. Allie was wearing a stop sign red shirt and was furiously working on his phone, committed to slinging as many narcotics as humanly possible, even on a special Sabado noche.

Click Clack looked spectacular. Everything was smooth and polished. Tasteful lighting fixtures hung from the ceiling, enveloping the cosmopolitan crowd in a sexy hue. I ordered a drink and heard some bass-y rumbles coming from the nightclub below. There was a Greek restaurant on one side of the bar and a Japanese noodle joint on the other.

I downed a mojito and then led the squad towards an elevator that was cordoned off with a velvet rope. A brick shithouse of a bouncer ticked our names off the list then took us down.

The room was big and loud. Lasers, smoke machines, strobes. There was a real authentic warehouse rave vibe in the place – a major departure from the tasteful elegance of the main bar. The bouncer snaked through the sweltering crowd. Ricardo had hooked us up with our private booth and bar. There was a bottle of champagne on ice waiting on the table for us next to a card that read *ForeverCoin*. We had the perfect view of the stage. All the peasants on the dancefloor looked up at us pitifully. Feeling wired, I shook up the bottle and sprayed a bit of champers down onto the crowd.

We monkeyed around in our little booth for a while. I did key bumps and Brian kept saying, "We're gonna be so fucking rich dude," right into my earhole which was annoying as fuck. The DJ was playing hard trance. More and more fuckers kept piling into the club. I was trying to get Allie off his phone for two minutes and have a dance when I saw Marcela waving at me from down below.

I went down and got her in the VIP section.

"Hey baby!"

Marcela's mouth tasted like bubblegum. She was wearing tight white jeans, hooped earrings and a low-cut top. I gave her planet of a culo a playful slap and then I introduced her to the rest of the crew.

At around midnight the music stopped and Ricardo bounded onto the stage. We started whooping and hollering at him from our booth. Ricardo grabbed a mic and started blabbering away in Spanish. My half-cut brain tried to translate in real time.

Welcome everybody to Click Clack... My name is Ricardo Carranza Rios and I am one of the owners of the hotel... We aim to become one of the best nightlife destinations in Latin America... Thank you all for coming... it is our absolute pleasure to host you... I know many of you are here to see a special guest and I promise there will be more music very soon... But first, I need to thank some people... Without these folks, Click Clack would just be an idea... So please welcome to the stage, my friends...

I was on the verge of corralling everyone and was shocked when Ricardo started rattling off a bunch of Colombiano names. Some bland middle-aged fellas, Ricardo's business partners, walked up onto the stage. It made sense. The Poblado party scene was an old boy's club, and Ricardo had to give the OGs their due. On stage they all looked chummy as fuck. These old fogeys could go ahead and have their moment in the sun. The future belonged to us.

After a brief smattering of applause, Ricardo continued.

"OK, now let me all ask you a question... do you like reggaeton?"

"Si!" the crowd roared.

"I said, do you like reggaeton?"

"Si!" the crowd roared again.

"OK... Well, do you like... J Gomez?"

Everyone on the floor went apeshit.

"Ladies and gentlemen... Please welcome to the stage... Medellín's own... J Gomezzzzzzzzzzzzzzz!!!!!!!"

The DJ dropped the beat and J rushed the stage. He was a lot smaller IRL. Everyone on the floor surged towards the front. Marcela screamed and began twerking on my cock.

The little bloke sang three tunes, blew kisses out towards the crowd, then waved goodbye. He handed a mic to one of his proteges, a skinny black kid with a wave. Ricardo texted me and told me to bring everyone backstage.

/

Jhonatan opened the green room door and I gave him a big hug. J Gomez was standing next to Ricardo, sipping a bottle of water and dabbing his face with a white towel.

"T!" Ricardo bounded towards me. "What do you think?"

I grabbed Ricardo and kissed him on the cheek. "It's fucking amazing bro. Fucking proud of you, lad."

Ricardo smiled. "J, this is my friend Tony. El Australiano."

I shook J's soft hand. "Great job, man. Mucho gusto."

"Tony, good to meet you. Ricardo says you're a very smart guy!"

I waved him away. "Not sure about that." The dude had an extremely photogenic face. I guess that's a non-negotiable for a pop star. "You gotta be somewhere tonight?"

"Yes, man. I fly to Bogotá soon. I can only chill for thirty minutes."

"Damn, that sucks. Well anyway, here's the rest of the crew."

I pushed the others towards J and grabbed myself a beer from the fridge. I was sick of key bumps. Ricardo directed me towards the bathroom where I enjoyed a few hefty white caterpillars.

When I came back into the green room it was way more crowded. Ricardo's business partners, security guys, a few of Jhonatan's amigos, random whores.

I looked across at the gaggle of people and noticed Marcela. J Gomez had her pinned against the wall. I took a sip of beer.

Marcela saw me staring at them. She said something to J, touched him gently on the forearm, and then came over to me. Marcela nestled into my side.

J looked at me straight in the eye. After ten long seconds he rounded up his crew, said ciao to everyone in the green room, then bounced.

TWENTY-FIVE

I don't want a girlfriend, but if you want, you can be my main bitch... I enjoy fucking you, but I've got a strong libido, and I want to bring other girls into our bedroom... I'm not emotionally available, but I earn a ton of money, and I can buy you lots of nice things... I don't know how long this will last, but I promise to make the ride as fun as possible... If you ever tell me what to do, I'll never talk to you again...

These are all things that I said to Marcela's face. To her credit, she accepted everything like a champ. In many ways, my parameters simplified things – she knew exactly who to become to make me happy. I was curious about why she stood me up for our date back in 2018 but I never asked her for an explanation out of principle. That would be the epitome of small dick energy.

I moved all my shit into the mansion which I christened Forever 2. Brian ordered me a deluxe 8-ball table. He also started making enquiries about installing a huge projector and sound system around the indoor swimming pool.

Brian was under the impression that he'd be moving in with me, and was a bit miffed when I explained that I wanted him to remain at Forever. But he got over it quick enough. Brian liked the idea of keeping an eye on Steve and Allie on my behalf.

One Friday I clocked off around 8pm and met Marcela at Forever 2. We ordered a dirty blonde escort (my inner Patrick Bateman was pretty happy about that one) and fucked her brains out. I sent the escort home in an Uber, got some food delivered, then me and Marcela watched *Good Time* by the Safdie Brothers. The movie was surprisingly hilarious. Before the joint started, I was under the impression that old mate Robert Pattinson was just a pretty-boy teen idol, but holy shit, turns out the kid can act his balls off! If this story you're reading ever gets turned into a flick, I want the posh bastard to play me, assuming he can cobble together a serviceable Strayan accent.

The next morning me and Marcela picked up one of her amigas, Paula, this cute-as-a-button bitch with amazing pins, and we headed up to the El Tesoro mall. I went full Tony Soprano – Gucci slippers, 80s style running shorts, cotton wifebeater, silver Pentagram necklace and a big white fluffy robe. Marcela looked tasty as fuck. She wore heels, black jeans and a t-shirt with the Pornhub logo on the front.

When we got to the mall, I asked Marcela to find me somewhere where I could get my hair done. Marcela translated to the middle-aged hairdresser lady that I wanted my hair dyed peroxide blonde. I pulled up a picture of R-Pattz from *Good Time* on my phone. The hairdresser looked bemused but ushered me towards a spare chair. I gave Marcela a wad of cash for a shopping spree.

The hairdresser did a good job. This wasn't my first hair bleaching experience. When I was a kid I got inspired after watching the Romanians at the World Cup 1998. The next day I took my pocket money savings and marched myself down to the local barber at the Mindarie Keys shopping complex. The dumb bitch hairstylist managed to burn the fuck out of my scalp and had to abort the mission halfway through. I ended up with dirty streaks rather than the full head of bleach that I was after. All my soccer pals gave me endless amounts of shit about it. The coach even held a vigil for the death of my barnet! When cunts get money, they become sentimental. Not only do you want to protect your future – you want the dosh to magically alter your past.

Once my hair was done, I found Marcela and Paula who were clutching a bunch of shopping bags outside some perfume place. We were deciding where to eat lunch when I saw Dani out the corner of my eye.

I locked eyes with Dani. She was walking alongside her ex, Joaquin, who was in mid-sentence. Joaquin was tall, dark and handsome, with fantastic cheekbones, like a Mills & Boon hero. Dani looked the same – effortlessly gorgeous. The two of them would undoubtedly make stunning babies. Dani has a brilliant poker face. Her flawless features stayed still and serene. Yet there was an intensity to her glare. She was imploring me not to make a scene. Joaquin didn't notice our private moment, nor did Marcela or Paula. When Dani realized that I was going to stay in my lane like a compliant little boy, she looked away and kept striding down the thoroughfare.

It was fitting that we were reunited with one another in this way; our true colours on full display. Tony, the eccentric horned-up clown, gangster cosplaying in public with two ditzy whores. Dani, strolling happily with her local beau like she's in an organic yoghurt ad, whimsically plotting her next international holiday.

Me and the girls ate lunch at a steakhouse. Paula caught a cab home. I took Marcela back to Forever 2. We went straight to the bedroom – I choked her and fucked her juicy snatch aggressively. Then I decided to cruise down to Forever. I needed to get a jump on the copy for our new line of products. I was listening to 'Sports' by Viagra Boys on my headphones when I got a call from Mono.

"What's new, Tones?"

"Not much, mate. Working hard. Playing hard."

"Good lad."

"Yourself?"

Mono sighed. "Can't complain. Getting a bit sick of Florida, to be honest. Fuckin' Trump keeps putting his foot in it. Prick's gonna start a race war."

"Oh yeah. Old mate Darth Vader. Loves to stir the pot."

"This country's great for business. Terrible for a family. Health and education systems are a shambles. You've got it great down there, lad. It's fucking paradise. Hope you're enjoying it."

I man-spread in the back seat of the Uber. "I'm definitely having fun."

"This week's numbers look good, Tones. Everything on track with the new SKUs?"

"Yep. I'm actually gonna do some final tweaks this arvo."

"Good lad. And what about the team? Everyone alright?"

"Yeah, mate. We're sweet."

"Good lad. Listen, if you need anything, give me a call, yeah?"

"Will do."

"It's not easy being the boss."

I checked out my new hairdo in the mirror. "Heavy is the head that wears the crown."

Mono chewed on this for a moment. "Heavy is the head that wears the *hollow* crown."

/

Months passed. We all went crazy in our own ways.

Everything with the biz went from strength to strength. We were generating a crazy amount of cash, and thanks to Steve's wizardry, we automated a lot of our processes. This freed everyone up to pursue extracurricular activities.

Steve leaned big time into the PUA stereotype. He bought a new blue Porsche Boxster convertible so he could stunt around Poblado. Marcela hooked him up with this stylist homo, and he began dressing like a preppy version of Dan Bilzerian, everything custom-made because he was so fucking small. The dude also started getting mad into pornos. Initially he was just helping a few camgirls with their live shows, setting up all the tech shit, helping them figure out how to accept donations. But then he started directing gonzo flicks, gangbangs, Taxi Cab-style public shoots. Steve was earning a bit of cash with the smut, but it was pennies compared to ForeverCoin. I guess you could say it was for art, not money.

Ricardo threw himself into planning a huge music festival for 2020. He wanted something massive that would rival Estereo Picnic in Bogotá. Click Clack seemed to be a hit – it was by far the best hotel and club in Medellín. But Ricardo was desperate to make a dent internationally. Ricardo believed that if more big-name artists played shows in Medellín, it would help cleanse the city of its bloody past. The dude was obsessed. I was happy for him. It didn't matter that he wasn't directly involved in 'our little thing'. There's no way I would've felt comfortable doing what I was doing in Medellín without him in my corner. Plus, if he could get a huge festival off the ground, this would give me and the boys another legit business we could hide behind.

Predictably, Brian found the sneaky nature of our operation difficult to deal with. His frustration reminded me of that classic quote from Bill Murray: "I always want to say to people who want to be rich and famous: 'try being rich first'. See if that doesn't cover most of it." Brian was on $20k a month, which in Medellín is a fucking fortune. But being loaded wasn't enough for Bri Bri. His newest hustle was a Social Coaching program. Our VIP experience at Click Clack tricked Brian into thinking he knew something about networking and climbing social ladders. He hired Marcela and a bunch of her amigas and shot a promo video at Forever 2 around the pool, where he hawked some overpriced video course on social etiquette in the age of Insta and Tinder. Plenty of tits and arse and Brian's goober face cheesing down the camera. Dating, friendships, business relationships – Brian was apparently an expert on everything, and his course was going to help solve all of your problems. I gently tried to push him in a different direction.

"Have you ever thought about putting together diet and exercise vids?" I said to him. "You've done a fucking amazing job with my training. Why don't you focus on that with your YouTube channel?"

Brian reconfigured his man bun. "Damn dude. That's awesome feedback. Super-stoked you're enjoying the program right now! And I appreciate the suggestion. But the fitness vlogger space is pretty crowded. Not sure I'd be bringing anything new to the table."

"Fuck it dude. People were selling drugs on the dark web before us, too. But we just found a way to do it better. You could do the same with your fitness vids. If it's something you enjoy, what could go wrong?"

"Really digging these suggestions bro… but I'm pretty happy with the social coach niche I've landed on. Feel like I can draw on my years of experience across different fields and create engaging content that people will connect with. What can I say, I've been bitten by that damn entrepreneurial bug and I'm *loving* how I'm feeling right now!"

During this period, I was giving the boozing and the snorting a red-hot go. Yet compared to the old Tony, I was far more considered in my debauchery. I was enamoured with the svelte figure I had attained under Brian's tutelage, and I didn't want my lifestyle to start ruining my looks. If I was feeling groggy and dehydrated, I would avoid caffeine and start my day with herbal tea. After a heavy day of body weight exercises, I would take magnesium with a protein shake which helped reduce muscle soreness. To limit my time hunched over a lappie I would pop modafinil if I needed to get through a ton of copywriting. If I was feeling stressed or paranoid, I would eat Valium, shag Marcela and then take an arvo nap as a way to reduce my cortisol levels. I remembered reading once that old mate Hunter S. Thompson got off the Chivas Regal towards the end of his life and switched to clear spirits, so in honour of the legend, I followed suit. I allowed myself two or three beers to start each session and then I quickly moved onto white rum, tequila or aguardiente sin azucar (over ice and lime only, no mixers). Ricardo hooked me up with an ounce of Grade A powder every couple of weeks and I started doing tiny bumps several times a day like they were cups of tea. I ate clean and trained hard with Brian. After a lifetime of obsessing within a paranoid fantasy world, I was sick of thinking. It was time to get grounded in my meat vehicle.

I also started buying clothes compulsively. Vintage Adidas tracksuits. Hawaiian shirts. Designer bucket hats. 80s-style running shorts. Lou Reed-esque black shades. Linen suits. Velour bathrobes. Bowling shirts. Fred Perry flats. A whole drawer full of sterling silver chains. I've got this theory that, at a certain point when you go too deep with an addiction, the drug ends up dressing you. Middle-aged alcoholics all look like Jimmy Buffett at a Margaritaville. Meth Heads go full chav. Stoners commit to tie-dye hoodies and loud sunnies. At this time the cokehead and the boozebag within me were duking it out like Conor McGregor and Nate Diaz, and so naturally I ended up buying some pretty outrageous shit.

The biggest surprise packet was Allie. One day the sly old fox popped over to see me and Brian at Forever 2.

"I've got some news lads," Allie said as he played air keyboards on my kitchen counter.

I sipped my black coffee. "Oh yeah?" I was doing intermittent fasting at the time – no calories til midday.

Brian rolled up his mat. We'd just finished a quick twenty-minute power yoga sesh. "What's on your mind, homie?"

Allie cleared his throat. "I've started seeing Melissa."

Melissa? Who the fuck was Melissa? "Nice," I said, playing it cool.

"We bumped into each other randomly at Exito. Then we caught up for coffee, one thing led to another…"

I was wracking my brain… who the fuck was Melissa?

"I know you both have some history with her," Allie continued. "For different reasons, of course."

It clicked. He was referring to Mel, the pink-haired chick from Dancefree. Dani's mate.

Brian put his hand on Allie's shoulder. "Damn dude. I'm super stoked for y'all! Mel is an absolute sweetie. And just so you know, nothing ever happened between us. We were just really great homies. Be sure to say waddup. It's been a minute!"

Allie nodded. "I will." He turned to face me. "We're gonna move in together next week. She's got a cracking little place near Centro. I'll keep coming to Forever every day, of course. And it goes without saying, Mel doesn't know zilch about the business. I told her it's crypto stuff. She won't be hearing nuffin' more about it."

"No worries man." I took a sip of coffee. "She still mates with Dani?"

Allie rubbed his chest. The scar tissue from the stabbing gave him grief every now and again. "No, not anymore. Dani ghosted her a few months back. Ain't heard from her since."

Dani was probably too busy canoodling with Joaquin, her Paisa Prince Charming.

I shook Allie's hand and thanked him for his honesty. The kid was a walking, talking advertisement for ayahuasca! I thought the old demons might come back after a while. But alas, there was no ego, no aggression, no deception. He was zen as fuck and becoming a better criminal with every passing day.

/

The fact that we were doing something illegal didn't bother any of us.

Drugs were gonna be bought and sold on the dark web regardless. We were just the facilitators. The *marketers*. And the best marketers are amoral. If you interview someone for a marketing position, and you sense that they genuinely love your product, or perhaps they legitimately detest what you're selling for some reason, be sure to run for the hills. You want someone completely neutral. That way they can focus on the task at hand. They're going to be too busy swaying others with bread and circuses to be swayed by bread and circuses.

We had absolutely zero connection to the poor fuckers manufacturing the coke in the wilds of Colombia. Nor did we have any connection to the puritanical pilgrims hoovering up the final product in Trumpistan with hepatitis-ridden dollar bills. We were independent contractors who knew how to optimize product listings on illegal online marketplaces. That's it. Morals or ethics didn't come into the equation.

I didn't feel bad about it then and I don't feel bad about it now. My personal view, for what it's worth, is that all drugs should be legalized and taxed. The internet has made it incredibly easy for anyone to acquire anything. The dam is about to burst – governments should get on board the gravy train and snag themselves some additional tax revenue. I always come back to booze. If governments really cared about their citizens, why on earth would they allow booze to be sold legally? Surely alcohol is the most dangerous substance of all time?

I'm boring myself here. Everyone's heard this argument a million times. Either you get it, or you're a retard.

The point I'm trying to make is that we were simply early adopters. The Kennedys were bootleggers, and then a couple generations later, they were in The White House. Allie was the only one who I thought might feel a little guilty about profiteering from the human impulse to get fucked up. But if anything, Allie's chequered past only seemed to fuel him. Coke had taken so much from him over the years. Now, with ForeverCoin, he was getting something back.

/

In September, old mate Jordan Belfort, *el lobo de Wall Street*, came to Medellín to give a seminar at the Plaza Mayor, this convention center just to the south of Centro. Considering our dodgy hustle I felt obliged to attend, so I asked Brian to get some tickets for Belfort's Sunday arvo session. I went with Brian, Marcela and Paula. I wanted the girls on our arms, all gussied up and hot to trot, so we could make a big impression upon arrival.

The foyer was only half-full. Everyone gawked at us. I was wearing a 2018 Independiente Medellín Puma third replica kit, purple John Lennon specs, Dunlop volleys and a white Kangol bucket hat.

The attendees were split right down the middle – half Colombian sales guys and half beer-bellied retiree gringos. In Colombia the jackpot is your child graduating from a good university and getting a stable corporate job at some dull multinational corporation. To them, entrepreneurs are the lowest of the low. Pimps. Conmen. Drug dealers. There's nothing sexy or cool about starting a business in Colombia.

The locals waiting to see Belfort talk were extra-scummy. These dudes (and yes, they were *all* dudes) grew up in a culture that denigrates everything about sales, advertising and marketing, yet they were still drawn to the vocation, like big stupid moths to a streetlight in a brand-new suburb. The only familiar face in the crowd was dumb Joe D'Angelo. Joe shook our hands and introduced us to a few of his ex-military gringo buddies as if we were his children. I felt an urge to blurt out that I'd seen his beloved whore of a wife get spit-roasted about a year beforehand. But getting kicked out of Forever would be a massive pain in the dick, so I let my sharp tongue simmer.

The four of us were led towards our seats, which were at the very back of the room. In honour of the Marty Scorsese joint that my life was starting to resemble to a frightening degree, I wanted to get my hands on some quaaludes, but they don't really exist anymore. Brian did a bit of research and figured out the closest thing available was meprobamate. I washed down a bunch of tabs with swigs of aguardiente from my hip flask.

Belfort bounded onto the stage like a beaten-up old marionette doll. He launched into his tired 'Straight Line Persuasion' bullshit which I had watched years ago on YouTube. The pills were doing something – I felt spacey as a motherfucker.

"Tony." Brian was poking my arm. "Can I try some of that?"

I pursed my lips. "Motherfucker." I handed him the flask. "I told you to bring something. This is gonna go for three hours."

"Sorry dude... I thought there'd be refreshments for sale."

The meprobamate turned me into a mong and I daydreamed the entire show. Brian and the girls drank the rest of my liquor and promptly all fell asleep.

During question time I began to wake from my stupor. Someone asked Belfort about crypto.

"Bitcoin, bitcoin... everyone's still talking about bitcoin!" Belfort was buzzing all over the stage like a maniac. Cunt was probably on some of the local produce. "A lot of people are gonna tell you to buy bitcoin in the next few years. Let me tell you right now. Do *not* buy bitcoin! You wanna know why? Because I guarantee you when you buy bitcoin, there's some little greedy shit out there, who probably idolizes me, profiting off your stupidity."

The crowd chuckled.

"It's a bubble folks." Belfort waved his arms around. "It's one big bubble. If bitcoin was around when I founded Stratton

Oakmont, I would one hundred percent be selling it to dummies all around the world! But, it's worse than penny stocks or the subprime mortgage crisis... you wanna know why? Because bitcoin is being used by criminals all over the world to launder dirty cash! And when the governments cotton on to the scheme, the bubble's gonna burst, the value of crypto is gonna drop to zero, and they're gonna audit absolutely everyone holding dirty digital assets."

I suddenly felt a tightness in my chest. Belfort kept barking into the mic.

"If you're holding bitcoin, or any crypto for that matter, don't be an idiot. Get out *now*! While you still can! It's just a matter of time before that whole scam falls apart."

TWENTY-SIX

"These fucking guys man… it's like they've already forgotten how I saved their asses."

Ricardo broke angrily. We were playing pool on my new table at Forever 2. 'High Highs to Low Lows' by Lolo Zouaï was playing softly out of my Bluetooth speaker. Jhonatan was chilling on my La-Z-Boy, smoking a joint, talking to skanks on WhatsApp.

"And now they want me to spend more! I'm keeping the whole thing above water. Without me there would be no fucking Click Clack."

I took a shot and sunk a ball. I was getting better. There are some amazing 8-ball tutorials online. Every morning I woke up, did a little caterpillar, and then hit balls for a half an hour. It prepped me mentally for the day ahead. Another ball sunk. I took a sip of my tequila and lime.

"I'm guessing the hotel isn't making much money yet?"

"No, man." Ricardo lit a fag. "We launched too close to Christmas. Everyone already booked somewhere else. January is looking better. But it's going to be quiet until then."

I lined up my next shot. "If you assumed majority ownership just before the launch, aren't the others now essentially silent partners? Couldn't you like, make them pay you? And if they don't cough up the loot, kick them off the board?"

Ricardo scoffed and a plume of smoke escaped from his lips. "You keep forgetting where you are, amigo. They're all 'made' guys. I can't kick them out of anything! When I first started throwing parties in Poblado, they helped me out. They will own me forever."

"Damn dude."

"It's fucked up man. I'm trying to do all this music festival shit and these fuckers keep asking for *more* money."

Poor fucker looked fried. Cunt needed more than a cigarette to calm his farm. I did a line and then waved the metal straw in the direction of Ricardo. He shook his head.

"What about you? How are things with the boys?"

The black ball was in a danger zone. "Yeah, good man. Revenue's plateaued over the last couple of months. But that's been a blessing in disguise. We know how hard we can push in terms of workload. Now, the focus is profitability. When Mono's here I'm gonna suggest we just niche down on the best products, slowly discontinue the rest of the inventory. That way, we know we're getting the most bang for our buck. There'll be some seasonal fluctuations, and when someone invents something new, like fucking bath salts, we obviously wanna jump on that asap. But for the most part we'll just niche down on the winners, make some mad bank. 2020 should be fucking mega."

"What about the boys?" Ricardo repeated. "Everyone good?"

I accidentally ricocheted the black ball into the bottom corner. "Fucking cunt!" I put my cue down on the table. "Yeah dude, everyone's good. Same old shit. That reminds me. Gonna throw a big party here. November 30. Save the date."

"November 30?"

I took a swig of tequila. "Yeah dude."

"That clashes with the next big show at Click Clack. I told you about it. A bunch of reggaeton guys are flying in from PR."

"Ahhhh man," I exhaled. "I'm fucking sick of reggaeton. Aren't you? I wanna have a huge party here and play my own music for once. I'll play a bit of metal for you as well."

Ricardo was wounded. "But this could mess up my business even more, man. Couldn't you throw your party on another night?"

I reached for my little hand mirror. I guess it really didn't matter when I had my party. "Sure." I hoovered up another caterpillar. "Sorry for missing your message."

"All good man… Fuck. It's been a long day. Rack me."

"Powder or balls?"

"Powder."

Marcela came up the stairs and gave me a big wet kiss. She was in her ravishing real estate get-up, the blouse and skirt combo. At this point she was only doing part-time hours. Her agency only wheeled her out when they needed to wave some tits and arse in front of a naive gringo. Most of the time she spent lounging around Forever 2, or shopping at the mall with her mates.

I was Marcela's el marrano sapiens, or 'clever pig': a rich gringo who knows he's getting used, but doesn't care in the slightest, because he's getting a great deal too. Marcela was grooming Paula, who evidently turned out to be happy-clappy Hillsong Christian, and didn't partake in anything too naughty. No drugs, no lesbo shenanigans. Yet, I was desperate to find out how her arsehole tasted, so Marcela was working her charms on the bitch for me. It was only a matter of time.

I poured Marcela a stiff drink. Ricardo did a few toots.

"Thanks bro." He handed back my straw.

"Another game?"

"Sorry dude. I gotta head back to Click Clack," Ricardo kissed Marcela on the cheek and slapped me on the back. "Let me know what date you land on for your party, okay?"

/

The next morning, I caught an Uber to Olaya Herrera, the tiny little airport in the middle of the city. Brian, Steve and

Allie were waiting by the security check-in. The complex was quaint and provincial – it looked like it hadn't changed much since the 70s. Allie was holding two bulging Adidas duffle bags, locked shut with padlocks. We showed our private charter tickets to the guards. They let us through and then some hombre took us out to the plane.

I used the sixty-minute flight to write an email to Dunc.

Hey buddy

Long time no speak. I'm gonna take responsibility for that one. Life is what happens while you're busy wondering why grown men still wear Vans... all that jazz... Sorry for taking so long to respond. I've been busy. But we both know that's not a real excuse.

Colombia continues to surprise me. Coming here I knew I was in for an adventure, but the reality has exceeded my wildest expectations. It's crazy to think I've been in Medellín for sixteen months now. In many ways, it feels like I've just arrived.

I guess I should start by telling you about the thing that's been eating up all my time. I, along with a few friends, started, wait for it... a crypto business. This is a living, breathing example of staring into the abyss for too long. When I got to Medellín, every gringo cunt and their dog was talking about crypto nonstop. As you will recall, I was not exactly crypto's biggest cheerleader. But one of my old roomies knows a lot about it and we randomly stumbled upon an idea. We launched something real quick, just as a laugh more than anything. Long story short, turns out our idea has legs. It's basically just betting on the long-term utility of blockchain technology more than anything else. We haven't made any real money from it, but through another housemate we were able to get connected with some VC investors in the States, and they've given us a bunch of funds to try and scale the business. Still early days, but I'm pretty sure we're on track to create something pretty special. So, I've been nose to the grindstone for about six months now, trying to convince the investors that they've backed a winning horse. If you're interested, you can check out our website – forevercoin.co

In terms of other news, I broke up with that Dani girl a while back. She was pretty but beige as fuck. Now I'm casually seeing this other Colombiana chick called Marcela. She's kinky. Toys, threesomes, other wholesome stuff. I'm a lucky lad :)

Medellín is a pretty crazy place to be as a single fella, especially if you've got a bit of coin. We are all programmed to be good little obedient slaves. Get degree, get job, get married, get children. But it's such an antiquated system. Now with the internet there's nothing stopping cunts from doing their own thing – apart from convention and fear.

The obvious exception is someone like yourself who found a compatible partner like Kel at an early age, and over the last fifteen years you've grown around one another and built up a tremendous amount of tenure. Because I've known you both for so long, I guess it just seemed normal to me, but recently I've been thinking about how unique your relationship truly is.

For someone like me, I'd really be sacrificing a lot if I was to get back into something serious. Di was a sweet girl and everything, but I couldn't truly be myself around her. If I gave her what she wanted and settled down, there would be that base level of companionship and security, but I would be giving up so much personal freedom. For better or worse, I am who I am at this point, and that's fine. We definitely needed a direct support network of other humans to survive when we were mucking about in the wilderness as hunter-gatherers. And then agriculture came along and turned women into property (yep I know, I'm on my 'Sex at Dawn' bullshit again). Now marriage and love is a literal commodity, and a lot of dumb cunts are taking out a mortgage to afford a cow, when instead you can just plug in and buy a couple litres of milk whenever you get thirsty.

I'm not too sure what the point of this rant is. One, I'm probably trying to let you know that, in case you've temporarily forgotten, your relationship with Kel is sacred, and you should be doing everything possible to keep that going. And two, I know that I've missed my window of opportunity, and I'll never find a girl that will be worth giving up my independence for, and I'm perfectly happy with that. There was a lot of resentment bubbling beneath the surface when I was with Di, but I feel like that's been exorcised since I got to Colombia. This probably made me selfish and as a result I neglected our friendship in some ways. I'm sorry for that. Next time we hang, you'll see that I'm a different person.

Speaking of which, y'all should really try and make it out here at some point. Next year I'll have to do a bunch of trips over to the States to meet with investors and potential partners, gonna be a long time before I get an opportunity to make it back to Straya. If you guys could take three weeks off, I think you'd be able to see all the best parts of Colombia. You could obviously stay with me in Medellín – I have an incredible spot with plenty of spare bedrooms – and I could show you around town. Tayrona in the north is this amazing national park that you'd both love. And there's actually a ton of places to do ayahuasca in rural Antioquia – so if you wanted to go full Graham Hancock and unlock the mystical secrets of Latin America, that would be totally possible.

How are things going with you? Everything all good at work? What are you writing about these days? I promise it won't take me half a year to respond to your next email.

Pass on my love to Kel and Fray.

Mwah, Tony Tissies

P.S. It's true that blondes have more fun. Check out my new look in the attached photo, me and Marcela chilling by the pool at my new spot.

I finished the email as we landed and sent it the moment I got service. As the plane taxi'd on the runway I checked Insta.

Result! La Bomba had posted a tearful selfie. Some anonymous troll had managed to get her OnlyFans account shut down by claiming she was profiting from sex with animals… I laughed to myself. Since she ghosted me in Miami, I'd submitted new complaints once a week under fake names. Serves the bitch right for stealing my cash. Dumb fucking cunt.

It only took us about an hour or so to get down to Tuluá,

which is a small city not too far from Cali. The driver was waiting for us with a van at the airport. We loaded up and made our way due west, up into the mountains. I took a few nips of aguardiente and put on 'Something Else' by The Brian Jonestown Massacre. Old mate Anton Newcombe had done it again. 'Who Dreams of Cats?' became my new favourite song the moment I heard it.

A proud old couple were waiting with the agent by the front gates of an abandoned estate. They opened the padlocks and started giving us a tour of the property. A short driveway led to a humble little bungalow with a stable at the rear. The property was approximately a hundred acres – the old boy had been growing coffee and avocados for forty years. He pulled out some handwritten notes, a list of tips and tricks to get the most out of the soil, and was about to launch into a big spiel, but Allie told don't him not to bother. We weren't planning to reboot the farm for a while.

"Documentos, por favor," I said to the agent.

With a heavy heart, the old man signed over his life's work to a bunch of entitled gringos. The four of us needed to buy property in order to qualify for two-year Colombian visas. I wanted somewhere outside of Antioquia just in case shit got hot and heavy in Medellín. Someone at Marcela's work got us hip to the farm. It seemed like a good deal, so we pulled the trigger.

We ushered the agent and the couple off the property and started looking for a good place to bury the loot. Heeding Belfort's warning, I'd converted about half of my crypto wallet into cash and convinced Allie and Brian to do the same. It seemed risky to have so much cash sitting in my safe at Forever 2. We found a good spot and some rusty old shovels and started to dig. Steve, the true believer, had no interest in cheating on his beloved crypto with some plain old traditional currency. He fell asleep in a hammock as we toiled away.

The driver returned half an hour after the agreed time (not a bad effort for a Colombian), and we piled into his van all sweaty and fucked. He looked at us with a bemused expression – cunt probably thought we were all christening our new property with a sneaky four-lad gangbang! I fell asleep on the drive back to the airport.

/

"Rise and shine, homie." Brian's punchable giraffe face was right in my grill. "You got a plane to catch!"

I sat up and stretched.

"Sorry dude. Forgot to tell ya. I'm gonna spend a few nights solo in Tuluá."

"Oh…"

"Yeah, I'm gonna give my novel another crack. Tuluá seems like a great place for a little writing retreat."

Brian looked ecstatic.

"Dude, that's awesome! Super proud of you."

I waved him away. "Safe flight. I'll be doing business stuff every day too, obviously. Hit me up if you need anything."

Brian gave me a thumbs up. "Smash it bro. Can't wait to read this novel!"

TWENTY-SEVEN

"Uno, dos, tres, cuatro! Uno, dos, tres, cuatro!"

Mel was leading us through our dance routine poolside at Forever 2. Brian's idea was to do an earnest step-for-step version of the 'I Want It That Way' music video by the Backstreet Boys. It was a retarded idea for several reasons. Firstly, there were five Backstreet Boys and only four lads on the ForeverCoin team. Ricardo, our esteemed silent partner, gracefully declined Brian's offer to take part in the shoot. Secondly, it's an incredibly boring music video – just a bunch of meandering shots of the squad loitering around different locations wearing ridiculous outfits. Finally, Brian insisting that we prance around to the Backstreet Boys was not helping his spurious claim that he was a red-blooded heterosexual male.

I was gonna put the kibosh on the whole thing. But having a goofy video plastered all over our website did have a utility. No one expects four fuckheads dancing around to 90s pop to be filthy rich dark web drug traffickers.

So, I agreed to the video, on the condition that we turned the thing into an *American Psycho* pastiche. The four of us would dance around by my pool wearing white suits for about a minute. And then Marcela, Paula and a few other hot sluts would sneak up behind us with pickaxes and start hacking us to pieces. We'd all fall into the pool and the whole thing would become ultra-schlocky. Cleavage, fake blood, detached limbs. Good, clean fun for dirty chicos and chicas.

Allie suggested that we hire Mel to do the choreography, and she did a stellar job. Brian also found this coked-out Italian fella called Giuseppe who had experience directing music videos and was now based in Medellín. The whole shoot was a gas. Afterwards we had an impromptu kick-on in my backyard.

Brian got stuck into some caterpillars with me and Giuseppe. Then Bri Bri started pestering me with his half-baked plans.

"We should start making plans about going legit real soon," he said right into my earhole as I grilled some steaks on my barbie. "Lay some foundations."

I sprinkled salt over the meat. "Still a lot of money to be made doing what we're doing, man."

"Of course! I'm just saying we could start thinking about the future."

I glared at Brian. "I'm always thinking about the future. Are you?" I flipped a steak. I was loving my new barbie. "Just relax. We'll talk about this another time."

After dinner I got stuck into some vod. Grey Goose straight from the bottle, like a Ruski. I began talking to Steve about Jordan Peterson.

"That quote," I began, "It's something like 'Be attractive to many women but only choose one'. Did Peterson actually say that? Or is that like a fake quote?"

Steve sipped his glass of water. "No. Dr Peterson definitely said that."

"You think that's good advice?"

"I do."

I took a greedy slug of Goose. "But come on. What about all this porn stuff? And the PUA nonsense you did back in the dizzay with Tyler? Seems like you're trying to be attractive to many women and picking a lot more than just one."

"Dr Peterson's messages can't really be boiled down to just single quotes. He has long, complex thoughts. You need to interpret his words in context."

I looked across my backyard. There was a slight breeze in the air. Marcela was combing Paula's wet hair. "OK, tell me. What's the broader context of that specific quote?"

Steve rotated from side to side, loosening his miniature spine. "You would have to watch the lecture in full to get a complete understanding. But fundamentally, Dr Peterson believes that personal transformation is slow and extremely difficult. It's important to set goals to better oneself, but at the same time, you have to be realistic about what's attainable. He also espouses the Jungian principle of confronting your demons head-on. With action, rather than just hypothetical thought experiments. This is how true change occurs."

A potato-y burp crept out the corner of my mouth. "I think I get it. You're fucking and sucking like crazy now to test yourself. You're figuring out how to be attractive to women. And once you've got that under control, you're gonna pump the brakes, find a nice girl, settle down. Is that the gist of what you're doing?"

Steve shrugged. "Something like that."

Most of the party cleared out. I sat cross-legged on the grass and chatted with Allie and Mel. At that point Mel's hair was green. The pair of them looked like young lovers in a Jean-Luc Godard joint.

"Look at her." Mel showed me a picture of Princess Snuggly. "How can you not fall in love with that face?"

"Cute cat," I said to her. "You officially adopted her?"

Allie nodded. "Was always more of a dog man. But she's a special little creature. Takes away all your negative energy."

I was sick of vodka and had moved onto Bacardi. "I've been thinking about your ayahuasca trip."

"Oh yeah?" Allie said.

"The lady screaming in her sleep. Avoiding you when you

walked into the room. And then at the very end she says all your bad vibes were gone."

"Amazing," Mel said. She kissed Allie on the cheek. "God bless the native healers in this country!"

"I've been wondering," I continued, "Do you think that was maybe some type of confidence trick? Like, even if you came in full of positive energy, buzzing like fucking Brian after his morning coffee, they would've still pretended that you were a massive downer. And then at the end she says your bad vibes have been vanquished by the spirits. It could be like some type of conditioned response thing. They might do it with everyone. The wife's stand-offish, her husband is the more approachable one. Good cop, bad cop. No doubt that the drugs made you trip your balls off. I'm not saying that the medicine was a placebo. But maybe by framing the experience in this way, they could influence the participant to think they've been successfully healed?"

My observation seemed to rattle Allie. He went inside to grab some leftover BBQ.

I was starting to slur. "Allie says you don't talk to Dani anymore?"

Mel sucked on a dart. "No."

"That's lame."

"I know. She totally cut me out."

I ran my fingers through my chlorinated hair. "Did Dani tell you what happened between me and her?"

Mel put out her smoke. "No. She didn't go into details. I was shocked when you broke up. She *really* liked you."

"She did?"

"Si. It was obvious." Mel leaned back and looked up at the night sky. "People change y'know? I thought she was my friend. But then one day. Nothing. Out of my life. So don't worry about her, okay? You are doing so well. Crypto. Marcela. This house. Your friends. Don't worry. Be happy."

I felt like I was gonna vomit.

"For sure. I'm looking straight ahead, babes. Always. Forever."

TWENTY-EIGHT

"Why can't you move the date?"

My head was pounding. Too much booze. Too many caterpillars. Not enough sleep.

"I don't know, man. Ask Brian."

It wasn't an amazing night or anything. Just chilling at Forever 2 with Marcela. We took a swim, fucked, had dinner. She went to sleep. I stayed up, listened to an old Rogan with Bill Burr while I shot balls by myself. Usually Valiums would knock me right out after a night on the sauce and sniff. But it took me ages to get to sleep. Maybe I was building up a tolerance?

Ricardo lit a fag. "It's your fucking party. I'm talking to you."

"Don't smoke in here," I said. "It's a rental."

We were heading out of the city towards Mono's compound on the outskirts of Retiro. Ricardo was driving like old mate Kowalski in *Vanishing Point*.

"I don't give a fuck," Ricardo said. He took another drag. "Since when did you become Brian's bitch?"

I rolled down my window. "Look man. I fucked up. I should've remembered that your thing was on the 30th. My bad. But Brian's already hired a bunch of shit. Speakers and lights; I think caterers too. If I could change the date, I would. But I can't. I don't know what else to tell you. Next right."

Ricardo took the exit at max speed. He hissed under his breath in Spanish.

"Like I told you, just do the event on Friday instead. Fly the Puerto Ricans in earlier if you have to."

Ricardo threw his fag out the window. "Sure. No problem. Whatever you say, boss."

I turned and faced him. "Bro, what's the problem here?" I said, much louder than I was intending to. "I made a mistake. You can still do your party. Why are you being a dick?"

Some final tendrils of smoke came out of Ricardo's nose. "You're right. I'm stressed." The nicotine seemed to mellow him out. "Forget it."

"Is it more bullshit with Click Clack?"

"No." Ricardo tried to keep everything under wraps. He quickly caved. "It's the festival. Booking agents think Bogotá is the only city in Colombia. They're too scared to send musicians anywhere else. Stupid fuckers."

"Maybe for the first year you should do something small? Like a boutique festival. And then the following year it'll get bigger."

"No." Ricardo shook his head aggressively. "Medellín needs a big music festival. International acts. I'm the only one who can make it happen."

/

We made excellent time because of Ricardo's lead-foot. Diego and three others were waiting in a car by the front gate. When we pulled up, they hopped out of their vehicle. All four of them were carrying handguns. I felt my scalp prickle.

Diego confiscated our phones and his buddies patted us down. My stomach was lurching. For some stupid reason the night before, I'd decided to break my clear liquor streak and get on the whiskeys. What a dumb cunt. Ricardo was wagging his finger in Diego's face.

"Solo el gringo," Diego said.

"Por qué?" Ricardo said.

Diego was adamant. "Solo el gringo."

Ricardo looked at me, bewildered. I shrugged. Mono told me to come alone, but I knew this would rub Ricardo up the wrong way. I brought him along hoping it wouldn't be a problem. One can only try.

Diego opened the gate to the compound. The three others took Ricardo as collateral and got back in their car. Diego walked me onto the property and the gate closed behind us. There was a beautiful double-storey family home at the end of the driveway with a cute little pond and a kid's playground out the front. Around the back of the property there was a huge garage; I guess it was actually more of a barn. There were a couple of Land Rovers off to the side, and several stacked pallets of dog food. Mono was waiting for me in the office at the back of the barn. Diego said a few words to his boss then pissed off, leaving us alone.

"G'day mate," I said to Mono as I sat down. There were a bunch of West Bromwich Albion posters on his wall. "Fuck. I didn't realize West Brom won the cup in '68. Nice."

Mono looked at my hair with thinly veiled disgust. My roots were coming through – I needed to get it bleached again.

"How are things with you, Tones?"

"I'm good. Moved into a new place a while back. Got an indoor pool. I've been swimming a lot."

Mono was wearing a purple polo shirt. A bit of grey stubble was coming through on his face. He pulled out some papers from a drawer. Performance graphs.

"Me and you need to have a little talk about something, Tony."

Mono grabbed a pen and circled the last couple months of flat growth. "What exactly am I looking at here?"

I quickly glanced up from the sheet. "I told the boys to focus on profitability. We pumped the brakes on the new product launches for a bit. It's been cool. We figured out exactly which products bring us the most money for the least amount of effort. Today I was hoping we could look ahead to 2020. Figure out how to build on this good start."

Mono rubbed the top of his shiny dome. "I think I get it. You're saying we should relax a bit, just stick with the best performers?"

"Exactly. I'm not sure if you have it here, but we also sent across our own profitability figures too. That trend line has been extremely positive over the last six to eight weeks. We can keep that going, but not worry too much about volume, because that doesn't really represent—"

I didn't see Mono's arm fly across the table. His palm hit me square in the Adam's apple. He closed his hand around my neck.

"You taking the fucking piss or something?" Mono's face was pulsing with fury. He looked like Allie after a night on the rack. "You think I'm running a charity here?"

The pain was immense. I let out a guttural cry. He squeezed as tight as he could for five more seconds and then finally let go. I fell down on the floor and started gasping for breath. Tears welled in my eyes. I was on the floor for two minutes. Eventually I was able to sit back on the chair. I massaged my throat, protecting myself from another surprise attack.

Mono's face relaxed.

"Let's try that again, shall we?"

/

I opened the front door to Forever. Me and Ricardo stormed inside. Allie was showing Brian pictures of his cat. Steve was watching some raw footage from one of his latest gangbangs. I threw my keys on the dining table.

"Sup boys!" Brian said. "Y'all gotta check out Allie and Mel's kitten, so damn cute! Holy shit... what happened to your neck homie?"

I walked over to the fridge. No beer. Typical. I started slamming the fridge door like Tony Soprano after Carmela forgot to buy his favourite salami. When the thing was nearly off its hinges I stepped back, took a deep breath, and ran my fingers through my hair.

"Stop what you're doing. Time for a team meeting."

TWENTY-NINE

If you're not getting bigger, you're dying. Right?

This idea underpins our glorious capitalist system. I don't see a problem with that line of thinking. Life is just like *Whose Line is it Anyway?* Everything's made up and the points don't matter. That doesn't mean there ain't rules. Me and the boys thought we were doing the right thing by taking our foot off the gas with new products. But we didn't understand the bigger picture.

Because of all the chummy phone calls, I was under the impression that I was Mono's golden boy. The prodigal son. Why would I, an upwardly mobile millennial, need to consult his geriatric Boomer arse about anything to do with selling drugs online? That was my domain. Mono was just an old man trying to keep up in this brave new world. A dangerous drug kingpin with years of experience annihilating competitors by hook or crook. Nah. In my head, he was just the schmuck client. We had the secret sauce. The ketchup for his dry polony sandwich. If I wanted to change direction, that's exactly what I was gonna do. He'd be sweet. What was the alternative?

Don't undermine the cunts who are writing your checks. I needed to get smacked in the throat to learn this valuable lesson. Years of working in the corporate world turned me into a cocky little shit. At Fairfax, whenever they wheeled out some dusty suit to take over the terminal Sales division, I would embarrass them publicly during team meetings. It would always be done under the guise of "please don't take this as a personal attack, I'm really just trying to draw attention to a few holes I think I noticed in your strategy". I was a failed artist looking for cheap ways to entertain myself and my peers in that godforsaken office. There's this Strayan expression called 'white-anting'. It describes bad actors wreaking havoc internally through gossip and misinformation. I knew in my heart that if I progressed and climbed the ladder at Fairfax, I would one day end up killing myself, probably in my corner office. So instead I became The King of the White Ants. In Straya, you need to do something horribly egregious to get yourself fired at a white-collar workplace. Even though all the Directors hated my guts, and knew exactly what I was doing, they had to stand in front of everyone and get humiliated. That's why the big dogs earn the big bucks. Not because of their skill or enthusiasm for the position. Rather, they're the ones who can deal with all the incompetence and laziness and preciousness that runs rampant within any fractured corporation. That shit doesn't fly in the real world. There's no performance plans or HR workplace dispute policies. There's angry middle-aged British cunts who don't think twice about attacking you with their bare hands to prove a point.

After he punched me in the throat, Mono started fleshing out the bigger picture. For starters, he tore me a new arsehole for bringing Ricardo to his compound. He repeated, for the final time, that I would be his only point of contact moving forward. Then, Mono explained that although pursuing profitability was a good move in principle, it didn't account for the nature of the operation.

"Pretend I run a fruit stand," he said. "Maybe I make more money selling mangoes. Everyone loves mangoes. But it's hard to grow mangoes all year round. Sometimes you ain't got no mangoes, but you've got a truckload of oranges. If you sit around waiting for more mangoes, and don't pull your finger out and start fucking selling oranges, the business goes under, you dopey cunt."

Finally, Mono showed me his own profitability analysis. Steve and Allie had just assumed the wholesale price for each item was consistent all year round. Mono's tech guy was sending Tweedledum and Tweedledee updated figures every day, yet they had completely ignored this data. The net result was that all of our estimates were based on bad assumptions. As I was leaving, Mono gave me a parting message.

"Before you go, Tony lad, I want to remind you that you're not the only game in town when it comes to this type of thing. Fair play, it's gonna be a big headache for me to change providers. Things might get a bit messy. It always does when things end suddenly. Get your house in order, lad."

In the interest of full disclosure, as Diego escorted me back to the car, for the first time since the whole ForeverCoin experiment blew up, I thought about running away. That would've been the right move. I could've returned to Medellín for a few days, told the other lads that things were sweet with Mono, and then jumped on a flight somewhere, preferably to a different continent, most likely to Madrid. The idea was definitely locked and loaded in my head.

But when me and Ricardo got back to Forever, the terrifying reality of my confrontation with Mono started to soften in my mind. I channelled all of my negative energy and berated Steve and Allie for half an hour. This transference set me at ease. After I was done ranting and raving, we pulled an all-nighter. We identified all the problems with our current processes. And then we put together an ambitious plan about how to set things right. The next morning, just as the sun was rising, I caught a beer-soaked Uber back to Forever 2. I was frazzled and janky because of too much sniff, so I necked a handful of Valiums and crashed hard.

I woke in the late arvo. Marcela was slinking around the pad in a new bra and panties combo. She made me an omelette and fussed over my bruised throat. I watched some ESPN and had a Pilsen. The idea to run away to Spain was still there, lingering in the background of my brain. But I wanted to give it a few days. Maybe things would go back to normal?

/

You're escaping a labyrinth, and there are three doors in front of you. The door on the left leads to a raging inferno. The door in the center leads to a deadly assassin. The door on the right leads to a lion that hasn't eaten in three months. Which door do you choose?

I woke up. The labyrinth riddle was sneaking into my dreams at least once a week. I would stare at the doors, understanding exactly which exit I needed to take. *The door on the right... A lion that hadn't eaten in three months would be dead.* Yet when I tried to move towards the door, I'd be paralysed. Perhaps my subconscious didn't have the adequate scaffolding to create a rotting lion carcass on the other side of the door? That didn't seem plausible – I've seen some pretty berserk shit in my dreams over the years. A dead lion would be a breeze. I remained rooted to the spot, unable to save myself. Then, the panic of being stuck in the maze forever would startle me back to the land of the living.

It was November 30, the day of the housewarming party at Forever 2. I went downstairs and made two cups of coffee. I added three sugars into one of them and brought the cup out to Humberto. Poor fucker had a long day ahead of him.

I did a quick power yoga sesh in the living room and was about to go take a shower when Mono called.

"Hey mate, how's it goin'?"

I heard Mono put his feet on his desk down the line. He was back in Florida. I only saw him the once while he was in Colombia.

"I'm good Tones… sorry to bother you on the weekend."

"No worries. What can I do for ya?"

"Just a quick one. It's about that stuff you sent over yesterday. I was wondering if you needed anything else from me to get it going?"

Mono was referring to the real-time inventory tracker that I'd developed with Steve and Allie.

"Nah mate. We built that using your original spreadsheet. Whenever you get a new shipment, just add the inventory details in. We've linked it to all the order data. It helps us figure out how aggressive we can be with paid advertising for the products on hand. And we've set up automated stock-out alerts. On your end you'll get an accurate estimate of how many days of inventory you have left for each SKU based on current order velocity. We used to pull these projections for our weekly reports, but now we can track everything in real time using this sheet. Way more accurate."

Mono chuckled. "Fair play lad. That's fucking brilliant."

I nodded to myself. "It's gonna be a gamechanger."

"Look Tones… I just wanna say how impressed I am with the effort you've been putting in these last few weeks. The numbers are looking much better."

"Cheers."

"And I'm sorry about how I handled things when we met in person."

My throat was still a bit tender. "That's cool."

"It's not easy being the boss." Mono paused for a moment. "If anything comes up with your team, and you wanna have a chat, don't suffer in silence lad. Give us a call."

"Will do."

I showered and dressed. The party was coming at a good time. We'd been grinding hard for several weeks on end. Twenty-hour days, seven days a week. Our numbers were looking good again. Mono was happy, and it was time for us to let our hair down. Ricardo wasn't able to reschedule his reggaeton night – his Puerto Rican homies didn't want to fly out to Medellín earlier. He was forced to postpone the show to 2020. It was a blessing in disguise. Click Clack was haemorrhaging money, and Ricardo was desperately trying to get his festival off the ground. I was looking forward to spending some time with him at the bash. It'd been a hot minute since we'd partied together.

I had about four hours until all the caterers were gonna start arriving, so I did a little bump and got stuck into some work. Modafinil's alright, but nothing increases my focus and productivity quite like A-grade Chuck E. Cheese.

There's two schools of thought when it comes to substances and output. You can be like Ernie Hemingway – smash out your work, then drink until you pass out. Or you can be like Hunter Thompson – get fucked up all day long, and then when you're nice and sozzled, whip out the typewriter and let the weirdness flow right onto the blank page. I'm definitely in the Thompson camp. I have my best ideas when I'm fucked up, so why would you let that go to waste? Now that I'm hashing this out, I realize there's a third option. You could go full straight edge – no stimulants or magic potions before, during or after. No gracias.

I did a few more toots and was able to get through all of my shit with about twenty minutes to spare. As a little reward, I pulled up YouTube. I wanted to read the top comments on the recent Rogan ep with Tim Dillon. There's a real artform to YouTube comments. Even if I'm not interested in a particular Rogan episode, I'll always read the top comments. Zingers. Burns. Hot takes. Aggregated, bite-sized takeaways for professional media junkies. They're often more entertaining than the content itself.

I was about to click on the Dillon ep when I saw that Brian had posted a new video. I did a double-take when I saw the thumbnail. Brian was winking at the camera in his trademark goofy style. The caption read 'SEO for the DARK WEB???'.

Please no. Surely he can't be that stupid.

Brian's video started playing.

"Wasssssssup guys! It's your boy Bri Bri the Hart Man, Social Coach and CEO here at Elite Society Networking... Today we're gonna be taking a little detour from our typical subject matter... As y'all know on this channel I'm always sharing exclusive tips, hints and tricks about how to grow your network and social status... But in this video I want to be talking to you about, wait for it, the dark web..."

The stupid fucker.

"Now, I know a lot y'all are sitting there thinking, 'Damn Bri Bri, the dark web, isn't that like the super-shady part of the internet?', and I totally get that... But today, I really just want to use the dark web as an example to make a broader point about expectations... Y'see, most of us just think that there's one internet... You got your Google, you got your Facebook, you got your Amazon, you got your YouTube... But the reality is that there's a whole flip-side to that coin... The dark web is just like the regular internet, except it's unregulated and there's a strong focus on anonymity..."

I'm gonna fucking kill him.

"Let's say you're an SEO expert on the regular internet... You know how to get products ranking and selling on platforms like Amazon... But what a lot of folks don't know, is that those exact same skills could be applied to the dark web... Sure, you might be selling a different type of product, but the fundamental principles are exactly the same... Pretty neat, huh?"

How did he think this would be okay?

"My point here is that when many of us look at the world, we only see one side of things... We think we've maxed out our potential... But what we don't realize is that our skills could be applied in many different environments... Just like an SEO marketer needs to find the right part of the internet to work their magic, individuals need to find different arenas that will help them grow their personal and professional networks…"

He's dead.

"So that's it for today fam! Hopefully this gets you thinking about different untapped areas of your life you could be exploring… Don't forget to like and subscribe! Bri Bri out!"

The video only had seven views. I took a deep breath and picked up my phone.

"Hey bud!" Brian said. "Ready to *par-tay?*"

"Hey." I closed my eyes. "I'm calling about the video you uploaded to YouTube this morning."

"Oh yeah?"

"Yeah." My voice was steady and calm. "Why did you do that?"

Brian bit into an apple. "I'm moving away from longer form content. I'm more focused on creating snappy little videos, pumping them out several times a week. And that–"

"–No. I mean why did you release something about the dark web?"

Brian took a moment to think. "I guess I'm trying to use more parables and left-field references in my storytelling. Makes things super-memorable."

"Dude," I said, my heart pumping. "We talked about this when this whole thing started. No mention of what we do. To anyone."

There was a moment of silence down the line. "Of course, dude," Brian said earnestly. "I would *never* do that. I didn't mention anything about our thing. I was just using the dark web as an example to make a point about–"

"–I understand. But it's not cool, alright? Could you take it down?"

Brian was cottoning on to the fact that he'd done something incredibly stupid. "Sure. I'll do it right now."

"Gracias."

/

The caterers began to arrive. I changed into my running gear and went for a jog around Poblado.

There are so many times where my anger problem has backfired massively and bit me square in the arse. It used to happen all the time with Di. She'd do something minor that would slight me, I'd fly off the handle, and then – because my reaction was so over-the-top – her original indiscretion would get completely overlooked. Over time, I've gotten craftier.

I didn't have a specific route in mind – I just wanted to let off some steam. I found myself at the top of Calle 10, 'Oedipus Race' by Native Sun blasting into my earholes, when I ran into Kat Volker. She was walking down the sidewalk holding little Bobby's hand. We made eye contact. I stopped running.

"Hey," I said, as I pulled off my headphones. "How's it going?"

"Hey Tony!" Kat smiled broadly at me. "How are you?"

"Yeah, good. Can't complain. How are things with the biz?"

"Busy! But good." Kat looked stunning. She was wearing a tight shirt that showed off her heavy naturals. "And how about yourself? Chris tells me that you're doing crypto stuff these days?"

"That's right. Things are coming along great."

"Awesome."

"You guys heading back to Oz for Christmas?"

Kat glanced involuntarily at my moist shoulders. Sly bitch was checking me out!

"Nah. Bit far to go with a little one."

"Fair enough. I'm having a party at my place tonight. I know Brian got an invite to Chris and Lamonte. You guys gonna make it?"

Kat looked at me with bedroom eyes. "No. Sorry. Tomorrow morning we're taking Bobby to Parque Explora, Lamonte's gonna tag along too. Can't have a late night. But appreciate the invite!"

"No worries." I bent down and got on Bobby's eye level. "How are ya, Bobby boy?"

The little guy was clutching a green lizard action figure. "Good," he squeaked.

"Good onya, mate." I ruffled Bobby's hair and stood back up. "Well I better be on my way. Gotta get ready for this bash!"

Kat beamed. "Good to see ya, Tony." She leant towards me and gave me a peck on the cheek.

"Ciao."

As she kissed me, I reached around and groped Kat's shapely arse. I felt her entire body freeze up. She pulled away from me in disgust – her eyes were white with fear.

I laughed nervously then bolted.

/

When I got home, I was fuming. Marcela accosted me the moment I walked through the door.

"Tony. Where do you want the comida?"

"I don't care."

"Because they say maybe the outside would be better. The kitchen will get too crowded."

"I don't care."

"But I don't know if people want to stand outside and eat food–"

"–SHUT UP YOU STUPID CUNT."

There it was. The first spurt of lava.

"FIGURE IT OUT YOURSELF."

And another.

"LEAVE ME THE FUCK ALONE!"

Marcela stood there like a stunned mullet. I ran up to my bedroom and slammed the door shut.

/

"I'm really sorry man," Brian said. He was dressed up like Russell Brand in *Forgetting Sarah Marshall*. "I don't know why I couldn't see the conflict of interest with that bad boy. My bad."

We were standing in the hallway that connects the two halves of Forever 2. It was early in the night, but the place was already starting to fill up.

"It's alright." I felt mellow as a motherfucker. I was on a large dose of meprobamate. "Just be careful what you're putting out into the world, alright?"

"For sure. You didn't tell the other guys, did you?"

There was a knock at the front door. Marcela and Paula (slutty police officers) breezed past us and let the newest batch of arrivals into the house. Marcela was giving me the cold shoulder. It didn't bother me – I deserved her temporary wrath.

"No. I didn't tell anyone."

"Thanks, bro." Brian looked me up and down. I was wearing a red FUBU jacket and one of my oversized silver chains. "Who are you meant to be, by the way?"

"Robert Pattinson in *Good Time*."

"Oh... Right on."

I glided into the kitchen and asked one of the dudes behind the bar to make me a mojito. Allie and Mel (Minions) were chatting to a bunch of Allie's old soccer pals. They were still loved-up something chronic. Allie saw me looking in his direction. He gave me the thumbs up sign and I winked back at him.

I went up to the billiards room. I was about to shoot some balls with Justin (Conor McGregor), when I noticed Ricardo (Cristiano Ronaldo) and Jhonatan (Captain Jack Sparrow) smoking on the balcony.

"It's *el jefe*!" Ricardo exclaimed. "How's el Australiano?"

I grinned. "Can I bum a smoke?"

Ricardo passed over a cigarette and lit me up. "Dude. I have news. I got my first headliner. Major Lazer!"

I raised my eyebrows. "Holy shit dude. Nice."

Ricardo was buzzing. "That was the hardest one. The first big name. Now the others will follow. I guarantee it."

"Sick. Top effort, lad." I leaned over and tapped Jhonatan on the knee. "Hola. Jhonny Depp. Cómo estás?"

Jhonatan blew out a huge mouthful of weed smoke. "Tony. Mi amigo." He bumped my fist. "Bien. Y tu?"

"Bien." I turned and faced Ricardo. "Can you ask him if everything's under control with security?"

Ricardo and Jhonatan had a brief exchange in Spanish. "He says everything's good. His guys have been at the front gate since six. And there are ten more guys arriving now. They are gonna stay in the house, make sure no one steals any of your shit."

"Nice."

"And I already told the cops about the party," Ricardo added. "They know not to send anyone."

"Cheers dude. How much do I owe ya?"

Ricardo waved me away. "It's nothing."

I wandered back downstairs. I wanted to eat something to line my stomach, but I had zero appetite. I ran into Steve (Joaquin Phoenix's *Joker*) and three of his camgirl whores (Harley Quinn, all three of them). One of the chicas looked way too young for the adult entertainment industry. Me and Steve had a brief, hushed conversation about some work shit. I went and checked out the pizza station in the backyard. The smell of cheese floating in the air made me feel nauseous, so I opted for an ice-cold Pilsen instead.

As the meprobamate wore off I began to simmer. I noticed Billy Hughes (Harry Potter), the gringo futbolista for Envigado FC. And the fat-necked Midwesterner (Batman), one of the blokes I'd spied on at 37 Park a year beforehand.

All of these random fuckers at my house didn't give a fuck about me. I was just the rich crypto guy with the cool house.

Take, take, take. That's what we all do. I'm certainly guilty of it. Apparently humans are highly social creatures. But do we truly care about one another? Or do we just need some minor, two-dimensional characters to add some conflict, flavour and the illusion of depth to our own hero's journey? *Every living creature dies alone*, says Grandma Death. Most of us spend a lifetime trapped inside a lonely, hellish prison of our own design. Knowledge comes with death's release. As we break on through to the other side, we realize that it's all been in vain. Nothing lost. Nothing gained.

We were playing with ourselves the whole time.

/

It was getting close to midnight. The house was packed. I was on my fifth mojito and starting to feel a little buzzed. Dark vibes were swirling around me. I heard 'Another Love Song' by Queens of the Stone Age coming from the dancefloor.

In the middle of the room Brian was salsa dancing with Paula. A circle had formed, and everyone was clapping along to the beat. Paula shook her tight culo and smiled effervescently, savouring all of the attention.

Brian saw me watching them. He ran towards me.

"Dude! Could you film?" Brian handed me his phone. "Thanks bro, this will be dope for my channel. Wish me luck!"

Brian started spinning Paula's delectable rig around the room. I glowered at him through his screen. Stupid fucker. That arvo I'd managed to talk myself off the ledge. But I was sick of diplomacy. No more Mr Nice Guy.

His time had come.

/

Me, Brian, Allie and Steve were all standing on the makeshift stage next to the indoor swimming pool.

"Everyone having a good time?" I said into the mic.

The crowd roared.

"EVERYONE HAVING A GOOD TIME?"

The crowd roared marginally louder.

"OK. That's good. Now, I want to take some time and lead everyone through a guided meditation…"

Confused silence.

"Jokes! There will be none of that hippie shit in my house."

A few cunts laughed.

"In case you're wondering, I'm Tony Fletcher, I live in this beautiful casa here in beautiful Medellín, and I'm one of the founders of ForeverCoin." I gestured to the others. "Here's the rest of the team. Allie Phillips, Steve Dobkin and… my right hand man, Brian Hartman." I paused and took a sip of my cocktail. "Don't worry, we're gonna get back to the festivities soon. But here's a little something we prepared earlier."

I tapped my lappie. The projector played our Backstreet Boys music video. The crowd seemed to dig it.

"Not too sure why we did that," I said after the video ended. "I guess we're trying to shed our image as crypto nerds." I finished the rest of my cocktail. "Just one more thing real quick before we get back to having fun. Tonight, ladies and gentlemen, I wanna say a few words about the word 'faggot'."

The crowd stopped chattering.

"My apologies if you don't speak English, this might be difficult for you to follow." I cracked my neck and continued. "See, when I was growing up in the humble northern suburbs of Perth, West Australia, the word 'faggot' was thrown around all the time. If you dropped a pass while you were playing basketball, you were a faggot. If you came last in Mario Kart, you were a faggot. If you didn't know how to tie your shoelaces properly, you were a faggot."

At this point the crowd was pretty much silent.

"I learnt later on, maybe the second year of high school, that the word 'faggot' was actually a derogatory slur for a gay person. That shit blew my mind! I didn't care if anyone was gay. I didn't have a homophobic bone in my body. Still don't."

I felt the hot glare of Brian, Steve and Allie on the side of my face.

"Now we live in this supposedly 'woke' society, and the word 'faggot' has been taken off the table, especially for straight, white, cisgendered males like me. The intentions behind the word don't mean a thing. It's simply contraband, no longer fit for use. Now, I would never want to offend a gay person, but I find this change a little bit annoying. Allow me to explain."

I began pacing back and forth like Bill Hicks.

"Y'see, you just can't throw the baby out with the bathwater! Some situations call for certain words. There's no way of getting around it." I walked back towards my lappie. "Don't believe me? Let me show you what I mean. Here is a prime example of a total faggot."

I cued up the next video and hit play. It started off blurry, but soon the footage of Brian and Nathan Condie settled on the projector. A wave of shock pulsed through the crowd. There were a few nervous giggles.

I turned and faced Brian. He was white as a sheet. Take that, you cunt!

After plenty of tongue kissing, Nathan grabbed Brian's head and pushed it down towards his crotch. I hit pause.

"I think we all know where that's headed." I chuckled into the mic. "I know some of you aren't as open-minded as me, so I'll spare you all the gory details. Y'see folks, my buddy and esteemed colleague Brian Hartman here is a massive faggot." I pointed at Brian. "Not because he's a closeted homosexual. No no no. There's nothing wrong with being gay! There is, however, something seriously wrong with lying to other people about your sexual orientation. That, my friends, is total *faggotry*!"

Brian looked broken. For a split second I thought he was going to charge at me. Instead, he ran off the stage and bolted towards the exit.

"That's all the housekeeping for tonight, folks. Thanks for coming! Let's get loose!"

I dropped the mic like Dave Chappelle and jumped off the stage. 'Does It Make You Feel Good?' by Confidence Man started blasting out from the speakers. I felt lighter. I went straight to the bar and got myself another mojito. Allie chased me.

"That wasn't cool, mate," Allie said.

"Fuck him," I said dismissively. I did a quick key. "The amount of shit that cunt's put us through. He doesn't realize it, but I'm actually doing him a favour. Trust me."

"There's a different way to go about something like that..."

"Are you telling me you didn't have suspicions?"

Mel was standing about ten feet behind Allie. Her hair wasn't green anymore – it was purple. She watched our interaction unfold nervously.

"Sure. I wondered," Allied said. "But at the end of the day, it's none of me business."

I turned away from him and leaned on the bar. Allie came to my side and put his hand on my shoulder.

"Look mate," he began softly. "I think you could benefit from a plant medicine ceremony. I could put you in touch with some really great people and–"

"–Not now dude." I scoffed. "I'm not having this discussion now."

The rest of the night was messy. There were eyes on me everywhere I turned. I went hard on the drinks and gak. Quite a few heavy looking fellas showed up – I wasn't sure if they were part of Jhonatan's security team or just wannabe gangsters. Steve and his three Harley Quinns started fucking on the couch in the living room. People were filming on their phones, and before too long it descended into a debauched orgy.

'Sick' by SALEM was playing when I ran into Marcela and Paula in the hallway. They were both rolling, hard. Marcela had her hand up the front of Paula's skirt. I popped a Cialis

273

and manoeuvred them up the stairs into my bedroom, locked the door behind me. Marcela went to town on Paula's cunt, and then Paula returned the favour. I played with my shaft and balls for a while and then shoved my cock into Paula's stinker raw.

After I pulsed, I collapsed on the bed. Paula kept munching away on Marcela's box, seemingly unaware of the load that I'd just dropped into her back hatch. I started to doze. The music made the walls of the house reverberate. Before I even fell asleep, I was back in the labyrinth.

THIRTY

"What can I say man. I'm sorry for doing that to you."

I was in Brian's bedroom at Forever. He was sitting on his bed, avoiding eye contact like a battered orphan.

"But just for a second, think about it from my perspective. You put that retarded video on YouTube. I don't think you understand how stupid that was. Because of this thing of ours, we're involved with some *heavy* fucking people. If anyone saw that, our lives would be in danger. You. Me. Allie. Steve. Ricardo. Everyone. You're lucky that you don't have a following. I was just gonna let it slide. But then I couldn't control my anger. You hurt me with a video. I wanted to hurt you with a video. Eye for an eye. That was wrong. I fucked up. I shouldn't have done it so publicly. Do you at least understand what I'm saying? Why I was so angry?"

Brian stared out his window. "Yeah."

"Good." I scratched dandruff from my dry scalp. I needed more Head & Shoulders. "Look. You've been an amazing asset since you joined the team. We're still on track to give you a big raise in Jan. There's no reason this should derail our professional relationship. Are you willing to put this behind us?"

Brian finally looked up at me. "I'm not gay you know. That thing you filmed in Miami, it was just a one-off. I was drunk. Nate took advantage of me."

I held my hands up. "Fair enough. It's none of my business, dude. I couldn't care less if you're gay, straight, asexual. If you were a nympho like Steve, that would be annoying. I can only work with one of those at a time!" The joke fell flat. "It's your life, bud. I won't be interfering again. There's too much money to be made. We good?"

Brian looked out the window again. "Yeah."

I took a step forward. "Look me in the eye man. We need to fix this properly. For good. Right now."

Brian stared up at me. I held out my hand and he shook it.

/

When I got back to Forever 2, the cleaners were finishing up. Apart from a few broken glasses and some bodily fluid-stains on the couch, there wasn't too much property damage, which was wild considering the carnage that had unfolded over the course of the night. Jhonatan's crew clearly did a good job keeping the masses of rowdy cunts under control.

I was about to go take a lie down when Humberto buzzed through to the house.

"Señor Tony," he said. "There is man here. Chris. He want see you."

I looked at the security screen. Chris Volker was waiting in front of Humberto's office next to the front gate. He looked furious. "Sin entrada," I said to Humberto through the buzzer.

When Humberto told him that he couldn't come through, Chris went apeshit. He started repeatedly punching the glass window.

I opened my front door. "Hey!" I screamed. "What the fuck are ya doin'?"

Chris scurried around to the gate. "THINK YOU CAN GROPE MY WIFE, CUNT?" He waved his fist at me. "IN FRONT OF MY KID? LET ME IN YOU WEAK CUNT!"

I waved him away. "Fuck off."

Chris started laughing. "Hiding in your rented mansion! Good one, you fuckin' clown."

I wheeled back around. "Go home Chris."

"You better tread carefully, cunt!"

Humberto came flying out of his office. He tried to pull Chris away from the gate, but the frail old bugger stood no chance.

"You can't do shit like that, Tony. She's my wife! Next time we run into each other I'm gonna FUCKING DESTROY YOU."

Just as I was closing the door, Chris lobbed over a final insult.

"You're pathetic, mate. Fucking poseur. Escobar wannabe..."

I turned around. "What the fuck did you just call me?"

There was a big shit-eating grin painted across the cunt's face. "Pablo wannabe."

I started charging towards him. "Say that again, cunt. I *dare* you!"

"PABLO! PABLO! PABLO!"

"SHUT THE FUCK UP!" I barked. Spit was flying everywhere. "I'M A CRYPTO TRADER, CUNT!"

Chris backed away. "Yeah yeah... Sure you are." He started walking towards the main road. "See ya 'round, cunt."

Humberto looked at me fearfully. I charged back inside and picked up my phone.

Who does that cunt think he is? Talking to me like that. I know where he lives! Private building. No portero. A sitting fucking duck. I'm sure one of Jhonatan's guys would help me out...

I was about to give Ricardo a call, when an image of sweet little Bobby Volker popped into my head. Those deep blue eyes and gorgeous blonde locks. His whole life ahead of him. Two doting parents. That poor little fucker hadn't done a thing wrong. Why should he suffer?

I put my phone down, popped some Valium and went back to bed.

THIRTY-ONE

Colombians are mad into Christmas.

Everyone throws up tons of lights at the beginning of December. It's called 'The Lighting of Medellín'. Malls, homes, parks – the whole city becomes one big Christmas tree. On top of all the ornaments and decorations and the Jesus bullshit, it's a time for family and tradition, way more so than the average Western country. What's the point of working hard all year round if you can't celebrate with loved ones?

No such joy for the ForeverCoin boys. Cunts want drugs 365 days a year. And with rev share deals, you're always singing for your supper. If you don't make money *you don't make money*. You convince yourself that your workload will flatten when you hit the next milestone, but that's a fairytale. There's always a new challenge. The grind, baby. It never ends.

If you've ever worked a corporate job, you'll be familiar with the concept known as 'The Fear'. It describes the existential crisis that kicks in for weekend warriors at some point on a Sunday arvo. *How can I go in to work tomorrow morning? I've taken far too many drugs this weekend. I'm a broken person. There's no way I can continue fulfilling all of my adult responsibilities. And even if I could rehydrate and get my brain chemistry back in working order, do I even want to? Who do I become when I sit down at my desk on a Monday morning? Is that the real me? Or am I wasting the best years of my life pretending to be someone else?*

This internal dialogue keeps you up all Sunday night. You come into work the next day feeling burned, emotionally exhausted, 'Blue Monday' by New Order swishing around your ears. But then you get on with it. You need coin. Lunch is only a few hours away. The job ain't that bad. Rinse. Wash. Repeat.

The desperately sad thing is that even if you find a way to earn money working for yourself, 'The Fear' never really goes away. And it doesn't just freak you out for a few hours every week. No, no, no.

This type of 'The Fear' stays with you all the fucking time.

/

At the beginning of December, things were still a little frosty between me and Brian. I knew it was gonna take a while for things to be the same again. Steve was getting more and more obsessed with his pornos. It didn't matter too much, because by this point, Allie knew how everything worked from a tech point of view. Ricardo started showing his face at Forever a bit more. I think he sensed how stressed I was about everything, and wanted to support me as a mate, which was cool.

One day, all five of us were working silently in the main living space at Forever, when Ricardo swore loudly and threw his phone across the room.

"What's goin' on?"

Ricardo stood up and started cursing in Spanish.

"What's goin' on?" I repeated.

Ricardo rubbed his tired eyes. "Major Lazer pulled out. Those *motherfuckers...*"

"Fuck." I struggled to find the words. "Why?"

"Some bullshit about a schedule clash." Ricardo lit a cig angrily. "Those fucking agents! They're all scared of Medellín!"

Out the corner of my eye, I saw something that didn't look right. I turned my head and looked to the end of the dining table. Steve was staring at his lappie screen, headphones on. His hands were under the table.

I stood up and walked towards him to investigate further. The cunt was enthralled by whatever was playing on the screen. Steve didn't notice me sneak up behind him. Just as I suspected, the sick bastard was watching himself fuck a couple of his cumslut grillas and tugging himself under the table.

"Hey!" I said as I ripped the headphones off Steve's head. "What the fuck are ya doin'?"

Steve looked at me like a lost dog.

"Go to the dunny if you're gonna do that!"

Without saying anything, Steve put his cock away and pulled his pants up. He closed the video and went back to his spreadsheets. Brian and Allie returned to their lappies without missing a beat, as if Steve whacking off at the dining table was a normal part of everyday life.

Ricardo, on the other hand, was horrified. He took a slow drag of his smoke. We acknowledged one another like two shell-shocked diggers on the front line.

/

Around this time, I received an email from Dad.

Anthony

Colombia, eh? How's it treating you? I'm sure the weather's a bit better than Melbourne?

We just moved into a new place last month. Still in Kuta, but a more secluded part compared to the old place. We've got a spare bedroom if you're interested in visiting.

Let me know how you're getting on. I have Skype now if you want to do a video call.

Love, Bob & Pam

I let his email fester in my inbox. Even if I wanted to respond, I would have no idea where to begin. Knowing my old man, he'd find a way to story-top my sprawling tale of black market crime. "Oh yeah, I've heard of that dark web thing... Anyway, back to me. I'm gonna get a new flat-screen installed so I can watch all the horses. I know a bloke in Denpasar who can hook up every channel in the world for only $10 Aussie every month. Not bad, eh?"

I made myself a black coffee and went up to my billiards room. A call came through from Allie.

"Brian's gone."

I put down my cue. "What?"

"I just got to Forever. Steve said he woke up and Brian wasn't around. We checked his room. Suitcase is here. But no passport, laptop or backpack. Tried calling him, no answer. Looks like he's flown the coop in the middle of the night."

I thought for a moment. "Stay there. I'm on my way."

I hung up on Allie and called Ricardo.

"Brian's gone."

"What?"

"Allie just called. They think he slipped away in the middle of the night."

Silence.

"Fuck."

"Hopefully he's just at a finca somewhere," I said as I bounded down my stairs. "Can you call one of your local police buds? See if they know whether he jumped on any flights?"

"OK."

"His full name is 'Brian David Hartman'. I've got his passport number too. I'll text it to you."

"OK."

"Don't incriminate yourself. Maybe Brian went to the feds."

"It's ok. I know what to say."

"Can you meet me at Forever?"

"I have meetings all morning..."

"Alright. Just stay safe. Keep me posted."

I caught an Uber to Forever. The harsh realization hit me. Brian needed to go. Even if he was just lounging in a hammock somewhere, the cunt had broken our number one rule – never go rogue. Stay in touch no matter what.

We spent a nervous day at Forever. I thought about calling Mono for advice but didn't want to rock the boat. We tried hacking into Brian's email and WhatsApp but didn't have any luck. Steve was too good at his job – he'd encrypted and blockaded the fuck out of everything.

I got some good news from Ricardo just after lunch. He knew almost for certain that Brian hadn't stepped on a flight at either of the Medellín airports, domestic or international. Brian also wasn't being held at a police station anywhere in Antioquia. He was probably hiding somewhere, likely nearby.

/

On Tuesday, Brian still wasn't anywhere to be found. We decided to wait until Wednesday, and at that point we'd catch a private charter to the farm outside of Tuluá with some of Jhonatan's guys. Maybe Brian was holed up there, and if he was, we could take care of him. If he wasn't, it would be the perfect place for us to tread water and figure out next steps.

I met Marcela for a highly paranoid lunch at a Vietnamese spot near Selina. It took me a minute to realize, but the waitress who served us was the first prepago I slept with in Medellín. As she took away my half-finished bowl of chicken pho, she beamed in my direction, appearing to remember me.

After settling the tab, I gave Marcela a peck on the cheek and she jumped in an Uber. On my walk back to Forever, I thought about the smiling waitress. Maybe once all the Brian bullshit was sorted, she could be my side chick? The fact that she'd graduated from fucking strangers to serving pho indicated that she was something of a go-getter. Her journey made me wonder if capitalism was that evil after all. I allowed myself to get lost in an erotic daydream.

Gunshots.

Glass shattered behind me and a bunch of people screamed. I hit the pavement. Bullets flew over my head. A car sped off, tires screeching.

I stood up slowly, in a daze. A bunch of people from a nearby coffee shop came out to help me, but I was unscathed. No other bystanders were hurt either. People were imploring me to sit down but I brushed them off. I hailed a cab and told the driver to head towards Forever.

I lay down flat on the backseat and called Ricardo.

"Hey. Someone just shot at me."

A ghastly silence. "Oh God," Ricardo said finally.

"I was walking down the street, and then this car did a drive-by."

"Are you okay?"

"I'm fine. Just in a bit of shock."

"We're in trouble," Ricardo said. He was crying. "Allie just called me. Someone broke into his house. They killed his cat."

I felt faint.

"He's on his way to Forever. Meet him there. Get Steve. Drive to my finca." Ricardo collected himself. "We need to get the fuck out of Medellín."

THIRTY-TWO

Steve drove me and Allie out to Ricardo's finca in his Porsche.

Allie took the passenger seat, so I hopped in the boot, a throwback to when I was broke, drunk and eighteen years old. On those lairy nights out, when there were always a few too many bodies for whatever vehicle would be transporting me and my fellow droogs about, I always appreciated the quiet solitude of the boot. Whatever the opposite of claustrophobia is, I have that. A love of womb-like enclosed spaces. Jesus Christ. Old mate Siggy Freud would have a field day with that one!

Here's why. If you're riding shotgun, there's a good chance you'll experience a few seconds of sheer existential terror before the 4WD tee-bones you at the intersection. Or the panic when you see the booze bus up on the horizon. In the cosy darkness you avoid all that malarkey. You're not immune from whatever bad shit is up ahead, but at least there's nothing to anticipate. Old mate Tom Petty was right. The waiting *is* the hardest part.

On the ride out to Guatape, I played 'No Werewolf' by Allah-Las repeatedly on my phone and tried to figure out who was trying to kill me.

The number one suspect in my mind was Mono. His credits were undeniable. Seasoned drug trafficker. Greedy. Violent.

There were a bunch of guys in Medellín who would love to get their hands dirty for him. In terms of a motive, the guy was probably sick of outsourcing the digital arm of his business. Mono let me and the boys hit the point of diminishing returns, and it was time to bring things back in-house.

Number two was Brian. There's no denying it, punking Bri Bri with my sneaky little home movie was a dog move. And there was the money side of things – I always worried that keeping Allie and Brian as salaried employees and not making them fully-fledged partners would bite me in the arse. Perhaps Brian faked his own disappearance as a diversion and was trying to pick us off, one by one? I tried to look at this possibility as objectively as possible, but it seemed incredibly unlikely. There was the needy, starving lion part of Brian, who wanted mainstream acceptance and adoration more than anything else in the world. The guy knew we were balls-deep in illegal activity but separated himself from any of the grubby details. There was no way he had the cojones to set up hits on our lives.

J Gomez took out the bronze. When Marcela chose me over the hometown hero backstage at Click Clack, I gloated like a motherfucker and stuck my chest out at the little fella. One assumes that you don't become a huge star in Colombia without becoming amigos with a few naughty operators... Maybe he'd taken umbrage with my cocky gringo arse and called in a favour? There *were* a lot of tough-looking geezers at my party who didn't seem to be associated with Jhonatan's crew. But this storyline seemed tenuous. I remember a time in the 90s when rappers were actual thugs. The good old days. Now you gotta be a squeaky-clean family-friendly influencer with a ton of legit side-hustles. I've said it once and I'll say it again; entrepreneurship ruins everything. J Gomez was probably more interested in getting himself on the Forbes list than having me whacked.

The final contestant, the dark horse roughie, was Chris Volker. This seemed completely implausible, but when he tried to confront me at Forever 2, I realized that beneath his pea-brained, creatine-laden exterior, old mate still had a bit of Bundy in his belly. You can take the boy out of Queensland but you can't take Queensland out of the boy, evidently. In all likelihood, his outburst was completely in line with a man looking to protect his wife's honour. But maybe, just maybe, my indiscretion had awoken something heinous within Chris The Wanderer.

Who've you got your money on? I bet you've got a hunch. When it comes to sniffing out danger, we all consider ourselves gifted. That's how you've made it this far, right? Your ability to read people's motives. Or maybe you're into some next level woo woo psychic shit, like that waxy cunt who used to be on telly, John Edward. Intuition, fool. If you can't trust your own gut, what can you trust?

That's all a crock of shit. We bumble our way through life, smashing into one another, getting distracted by shiny things, losing focus quicker than a *Half Baked* fan with amnesia. *Things just happen.* It's only afterwards that we assign some order to the chaos. If you're lucky, you can hone your gut just enough to figure out who's keen to jump your bones. But that's it fuck-o, that's the fullest extent of your superpowers. Forget all that nonsense about sniffing out danger. No one does that. You're here because of luck and chance. Danger hasn't paid you a visit yet.

But one day, it will.

/

"Relax, man. Relax," Ricardo said to Allie. "Drink some water."

Poor fucker was inconsolable. "They dismembered me cat," he sobbed. "How the fack am I gonna tell Mel?"

I couldn't look at Allie a second longer. He was dripping with fear, completely exposed like a raw nerve. Steve was sitting at the dining table. He was quietly muttering prayers to himself in Hebrew. I found this pitiful regression to be more confronting than Allie's full-blown breakdown.

Ricardo and Jhonatan were doing their very best to calm us, but they weren't looking too hot themselves. I took a sip of whiskey and steadied my ship.

"What about your Click Clack partners?" I said to Ricardo. "That bad blood you told me about. Maybe they took Brian to get back at you?"

Ricardo's eyes were bloodshot. "No, man." He was on his haunches, rubbing the top of Allie's back. "They owe *me* money. But it's not serious. No one wants to fight." Finally, Allie stopped crying and took a sip of water. Ricardo stood up and walked towards me. "Think about it. Brian's gone. They broke into Allie's home. They tried to shoot you. It has to be Mono! He's trying to take you out, one by one. When was the last time you spoke to him?"

"A few days ago," I said. "He seemed fine."

I took another sip of whiskey. I was about to ask Ricardo for a fag when the buzzer went off and scared the bejesus out of everyone. Jhonatan scurried up to the front door to check the security cam.

"Tranquilo," he called out. "Son mis amigos."

Jhonatan opened the gate. Four geezers carrying guns came into the house – I recognized them from my party. They all looked a bit rattled. Having them around helped a little with the whirlpool of fear that was churning around my gut. They seemed like street thugs – armed, aggressive, loyal, but completely untrained. Ricardo's finca was really isolated. If another force stormed the property, I didn't like our chances.

I drank more whiskey and brainstormed a plan with Ricardo. There was an airstrip in Guatape. The next morning we would fly down to the farm in Tuluá, dig up all that cash we buried, keep flying all the way down the coast until we reached Ecuador, bribe an official, and sneak over the border. Ricardo knew a dude in the town who did scenic flights for tourists. He stood up to call him. There was a thump behind me.

Steve was slumped face down on the dining table.

"Steve-o." I ran towards him. "You good mate?"

Steve had tipped his glass of whiskey over on his way down. Cunt was passed out, cold. The little fella rarely drank, and the combination of the booze and all the stress was likely too much for his hobbit-sized system. We hoisted him off the chair and laid him in the recovery position on the floor. Steve was dead to the world, snoring like a long-haul trucker after an overnight drive.

There was a commotion behind me. A few of the hard men were trying to prop Allie up. His legs had given way.

"What the fuck!" I moved towards him. "Oi! Allie! Allie! Wake up!"

He was already under.

"What the fuck's going—"

And then, it sidled up, suave as fuck in a crisp Armani suit, and kissed me right on the mouth. *The devil's breath.*

My mouth went dry, my eyes blurred, and I hit the deck. Paralysed and blind, I heard voices for a little while, and then, right on cue, I went under.

It was my turn.

/

"Here he is… Here he is… The boss is waking up!… Rise and shine, Antonio."

Scopolamina. Gringos. So many cautionary tales in the expat group. *It's not a case of if… it's a case of when.* If you have a basic understanding of the laws of probability, and impulsive tendencies, you accept such fatalistic assumptions.

Yet, it never goes down the way you think it will. In my head, I was going to be drunk at a hooker bar. Some tantalizing fuck-house would trick me with a subtle sleight of hand while I was busy staring at her tits. The next morning I'd wake up with a sore head, a missing wallet and phone. I'd shake off the cobwebs and count my lucky stars. That was going to be my scopolamina story.

What a conceited arsehole! In control even when he's not in control. The writer, slaloming down the artificial slope that he's created for himself. Every part of the course has been plotted out way ahead of time – from grand identity breakthroughs to skirmishes with death. Playing God with your own life. What could possibly go wrong with that line of thinking, Tony boy?

Reality doesn't care about your desires. Reality doesn't care about your trauma. Reality doesn't care about your plans. Reality doesn't care about your ego. Reality doesn't care about your fears.

Reality. Doesn't. Care.

"Wake up motherfucker. Time to meet 'The Shaman'!"

'Hero' by Mariah Carey was playing. The air felt a lot cooler on my skin. Hours must've passed.

I slowly opened my eyes. Ricardo's gakked-out face was an inch from mine. He slapped me across the cheek with an open palm. My brain bounced around like a Lotto ball.

"Come on Antonio! Your amigos are waiting for you!"

I was sitting on a chair. My arms were zip-tied behind my back. It was the middle of the night. The only light was coming from a standing lamp. We were still in the living room at Ricardo's finca. The air smelled like weed and vomit. Steve was to my left. Allie was to my right. Both of them were gagged. Neither seemed to be struggling.

Ricardo massaged my shoulders. He ran over and turned off Mariah. "Finally. The captain's awake! El conquistador!"

"Bro," I croaked. My throat felt like it was made out of sandpaper. "What are ya doin'?"

"Jhonatan!" Ricardo yelled out a demand in Spanish towards the front of the house.

I was suddenly overcome with nausea. Chunks of whis-key-infused vomit started tumbling out of my nose and mouth. Ricardo slapped me again on the back of the head.

"Typical fucking gringo." Another slap to my face. "Wher-ever he goes, he leaves a big fucking mess!"

Footsteps. I turned my head. It was like seeing a ghost. Jho-natan led Brian into the room at gunpoint. He sat him down in the seat opposite me and tied him up. Brian looked grey and emaciated. Once he was safely secured, Jhonatan took the gag out of his mouth.

"Tell him," Ricardo said to Brian. "Tell him what you did."

Brian closed his eyes and breathed in through his nose. The soft light made him look like a medieval knight. Brian opened his eyes and looked at me. "I tried to run away," he said to me.

Ricardo racked himself up a huge line on the table. "Like a rat escaping a sinking ship." Ricardo snorted up the caterpillar. "And then what happened?"

Brian held my gaze. "They caught me just before I reached the airport."

I blew more chunks down onto my lap. My whole body ached.

Ricardo lit a fag. "We sure did."

I felt a flash of anger pulse through me.

Let it go. Not now. It's not the time nor the place.

Ricardo kept going. "I was planning on inviting the whole gang out to the finca again, anyway. Brian just got to the ceremony a little earlier than everyone else!"

Oh boy. Here it comes...

"You stupid fucking cunt!" I screamed hoarsely at Brian. "Why the fuck would you do that?"

Ricardo clapped his hands together. "El jefe!"

"And surprise surprise," I continued, "you couldn't even figure out how to run away, you fucking dolt!"

Finally, Brian showed his teeth. "I WAS TRYING TO

GET AWAY FROM YOU!" he screamed. "I THOUGHT YOU WERE GONNA KILL ME!"

I scoffed. "Fuck off. You're the one who nearly fucked everything up–"

"–NO." Brian started shaking his head aggressively. "I'M NOT LISTENING TO THIS SHIT ANYMORE. NOTH-ING'S EVER YOUR FAULT. YOU TREAT EVERYONE LIKE SHIT. YOU'RE A BULLY. YOU'RE SELFISH. YOU'RE MEAN. YOU'RE LAZY. YOU'RE A NAR-CISSIST. YOU'RE AN ALCOHOLIC. YOU'RE THE REASON WE'RE ALL IN THIS MESS. YOU'RE THE REASON WE'RE ALL GONNA DIE. SO SHUT THE FUCK UP. SHUT THE FUCK UP."

Brian's outburst hung in the air like a bad fart. Ricardo racked himself up another line. "I've been looking forward to that." Another caterpillar down the hatch. "You know what Brian, I've been thinking a lot about Tony recently, and what can I say – you really took the words out of my mouth." Ricardo rubbed his hands together. "So, amigos, let me tell you what's going on here. After the party at Antonio's house, I started getting a little concerned about our business relation-ship. The video of Brian and that other faggot… I mean, wow! Talk about airing your dirty laundry in public! I don't care how much money you're making, it's impossible to come back from that. ForeverCoin was going to fall apart. For me, the solution was simple. Find someone to drive you out to the forest, a few bullets, leave your bodies for the vultures. Muy fácil. I can go back to my life, forget about all of this stupid shit."

Ricardo began circling us.

"But then I remembered more things about the party. Anto-nio wasn't the only one causing trouble. I saw a lot of broke gringos acting like assholes. Clicking their fingers at waiters. Treating women like animals. Complaining about Colombia – the food, the weather, the traffic, the pollution… everything is a big problem. I started to feel guilty. Why do I hate my own country so much? Why do I let all these assholes call the shots? Disrespect everything we've built here?"

Ricardo put his fag out on my forearm. I grunted and squirmed in my seat.

"I had an idea. If I kill these gringos quick and easy, is that enough? Do they deserve more pain? I thought to myself, 'What would a gringo do if they were in my position?' And then it hit me. I need a *slave*. My own personal Jesse Pinkman. Someone who can keep making me money but won't cause any trouble." Another caterpillar went down Ricardo's hatch. "But they can't be weak! A weak slave is good for nothing."

Ricardo told Jhonatan to get something ready in Spanish.

"So chicos, I've put together a little challenge for you. Another video. I know you enjoy video games! Something to separate the men from the boys."

Ricardo and Jhonatan dragged each of us until we were lined up, side-by-side in front of the telly.

"Rick," I pleaded. "Don't do this."

Ricardo smacked me in the back of the head a final time.

"I'm not Ricardo anymore, you dirty gringo. I'm 'The Shaman'!" Ricardo gagged my mouth shut. Then he did the same to Brian. Jhonatan turned on the TV. "It's time for the ceremony to begin!"

Graphic child porn began to play at full volume. I closed my eyes the second I realized what was on the screen. The problem was that I was still tripping hard off the devil's breath. In my mind's eye, two alien figures who quickly morphed into Dad and Mono trapped me in a cocoon of pulsing testicles. The two of them fought for a while, and then they began to 69. Septic yellow cum went everywhere. Soon the pair of them grabbed me by the legs and started trying to eat me alive, arsehole first. I felt like I was going to have a heart attack, so I opened my eyes and when I did, I caught a glimpse of two hairy Arabs spit roasting a boy who looked to be about five years old. I flinched – the boy's screams lacerated my spinal cord. I closed my eyes again and was subjected to another hellish, hyper-realistic hallucination of my mother eating newborn puppies. Again and again and again. I saw other things that I don't want to repeat. I'm not sure how long the ordeal lasted, but if I were to guess, I would say two hours.

These things will *never* leave me. This is my burden to bear.

/

"Any last words, amigos?"

We were lined up like lambs to the slaughter on the lakefront. Ricardo had a throwing knife in one hand and a handgun in the other. Jhonatan and his men had their guns locked on us.

"Silly me, you're all still gagged! Hard to say anything when you can't make a noise. Maybe we should just get down to business? It's getting late."

From what I remember, it was a full moon. Or maybe the deck lights were on. I could definitely see everyone's faces. Me and Allie were bawling uncontrollably. Steve looked like he'd been lobotomized. The only one with a stiff upper lip was Brian.

"Hmmmm. Who should be my slave?" Ricardo paced back and forth in front of us. "Who should be my slave?" He stopped in front of Steve. "Could it be this little fucker? Hmmm. The crypto guy. The tech guy. Great with computers. Not so good with people." Ricardo looked over at Jhonatan. "You know what, I'm not so sure about this guy. He jerks off all the time. Like Louis CK. But he's not funny! I don't want a dirty gringo slave that cums all the time. Especially if he can't tell a joke! ForeverCoin chicos, say goodbye to one of your precious co-founders!"

Jhonatan made his way towards Ricardo and Steve. I grimaced and waited for the gunshot. Instead, Jhonatan stood behind Steve and put him in a chokehold. Ricardo pulled down Steve's pants, exposing his hairy cock and balls. He

293

grabbed Steve's package and sliced off his prick with the throwing knife. Ricardo waved his war trophy in the air.

"Viva Colombia!" Ricardo yelled towards the mountains, before launching Steve's pecker into the lake.

Steve dropped and began to scream like an impaled goat.

Ricardo continued to pace.

"Who's next. Who's next. Who's next…"

For those interested, while I stood there, awaiting my fate, I didn't pray to God. I thought briefly about my parents and my childhood dog. I thought about whether my funeral would be in Melbourne or Perth. But that was it. God didn't make an appearance.

"Antonio!" Ricardo locked eyes with me. "You are not a good person, my friend. It's time for 'The Shaman' to teach you a lesson!"

Ricardo pulled down my jeans and boxer shorts. Fittingly, I had a chronic case of pebble dick.

Someone yelled something out in Spanish. I thought it was one of Jhonatan's guys. More yelling. I cottoned on to the fact that it was coming from the darkened little ridge on the east of the property.

Ricardo put his gun to my temple and told everyone to stand back. I stood there, half-naked and trembling. Jhonatan and his guys all had their guns drawn towards the darkness. Ricardo repeated his threat to kill me if anyone took a step further.

Silence. Nothing happened for a while. Out the corner of my eye, I sensed a bit of movement.

Ricardo screamed, pleading for the strangers to come forward with their hands up. There was something moving just at the edge of my periphery. Brian was also slowly creeping towards me. I closed my eyes and willed him to stay put. Ricardo pressed the barrel of the gun into my temple. He tried yelling in English.

"WHO'S OUT THERE? GUNS DOWN! HANDS UP!"

Brian seized the moment and bolted towards me. Ricardo clocked him at the last minute. He pulled his arm down and fired off a few shots. Brian fell like a sack of shit.

There was a brief vacuum in the space time continuum. Then the floodgates opened.

Yelling. Automatic gunfire. Screams. I threw myself down and joined Brian on the dirt.

The danger, baby. It had officially arrived.

THIRTY-THREE

The sleeping pills wore off around mid-morning.

I was lying on my king-sized bed at Forever 2. There was no sense of, "fuck, was that all just a dream?" The moment my eyes opened I remembered everything from the night before. Maybe one day these memories might be relegated to an ambiguous fugue state in a back closet of my psyche. I am not hopeful. There is a tender spot between my eyes where the trauma has gathered. It seems unfair that it hasn't blown up into some unsightly boil. Like a toddler, I want a physical reminder of my ouchy. I sometimes wonder if I gave myself a homemade lobotomy, whether any dark matter (real or imagined) would be released? Probably not. Telling my story may relieve some of the pressure, but again, I'm not hopeful.

Do you know who my angel was? I certainly didn't. In most life-or-death moments, folks hold out hope for salvation. Not me. My ordeal at Ricardo's finca was a legit existential crisis. The end of the line, baby. In my mind, no one was coming to save me. I didn't buy Ricardo's whole 'I need a Jesse Pinkman' trip, I thought he was gonna kill us all, but even if he did decide to spare one of us, it definitely wasn't going to be me. I've poked my beak into the black hole and now I'm back, walking amongst all the other modern users and abusers like an impaired zombie.

I stumbled down the stairs and went through to the kitchen. There she was. My angel.

/

Dani was dressed for success. Long black pants, heels, light blue blouse, ponytail. New angular reading glasses. She was peering over Allie's shoulder – he was showing her something on his lappie. Needless to say, she looked stunning.

"Good morning," I croaked.

She looked my way. "Buenas dias."

There was quite a motley crew in la casa. A nerdy young guy with a bulbous head worked next to Allie on a lappie of his own. Several militia guys were lounging about in the TV room, mindlessly scrolling on their phones. All their guns were piled on the glass coffee table in the middle of the room. Humberto was slouched on the kitchen bench, looking glum, but he perked right up when he saw me.

"Señor Tony!" he said. "Cafe?"

"Si, gracias."

"Before that," Dani said, "I need you to call your old boss." She handed me my phone.

I looked Dani up and down. She was wearing more makeup than she used to.

"Sure." I unlocked my phone. "Here?"

Dani nodded. She called out to one of the militia guys. He popped up, grabbed his piece off the table and made his way towards us. Then he set the gun on me.

Mono answered after the second ring.

"Tony, lad."

My neck prickled.

"Hey mate."

"Everything alright? Been trying to reach ya since last night."

"Yeah, mate. Everything's cool. Just been dealing with some

297

food poisoning. Went to Mondongos last night and we all came down with something. Sorry for goin' MIA."

"Ah shit. Fair play. Both ends?"

"'Fraid so."

Mono chuckled. "I've been there my friend. That's what you get for noshing on tripe!"

"I know. Never again."

"You better now?"

I looked at Dani and nodded. "Yeah. We're all on the mend."

"Nice one. Was starting to get worried. My blokes said they were having trouble reaching your fellas online."

I spoke with Mono for five minutes. There wasn't too much substance to our convo – it just seemed like he wanted to chat. Mono bought my food poisoning excuse and didn't suspect a thing. I ended the call.

Dani nodded at the militia guy. He lowered his gun and returned to the couch.

Enough teasing. This thing's ready to come out of the oven.

/

Dani's father, Alvaro Flores Márquez, was a senior member of the Cali cartel back in the dizzay. He went 'legit' in the 90s with the plastics business. But at some point, he got back into powder in a big way. Or maybe he never stopped fucking around with the white girl. I always suspected Dani had a man in her past that she wasn't telling me about, but I never suspected it would be her pops! This explains Dani's wanderlust – she wanted to get away from the family business. Talk about failing miserably at spotting danger. I cheated on an incredibly powerful narco's daughter with two rank hookers. And I filmed it!

As you know, when me and Dani broke up, I went on my merry way and started building my nefarious little empire. By this point, you know just about everything about our thwarted business venture, my esteemed reader. There is, however, one tasty little morsel I've saved for dessert.

Tony, the depraved, power-hungry unofficial CEO of ForeverCoin, thought it would be a good idea to investigate the possibility of acquiring his own inventory for export to the States. This was clearly against the terms of service outlined by Mono and the other members of ForeverCoin conglomerate. Tony's motives were, and still are, unclear. Conceivably Tony was aware that, at the end of the day, the ForeverCoin team were merely consultants, hired guns, and at any point the working relationship with Mono could come to an end. This rubbed Tony up the wrong way, and this is why he considered going out on his own.

After burying the cash on the farm with the other boys, instead of committing to a solo writing retreat in Tuluá, Tony spent a few days trying to sniff out a local cocaine distributor. Due to his substandard Spanish and complete lack of local contacts, Tony struggled to make any meaningful headway in Tuluá. The only meeting he managed to finagle was with a middle-aged gentleman called Gabriel in the back room of a dusty pool hall. Gabriel claimed to be a distributor for the entire department. But Tony, the cocky prick, wasn't convinced. He took Gabriel for nothing more than a small-time local dealer. Realizing that his solo venture was going to take a lot of time and effort to get off the ground, Tony abandoned the idea and returned to Medellín.

Turns out Gabriel wasn't bluffing. He was indeed someone who facilitated the mass transfer of inventory to and through the port of Buenaventura. Gabriel spoke with his boss, Alvaro, about Tony, the blue-eyed, blonde-haired Australian from Medellín who wanted to buy hundreds of thousands of dollars' worth of powder and ship it to the States. Alvaro was convinced that it must be a coincidence. Señor Azul, the Australian Tony that stayed at his casa with Dani for Christmas 2018, was an eccentric artist-type, not a budding cocaine cowboy. And besides, Tony's hair was brown, not blonde. However, just to be on the safe side, Alvaro gave Dani a call.

As chance would have it, Dani had recently bumped into Tony in a shopping mall. His hair was now blonde, and he definitely seemed... *different*. Alvaro explained the situation with Gabriel to Dani. If Tony was indeed intending to buy a large quantity of cocaine and export it to the States, there was a good chance that he was in a lot of danger. Alvaro suggested to Dani that they could instruct some of his men in Medellín to trail Tony.

Now, this put Dani in something of a quandary. Alvaro knew that his daughter and Tony were no longer an item, but Alvaro had no idea that Tony had broken Dani's heart in the most callous and disrespectful way imaginable. If she revealed the truth, Alvaro would likely have Tony murdered immediately. The second option would be to tell Alvaro not to bother with any surveillance, and let Tony collide with whatever fate awaited him. The third option was to accept her father's offer and learn exactly what mischief Tony was getting up to.

Thankfully for your disgraced narrator, Dani went with option number three. Over a couple of months, Alvaro's guys figured out the true nature of the ForeverCoin enterprise and all the parties that were involved. They crashed the housewarming bash at Forever 2. They uncovered Ricardo's mutinous plot and watched him kidnap Brian before he could reach the airport. They trailed Steve's Porsche to the finca. And they got the order to intervene from Alvaro and Dani just after Ricardo threw poor old Steve's cock into the lake.

/

"Drink your coffee," Dani said to me. "I want you focused."

Me and Allie worked with Dani and her tech guy, explaining everything about our business. It was a cathartic experience. No more secrets. Me and Allie really knew our shit.

Our scrappy start-up had essentially been acquired by a larger, more established player in the space. Unlike many fairytale acquisitions, it wasn't the deal of our lives. It was a deal *for* our lives.

"That's enough for today," Dani said. It was around midnight. She closed her lappie. "Let's finish up first thing tomorrow."

"Dani," Allie said. "Before I go to bed, can I make a quick call to Mel?"

Dani rubbed the back of her neck.

"Please. I promise to be quick…"

Dani sighed. "OK." She told one of the militia guys to point a gun at Allie. Once the gunman was set up, Dani handed Allie his phone.

It was a devastating call to listen in on. Allie spoke to Mel in Spanish, so I didn't get everything, but this was the gist of the conversation.

Hi baby… no I'm fine… I'm sorry for being out of touch all day long… I'm at an Airbnb outside the city… yes, all the other boys are here too… I know, I can't stop thinking about it too… I don't know what type of sick fuck could kill a kitten like that… It's alright… We are taking control of the situation now… It's just a minor misunderstanding… no, please don't return to the apartment for a few more days… because we want to make sure everything is one hundred percent safe… I will let you know when we can go back… it will be a few days, just stay at your parents' place… no trust me, no one is in danger… it has nothing to do with the business, I think it was an old co-worker I had a problem with… I have some friends taking care of the situation… just relax, in a few days we'll both be home and we'll have a funeral for Princess Snuggly… yes we can get another kitten just like her… I promise…

Dani gave Allie the sign to wrap up the call. He glumly complied. The man was inconsolable. Dani force-fed him a cocktail of sedatives. Then some dudes led Allie through to his room.

"OK," Dani said to me. "One of the guys will take you up now."

"You can have the master bedroom if you want," I said. "It's the least I can do."

"No thanks." She untied her ponytail. "I'll see you tomorrow."

"Am I good to drink some water before I go to bed? Dehydrated as fuck."

Dani looked at me like I was a piece of vermin. "Hurry. You need to be up at six." She went through to one of the spare rooms to crash.

I drank a few glasses of orange juice and water. I was about to head up when I heard the front door open. A few seconds later, some special forces-looking motherfucker pushed Steve, who was in a wheelchair, into the living area. Brian, who was on crutches, entered immediately after.

"Holy fuck!" I said as I rushed towards them.

Brian was beaming. "Wassup homie?"

The night before, I was convinced both of them were on the way out. Steve's screaming was the first thing I heard by the lakefront when the gunshots stopped. I opened my eyes and stood up. Ricardo's face was like mincemeat. Jhonatan was crumpled on top of himself like a broken puppet. Dani's guys had taken out everyone except us four gringos in a short, diabolical blast.

After all the targets were dead, the unit swooped down onto the lakefront. Me and Allie got led to a Hummer and were taken straight to Forever 2. Steve and Brian got loaded into a separate vehicle and were taken elsewhere. I was too fried to ask any questions, and just assumed the dudes with guns were mercenaries working covertly for the CIA. When Dani opened the front door of Forever 2, I thought I'd died and gone to heaven.

"It was Dani!" I said to Brian and Steve. "Dani was the one who saved us!"

Brian nodded like an eager Labrador. He seemed loopy, like he was dosed up on something real strong. "We know dude! She spoke to us over the phone on the ride over. Told us all the rules of the deal."

"How are you feeling?" I said.

Brian rubbed his stomach. "Not too bad, man. Never been shot before. Hurts like crazy! We got fixed up in some fancy hospital just outside the city. Me and Steve had the whole floor to ourselves!"

I looked down at Steve. He looked gaunt and blue, like a sickly Smurf. The dark truth dawned on me. I thought of my favourite quote from *Donnie Darko*: "What's the point of living if you don't have a dick?"

"Hey buddy," I said to Steve. "Glad you're okay."

Steve looked at me with unbridled disgust.

"Fuck you," he said, the words tumbling out of his mouth with sincere precision.

Before I had a chance to respond, the special forces lad wheeled him away.

"About what I said last night," Brian started. "Y'know. Before we got taken to Crazy Town. I'm so sorry, bro. I was sleep-deprived, and hungry, and I–"

"–It's okay," I said matter-of-factly. "You were right. Everything you said was right."

"I'm not sure about that, homie, I was pretty–"

"–No, you were right about everything," I insisted. "Thanks for saving my life."

Two of the guards told Brian to move along.

"De nada, parcero." The kid's eyes were as big as saucers – Brian was higher than the sun. "Time for me to crash, homie! Sleep tight bro-seph. Catch you mañana!"

/

Dani let me know that I was done just after breakfast. Her tech guy was satisfied that he didn't need any more info from me. It was a shock to the system. I was expecting to be holed up for at least a few more days. Dani cleaned out my bank accounts and crypto wallets (leaving me $15,000 AUD, exactly what I had when I arrived) and got me a one-way ticket back to Melbourne, the first leg departing from Medellín that arvo.

My hair was long and straggly, dark regrowth coming through something chronic, so I asked Dani if she could give me a haircut before I got on the plane. One of the guards produced a pair of clippers. We went up to my ensuite bathroom. The guard offered to keep an eye on me, but Dani waved him away.

She started buzzing my scalp.

"I'm sure you know this, but Ricardo has business partners at Click Clack," I said. "He wasn't super-tight with any of them. But it's been a couple of days now. They might start getting suspicious."

Dani was concentrating on doing a good job with my hair. Her mouth was open ever so slightly. "We're moving locations today."

"Oh cool. Those Click Clack dudes know a lot of local cops too."

"My father has the police under control."

I didn't have much time.

"This is difficult for me to say, so I'm just gonna say it." I looked down at my feet. Dirty clumps all over the white tiles. "I want to thank you for saving me. And the others too. We owe our lives to you and your father."

Dani kept buzzing in silence.

"I know our relationship ended horribly. It's just, when I saw you last night, I remembered how much I loved you. The fact that you chose to save me even after what I did to you… it says a lot about what we had."

More clumps fell to the ground.

"This isn't your world, Dani. I dragged you into this. I hope after you've sent us all home you can go back to your regular life. You still seeing Joaquin? That was Joaquin you were with at the mall, right?"

Dani lifted the clippers off my scalp and clicked them off.

"Let me make something clear," she said. "I didn't get involved in this to save you. I was curious about what you were doing. When I learnt the truth, I saw an opportunity. Now I have what I need, I'm sparing you. Just like I spared you when I found that disgusting video."

With only a portion of my head shaved I looked like a street beggar.

"But Dani," I whispered. "You don't want to get involved with any of this stuff. Trust me. This isn't your world."

She scrunched up her perfect face. "Not my world? I grew up in this world."

I tried to get the conversation back on track.

"Look, I know you did this to save me. But just because your father's a narco, doesn't mean you have to be. Anyway, isn't Joaquin a lawyer? You're probably putting him in a pretty weird situation right now."

Dani laughed.

"You gringos are all the same. No loyalty. No sense of obligation. I thought you were different Tony. But no. You're just another man-child living out some stupid fantasy in Medellín. I've tried running away from my family. I've tried running away from duty. It's not right." Dani turned the clippers back on and kept buzzing. "Maybe you should stop running away too?"

/

I wasn't allowed to say goodbye to the others – everybody was being held in separate rooms.

Dani instructed me to call Marcela and let her know I was headed back to Australia for a while. Marcela swallowed the news like a bitter pill. I wanted to comfort her, tell her that it wasn't her fault, not to beat herself up. But I was too exhausted. I ended the call quickly. I gave Humberto a hug and got in the Hummer.

One of Dani's guys drove me to José María Córdova. The weather was exactly the same as the first day I arrived. My sense memory kicked in. That palpable feeling of excitement and positive tension. It was all ahead of me, back then. Everything to gain, nothing to lose.

Dani's guy followed me into the terminal. He loitered at a gift shop and watched me pass through security.

And then, just like that, I was free.

THIRTY-FOUR

"You're looking like Christian Bale in *The Machinist*, bro."

Even though it was the middle of December, Melbourne was cold and drizzly.

I laughed. "You don't like me with cheekbones?"

"Depends how you got them. Colombian supplements?" Dunc asked.

The freeway was pretty fucking hectic for ten in the morning.

"There was a bit of that. But nothing too wild. I'm getting old, mate. Not as crazy as I used to be."

"No checked luggage is a surprise too." Dunc took a sip of coffee from his Thermos. "Didn't have you pegged as a minimalist."

"What can I say. I'm full of surprises."

Dunc and Kel weren't in Abbotsford anymore. Their new place was in Ashburton, right near the public golf course.

"This is us," Dunc said as he pulled into a rundown-looking rental.

Just as Dunc was about to jump out of the car, I grabbed him by the arm. "Hey dude. Sorry for not keeping in touch while I was away. I'm a shit bloke."

Dunc waved me away. "You're good, buddy," he said genuinely. "Stoked to have you back."

The moment I walked into the house, Fray jumped on me and began to lick my face. I gave her some smooches and then Dunc pulled her off me. I wandered through the house. Kel was out the back near the chicken coop. It was only when I opened the flyscreen door that I saw her bump.

My pipes nearly burst. But I managed to keep my shit together, like a man.

/

"How far are you along?"

Kel took a sip of juice.

"Five months."

I nodded. "You still teaching?"

"Term 4 just finished a few weeks back. I've got a bit of admin to do over the next week, and then I'm done for a while," Kel said. "I'm gonna be a full-time mum for the next couple years."

I smiled. "Lad or ladette?"

"We're gonna keep it a surprise," Dunc said.

"Nice." I took a sip of VB. "Congrats fam. Can't believe you're gonna be parents! Fucking bonkers."

"Cheers bloke," Kel said. "Now come on! Tell us about your adventure!"

I relayed a heavily edited version of my eighteen months in Colombia.

"Wow!" Kel said. "Sounds like an amazing place. Think you'll go back?"

Dunc tried to pass me a joint, but I waved it away. "Maybe one day. We'll see."

"That's cool so many people work remote over there," Dunc said. "I'm actually planting the seeds for that with my gig so we can move up to Daylesford."

"What's your title these days, big fella?" I asked Dunc.

"Head of Content."

"Sounds important."

"To you maybe," Dunc said with a smile.

"Di said she sent you an email," Kel said. "Told you her news. Did you read it?"

"I did," I said. "Really stoked for her. Didn't get a chance to respond yet. Life's been nonstop crypto hustle! But I'll definitely send her a note over the next couple of days."

"It's great to have you back, T," Kel said. "Maybe you two boys could start writing together again?"

/

Me and Dunc sunk beers and talked shit all arvo. We ate dinner then Dunc and Kel crashed early – they both had work the next day.

I lay on the couch and watched some 20/20 cricket on the telly. Big Fray snuggled into me. All the players looked like tradies in their high-vis gear. Straya, mate.

It felt utterly ridiculous to be back in Melbourne. Third-wheeling with Dunc and Kel like it was 2011 again. At some point I'd be forced to interact with Di and her beige fiancé.

Fuck.

I suddenly remembered that Dani had a Colombiana amiga in Melbourne, the chick she FaceTimed with. She'd be able to spy on me, send updates back to Medellín.

This ain't gonna work. You know what needs to happen, Tony boy.

Exhaustion was kicking in. I desperately wanted to conk out on the couch, but I forced myself to sit up and find my phone. There was a red-eye leaving in a few hours.

I wrote a note and left it on the dining room table.

"Good to see you again," I whispered to Fray. "Wish I could stick around a bit longer."

/

As a north of the river boy, I didn't know exactly where Spearwood was, but I sensed that it was right near Freo, so I asked the cabbie to drop me off at Bathers Beach.

It was one in the morning and the beach was completely deserted. Unlike chilly Melbourne, Perth was balmy as fuck. I took my shoes off and dipped my toes in the Indian Ocean.

All the pent-up angst poured out of me. I sobbed for thirty minutes straight. I was right near 'The Round House', the oldest building in WA, a prison from the 1800s. This particular stretch of coastline has seen and heard broken men crying for hundreds of years, making my outburst laughably insignificant in context.

Turns out Spearwood is a lot further from Freo than I thought. It took me an hour and a half to get to Mum's on foot. Either way, I arrived just before dawn, as I intended to.

Mum nearly dropped her cup of tea when she saw me. Her hair's silver now. After a bunch of tears and bearhugs, she force-fed me a Full English.

Then I slept for a long, long time.

/

I've spent Christmas and New Years at Mum's.

She's over the moon to have me around. These days, she works as an office manager for Notre Dame uni in Freo. Mum's on her end of year break, so she's been cooking around the clock, trying to fatten me up. Apart from eating, I've been going down to the beach for swims by myself. I've also been watching a lot of TV. After so long in Colombia, it's a novelty to understand what's being said on the box at all times. This coronavirus thing that's kicking off in China looks fucking hectic.

Kel sent me an email the other day. She wished I hadn't done an Irish goodbye, but understood why I wanted to go back to Perth for a while. I haven't heard anything from Dunc.

Of course, the moment I touched down in Oz, I started frantically checking the main Medellín news sites. A couple days after arriving in Perth the story emerged. I put it through Google Translate.

The body of Ricardo Carranza Rios, an eminent nightclub owner and promoter, was found dead in the Peñol reservoir, alongside five of his business associates. Police raided Mr. Rios' nearby finca which exhibited no signs of foul play. Investigations are ongoing.

That was it. No more stories came out. Dani's guys must've done a solid job cleaning up the bloodbath. Or they paid a bunch of people to shut the fuck up. Either way, the story died.

I think about Ricardo a lot. Did you pick him as the 'bad guy' of this story? I certainly didn't. The drug dealing, black-clad, heavy metal fan, whose father was brutally murdered by narcos... on paper he seems cartoonishly dark, but I assure you that he wasn't. He was just like me – a lost man-child with a chip on his shoulder. That's probably why I dug him so much.

And of course, I think about the other dudes. Allie in London. Brian back home in sunny San Diego. And mutilated little Steve in Toronto. Picking up the pieces. Starting again. The expat Facebook group has probably gone into overdrive with gossip and speculation about what really happened to the ForeverCoin crew. I wouldn't know. I'm finally done with wasting my life lurking on social media.

I'm not sure if this story has a hero, but if I had to nominate one, it would be Brian. If that fucker hadn't charged at Ricardo when he did, I'm not sure I'd still be walking the earth. After all the abuse and bullying I subjected him to, he still found the courage to try and save my life. I hope things work out OK for that poor bastard.

Dani's parting instructions were clear. No communication with any of the ForeverCoin crew. No communication with Mono. No communication or cooperation with the police. No selling drugs online ever again. No returning to Colombia. No sharing the story with *anyone*. The punishment for any transgression would be death.

Finish strong, Tony lad. Finish strong.

Since I got back to Perth a few weeks ago, I've been sitting in Mum's study, listening to 'Street Worms' by Viagra Boys on repeat, writing this story on her old lappie. Now it's done, I'm not sure what to do with it. I could put it on Reddit anonymously and see what happens. I don't know. We'll see. I'm too close to my story to understand what it means. But, if there's anything I'd like you to gleam from my tale, it's this…

For the longest time, I believed that I was incapable of changing myself. I wanted the world to shape me. Don't wait for that to happen. Any day you can die. There's no reason to carry on if you don't want to. Crucify the old version of yourself. Laugh and throw rocks as he pleads for mercy. Fuck that clown. That was the old you! It's time for a costume change. Out with the old, in with the new. Good riddance to bad rubbish. There's no one stopping you, except yourself.

What are you waiting for? Look at me. If I can die and start again, why can't you?

ABOUT THE AUTHOR

Thommy Waite is an Australian writer and host of the podcast 'Thommy Waite's Square Record'. He *was* based in Medellín, Colombia. But like many others, he scurried back to his home-town (Perth, Australia) during the COVID-19 pandemic.

His future whereabouts remain undetermined.

NOTE FROM THE AUTHOR

I had a lot of fun writing this book.

Considering you made it to the bitter end, I'm hoping you got something out of it too.

The days of writers and readers being separated by carefully crafted mystique are gone. If you dug this book you would probably dig me. And I would probably dig you.

With that in mind, let's hook up. You can find me on social media. If you really want to get to know me, listen to my podcast. Sign up to my email newsletter so I can send you occasional love letters. Or sling me a note of your own. It would make my day to hear from you.

If you're so inclined, there are many ways you can further support me. Here are a few ideas: write a review of this book on Amazon or Goodreads, give a copy to a like-minded pal, or simply keep your eyes peeled for my next project.

You can find all the right links on my website.

Until we meet again.

TW
December 2020

THOMMYWAITE.COM

ANY DAY YOU CAN DIE 2

Tony Fletcher has the story of a lifetime up his sleeve. The problem is, no one can know the shocking truth about his stint in Medellín, Colombia. Tony has vowed to take his drug trafficking escapades to the grave.

Whilst visiting his father in Bali, Tony gets a call from an old friend. Plans have changed – the ForeverCoin crew are getting back together for an unlikely reunion tour.

Amidst the escalating COVID-19 pandemic, Tony embarks on a perilous trip across several continents. Soon enough the boys are up to their old tricks again. But this time around, the stakes are much higher.

Tony gets unwittingly dragged into the 2020 United States presidential election, and learns the sordid truth behind a bonkers conspiracy theory. He is faced with a dilemma – slip back into obscurity, or risk everything to alter the course of history.

Every choice has a consequence. Every hero needs a villain. Every life ends with death.

COMING 2021

SUBSCRIBE FOR EARLY ACCESS
AT THOMMYWAITE.COM/NEWSLETTER

Lightning Source UK Ltd.
Milton Keynes UK
UKHW010723210321
380707UK00001B/32